# The Heritage

# The
# HERITAGE

# Siegfried Lenz

TRANSLATED FROM THE GERMAN
BY KRISHNA WINSTON

SECKER & WARBURG
LONDON

*Originally published in German under the title* Heimatmuseum
© *1978 by Hoffmann und Campe Verlag, Hamburg*
*First published in England 1981 by*
*Martin Secker & Warburg Limited*
*54 Poland Street, London W1V 3DF*
*English translation copyright © 1981 by Farrar, Straus & Giroux, Inc.*

*ISBN 0–436–24424–1*
*Printed in the United States of America*

This English-language edition has been shortened
with the cooperation of the author

# The Heritage

# I

No, it was not an accident. I was the one who laid the fire one night, the night of August 18, to be precise. I had no choice but to destroy the museum, the only existing museum of Masurian history, over there in Egenlund, near Schleswig, more than 600 miles from my home town, Lucknow. No, not an accident, young man. Once it had been my dream to construct the museum and build the entire collection; now it was my decision, and mine alone, to burn it to the ground, with all the papers, memorabilia, and documents which my helpers and I had so painstakingly gathered after the war.

Go ahead and smoke, here's an ashtray . . . What did you just say? It's so hard to hear you through all these bandages . . . Oh, yes, the nurse is the sort who would disapprove, at least to judge by her voice, but maybe you can manage to head her off when she comes in—send her to get me a glass of orange juice—and while she's out of the room you can open the window . . .

Anyway, I set the fire with scraps from the weaving studio, if you want to know. I poured gasoline on them and lit them in the rug room, as well as in the room where the old Masurian toys were displayed: rag dolls and wooden instruments, carved and painted birds, which would burn readily. The only person I had confided my plan to was Simon Gayko, a carpenter and cartwright. He came from Lucknow, on Lake Lucknow, like me, and it was Simon who had built the museum to my specifications, in the form of a bower house with a wooden veranda around it . . . No, we were not the only witnesses. Several people saw the museum burn down: my wife Carola, the master weaver Marian Jeromin, who had once been my favorite pupil, as well as my daughter Henrike, and, as I mentioned, Simon Gayko, who went down on his knees when the flames came spewing out of the windows, fanned by a breeze that sprang up as if on command. No one made the slightest attempt to extinguish the fire. My wife leaned in the doorway of our house and shaded her eyes with her hand. Marian stood there still as a statue under the red beeches. My daughter, Henrike—who, by the way, had been the only one to protest my action and had even pummeled me with her fists, begging me to do something about the fire—she huddled halfway down the path that led to the water and wept . . .

In a little while, young man, in a little while you can peel an apple for me. Thanks.

I had laid the fire at night—I mentioned that already—after our seven weaving pupils had gone home. Now there was a moderate northwester blowing, and it wafted the sparks and smoke out over the Schlei River, just as I had intended. No one was in any danger, even when the fire reached the document room and a sudden gust whirled the papers into the air. They floated away like huge snowflakes, and came to rest on the water or landed in the white hawthorn bushes which covered the steep riverbanks. A strange thing happened: while the museum was burning, two fishing boats sailed out past Egenlund; apparently their crews deliberately ignored the fire, for they glided on through the cloud of smoke and black flakes toward the mouth of the river.

The last room to surrender to the fire was the one with the jewelry display. It contained, among other things, the Drygallian silver arm bracelets and horseshoe brooches, and necklaces of wooden beads with horizontal and vertical fluting, a burial treasure from the area of Sudau, you know. Probably the fire spared the jewelry room for so long because Simon Gayko—one of these days he will drop in to see me and then you'll meet him— he's wiry and crookedly built like a Bosnian, and he has that typically Bosnian determination and persistence in everything he does—but what was I starting to say? . . . Oh, yes, because Simon Gayko had taken my suggestion and equipped the jewelry room with a door sheathed in sheet metal which we kept locked except during visiting hours . . .

That's true, you're perfectly right. Even though no one dared to extinguish the fire so long as I was present, some attempts were made to rescue individual items just before the fire reached them.

For instance, my daughter Henrike begged me to let her salvage the index of Masurian dialect which she had compiled and then transcribed in her best handwriting. I refused . . .

Henrike told you about that? Well, all right . . . I had to refuse to rescue the old carved butter churn for my wife. She was so attached to it. And Marian Jeromin wanted to go in after my big blue and white wedding rug . . . The blue and white wedding rug I had submitted forty years ago in Lucknow for my master weaver's examination; it had vanished and mysteriously reappeared several times. The wedding rug was the only one of my works to bear my initials, Z.R., for Zygmunt Rogalla. With all my other works I insisted on strict anonymity . . .

You don't see why? Just wait, my boy, and listen well, and when you've heard the whole story you'll understand . . . But what was I going to say? Oh, yes, when the museum roof curled up in the heat, when it split open and caved in, there was an explosion in the weapons exhibit—Russian infantry munitions left over from the Winter Battle in Masuria. That shows you how long such things keep! In that same room, Polish, Tartar, and Lithuanian weapons were melting down, as well as the two scimitars with which my ancestors had killed the missionary Bruno von Querfurt and the seventeen men in his party who had come to introduce milder ways to the inhabitants of Lucknow. That was the expression they used: milder ways . . .

No, I'm not mistaken; everything would have subsided into ashes without further ado if the wind had not shifted. The moderate northwester shifted to a brisk southwester, which drove biting smoke into our eyes, ripped through the curtain of smoke hovering over the water, and fanned the dying embers, sending sparks and flames shooting from every dark crevice. And then sparks began to fly, something we had not anticipated. The updraft created by the fire swept lighter objects into the air, where they flared up brightly for a moment before darkening into ash. But they began to glow again as soon as the wind had dropped them onto the straw thatch of our house. Then all at once the weaving studio shot up in flames and its roof became a sheet of fire. The fire licked along the roof joists, leaped through the open windows of the rooms under the eaves, sending down a shower of straw torches, which the southwester swirled around the house, igniting a beam with them here, depositing them in front of a door there . . .

No, you're mistaken. When the fire crossed over to the main house, I was the one who organized the fight against it. We quickly formed a bucket brigade, taking up positions in the front hall, on the stairs, in the story above the weaving studio, and passing the buckets along from the spigot, where my wife filled them, to Simon Gayko, who heaved them up to me under the roof. At first it looked as though all the water I was pouring out in sheets might check the fire. But that infernal smoke forced us to abandon the attic. The smoke also frustrated our efforts to break through part of the burning roof. With ax and crowbar we tried to chop open the gable over the weaving studio, but the angle irons in the old beams held fast, and when wet handkerchiefs over our noses and mouths no longer helped, we had to retreat. From a window I glimpsed our own trail of smoke and sparks, the wake of the fire. Down below in the pasture, the animals panicked and set out at a gallop for the estate, toward Holmbek . . .

Pardon me? But of course we had. Marian Jeromin had called the fire department . . .

Since nothing more could be done, we made individual or group sorties to rescue some valuables and to drag whatever we could outside, especially bedding, furniture, and clothing, even the pieces our weaving pupils had been working on. We kept this up as long as the heat and smoke permitted. Only my daughter refused to help; she huddled near the dying embers of our museum and none of us could persuade her to budge from the spot.

Suddenly a stranger appeared under the beeches. Without asking our leave, he rushed into the house and began carrying to safety whatever he could lay hands on. And it was he, the stranger, who helped Simon Gayko and me unbolt the looms, while all around us flaming rafters were crashing down; but even with his help we were unable to heave any of the looms out of the building. We were driven out by the unbearable heat from the burning wool in the storeroom . . .

That was you? You were the stranger who came to our aid? You had come for Henrike? I didn't know that . . . I didn't recognize you . . . But what was I saying?

Out, yes, that was it. We were just catching our breath under the beeches, surrounded by the objects we had rescued, when Marian Jeromin, whose hair and eyebrows were singed, checked over the chaotic heap and suddenly realized that the book was missing. No sooner had he mentioned it than I was already soaking my handkerchief and wringing it out over my head. I turned a deaf ear to his warnings and his offer of help. With the handkerchief over my face, I rushed to the door of the house, from which yellow and blue smoke was billowing. I had not even reached the worn stone steps before Simon Gayko and Marian Jeromin seized my arms from behind and pulled me away, remonstrating with me. I acted as though I were giving in; actually I was only waiting for them to think they had dissuaded me and loosen their grip. Even if there had been four of them, they could not have held me. All I had to do was twist a bit, give one shove, and I broke free and dashed through the smoke into the house and up the stairs to the cupboard where I kept the book . . .

Yes, it meant that much to me, and there was good reason for it's not being part of the museum inventory.

Sonja Turk had taken thirty years to write the book, in her self-righteous old German script, and I had trimmed the pages myself and bound them in red kid before she passed it on to me, the only pupil she had ever consented to take on . . .

And who was Sonja Turk? The greatest, most singular rug-maker in the history of Masuria.

I pressed the heavy book close to my body. Those blotched pages contained everything that had once produced the threefold flowering of our rugmaking art: the combination of symbols, with their proven magic effects, the secrets of deriving dyes from the kaddik bush, dye camomile, and madder, and of course also the patterns and techniques for our double weaves and knotted rugs. Although the staircase swayed beneath me, I managed to get back down to the vestibule—holding the book, Sonja Turk's unique bequest, which I had gradually committed to memory, with all its little errors and quaint turns of phrase. And then, at the foot of the stairs, I was hit by a piece of flaming banister on almost the same spot where the bullet struck that time they tried to execute me. I fell down, thinking I had the book firmly in my arms as I fell. I still believe, my boy, that I buried it beneath

me, but none of the men who carried me out of there could find
it in the vestibule, not even Marian Jeromin, who helped get me
outside and then went back in, as I expected him to, and as he
expected himself to, and searched until the smoke forced him to
quit . . .

Yes, Martin Witt, that's what I'm afraid of; I assume the book
itself burned. But it is not completely lost, at least not in the same
final sense in which the objects in the museum are lost. I have it
stored in my memory and intend to record it again, in Sonja
Turk's own language . . .

Pardon me? Too much was lost? Irreplaceable objects? The
very thought of such a loss pains you? If one wants to set a
record straight, Martin Witt, often pain cannot be avoided. And
I had to set the record straight, after all that happened . . .

Well, they carried me to the heap of rescued household objects
under the red beeches, and they bedded me down so I was looking not toward the fire but out over the water, but whenever I
came to after brief periods of unconsciousness, I saw the fire
reflected in the treetops and in the many unfamiliar faces, and the
faces revealed the true state of affairs. One face finally showed
what had happened to me. It was my wife's. She found me at last,
and even as she bent over me, she drew back in horror and alarm.
She summoned up all her strength to look at me for a moment,
then covered her face with her hands and hurtled away, without
a word . . .

Let's hope so, my boy, let's hope the new skin heals well, the
islands of new skin which they have grafted onto me . . . I'm
prepared for the worst; even skin has memories, after all. In any
case, I'm grateful that you're here, at least. I predicted that Henrike would not come . . .

Did you say Henrike doesn't know you're here? Then I'm
even more grateful to you. I just hope she hasn't done anything
rash—I know she's capable of that . . .

She's living at your house? That reassures me. I know how
much influence you have over Henrike . . . She told me a lot
about you . . . Yes, your influence. It was so great that she even
lit upon oceanography one day—as a possible field to study, I
mean . . .

You don't understand why I set the fire? That's just because you don't know what led up to it. Wherever one chooses to start, things have already happened, the course has been laid out, conditions determined, premises established; we come on the scene only to carry something to conclusion, or to grow into a shape which chance has long since selected for us ...

Certainly I'm willing, with all it entails, yes. I'm willing to tell you the whole story, even if it brings back all the old pain, the old emotion—but where should I begin? The fact that I am lying here could be traced all the way to those white-caped men with the Balkan Cross, the Grand Masters of the Teutonic Order who subjugated my people in order to confer the blessings of their highly developed administrative system on them, as well as their cross and their exemplary system of finance, which, as you may know, was based on four sources of income. But I might also begin with Hyronimus Rogalla, a documented early ancestor of mine, who achieved renown as a beekeeper and distiller; one day he was under a bee tree sleeping off a drinking bout from which only he could have recovered, and thus he survived the second Tartar attack on Lucknow, in which all the males were slaughered.

Another figure to begin with would be the false priest who called himself Johann von Rogalla and turned up here and there in Masuria after the plague, where he ordered the bewildered survivors to worship him; his passion for gambling proved his undoing ...

No, no, I understand your interest, and I acknowledge your special right to seek information about all this ... It's simply that I probably won't be able to locate the exact point at which this whole development began, because no matter where one starts, one is always dealing with results, never with primary causes, yes ... There is too much along the way—people, constellations, atmosphere, or simply the lost country, Masuria—too much forces itself upon one's attention and demands explanation ... Where should I start, what should I focus on first ...

Maybe I should start with my grandfather, the estate manager Alfons Rogalla, who always asserted he would die only with his own permission; a domineering, driven man who thought every job got done too slowly and daily cautioned his help to speak as little as possible, because idle talk simply wasted time. Although he was only an estate manager, he had assumed the habit of regarding the entire estate as his own, and he treated the horses, the stablehands, and even the pigeons accordingly. Perhaps it was because of his immoderate pretensions that we were all afraid of him. Alfons Rogalla with his crippled leg . . .

But now I see someone else beckoning to me, my uncle Adam Rogalla, the self-styled local historian, the gently agitated mole grubbing through our Masurian past. He invites me to delve into the abundant bog with my blue and yellow shovel; he teaches me, if not reverence, then awe for the eloquent relics of our early times; in the course of years of fanatical collecting, he has transformed his house into a museum of regional history, and there I learn that any understanding of the world must begin at home— or end there. Since he died without issue, one fine day I inherited the house and the collection. To him, who so successfully instilled enthusiasm for all these things in me, I owe a great deal, or enough, at any rate, so that it would be fitting to begin with him . . .

But there is another person I really can't avoid mentioning, a person who certainly merits being placed at the beginning of my tale: my father, Jan Rogalla, the most famous distiller and vendor of marvelous elixirs who ever roamed Masuria. I was allowed to sit beside him in his elegant two-horse conveyance, dressed in my faded sailor suit, holding the homemade cage that contained the adder Ella. Our horses' heads were decked out with nodding bunches of artificial flowers, and wherever we appeared, we were immediately surrounded by spectators; everyone wanted to secure a good spot for the high point of our presentation, the moment when my father would bare his arm, revealing dozens of blue and red bite marks, plunge it into the cage, and provoke the adder until she lashed out and sank her fangs into him . . .

Or Sonja Turk. Without Sonja Turk I would not even be here, for it was she, our greatest rugmaker, who waded into the Lucknow River one day, extended a long branch to a boy caught in the current, and dragged him to shore. I regained consciousness on her drying meadow, amid all the glowing skeins of wool in indigo blue, white, and red . . .

Yet when I think of it, there is someone else who played a major part in my decision: Conny Karrasch, the great Konrad

Karrasch. Whenever I remember him, I feel a stab in my upper arm. We are standing solemnly on the old Castle Hill, at the spot where the mountain falls away into a wooded gorge. All this was long, long ago, on the first day of the First World War. I can feel the knife stab and see my blood oozing out, almost reluctantly, only a few drops, into which he repeatedly dips the knife point until the blood clings; then he holds out his own arm to me. He seems less serious than I was, just curious, and I take the knife and place it against his arm just under the vaccination mark. A bit of pressure, a short downward cut, and I dip the knife point into the dark red substance which dribbles jerkily down his arm as though searching for something. Then we place our hands on top of each other and look at one another, standing there by the seven giant spruces . . .

In spite of all that came later, we never canceled that pact; neither one of us declared it void, that brotherhood bond concluded up there on Castle Hill . . .

Yes, all in all, it was probably Conny Karrasch who forced me to make the decision I did, who left me no other choice . . .

Someone's coming? Well, put out the cigarette and close the drawer . . . May I ask how old you are? I would guess about twenty-two. Twenty-four already? I didn't hear any footsteps; you must have been mistaken . . .

Louder, you'll have to speak a bit louder . . . You're right, one has to make up one's mind. Since that's the case, I'll begin the way I have to, with swirling vapor clouds, multicolored mists which eddied out of my father's so-called laboratory through every crack and cranny into our living quarters, where, depending on the substances and combinations of the moment, we had our violet periods or brown periods, or our poisonous yellow periods. The gases released by heated sulfur, by mercuric chloride, by distilled rosemary billowed about and worked their way through the keyholes, along with the fragrances of all the dried herbs he heated in a pan or boiled for an infusion. We sat there patiently, and as the vapor clouds darkened the rooms and obscured our view of one another, we listened timorously to the sounds: pans being scraped, test tubes tinkling, filters gurgling, and colanders vibrating as they were beaten. And since our livelihood depended on the potions he brewed and distilled in his laboratory, we sat there and tolerated all kinds of ills—speech disturbances, coughs, vomiting, and even colorful visions—symptoms he himself was apparently completely, or almost completely, spared . . .

Don't think for a moment he was just boiling and mixing at random in there. No, with the help of his mysterious and venerable tomes he was systematically searching for the *magisterium*, the substance that can heal all diseases, and his chief guide on this venture was Basilius Valentinus, a painstaking visionary who had worked with ammonia, fulminating gold, and lead sugar, adapting them for the practice of medicine . . .

Yes, in the beginning were the vapor clouds, which spread inexorably and suffocatingly through our little whitewashed house on Lake Lucknow, powerful vapor clouds which drew festering saltpeter flowers out of the walls and etched the beams and turned our skin dull and yellowish. The two cats had long since run off; birds and butterflies gave the house and grounds a wide berth. Guests would quietly keel over and have to be carried out to the crooked boardwalk down by the water—this usually occurred during mealtimes. The moment someone began to babble at the table or halted in mid-sentence or complained of a mysterious loss of appetite, we knew what was about to happen, and without a word I would go out and sweep off the walk. My mother, who always smelled of sulfur and ammonia, seemed to have resigned herself to the situation. She never complained or showed anger, and she accepted the multicolored vapor clouds as a necessary by-product of the miraculous oils, powders, and essences. In my mind's eye I always see her brushing the blooming vapor clouds aside with a limp hand, materializing out of them in slow motion, and then plunging into them as if for good, her apron strings fluttering in the breeze.

We never saw her agitated, and I was already convinced that nothing whatsoever could excite her, when suddenly I myself began to suffer from lack of appetite and dizzy spells, this in spite of having been accustomed to the vapors from earliest childhood. I turned an ominous yolk-yellow, and in less than a week had lost the strength to drag my footstool by a string down to the lake where I regularly washed it. Much disturbed, my mother moved my bed under the window, which she left open. She stuffed me with milk and honey. She bought me currants on the sly; but all these measures could not prevent my fainting dead away one afternoon, falling off my footstool after attempting to capture some particularly heavy vapor clouds in those cones of paper the vegetable women used at the marketplace. When my mother found me lying there, she is supposed to have uttered the one and only shriek of her life. She picked me up, carried me down the stairs (I was already coming to), kicked open the door to the laboratory, although we were all strictly forbidden to enter, and bore me in a sort of solemn indignation to a scarred and blackened workbench, where she deposited me with the words, "Looka-here, you've done in our Zygmunt, our little mouse." Her accusatory gesture was intended to call his attention to the first victim of his fantastical science.

From behind a test tube my father looked at us dumbfounded, squeezed his eyes shut, and opened them, looking more dumbfounded still, but not because the first victim of his vapor-releasing science had just been carried in, but rather because his entire family had flouted his ban and set foot inside his laboratory. Nothing worse could be imagined, and thus he listened in a daze to the plan my mother had hatched posthaste for rescuing me from his vapor clouds. Twice a week, that is to say, at those times when he attempted to draw the innermost secrets out of substances with the aid of heat and biting acids, I was to accompany Uncle Adam to the bog, the soggy meadows beneath Castle Hill, where only clean winds blew and "there isn't anyone sulfuring around." Out there by the seven spruces I was supposed to lose my yellowish yolk color, be freed of my hiccuping among the meadow herbs, and there, where my Uncle Adam dug and delved with his wooden spade, in the shelter of the warm peat terraces, I was to be cured of my dizzy spells. Jan Rogalla, my father, just stared at me with pained astonishment, as if I were a chemical compound that had gone wrong, a compound that made sense on paper and yet had failed ...

For fuel, you say? Oh, you want to know if the peat was dug for fuel? Certainly, but not by Uncle Adam. He carried not a crowbar but a wooden spade, which he used with utmost care, as well as a trowel, a scraper, and even brushes. All these implements came in handy for his tenacious work in the bog, at the foot of Castle Hill. You want to know what he was up to? He was excavating our past, the most industrious mole ever to unearth our early history . . . By the way, Uncle Adam was not my father's brother but the brother of my grandfather, that's right . . .

We met at the wild pear tree, whose fruit was hard and bitter, and whose branches frightened me when I was alone because they were so tangled and twisted. I, too, was equipped for the moor, with a dark loden coat like Uncle Adam's, a knapsack like his, and a shovel to match his spade, except that mine was a blue toy shovel, which I carried with its yellow handle over my shoulder. His greeting was extravagant, for he was an emotional man. He swept me off the ground, shovel and all, raised me up close to his large, owl-like face, jerked back his broad-brimmed hat with a toss of his head, and then kissed me here and there at random, pressing me violently to him. I had no sooner touched ground again than he seized my hand and dragged me wordlessly down the sandy path which led to Borek Forest, dragged me impatiently along the edge of the woods and up a hillock toward Castle Hill. Here he had to stop, look, and listen. But this was not the recently retired art teacher Adam Rogalla surveying the landscape. This was the self-styled local historian, and because he did not let go of my hand, but rather squeezed it convulsively, his excitement transmitted itself to me. The narrow spit of land between Lake Tartar and Lake Lucknow suddenly seemed populated; the air was full of the tumult of many voices and galloping horses' hoofs, and from the depths of Castle Hill came a rumbling and shaking as if heavy wooden gates were being stormed.

Anyone posted on Castle Hill could not help throwing up fortifications. One barely had time to man the walls and bar the gate before the tongue of land below was thronged with white capes, flashing against the background of black, motionless lakes and dull silver poplars. And their capes were barely spotted with red when down there among the grim kaddik bushes there was a whooshing and darting of Lithuanian arrows. One could take one's pick when it came to the attackers. Tartars on shaggy ponies, wretched Swedes, time and again fanatical Polish cavalry, and finally Samsonov's faltering infantry.

I have no doubt that Uncle Adam, standing there and listening, found himself involuntarily fortifying Castle Hill against an attack, or at least recalling how often and against whom it had been defended during those times for whose historic relics he delved.

In any case, from Castle Hill one could see out over the brown terraces, which he had carved out and cleared, an entire network of corridors, shafts, and tidy platforms, which began in the bog and extended toward the sparsely wooded slope of the hill; it looked as though he had saved the hill for later, planning to compensate himself with the innumerable treasures it surely contained for the slim yet informative pickings he brought home from the bog.

At the sight of the terraces, with their cleanly scraped plateaus and sharply carved-out walls, my shovel grew restless, quivering and flipping like a divining rod. I could barely wait to descend the slope and go to work.

We heaved off our knapsacks, and placed them neatly side by side. While he was removing the finer tools from their protective wrappings, I gulped down my raspberry fizz and ate the sandwiches with the thickest spread, for out there in the "unsulfured" wind amid the meadow herbs I had recovered my appetite far better than my mother could have hoped. Before we got started, Uncle Adam showed me shards of a jar, smoke-darkened stones, and a skeleton with a tale to tell, or rather, two skeletons, one of a large bird and the other of an even larger fish. Apparently the bird, whose claws were locked into the fish's backbone, had pounced on the fish and tried to pull it out of the water, but had not succeeded; nor had it succeeded in opening its locked claws, with the result that they had swum along together for some time with a great flapping of wings and thrashing of tail, until one had given up the struggle.

Then Adam Rogalla pointed out a corner in his system of trenches and showed me how to wield shovel and spade: never perpendicularly, never violently, but always at an angle and delicately; at the slightest resistance I should put aside the shovel and cautiously poke with trowel and brush, for, as he said, "There's nothing makes the archaeologist so bitter as finds he has botched up himself."

I dug. The little shovel grubbed and poked in the peat as if it were intent on uncovering our entire past in one day. There was much scratching, and a cracking sound when I chopped through the leathery old roots, and when I dumped the powdery soil over the edge of my pit, the wind whirled it in brownish clouds toward Castle Hill.

I would have loved to unearth animals, especially bear skeletons, but skeletons of lynx, martin, and beaver would have done, too. But I dug and dug, and nothing appeared, at least nothing that even faintly resembled a fang. Gradually my shovel went limp with disappointment, poking away more and more aimlessly. Along with the disappointment came exhaustion, and I sat down on a nearly dug-out step and watched the bent back of Adam Rogalla, who was carving brown pie slices out of a mound, surveying each piece with eagle eye, then deliberately moving on to the next one. As I watched him, I carelessly swung my shovel. Several times it struck broadside against the edge of the trench. Suddenly I was sure I had heard something, a brief echo that became more audible every time my shovel struck a certain spot in the wall. After repeating the experiment a number of times, I inserted the shovel horizontally, hollowed out a little cave, scratched and brushed, and soon coaxed a rusty but still shining gold urn out of the opening.

I shouted for joy and called Adam Rogalla. I banged the gold triumphantly with my shovel and danced and pranced around the object. He ambled over, far too slowly for my taste, showing much too little excitement, and instead of kneeling down and polishing and brushing until the treasure blinded us with its brilliance, he gave the urn a scornful kick with his heavy double-stitched boots. The urn received a sizable dent, and as it rolled away, the cover fell off and out tumbled a few bones.

I rushed after it, intending to gather up the bones, those sacred Sudauese and Prussian bones, perhaps the bones of my own ancestors, but my uncle held me back. He bent down to pick up a scrap of paper which the breeze swirled out of the urn and read expressionlessly, "Rogalla has already gnawed these bones." Then with barely contained rage, he collected the cooked and well-gnawed bones, flung them into the metal jam pail which I had taken for an urn, and hurled the container as far as he could.

He grimly scrambled out of the trench, and I did the same. He gesticulated threateningly in the direction of the kaddik bushes, and I, too, gesticulated mechanically at the green wall pierced with streaks of rust color. And wonder of wonders, our combined imprecations caused a stirring among the graceful canes, and we caught sight of a dull blond head in flight, then kneesocks with red bands, and we could trace the path of his flight by the parting and snapping back of the branches.

"Mischief, mischief," Adam Rogalla muttered, "just keep up the mischief, and one day you'll be all mischiefed out." As we descended the hill, he explained that there was one brat who kept "mischiefing up" his work, who took pleasure in burying nails and mousetraps and bicycle bells and flashlight batteries in his hallowed ground, with the specific intention of irking the awed researcher. My uncle mentioned the boy's name in tones of deepest bitterness: Conny Karrasch . . .

Pardon me? Yes, the ancient Prussians were our ancestors, and they were related to the Sudauese, gatherers of honey and remarkable hunters, I would imagine. It is to them that we owe the discovery that one can capture a drunk bear more easily than a sober one. Bowls of brandy mixed with wild honey accounted for the better part of their success at the hunt . . .

But what was I saying? Oh, yes, I knew Conny Karrasch before he knew me. He was the boy who teased and plagued Adam Rogalla, who desecrated the peat terraces, the little scoundrel whom my uncle pelted with threats and curses. And even before I met him, I knew that his father reigned over the white, thick-walled Lucknow Prison, which had once been a fortress of the Teutonic Knights. It had steep, unscalable walls that looked out over the lake. How I envied him for being able to live within those walls, with their gleaming glass splinters along the top! And what wouldn't I have given for just one glimpse inside! I would even have parted with my wild bird's egg collection. But for the time being Conny Karrasch was nothing but a dull blond mop of hair out in the bog, the occasion of Adam Rogalla's impotent rage out there beneath Castle Hill, where I was supposed to be recovering from the vapor clouds my father cooked up in his laboratory. And in fact I did recover.

I was eager to get well quickly, for the autumn fairs were coming up in Lucknow and vicinity, and that meant trips to Prostken, Malkihnen, Milucken, and Mostolten, as well as to Skomanten and Kobilinnen, the inhabitants of which places would dwell far into the cruel winter on two topics: the most recent jailbreak of Hugo Bandilla, the self-styled king of the Masurian smugglers, and my father's act with the adder Ella.

You may rightly assume that these trips yielded early and powerful impressions: the ride through the autumnal moors and heaths, beneath birches, firs, and birches again, over stony roads and stubble fields and narrow wooden bridges battered by the clumsy harvest wagons. Everywhere smoldering piles of potato vines. Mighty cloud formations in the sky. Woodpeckers hammering away madly in every clearing. Huge spiderwebs. Dusty thistles. Brambles and more brambles. Not a blueberry bush but might be hiding a wild-eyed vagabond who could lunge out at any moment. Wherever there were geese, there was also a mean-tempered gander. The farm dogs tugged at their chains when they caught sight of our horses crowned with nodding bunches of artificial flowers.

Breathless little crowds gathered to either side of the road wherever we were sighted. Lumbermen leaped to shore across their logjams and stared after us. Schoolchildren rushed outside as if their school were on fire. Old women gleaning in the fields straightened up and waved; and in the semidarkness of the fir forests, woodsmen waved their fur caps with turned-up ear flaps.

Jan Rogalla, my father, cast impassive eyes over the crowds, seeming to ignore the veneration and the greetings, as if external appearances meant nothing to him, who lived only to get to the bottom of things, to the bubbling, steaming bottom, that's right, where the *magisterium* lurked. You must imagine him this way: beneath a dull black peaked hat, a pale, lean face expressive not only of burning passion for the search but also of a marked lack of fresh air; a white scarf over his collarless shirt; a black velvet jacket with a double row of mother-of-pearl buttons, and tight, dark trousers which always hung at half-mast, so to speak. And me beside him in my worn sailor suit. The band on my cap identified me as belonging to the good ship *Alsatia*. On my knees rested the wrapped cage in which Ella dozed in unimaginative coils, forever tired out from her digestive processes. It was to be taken for granted that all the way from Alt-Kriewen to Zinschen the heavy carts moved aside to let our smart two-horse carriage pass, that bystanders greeted us quickly and somewhat nervously, and that whatever marketplace we rolled into, people seemed to have been expecting us. The moment we turned up, all other commerce seemed to flag or was simply suspended. Eggs and butter were left to their own devices, ducks which a moment ago people had been pinching and patting appreciatively were thrust head down into their baskets; whitefish, perch, and carp, which were slippery enough anyway, leaped out of the fishmongers' hands into the tank; that the apples were rosy-cheeked, the potatoes redolent of fresh earth, the plums juicy and shining, helped them not at all, and even blueberries and currants received no notice, simply because the news of our arrival had traveled like lightning along the endless row of vans, and everyone scurried to secure a spot with a good view. How they thronged around us, blocking our way: in huge kerchiefs, in felt boots, with whips under their arms, baskets and bundles clasped to their bellies; here a man with a colt on a halter, there another man panting because in his excitement he had forgotten to put down his sack of potatoes. Someone else was clutching a goose, another was brandishing smoked eels, and whether chewing, smoking, or sucking, what they all had in common was an expectancy in which hope mingled with fear.

At first Jan Rogalla would just sit on the box, sunk into himself, his shoulders hunched, his hands under his leather apron. Yet his eyes were open and scanned the crowd, while his slightly skewed face was lit by attentive receptivity, as though he were waiting for a message audible only to him. Then he jerked to his feet and almost too elegantly swept his hat through the air, to which the audience responded with varying degrees of enthusiasm. But that was simply his style of greeting; it gave him the air of a magician, although certainly nothing could have been farther from his intention. However, he immediately canceled this impression when he climbed off the box and whipped the waterproof tarpaulin from the shelves and cabinets packed with the marvelous elixirs he himself had distilled, poured into bottles, and labeled, each with its own mysterious and resonant name . . .

Yes, dear Martin Witt, we'll get to that, all in due time. A single gesture, an upward toss of his hand, brought his audience to attention. His speech was softly spoken, full of hesitations, as though he were talking to himself, and what he had to say

aroused astonishment in people who had never before been astonished. My father's thesis was that the true ruler of Masuria was
not loneliness, nor yet poverty, but sickness in all its thousand
manifestations.

He said what hardly anyone before or after him dared say, and
that is that there was basically only one sickness, the quintessence
of all sicknesses. One should picture it as an ancient crone, whose
only purpose was to command dread and respect under a multitude of guises; sometimes she came masked as fever, sometimes as
falling sickness; in one person she would appear as tooth decay, in
another as anthrax. Yet despite her many masquerades, he, my
father Jan Rogalla, had seen through her, hunted her down, and
discovered that behind them all lurked one basic force, that of
disease per se.

It was against her that he waged war with all his scientific
weapons. With the help of the *magisterium* he would worst her,
he hoped; yet until he achieved this, he unfortunately had to
make do with specifics as numerous as the manifestations of sickness itself. But, as he said, "better a small cannon than no guns at
all."

And you should have heard him when he drew a picture of
Masurian life as threatened on all sides by sickness, pain, and
affliction. There was not a merry mushroom gatherer who did
not risk being poisoned someday, not a farmer who might not be
struck down by lightning or a horse's hoof. The peat worker had
always to reckon with the danger of contracting swamp fever.
The butcher was constantly threatened by trichinosis, and every
barefoot boy behind the barn was just asking to be pierced by a
rusty nail. The civil servant, however important the papers that
crossed his desk, would not be spared a stroke. And the logger
could never be sure that his work in the dank woods would not
bring on boils. If one listened to my father, it became clear that
every Masurian was doomed to come down with a specific disease, a curiously fitting disease, which one could contract by
contagion, in a fight, in an accident, or through simple bad luck.

Yet despair was not in order, for he, Jan Rogalla, had managed,
in his scientific battle against disease, to produce medications
which would enable everyone to ease his lot, if not entirely escape it. He called the audience's attention to the contents of the

shelves and cabinets. He publicly thanked the substances for revealing to him their marvelous properties. The implication was that he had concluded a pact with the substances that went beyond the merely medical. And with sovereign modesty he let his audience know that fulminating gold had bared its innermost secrets to him, which put him in a position to offer them opportunities the likes of which they had never seen before . . .

No, no, no glimpses of the future . . . He had drops for sale which, added to cabbage soup, almost at once stimulated the God-fearing spirit. He had a salve against wounds dealt by Cossack sabers—apparently an attack by Cossacks could be expected any day. But the prize item in his special offer was a gritty, ammonia-smelling powder which could make a smuggler invisible. This brought the first reaction from the crowd; voices were raised, first shyly, then more boldly; how much did the powder cost? What was the recommended dosage: was one supposed to drink it with water: and finally, how long did the invisibility last and what had one to do to become visible again?

These questions Jan Rogalla waved aside as if they were premature, for before the actual sales got underway, one more thing had to be done. Proof had to be offered that all the drops, powders, and essences actually lived up to their claims. My father prepared for the test that would demonstrate his integrity. Slowly he pushed up the sleeve of his jacket, rolled up his shirt sleeve, and showed the audience his forearm with its blue and red spots. All those standing close by could attest that his forearm was dotted with marks from tiny, dagger-like teeth. His skin looked like a needlework sample, embroidered in blue and red, without the slightest trace of infection. He urged the audience to note the delicate patterns of dots, while he gazed out over the heads of the crowd toward the nearby forest and bog, and remarked somberly that in these times neither our forests nor our bogs were safe, for there, too, peril lurked, for the berry picker as for the woodsman. He meant the irritable, hissing adder, which puffed up when angered.

When he spoke the peril's name, that was my cue to bring him the covered cage. His face twitched as he took it, held it up, turned it, and then, again somewhat too elegantly, uncovered it, swirling the blue cloth two or three times through the air. There lay Ella, drunk with sleep as usual, her two-foot-long body so twined and twisted upon itself that it was hard to tell where she began and where she ended. By the way, we had named her after a sister of my mother's whose speech consisted of a barely intelligible hissing. Although Ella had played her part so many times before, she seemed to have forgotten her role each time, so that her master had to invent ever new approaches.

So now he opened the cage, held it up, and showed it around. There was no swagger in his manner; rather, he seemed grave and solemn and kept his lips pressed tightly together. He placed the cage on a wooden crate, made a fist, and thrust his arm into the cage. Several times he prodded the adder. Beneath the scales of her neck something began pulsing. Slowly the flattened head reared back, all the way to the wall of the cage. Now her whole body lifted. Her tongue darted at the forearm, and suddenly, with a rattling noise and with the full force of her muscles, she struck, once and then again, and Jan Rogalla's face quivered and his eyes clenched shut. Ella's longest, inward-curving fang was located in her upper jaw, and when that fang had dug in, you know, my father could pull his arm out of the cage and the whole snake came with it. And that he did. He extended his arm so that everyone could see the adder dangling from it, holding herself only by her fangs, and not letting go. Then came a firm squeeze on her throat, and Ella opened her jaws and tumbled back into the cage.

Oblivious to the applause, which was rather scanty anyway because most of the audience were in a state of shock, Jan Rogalla rolled down his shirt and jacket sleeves, and with remarkably steady fingers replaced his silver cuff link. Then he reached for a little bottle on a shelf, read the label, sniffed the cork for good measure, and before the eyes of the multitude poured himself three teaspoons of the viscous liquid, which he not only swallowed solemnly but appeared to listen to as it went down, as if he could hear the battle raging in his innards between the poison and the antidote.

With a satisfied smile, he indicated to the audience that his miraculous specific had triumphed—no need to keep an anxious eye on him for the next hour.

Only now did Jan Rogalla receive the applause his performance deserved. Clapping heartily, the audience moved closer, wondering aloud or to themselves which illness they wanted to relieve or prevent. I watched over the cigar box, which began to fill up with our revenues; I was responsible for seeing that each customer paid the right price for his medicine: a mere twenty-five pfennigs for forestalling tooth decay, while the remedy for falling sickness cost two marks. We cured swamp fever for one mark seventy, asked two and a half marks for putting the lame back on their feet, and for only a taler could banish St. Vitus's dance. Three marks twenty-five allowed one to laugh at the bite of an adder . . .

What's that? What did we charge for making the blind see? That was not on our list, not so much because we had overlooked the matter, but because of a strange reluctance on my father's part. For all his faith in himself, he refused to deal with amputees, and if you really wanted to put him in a rage, you had only to ask him to raise someone from the dead.

Don't smile too soon, my boy; there was a limit he respected absolutely, and he felt quite content with the successes he achieved in his clearly circumscribed field . . .

You want to know what these successes were. I could name you many; but the most momentous one, though more for me than for him, happened at the Lucknow marketplace about the time of the first snowfall.

It must have been that snow which set Ella on edge and kept her from sinking back into her digestive torpor immediately after the performance—after all, under normal circumstances she would have been deep in hibernation by this season. At any rate, she was slithering around restlessly in her cage, hissing and darting her forked tongue, forcing the tip of her hard, leathery tail out through the bars. Jan Rogalla was helping his customers, I was guarding the cigar box, and neither of us noticed Ella's irritability or the boys who had sidled up to the cage and were teasing the adder, counting her coils with a stick or trying to rob her of a few of her scales. Suddenly we heard a scream—it still rings in my ears: a sharp, shrill scream that broke off as if smothered in pain. At first all I saw was a dull blond mop of hair, a face daringly pressed to the bars of the cage, and another boy taking to his heels, pushing through the coats and jackets of the crowd.

But when I slid down from my seat on the box to trace the source of the scream, I realized that Ella had struck. The cheek had simply pressed too close, and the adder had darted forward and sunk in her fangs, not with all her might, for the bars were too close together for that, but deep enough so that her fangs pierced the skin of the cheek like fishhooks.

My father lifted the lid of the cage and gripped Ella from above, behind the head. He squeezed until her jaw locked; she released her prey and wrapped herself around my father's arm in furious coils. He skillfully brushed her off, eased the pressure a little until she dangled at full length, and dropped her back onto her bed of excelsior. When he had closed the lid, he threw not only the blue cloth but also a horse blanket over the cage.

Only a bit of blood trickled down the boy's cheek, which bore the precise mark of the adder's teeth, a sharp pointed triangle, which the onlookers pointed out to one another with awe. My father calmly set the boy, who kept up a mechanical moan, on the wagon seat, plucked the proper little bottle from the shelf, and pulled the hand-carved teaspoon out of his pocket. He forced the spoon between the boy's chattering teeth, made him take two doses of the miraculous liquid, and patted his head encouragingly. Not a soul objected when we suspended sales to drive the stricken boy home. And that was how I met Conny Karrasch; that was how our unequal fates were joined.

We placed the boy between us on the box, wrapping him in the other horse blanket, and rattled down the hill to Lake Lucknow and across the old bridge that led to the prison island. You see, the prison was housed in what had once been a castle of the Teutonic Order, built on an islet in the lake, and though nowadays there was a causeway and a bridge linking it to the mainland, it was still called the island. We drove along the whitewashed walls topped by shining bits of glass until we came to the wide-ribbed wooden gate. Here Jan Rogalla rapped rhythmically with his whip handle on a little shutter, and when nothing happened, he found and pulled a bellpull, whereupon several bells far inside the walls began to rattle and rumble, to such alarming effect that he involuntarily retreated several steps and stood there looking quite dismayed. Finally, the shutter opened, revealing a snout, two sleepy brown eyes, and a cockade. My father stood on tiptoes. Earnest whispering through the opening. A long, searching gaze from the brown eyes, and then at last the key turned in the lock. When the guard spotted Conny on the box, he hastened to help him down, gestured imperiously to my father, and steered the two toward the warden's residence, with its date in wrought iron above the door. Since he forgot all about me, I shut the prison gate from inside. I had reached my goal. I was standing where I had always dreamed of someday standing.

Let me tell you: if someone had put up a prize for the most beautiful prison in Masuria, our Lucknow prison would have won hands down. Slightly feverish with excitement, I gazed at the rough whitewashed walls. Ancient as they were, there was no crumbling at the seams. They stood there unmoved and definitive, the walls built to withstand Polish scaling ladders, Lithuanian catapults, and Tartar fireballs. Worn stone paving covered the inner court. Edging the main building were narrow flower beds, where blasted asters and marigolds whitened under the first snow. I looked up at the rows of barred windows, searching for a face, expecting to see an impatient signal or a brandished fist. But all the windows remained empty, and I sneaked around the beveled base of the east tower to the garden, the prison garden. Two apples lay on the path. Dropping them into my pockets, I resolved to keep them forever. In the garden I found straight rows of cabbages, late, frost-spotted tomatoes still hanging from their limp vines, and all the way down to the lake shore, down to the incandescent willows, overgrown turnips poked out of the ground. Why had they been left to rot?

Though not a soul was in sight, I felt myself observed, and not just by the crows flapping about in the alders. A stubby little boat was straining at its anchor. Behind bare berry bushes a walled hatchway led into the depths of the earth, and I thought this must be the entrance to the underground tunnel which was reputed to run under the lake. It went back to the days when the prison was still a fortress. I dared not continue my explorations. I fearfully searched the windows of the rear façade for a face, found none, even in the deep-set windows of the tower, but still felt I was being watched and decided it would be sensible to head back toward the gate. There I stood waiting and let the stern black and white stronghold work its spell on me from close up.

This was the sternness of the Teutonic Order, which eschewed all other colors—no red, green, not even that dark blue beloved of the Prussians—probably because the vow of poverty, celibacy, and unconditional obedience was best expressed by black and white . . .

Did you say simplicity? Unbearable simplicity? You have to speak somewhat louder, my boy . . .

Oh, you mean that black and white describes their view of the world? Well, that may be so, but you should remember that the Teutonic Order was started by prosperous merchants of Lübeck, and its original aim was the care of the sick.

Black and white, yes . . .

At any rate, after a while my father returned, looking rather subdued. He handed the guard who was with him the bottle of snake-bite syrup. He said not a word about price, merely instructed that the dosage should be two teaspoons three times a day, and with that we drove back, not to the marketplace, where the crowd was still waiting patiently in the falling snow, but home.

During the next few days Jan Rogalla had his meals brought to him in the laboratory, from which, for the time being, no multicolored vapor clouds issued, but only silence, an ominous silence which at times made us fear he might be dead. But whenever the door was opened, we saw him hunched over the massive volumes of Basilius Valentinus, staring haplessly, worn out by his search for an answer his visionary mentor could not give him. On the floor all about him lay a regular snowfall, scraps of paper covered with half-finished formulas, equations, alchemical symbols. Nothing could distract him, not even a letter from the Kaiser's chancellery in Berlin thanking him for the receipt of a medicine which had effectively banished the "royal migraines."

Five days later we received an invitation to the prison. I recognized the guard the moment he propped his bicycle against our fence, and I greeted him and led him to the laboratory, where he very matter-of-factly requested the pleasure of my father's presence at the prison and, on the point of leaving, added, "You can take that little puppydog"—here he gestured at me with his thumb—"by the tail and bring him along."

We were invited for teatime, and we reached the prison gate

half an hour beforehand and walked up and down there, my father pacing abstractedly. I stuck close to the wall, looking for bits of glass that might have broken off its top. When the moment came to knock, he held me up, and I pounded on the shutter with both fists. It hung by leather hinges and banged so convincingly that this time the guard opened before looking to see who was out there. He saluted, led us to the warden's quarters across a dusky, echoing, freshly scrubbed vestibule, knocked on a door beneath a stone arch, and tugged it open, saluted again, reported something we could not quite hear, then bade us step inside. All I could feel was ants, in the back of my neck, in my stockings, even in my hair; that was why I kept my eyes down as we entered.

What I saw was a massive gold watch chain with boar's teeth set in silver dangling from it; the chain looped across a dark blue, somewhat worn vest, which in turn girded a body that called to mind a clumsily blown bottle. Near the watch chain, at about the same height, two hands, chubby, freckled hands holding a little cloth bag just big enough to contain a handkerchief or a mess of sunflower seeds. And on the outer edges a gray pullover with a white stripe across the chest, a stripe which rose and fell with its wearer's regular breathing, and with it rose and fell the medallion which had been struck for the quincentennial of Lucknow: a hollow-eyed Janus head, one face with a curly beard, the other clean-shaven.

When I finally looked up, I was startled, as anyone would have been, for Conny Karrasch's father was all too much like the bearded half of the Janus head: the same furrowed brow, the same eternal grimness, but also the same expression of calm and determination; only their ages differed. The father was older than Janus; indeed at the time he struck me as too old to be a father, in contrast to Conny Karrasch's mother, who was endlessly animated and round-faced, so fond of talking that she repeated the last portion of every sentence.

Yes, I would have to say that we were received cordially. The warden thanked my father with all due ceremony, and then Conny had to demonstrate that he was fully recovered, free of fever, his tongue no longer swollen, only three red and blue dots on his cheek as a reminder. His parents agreed that the contents of the little bottle had saved him; there was a bit left over which they wanted to keep and pay for, but my father would not hear of this. He promised to have me drop off a sealed bottle someday. After that we had yeast pancakes powdered with sugar, and as always when my father was invited somewhere, the adults soon began trading stories about various illnesses. They shamelessly displayed their scars, dwelt on different forms of death, and once the ice had been broken, the prison warden topped all the other tales by bringing out a snuff box and passing around a kidney stone as large as a pigeon's egg which had been extracted from him. At the sight of the stone, the assembled company became deeply reflective.

Meanwhile, Conny, who was sitting across from me at the massive table, sensed my restlessness and smiled at me over the white candle, for he had caught me looking around the room and making a mental inventory of its contents. Seeing me so impressed, he put on an air of indifference. As cigars were offered, Conny nodded to me; we stood up and slipped out of the room and ascended a well-scrubbed flight of wooden stairs. The same cool, implacable cleanliness characterized everything—the staircase, the winding corridor, even the attic.

Up here a space was marked off, not by walls, but by tautly stretched ropes, a playroom under a dormer window which admitted only a bit of filtered light, so that the entire area was bathed in a greenish hue, a real underwater green, that's right. Still as coolly, Conny beckoned to me to follow him into the roped-off section, but I could already tell what he meant to bowl me over with. There in the greenish light stood a white fortress, a perfect model in plywood and cardboard, whose walls and towers left no doubt that it was Lucknow Prison, or rather a scale model of the same, about knee-high but equipped with every feature of the real one, even to tiny flower beds. We stepped over the rope and sat down in the prison courtyard, where Conny Karrasch reveled in my wonderment; he watched intently as I touched this and that, comparing the model with the original and delighting in the parallels. I could place my hand on the warden's quarters and point to the very dormer under which we were sitting, while Conny indicated the room in which the grown-ups were probably savoring their cigars and meschkinnes, the local honey brandy. But that was not all; Conny Karrasch tugged a bit at the roof, loosening it, and together we lifted it off.

There they were, some huddled close together, others sullenly off by themselves, some with twisted, distorted limbs, as if they had just been tortured—the inmates, with individual faces, but all in the faded prison overalls and the round twill cap. Conny Karrasch lifted them out one by one, looked at them severely, shook them, and lined them up, addressing each doll by name, in a column in the courtyard, apparently for roll call.

There were about twenty prisoners in the lineup. Their painted faces were clearly meant as portraits, and I can still see one with receding forehead and slanted eyes who could be none other than Hugo Bandilla, the self-styled king of the Masurian smugglers. Conny Karrasch took some pride in identifying them for me, all these fellows whom illicit urges or lack of moral sense had brought to this pass, the so-called undesirables of Masuria. He named each one and cited his offense: Heinrich Valendy, stealing poultry; Johann Skodda, fighting with a knife; Otto Michalzik, lèse-majesté; Hermann Hoyer, poaching on government property; Michael Skovronnek, arson; Gottlieb Naujok, smuggling and lèse-majesté; Ludwig Poerschke, don't know, something to do with Sodom; Oskar Dumschevski, boat theft; Eugen Lavrenz, homicide and arson.

With sudden impatience Conny Karrasch swept all the miscreants into a heap and pitched them back into the castle, any which way, face down, their legs painfully twisted. Once we had replaced the roof, he led me across the attic and through another set of cool, bare corridors. We went down several flights of stairs, passed through a dusky tunnel, and reached a door, on which he rapped sharply. An elderly guard in uniform opened it for us. At the sight of Conny Karrasch his sour face brightened. A confidential handshake, conspiratorial whispers. We were admitted into the prison workshop, where rows of tables were heaped with bundles of twigs, rolls of caning, stacks of brown paper, batches of broom straw, smeared paste pots, and piles of precut wooden soles and leather uppers for clogs.

As we entered, all the overall-clad men at the tables turned toward us with common accord, as though their heads were attached to a single string. When they saw who we were, they turned back to their work as if disappointed. But in this brief moment I had recognized the stars of the lot: Hugo Bandilla and the murderer Eugen Lavrenz.

Throwing out greetings left and right, Conny Karrasch went straight up to Eugen Lavrenz, held out his hand, whispered with him, pointed at me, and then I, too, was permitted to shake hands with the prisoner and gaze into his inscrutable face with its quizzical eyes . . .

His case? That I did not hear about until later; what came out now was simply that Eugen Lavrenz knew a story for every lake round about Lucknow—and that meant not only Selment, Sunovo, and Hertha lakes, but all ninety-two of them. Presumably Conny had already heard a good many. He begged for one now, but Eugen Lavrenz shook his head and alluded to some sort of payment which had apparently been made in the past. So firm was he in his refusal that Conny had no choice but to meet his price—a handful of cigar butts, which Conny strewed on the table, and which the man quickly counted and stuffed into his pocket before he served up one of his lake stories for us . . .

Why, of course! How could I forget it! The story flowed along as quietly as a log float on the Lucknow River, and you must realize that he told it without ever once pausing in his work. He took a precut wooden sole from the heap, ran it across the table with an undulating motion, and set it down carefully, transporting us to the fir trees that lined the lakes of Lake Tartar. We saw the black stork who nested there and heard the mysterious sighs and long-drawn-out shouts that anyone would hear if he walked there alone and listened hard enough. The storyteller made bubbles rise up out of the mud, made ducks alight on the water and paddle straight into the reeds in fright. And then from the sand ridge approached the sorry procession of humans and horses. It wove its way through the scattered fir trees, was etched against the always overwhelming sky. Horsemen on shaggy Tartar ponies constantly circled the file; their lances pointed into the air.

The shackled prisoners stumbled down to the lake. They were men and women from Lucknow whom the Tartars had taken captive out of disappointment or fury at not finding what they had hoped for: the buried silver, the livestock that had been turned loose in the forest. And down by the lake they halted the procession of prisoners, conferred with one another, dismounted, and tethered their shaggy ponies to the trees. With their finely plaited knouts they drove the prisoners into the circle which one of the Tartars had traced with the heel of his boot; soon the Tartars had fires going and sat morosely around them, roasting slabs of meat which they carried under their saddles.

Their silence, their fixed look of frustration, made the prisoners uneasy, but especially Maria Chlupka, the mayor's wife. Finally, she could stand it no longer. She negotiated briefly with one of the principal Tartars, then rode off with him and a few companions, though not for long. When they returned, some of the horsemen were balancing little wooden barrels full of honey brandy on their saddles, and tossed these down by the fires.

Only now did the Tartars realize why they had not been flaunting their talents for dancing and singing: the meschkinnes had been missing. So they knocked the bungs out of the barrels, got themselves warmed up, and then sang the songs and danced the dances of their steppes—until finally the mayor's wife and several other women asked whether they might join in, whereupon they were unbound.

They rubbed their wrists and ankles, took off their shoes, tossed away their long overskirts, and danced with the Tartars in the light of the fires, on the banks of the nameless lake. Honey brandy was poured for them, too, and they drank or made as if to drink, while the prisoners still in chains crouched on the sands and looked on hungrily. The Tartars drained the barrels to the last drop and keeled over, dragging the women down with them into the warm sand.

An hour before sunrise—mist hung over the lake—skirted figures rose and scurried about. They bent over the sleeping Tartars, who in the chill of morning lay huddled close to the dying fires. Those prisoners who were awake saw fists plunging down, saw feet raking the ground and bodies rearing up and collapsing, twitching, all without a sound, or almost without a sound. The women dragged the bodies of the Tartars into the water and pushed them under, still cautious and trying to maintain silence; they cleaned up the beach and only then went to the prisoners and cut them loose.

The men and women stood facing each other with a solemnity that came of its own accord; they sought each other's eyes, questioning one another wordlessly, while out on the lake the bodies of the dead Tartars spun slowly and sank.

The mayor of Lucknow, Ottomar Chlupka, was the first to embrace his wife and march up the sand ridge with her, whereupon the others, their limbs still stiff, still trembling and bemused, likewise stepped toward their wives, embraced them, and followed the mayor.

And laying out a line of staples on the workbench, Eugen Lavrenz traced the homeward file, as they went two by two back to the village, leaving behind the somber lake, which from now on was called Lake Tartar.

I was already determined to collect cigar butts; I wanted to hear the other ninety-one lake stories he had in reserve . . .

Yes, you may peel me an apple, but before that I would like something to drink . . .

It doesn't matter about the tea's being cold, thank you . . . Simon Gayko, if he comes someday, and he will come, as will the others—Simon will vouch for the fact that we never went into Lake Tartar barefoot, and this was even without knowing how the lake got its name. There were those bubbles in the mud, and those sounds of sighing, and besides, the minute you dipped your foot in the lake, a dozen leeches immediately swarmed over it. So we never went swimming there, or even fishing. The boat which my grandfather, the estate manager Alfons Rogalla, had brought there, rotted away at its mooring. You see, Lake Tartar was one of the five lakes belonging to the large estate which my grandfather managed, and so this lake belonged to him, too. For although he was only the bailiff, no one ever questioned that he was boss of it all—the horses and the dogs, the stablehands and the maids, and everything that was there. He had the final say, and everyone bowed to the authority of this crookedly built and driven man who had so little use for words that he would have done without them if he could have . . .

I didn't hear what you said, son . . . Did he pay his rents to the legal owner? Oh, yes, once a year he drew up the accounts; once a year he shut himself up in his room for ten days, always in January; his lamp burned almost until dawn, and those who knew him slightly were aware that he was preparing his balance sheets for the bedridden woman in faraway Königsberg on whom his hatred had fastened, as hers had reportedly fastened on him. It was her fixed conviction that he was cheating her, but she kept him on because he knew something that only the two of them knew. Each time she received one of his balance sheets, she responded with knowledgeable, sarcastic questions and ended with an allusion to her unchanging state of health. The whole process so riled him that for days he subsisted on nothing but liverwurst and the fiery brennabor; that was how he calmed himself. It never entered his mind to ask our help, although my father had made up a specific which worked in the area around Lucknow against all sorts of excitation. Its base was woodbine, high in prussic acid; it had to be picked when the moon was waning. My grandfather grudgingly permitted my father to park his two-horse carriage in one of the estate sheds and let the horses into the paddock, but no more. He had nothing but scorn for my father's visionary science, and further condemned us for introducing people to diseases they had previously not noticed, to which they then completely capitulated, as he put it. But that did not keep him from sending for us whenever some job on the estate became pressing, not for my father, to be sure—him he dismissed with a wave of the hand. The message was: "Ida should come help; we can't manage no more."

At the estate the wind seemed to be always swirling across the rutted clay courtyard, blowing about wisps of hay and straw. The two slavering dogs were checked in mid-leap by their chains. From the smithy the usual sound of hammering sounded. At the edge of the murky, manure-filled pond strutted the ganders, tails high. They stretched out their necks and came at one's calves, hissing fiercely. I always remembered to take along a stick to deflect their beaks.

At the estate things were always happening to furnish rich material for talk. Someone was always catching his arm in the straw machine or being kicked in the hip by a horse, falling off a hay wagon, being gored by the bull, or at least cutting himself on a rusty scythe. You catch my meaning, son. Every department offered its special drama, even the poultry house, especially during the duck slaughter, which you must picture as silent teamwork requiring great skill as well as exceptionally strong fingers.

Old Pivko, an outrageous braggart even by Masurian standards, had driven the flock of ducks into their pen, eighty or a hundred of them. The ducks fluttered about, trying to escape his staff, from which hung an oval loop of woven wire, a loop which he dangled and jiggled in front of the blackish-brown duck eyes, before he jerked it over a head and pulled it tight. That put an end to the quacking, but the bird could still beat its wings furiously, flailing wildly with desperately splayed feet, and in its terror defecating in a great arc. Pivko lifted the lassoed duck out with the staff. I was waiting and grasped the beak with both hands, feeling the bird's breath blasting out of its nostrils. I took care that the neck was stretched out good and long over the chopping block when Pivko raised the ax, measured the duck with his eye, and with a single blow severed the head. The beak tried to open, a bluish film spread slowly over the eyes. I carried the head to a canvas where the heads were lined up in rows of ten for easy counting, while Pivko handed the warm, twitching body to Regina Ziemek, who sat humming on a nearby stool with legs outspread. Still humming, she took the duck, slit the neck artery with a small knife, and let the duck's blood drain into an earthenware basin, stirring at frequent intervals to keep the blood from hardening.

Regina Ziemek, not only the ablest, most steady, but also the most untroubled girl on the estate, a girl whose only remark, no matter what happened, was "What's it to me," or "*Fschistko jedno,*" which amounted to the same thing. Her equanimity was so great, her balance so imperturbable, that she only very rarely lifted her head and glanced out across the farmyard, even now when her own future was at stake, even now when two men were negotiating before a considerable crowd—my grandfather was gone that day—over what name Regina Ziemek would bear in the future. She calmly stirred blood for black pudding, her favorite dish, smilingly handed the duck's carcass on to my mother, who plucked it, slit it open, and masterfully pulled out the entrails and sorted them.

And while this was going on, her future was being decided there in the farmyard, as I said. From where I stood at the chopping block I could clearly see the two rivals: Pravdzik, the chief milker, a stocky man, with a coarse, hard face, and next to him, in battered but stylish boots, Hugo Bandilla, king of the Masurian smugglers, who had taken a day off from prison just for settling this question. Apparently the entire procedure had been agreed upon beforehand by the rivals; they shook hands, and when old Pivko asked the girl, "Which one of 'em do you want to win?" she shrugged and said simply, "It's all one to me."

She went on passing the ducks to my mother at the same steady pace, while out there in the farmyard each of the men shouldered a two-hundred-pound sack of grain, walked over to a tall, springy ladder which led to the loft above the stables, and struggled up the sixteen wooden rungs. With one hand they drew themselves up, rung after rung, and the ladders swayed, rocked, and bent. The climber had to offset that motion, pressing his thighs against the ladder as he made it, rung by rung, up toward the opening, where he could not simply let the sack drop but had to lower it with full control, taking care not to let it tip backward and tumble to the barnyard below.

I should tell you the agreement that had been struck: each man would climb the ladder five times, each time with a two-hundred-pound sack on his back; yet it looked as though the weight were being added to each time, for in spite of the support of his boots, Bandilla could no longer straighten his knees, and Pravdzik made sounds on the ladder such as had never been heard from him before—sounds of distress and despair. When the climber began to tremble, when the load began to sway ominously, when it seemed he would never reach the loft and a little voice seemed to be urging surrender, the man would seek out the other with his eyes, fasten his gaze on him for a moment, and, as if restored by one of my father's miraculous elixirs, climb on, watched by a crowd whose cheerful excitement had passed and been followed by painful silence. Only Pivko, the old braggart, forever grinning under his sun-bleached cap, could not hold back his idiotic commentary; with every second duck he dropped into Regina Ziemek's lap, he gave a report of the way the contest was going, and added, "You'll prob'ly get Bandilla's earrings," or "Pravdzik —now there's a fine name for you."

Once Regina Ziemek squinted over at the rivals, sizing them up, smiled, and then turned back to my mother, intent on learning how she cleaned the pale-blue duck innards, twining and knotting them around duck feet that had already been scalded, to add to the blood pudding. She also wrapped intestines around duck necks, first running the guts through thumb and forefinger, pressing out their greenish, sometimes still recognizable contents; wings were similarly wrapped, but not stomachs; these were slit open, rinsed, and tossed into a wooden tub.

The girl did nothing to undo the impression that she was far more interested in the cleaning, scalding, and wrapping of the innards than in her own future; for even when the rivals began on the second stage of their competition—neither having emerged as a clear victor from the first—she sat there unmoved on her stool, made no effort to see what took place on the muddy bank of the pond, supervised by the ganders . . .

No, don't say that, dear Martin Witt. It was not so much lack of interest as fatalism, the fatalism typical of our region . . .

Well, anyway, the rivals took up their positions on opposite sides of the pond, shed their jackets, and stripped off their collarless shirts, Pravdzik removing his red-and-white-checked milker's shirt. They surveyed the pond, on whose surface little clumps of duck droppings floated. Dragonflies patrolled the area in monotonous swoops. The murky water gave no hint of its depth. Now and then the surface was broken by a carp snapping for insects.

The crowd had followed the rivals and stood by with thoughtful faces and crossed arms. Those who spoke, spoke in whispers. The two men looked at each other. They nodded challengingly from opposite sides of the pond, bent, and picked up the long, heavy whips, horsewhips, you know, the kind used for a four-in-hand, and looked at each other again. Anyone who knew what was at stake here could observe that they lowered their gaze and measured each other from the belt down. And when both had nodded again, they began to snap the heavy whips that came to so fine a point, first high over their heads, then lower and lower; they forced the whistling whips down, down, down, keeping their swings even, so low that sometimes the lash skimmed the water like a swallow. When the lash had achieved sufficient power and the moment seemed right, they struck. They let out the lash to its full extent and snatched it back at almost the same instant, so that the leather rolled up of its own accord or, to be more precise, had so much thrashing slack that it wound itself three or maybe even five times around an object, wrapping it right up with a cracking sound. They were reaching for each other's legs, trying to catch them around the ankles. Once the leather strand had bound the rival in the twinkling of an eye, it would be easy to pull him down and drag him in the mud.

You may well imagine that this was not the moment for laying duck necks on the chopping block; I simply had to see the duel down by the pond, where they were chopping the air in slices. The men seemed calmly and grimly determined, but by no means filled with hatred; a few times when their whips met in mid-swing and became tangled, the two rivals stomped over, breathing heavily but bearing no apparent grudge, untwisted the leather, and helped each other as much as permissible. And I still remember when the snapping and whistling down by the pond let up for a moment, Regina Ziemek leaned a bit forward on her stool, probably thinking a decision had been reached; she was not entirely uninterested, although I am sure she would never have let it be known how she expected the contest to end.

The rivals parted again, returned to their places, and whirled the whips. Suddenly Pravdzik succeeded in landing a blow of such tremendous force that Hugo Bandilla leaped in pain. The whip had only caught him on the top of his boot, but it had wound itself tightly around his leg, and if Pravdzik had pulled in sharply, his rival would probably have fallen. But Pravdzik did not pull, no; he stood there, holding the clear advantage and looking thoroughly bewildered. He let the whip sink to the ground, as if he had achieved all he had set out to do.

His gaze traveled past Hugo Bandilla to the tumbledown smithy, where the collection of worn-out harrows and cultivators lay rusting in the weeds and where suddenly two policemen had appeared. Apparently this was a planned operation, for they separated and advanced toward the pond, two policemen with short swords, whom the rest of us had now also spotted. Hugo Bandilla was the only one who had not; he stood there waiting for the deciding jerk which would bring him down. When our air of suspense finally made him turn around, it was already too late. They came at him from both sides, dashed the whip from his hand, and bound his hands behind his back, two policemen in ill-fitting uniforms, each with his whistle dangling by a braided cord. They tried to ignore the irateness of the crowd, its angry gestures and the scattered curses, because they feared for the success of their mission. Once before Bandilla had made use of a brush between police and bystanders to escape. They prodded their prisoner to move on, hustling him between them. At this moment Pravdzik tugged once on the whip, and the signal was so unmistakable that not only Bandilla but also the policemen came to a halt. Pravdzik sauntered unhurriedly around the pond, gathering up the whiplash hand over hand in uniform lengths, until it led him to the group, more precisely to Bandilla. There he bent down and unwound the whip from his boot. In fact, while he unwound the whiplash, he squinted up at Bandilla, frowning slightly, and as if some account had to be settled, said simply, "I just want you to know I'm giving up my claim, and the best of luck to ye." With that he turned away, a bit too sharply, and, dragging the end of the whiplash behind him, trudged across the yard to the stables; seeing him tramp stolidly past the poultry yard, Regina Ziemek did not need to ask how her future had been decided . . .

Just be patient, my boy. All this is part of the story, and I have to tell it to you, because I myself have often found the key in what seemed like minor details . . . But what was it I wanted to say? . . . The crowd, right, our people on the estate, yes: the maids and the stablehands suddenly began to clap. The applause was meant for both men, so it went in both directions, followed Pravdzik to the stables and Hugo Bandilla up the hill toward the kennels. And suddenly it broke off, like a drive belt that has jumped its track.

Through the open gate rode Alfons Rogalla, my grandfather. The policemen saluted him, but he did not even look up. Slung over his horse's neck in front of the saddle lay something limp and spotted, the body of his dead hound, Griffin. When he reached the crowd, he drew up, flung the body to the ground, seemed to awaken all at once from his brooding, and remarked acerbically that he hadn't, so far as he could remember, given anyone the day off. One impatient gesture from him and they scattered, going back to their jobs—except for a stableboy, whom his glance commanded to stay. He had himself helped off his horse, kicked the dead dog, said nothing more than "Bury him," and came limping toward the poultry house.

The dog had not performed well that day. Grandfather had been off shooting coots on Lake Tartar and had brought down several, who tumbled into the reeds that fringed the lake, where the dog should have retrieved them. But every time the brackish water reached the dog's flanks, he looked back and whimpered, his skin twitching all over. He had refused to obey . . . Yes, it was Lake Tartar, that's right . . .

What did you say? Not only that; my grandfather took time to explain to us: "Actually I should've shot him the first time . . ." So he had shot him the second time he failed to do his duty. But he brought the body home and had it buried behind the smithy, among the stinging nettles. So distrustful was he that he later went to the spot and trampled the grave with his boots. This gnawing distrust was his ruling trait and was forever driving him out to the fields, to the forest, and around the buildings of the estate, to make sure his orders were being executed. He even felt compelled to be present when we received in lieu of wages a milk can of duck blood and a basin of slippery giblets.

Ah, what a pleasure if I could invite you for a kaddik brandy and go over all the makings of a Masurian black pudding. But I realize you have to go now, son. With all its variations the recipe took up more than two pages in the *General Cookbook*, of which we had a copy on display in our museum, in the room devoted to Masurian eating, drinking, and work habits . . .

Yes, I know you have to go . . .

If I only knew where my people were—Carola and Simon Gayko and Marian; if I only knew where they have found shelter. But lying here I can't find anything out. Perhaps the people here just pretend not to have heard any news, in order to spare my feelings. Well, in any case, I know where Henrike is, and for that I thank you . . .

Do you really mean to do that? Well, you may have more luck tracking them down, finding out why they haven't been to see me. No reason to think they were hurt, is there, that something happened to them at the end, after they had carried me out of the range of the fire . . . Pardon me? No, no, don't worry. It's the way it always affects me, it comes from inside; this agitation has been with me for a long, long time; it's become part of me . . .

Oh, I don't doubt it for a minute; after all, you are almost obligated to visit again . . .

You have to go, I understand. I realize you don't want to say hello to Henrike for me. In any case, I'll be glad, very glad, if you come again. You needn't keep to visiting hours.

# 2

COME closer, move your chair closer, son, so I can hear you better and don't have to strain my voice. There, that's better . . .

So Henrike is taking the loss hard; that doesn't surprise me. In fact, I predicted it. Just between ourselves—I would be surprised if it were otherwise, because during those years when we were creating the museum, we were both inspired not only by the same ardor but also by the same conviction that Masuria, this dark, taciturn land, would be lost and given up for lost only when no one was left who remembered it.

Perhaps you've noticed the similarities between Henrike and myself—which became clear whenever we had to defend our museum against her older brother Bernhard's sardonic comments, his ridicule and his political objections. Henrike and I never needed to talk things over; as a matter of course, we found ourselves on the same side, despite the difference in age and experience . . .

Pardon me? No, I could not tell her my real reasons. Perhaps she never will comprehend that sometimes the only way to keep our hands clean is to throw away what we value most.

But what was it I wanted to tell you about? I had it all mapped out in my mind . . . The winter, right, the winter when I first became conscious of how things stood . . .

In the beginning, as I said, there were those multicolored vapor clouds. I stepped out of these artificial mists and, still somewhat lightheaded, discovered a Masuria which began at the white-washed walls of the prison and ended with the estate. And then came a certain winter. You must try to imagine a world snowed in for all eternity. Houses shrunken, forests shrunken, banners of snow swirling in the wind, exhausted crows battling the blasts, glistening sheets of ice. The frost itself sang and the brittle reeds and glazed meadows crackled. In the ice fishermen's creels, perch and whitefish froze, turned fragile as glass. The frost bit through the straw over the root pits and made the potatoes too sweet. Little birds dropped from the trees.

And now picture six sleighs in a row, gliding without bells over the trackless snow, across fields and meadows, parallel to Lake Lucknow. In them people all bundled up, headed for the Juschken inlet and the rugged hill on which stood the settlement of Little Grajevo.

No, that was not its official name. It was we who had given this cluster of moss-grown shacks the name of Little Grajevo, because the inhabitants had taken refuge there, cut off from the rest of the world—Polish farmhands and loggers who had been cutting rafters in our forests for generations. From my place in the last sleigh I saw shapeless, swaddled backs and rifle butts poking up; I saw the clouds formed by the horses' breath as they pulled us over hills and hollows, sweat forming black patches on their coats. Of course, my grandfather Alfons Rogalla was one of the party, as was Blask, the head forester, but also Heyduck, the sawmill owner, and Tuchlinski, the Lucknow town treasurer, and in front of us on the driver's box, massive as a stuffed sack, Conny Karrasch's father. He had finally given in to our whining: "Well, all right then, but you boys will have to behave—there might be trouble." Conny's sister, Edith, had not been allowed to join us under the fur lap robe.

The sleighs proceeded some distance into Borek Forest, past a stand of trees where the snow lay hip-high, and then turned off at a clearing and glided more rapidly down toward Lake Lucknow and Little Grajevo. They were expecting us—children watching behind windows blinded by frost flowers (Conny waved to some of them)—but also women peeping through cracks in their doors, and farther down, by the iced-up well where water had frozen into a hummock, men in heavy jackets, with fur caps and felt boots, in their hands wagon-wheel spokes, or clubs that looked like spokes. The sleighs drew up two by two and halted in the trampled square around the well. No greetings, not even a hand lifted in recognition, only an exchange of looks, guarded and contemptuous, and then one man stepped up to Blask's sleigh. He was a pale man with a dragging gait, Johannes Hauser . . .

You think that odd? You shouldn't, son, that was just how it was in our parts. Our own people had names like Konopatski, Piassek, or Sobottka, and here in Little Grajevo they had names like Gutkelch or Niedermüller or Hauser.

At any rate, I can still see Johannes Hauser's bent figure standing there in the milky sunlight; he was not the oldest of the men, but he was their spokesman or secret chief, and now he listened impassively to the instructions of the head forester, asked no questions, just nodded, holding his wagon-wheel spoke behind his back as a sign of deference. At one point he did smile; he threw back his head and responded wearily to Conny's wave. With a wink he seemed to hint at a complicated understanding. "My friend Johannes," Conny whispered to me.

Johannes Hauser listened until he was dismissed with a wave of the hand; then he walked over to his people and stood there watching with them as the sleighs pulled up and turned around, gliding up the slope through the crackling snow. Only when we were out of earshot did he gather them around him and seem to be talking to them with the same impassive look as before. I could see the men set out in small groups to follow us, weaving in and out of the sparse trees.

We drove to our prearranged posts, and the hunt could begin.

Every winter for as long as I could remember he had crossed the border with his obedient pack, and every winter, as soon as the rumors had been confirmed, hunting parties had formed to get him, the old one-eyed lead wolf whom they had named *Zatang czerno*—Black Devil—although he was not black but gray, a medium-sized animal, covered with scars, with a pelt like a piece of burned-over woodland. Often they had had him encircled, and aimed and fired their guns, and had sworn they had hit him. Some men even claimed he had rolled over before their very eyes, flailing and quivering in the snow, but in spite of these stories of prowess, not one of the hunters could produce his battered corpse, and that meant he could be expected to return the following winter. He came, so they thought, out of the forests on the other side of the border, from the Polish area of

Suwalki, and with his pack wreaked havoc on the game, made the roads unsafe, and besieged isolated farms.

This was the eighth hunt, or the ninth, according to my grandfather's reckoning, and some of the participants—Blask, Karrasch, Tuchlinski—had attended every one. For them the arrival of the old lead wolf was the high point of the winter, ushering in the same new sense of purpose, the same discussions and preparations, the same exciting expedition.

Well, we rode to our positions, first all together in single file through the snowy forest, then with one sled after another branching off and disappearing behind piles of cordwood and snow-laden fir trees. Our sleigh turned into a wood road that led to where the Borek thinned out. In the distance Castle Hill, with its seven giant spruces, at its feet the bog which Adam Rogalla had leveled and carved into terraces, whose outlines still showed clearly under the snow.

We stopped in the shelter of the underbrush. Conny and I extricated ourselves from our wrappings and prowled around the edge of the forest. Then we peered in all directions, over the frozen bog, over the plundered reed belt around the lakes, over the white humps of the brushland, but we saw nothing stirring, at least not yet. Conny's father sat there apathetic, his rifle across his knees. Perhaps he was already resigned to failure, after so many fruitless hunts. All he had done was to raise one ear flap of his fur cap. His hands were encased in bulky mittens. The way he sat there told us he did not want to be spoken to, so we drew the fur robe over us, leaving only a slit from which we could view the silent landscape.

I would not want to exaggerate, dear Martin Witt, but if you have not known the silence of a Masurian winter, you have no idea what silence is; it was not simply that the usual sounds were absent, even the most modest humming, gurgling, or trickling. Rather this silence made you feel you were at the very edge of the world, forgotten and abandoned, and it was as though time swept everything before it, every human effort, every hint of resistance. But that's enough of that; we must keep our eyes glued to the edge of the forest, waiting for a gray body to streak past or, wise from his many scars, to slink through the snow toward the brown belt of reeds. Finally, Conny's father turned up his other earflap and drew one hand out of its mitten. That was the signal for us to bob up again and stand in the sleigh listening into the depths of Borek Forest, from which shouts began to issue, strange shouts, a sort of toneless chant which made one think of weary lamentations. One could also hear the sound of wood being struck on wood; presumably they were beating their wagon-wheel spokes against the tree trunks. And between blows the first shot rang out, more like a little pop than a shot. The horses pricked up their ears, then laid them back to listen, and tossed their heads, awaiting directions. Conny's father calmly cocked his rifle and groped with his index finger for the trigger. The shouts did not draw nearer. They came in rapid tempo, the tempo of a wave that rushes forward and quickly crashes, and continued even after a hail of shots resounded dully like fireworks going off in snow. Blue jays fluttered up from the trees, a woodpecker dipped low over the lake. It was not the cold which made us quiver. We bobbed up and down in the sleigh, pounded on the bent iron handlebar, and waved our arms, because something went flashing by in a cloud of snow, fleeing, something which could certainly serve as a target but was not the target which Conny's father sat stolidly waiting for . . .

You're right: excitement makes us see more than is really there. The shouts, the thuds, the hail of shots so excited us that we saw movement where there was none. The delusion was strengthened by the early dusk, which wafted in a faint smell of smoke. Feeling excluded, we pictured ourselves in the depths of the forest, in the midst of the action, where the old, one-eyed wolf, blinded by the flash of the shots, drove his bewildered pack apart with growls, urging each wolf to flee separately, through the flailing wagon-wheel spokes, through the gleaming veils of snow which the vibrations of the rifle shots brought tumbling down from the boughs. Why had they banished us to this isolated post?

You can imagine how we felt when the din of the hunt died away, moved off; all we could do was strain our ears and feel we had been made fools of.

Something must have happened in the drifting circle of hunters and beaters; a few shots still rang out now and then, and the scattered cries still to be heard sounded like orders passed along in song, that's right, orders which seemed to apply to us as well, off here in our forgotten corner. Conny urged, pleaded, begged for us to join the hunt, but his father shook his head, only staring fixedly at the edge of Borek Forest, until finally dusk robbed everything of its clear outlines. Not until everything had melted together into a blue-black wall did he give the signal to move, but by then all was still again. The hunt really seemed over. There were no more thuds, no shouts, and we glided silently through the woods, edgy with disappointment.

We pulled up to the meeting place, a flat, treeless knoll in Borek Forest. As we approached, we saw a fire and torches lighting up the clearing. I could see through the branches that the sleighs had been drawn up in a semicircle and that men were standing there confronting each other, motionless and intent. We stopped beside the other sleighs, leaped down, and looked back and forth between the two groups of men, until suddenly we noticed two bodies lying on the snow, the corpse of the wolf, captured in mid-flight, paws outstretched, and beside it, the body of a man with a length of cordwood under his neck. They lay there as if both were the booty of this hunt, the wolf and the man, on about the same level . . .

No, I didn't at once grasp what had happened, either, and what was still happening, there in the semicircle of the sleighs. Most of the men just stood there facing each other defiantly, but a few were debating in whispers, or rather arguing with suppressed fury. Blask spoke for one side, while the people of Little Grajevo were represented by two men who looked like brothers, both with broad faces and high cheekbones, both wearing scarves of undyed wool around their necks. Back and forth it went—one side accusing, the other denying the charges; then the three went close to the fire, followed by the men with the torches and our people, who carried their rifles slung loosely over their shoulders, the barrels pointing downward. The men knelt in the snow beside the motionless man and began examining him, first the matted, coarse hair, then the back of his head and neck, and the circle of bystanders closed in as they stripped off the man's heavy jacket, two sweaters, and finally the two coarse, collarless shirts. Even when he lay there bare-chested in the snow, they did not accept the evidence of their eyes but ran their fingers over the body, searched the armpits, and then turned the body over, a yellowish, lean body with two sickle-shaped scars below the shoulder blades. Yes, they turned him over and groped about, down to the last vertebra. They held their hands up to the light. They were looking for traces of blood . . .

Pardon me?

Of course, that was what they were after, but they could not find any bullet wound. Even so, we could feel their suspicion, and their faces still wore that look of thwarted fury. They seemed to be waiting for something. Perhaps they themselves did not know what it might be, for, after all, the dead man had been found by some of his own party, who had carried him here and had already noted that he had no visible wounds. In any case, I sensed the violence of their expectation as I crouched beside the dead wolf, gingerly touched his pelt and his muzzle, shattered by the bullets, and found the broken-off tooth my father so urgently needed. And as I crouched there, I saw Conny force his way through the circle, bend over the dead man, and recognize him. He slowly straightened up with an expression of horror. Then he recoiled in shock, first looking at the man in the snow, then up at Blask, who simply returned the stare. Suddenly Conny seemed to have seen enough; with a sob that was more like a groan, he flung himself at our head forester and pummeled the man's ample fur coat, wildly, aimlessly, less for the sake of any effect he might have than to dull his own pain.

Conny Karrasch, the great Conny Karrasch, who probably more than anyone else is responsible for my lying here, for in fact no one influenced my final decision more than he—Conny might as well have used his fists against a sheet blowing in the wind on the clothesline, for Blask's coat blotted up all his blows. Blask did not even defend himself. He just gazed down at his assailant with patronizing surprise, and then, with one wide, deliberate swing of his arm, mowed Conny down. Conny buckled and curled up into a ball before he fell into the snow, whimpering. He whimpered over and over again, "You shot Johannes, you shot Johannes." He seemed oblivious as his father picked him up by the scruff of his neck like a puppy, shook him, forcing him to look up, and, as Conny raised his eyes, struck him in the face, once with his palm, then with the back of his hand, so that everyone could see Conny's head thrown back and forth by the blows. Then he let Conny go, and the boy fell to the ground, his hands covering his face. He refused to stand up.

They carried him to the sleigh, dropped him in like a sack, and threw the lap robe over him; now his whimpering could no longer be heard. I held the broken wolf's tooth tight, crept through the circle, scurried to the sleigh, swung up into it, and groped for Conny under the fur robe. He jerked away from me and hunched in a corner, doubled up. I let him be, for I wanted to watch the men around the fire. Through my peep hole I saw them still at loggerheads, the two groups edging farther apart and never saying any more than the bare minimum. Then Tuchlinski's sleigh drew up to the fire, and they loaded the man and the wolf onto the same sleigh, stretching the bodies out next to each other, but laying a covering over the man. They smothered the fire with snow, and slowly, so the people of Little Grajevo could keep up, Tuchlinski's sleigh turned into the wide wood road, accompanied by the bobbing flames of the torches.

No, he did not say much; but as he climbed into the sleigh, Conny's father pressed the shaft of his whip against the hump under the fur robe and hissed, "Polack lover!" We glided in silence through the darkness. The runners sliced the frozen track, and just past the estate, before he steered the sleigh onto the causeway, he said suddenly, as if there had been no other thought running through his mind during the entire ride, "Polack lover . . ."

By the way, the stuffed wolf in our museum whose panting plaster tongue greeted each visitor as he stepped into the exhibit on Masurian fauna was much smaller and scrawnier, and its pelt was completely worn away in places, where schoolchildren had stroked it . . .

What did you say? A world that is lost and gone? I see, all this strikes you as part of a bygone world, dead and forgotten, a world that has been put behind us, fortunately. I'm not so sure, son; for me there is no such thing as a world that is lost and gone, no time that has been canceled, simply plucked off the calendar of history. On the contrary, I am convinced that the past lives on, if for no other reason than that we cannot shake it off . . .

Yes, the past is with us, as pain or as potential . . . But what was I starting to say?

Right; on the way home, at the end of the causeway, the sleigh stopped, the whip shaft pointed toward our little house, and I jumped down and waited for some sort of goodbye, but all I heard was the crack of the whip. Perhaps Conny waved to me, I don't know, for I could not look after the sleigh for long. My father rushed excitedly out of the house, dragged me inside, and immediately stuck out his pale hand with its flaming scars: "Come on, did you get the tooth or not?" He did not even take time to feel my booty or sniff it; it went straight into a mortar, where, with a judicious admixture of silver thistle seeds, it was supposed to be pounded into yielding up its secrets.

Conny stayed out of sight all winter. He did not appear when the ice fishermen hauled up their nets out of the holes they had chopped in the ice near the prison walls. He was not among the bundled-up spectators when the ice sailors skimmed across Lake Lucknow on their sharp runners and performed their daring stunts. And later, too, when the great thaw came, when we poled along the banks on bobbing ice floes, ramming each other and boarding each other's floe, even then Conny Karrasch was nowhere to be seen . . .

Certainly, but they would not let me into the prison, no matter how often I stopped by. They simply sent me on my way, and after a while I gave up, although I could not forget him. I had already become addicted to hearing strange things from him, to his bold ideas, his intuitions. In fact, he had only to look at anything more intently or listen a bit longer than usual and already I was sure something remarkable was about to occur. I wondered if he was sick. Then sometimes I thought his father might have condemned him to an indefinite prison term for his impudence and that he was in there making twig brooms with Eugen Lavrenz and listening to the stories of our ninety-two lakes as he trimmed the branches for him.

But he reappeared. Conny turned up again, perhaps paler, but still with the same aloof look in his eyes and his way of suddenly interrupting a game or a discussion in order to follow up a new inspiration which promised to be more exciting. And, of course, he still had his habit of popping up unannounced and unexpected, even for the overdue celebration of Lucknow's five hundredth anniversary, on Juschken inlet; I mean to say, only the theatrical part was overdue, because my uncle Adam Rogalla had not fin-

ished his play *Wild Honey: Great Moments in Masurian History*
in time. I should explain that we celebrated the anniversary for an
entire year, and the play was its last major event, a concerted
attempt to portray Masuria in graphic form, to make us visualize
the darkness from which we issued, the trials history had imposed
on us, the suffering and exploitation we had undergone, and how
we had nevertheless managed to slip through all the traps that
fate had laid for us.

And now you must try to picture Juschken inlet: pickerel-
weed, swaying rushes, a belt of indecently lush reeds, the scent of
sweet flag, the cry of the bittern. There on the rugged, steep
slope above the shoreline, a landslide or some long-ago blasting
had scooped out a semicircular hollow, a sort of amphitheater
which looked out over the lake.

There were no stone seats, let alone wooden benches, but there
were little ledges where one could sit and have an excellent view
of the broad green stage, floored with thick sod and shaded by
poplars and willows. The sets were entirely provided by June,
and included dragonflies, grebes, and wild ducks.

As usual the Lucknowers had arrived too early. Hours before
the performance was to begin, the semicircle was crowded with
people exchanging the latest gossip and snacks, retrieving youngsters who had wandered off among the tiers of seats, watching
the waterfowl, or sitting in silent expectation, letting the light
from the lake dazzle their eyes.

We, the actors, were putting on our costumes under my uncle
Adam Rogalla's supervision—our dressing room a narrow, hidden
tongue of land, from which a wavering path had been trampled
through the rushes to the stage. You must try to picture the
confused scene there: men in white capes, with excessively long
swords; short-legged Sudauese in sackcloth tunics; Lithuanian
archers in ratty furs; Tartars with curved scimitars; Swedish
harquebusiers; Polish lancers, barefoot and proud; and then, of
course, ragged civilians from a number of historical epochs, the
ones who always got the worst of it, in Masuria as everywhere
else. Adam Rogalla bustled about among the different centuries,
author, director, and costume designer in one. With his own
hands he tied the belt around my coarse sackcloth tunic or

showed Conny's sister, Edith, just how she should hug her big, shapeless doll, which resembled a pregnant beaver.

Suddenly I spied Conny. He parted the rushes and looked long and intently at this living tableau of Masurian history. He did not come closer or even greet the two of us, Edith and me. Although he had applied, he had not been accepted for a role in the play; Uncle Adam had refused. Now Conny merely smiled condescendingly, and when I called out to him, he let the rushes spring back into place and slipped away with the smooth motion of a heron. Edith shrugged her shoulders and with a peevish gesture indicated to me that I should wipe the splashes of mud off her legs. This was the only touch she permitted; she would not let me take her hand or put my arm around her or test the weight of her thick coil of corn-colored braids, in spite of the fact that we played sister and brother, the children of a Sudauese prince, the children of the great, grim Wadoles, that's right. But that is how she was in those days, imperious and unpredictable, long before she became my wife, my first wife.

But now for a glimpse of our performance, in our green outdoor theater. Adam Rogalla gave the signal for the play to start and led us, the Sudauese and the Crusaders, along the path through the rushes, arousing great flutter among the waterfowl. Smoke-blackened stones, charred beams, smashed household goods made it clear that the scene took place in a castle, the castle of the great Wadoles on Lake Selment. It had been stormed and badly damaged, but still not taken, in this year of 1283. First the dead were sent out onto the stage, dead Sudauese who arranged themselves in a little heap that bore witness to their grim determination to defend themselves. But there were also dead Crusaders, their capes singed and spattered with red, who lay down and piled themselves into a decorative wall which illustrated the consequences of too much fighting spirit. Here and there one saw Sudauese and Crusaders dead in one another's arms, one of the director's inspirations. In any case, the corpses made a favorable impression on the audience and received the first round of applause.

In the midst of all the lifeless, or rather, shallowly breathing, fellow actors, Edith and I sat together on the warm sod. We sat there dreamily, children of the island, lost in our play, she with her bulky rag doll Skomanta, I with a collection of smooth, bleached little bones, mostly bird bones. Our innocence was such that we were supposed to be oblivious to the bodies that had arranged themselves so affectingly all around us. Only Wadoles, the grim prince of the Sudauese, was allowed a sort of choked lament. The part was played by Tuchlinski, the Lucknow town treasurer; as he crossed and recrossed the stage, he mourned the loss of his comrades, the women, his subjects, and his lands, wrested from him by the "thrice-cursed knights." His only hearer was Sygus, the Sudaueses' finest archer, who sprawled against a charred beam, exhausted from his effort to defend the castle and giving vent to periodic sighs which sounded more like hiccups.

After pacing about until he had unbosomed himself of his grief, Wadoles went on to curses and execrations. He stretched to his full height, gesticulating so fiercely at the horizon that he almost lost his balance, and swearing at the "thrice-cursed tribe in the white woven mantles" who were rounding up the remnants of his people and dispersing them as far as the Samland. Let the Crusaders come and try to take the last survivors, he taunted. And when Sygus the archer embraced him as was meet, he whispered loudly, foreshadowing our later history, "Many, Sygus, have met their deaths in gaining victory over us; let them be victorious this time, too, for the true victor will be the great wilderness."

This was the cue for a melancholy Grand Master—Ludolf, I think it was—to appear, swathed in his cloak. He strode up to the ruins of the castle and asked to speak with the great, most noble and daring Wadoles. The latter immediately swelled up with pride and went to receive his archenemy. He only regretted that he could not offer him any meschkinnes—you know, dear boy, how they do these things in the best circles—and asked, with remarkable sangfroid, to what he owed this visit.

Simple good sense, it seemed, had brought Grand Master Ludolf here, which was why at first he refused to sit down. He wanted to confront the facts from a standing position: settlements burned, the people vanquished and scattered to the winds, their chieftain left but a single companion and two children;

under these circumstances, he would think, submission was the only course.

But he had not counted on Wadoles's cunning. Blessed like most Sudauese with not five but seven senses, Wadoles suspected that this proposal of submission might be a trap. He considered long and hard, even consulting the little bones I was playing with; he laid them out and read their secret meaning. Finally, he informed the Grand Master with deadly courtesy that he would not capitulate. "It is not for us to prevent the fated demise of the knightly order. But in order that you may perish completely, you must first have triumphed completely. So come and take whatever you lack to make the victory complete." Hearing this, Ludolf, the Grand Master, seemed less melancholy than bewildered and bemused; presumably history had never before been interpreted to him in this manner, and into his bemused silence the grim Sudauese almost gleefully tossed an image of the future: first a barren land of no use to anyone; then, simply in order to hold on to the land, strenuous efforts at colonization with foreign folk from Masovia. In addition, he made unpleasant predictions about Polish kings and a number of rebellions and uprisings against the Order. He did not prophesy the Battle of Tannenberg in so many words, but he spoke of a battle that would remain in the history books for years to come.

Thereupon Wadoles turned to us, his children. He caressed us and asked us, loudly enough so that the Grand Master could not help hearing, whether we wished to make way for the total victory of the Order. We rose and nodded enthusiastically, whereupon he kissed us, and lovingly dispatched us with his dagger . . .

What did you say? Did we stand there quietly? Why, of course; but that is not all, dear Martin Witt. The stage directions called for Edith and me to sink to the ground with ecstatic smiles, and so effectively did we carry it off that several in the audience cried out in fury against the Grand Master. But there is something else you should know: Sygus the archer started up in sudden outrage, snatched a few arrows, and plunged into the rushes, apparently in the grip of a force mightier than himself, thereby clearing the stage for the two principals.

They stood facing each other in all their dignity, tragedy, and grandeur. As the author had directed, they kept their hands on the pommel of their sword and took measure of this classic tragic situation. I squinted up at them: the mighty opponents did not falter as they studied each other with meaningful looks. There was not a blink, not a swallow, not even a single human swat at one of the thrice-cursed local mosquitos. The director had insisted on this long, eloquent exchange of looks, which, after all, represented the moment where two epochs stared each other in the face, two epochs, one of which had to yield to the other.

The audience grew restive. Up front several could bear it no longer, jumped up, and demanded, "Come on, give the beast what he deserves, give it to him!" But Wadoles masterfully refused to lose his composure or drop out of his role. He calmly invited the death Adam Rogalla had decreed for him, challenging Ludolf to a duel and confining himself to only the essential defensive gestures, continually backing away until he was standing beside us, where he leaned toward his enemy to receive the coup de grace. As he fell, I thought I caught sight of Conny Karrasch in a hollow willow tree, mockingly watching through a knothole how our history hobbled on.

Anyway, Edith and I left the stage amid moderate applause. We ran through the rushes to the dressing area. There they took off our Sudauese sackcloth tunics and turned us into blue and white Mazovians, yes, colonists' children, another brother-and-sister couple with all too symbolic playthings: Edith was to ply a miniature spinning wheel, and I was supposed to scratch the soil with a miniature plow. The set: an ancient tree, an elm, of course, whose spreading branches would offer a pleasing haunt for the pagan god Perkunos.

We stepped onto the stage with our parents, Stefan and Anna Priezlav, and sat down at the foot of the tree, where we breakfasted with varying degrees of enjoyment. Stefan Priezlav in particular seemed the picture of gloom, for neither smoked trout nor crisply fried smelts nor corned beef with roasted potatoes appealed to him; he took a bit of everything and tossed it back into the enormous basket. He was definitely under a cloud.

Then he got up and paced restlessly around the tree, where as if by chance he noticed a very long hemp rope which might belong to Perkunos, the pagan god. In spite of which Priezlav worked the rope down, measured it length for length, and seemed to be wondering what such a rope might be good for besides hanging oneself. And suddenly all the torment vanished from his face; with an expression of vague bliss he walked over to us and ordered us to bind him to the tree. Since we did not dare to ask any questions, we did as he wished, drew the rope around him, coil after coil, around his chest, his middle, his legs, bending his arms back and tying safety knots around his wrists. And as we were fastening him, he sighed with contentment and explained the reason for his satisfaction.

Stefan Priezlav was a Mazovian, you see, one of the foreign colonists whom the Teutonic Order had invited to the great Masurian wilderness and enfiefed with fields and meadows and woodland, with no other requirement than that they settle and cultivate the land, free of tribute for the first ten years and with the assurance that they could retain their old religion. Here was a Pole who felt much indebted to the Order for this. But now other Poles were trickling into the territory, less with the purpose of learning better methods of agronomy than with seeing how much booty was to be had—an aim which could not but bring them into conflict with the Order. What neutral reports described as troubles were actually an undeclared war, and Stefan Priezlav, too, had to choose sides: with the Order against his fellow Poles, or with his fellow Poles against the Order, to which he owed his land, along with fish from Lake Lucknow, and wild honey from the bee trees. For a long time he had put off making a decision, unable to work up loyalty for the one side, or to cleave to the other out of simple gratitude . . .

Did you say something? Yes, that's right: it was a classic dilemma—on one side home, and all the rest; on the other ethnic solidarity, and all the rest. And he put an end to his plight by having us bind him to the tree and leave him to his fate . . .

No, not the way you think. He explained that he would go over to that side the sight of which gave him the strength to break his bonds.

We had not long to wait. Edith had no sooner set her distaff to humming, I had no sooner scratched my initials into the ground with my plow than they came riding up on horses with blue-black manes, flags fluttering from their lances. They were carrying a pole from which the picture of the Blessed Virgin of

Czestochowa looked down with universal forgiveness. This band
of shabbily clothed soldiers looked as though they could use a
rest. Although we were standing directly before them, they took
an amazingly long time to notice us—that's how it is sometimes
on the stage.

Their behavior toward us was not unfriendly. They merely
cleared out our pockets, devoured the contents of the basket, and
when one of them spied blowing white capes on the horizon,
they deliberated as to who would be more useful to them in
future campaigns, Edith or me. They settled on Edith, after they
had looked me over and found me too skinny. As a soldier con-
siderately bound her hands with a leather thong, Stefan Priezlav
strained his torso against the rope, jerked and twisted and sighed
up into the branches, apparently begging Perkunos for aid. But
the bonds held fast.

With their weapons, sacks, pouches, baskets, and especially
Edith, they plunged into the rushes, just in time to avoid being
found by the stern white capes and relieved of their booty.

These towering gentlemen saluted us with reserved politeness,
turned out pockets inside out—of course searching for concealed
weapons—thoughtfully surveyed the gnawed bones and fish remains lying about, looked up into the branches, presumably in
search of dangling bottles, and gave vent to their disappointment
at finding nothing worth taking.

Suddenly one of them thought he spied an entire Polish army
on the horizon and did a quick count of the advancing cavalry
and foot soldiers. This army apparently looked in a confident
mood, and in order not to disconcert them, the mighty gentlemen
also decided to take to the sheltering rushes. But before the green
stalks closed behind them, they came to the conclusion that for
some time they had been lacking a page, one who could perform
the lowliest duties for them.

That's how it was: one of the brothers placed his iron hand on
my nape, made a slight bow to my stage mother, Anna Priezlav,
and with an expression of regret led me away.

Now you should have seen how Stefan Priezlav writhed under
his bonds, how he snorted and strained, trying to thrust one arm
through, to draw up his knees to loosen the rope, but all to no
avail. The die was cast: neither the soldiers in rags and tatters nor

those in the white capes would have Stefan Priezlav on their side.
No longer had he any love for his old people, nor was he yet won
over by his sober new lords. So he abjured any warlike doings
and resolved instead to make a demonstration of a very special
sort . . .

You needn't try to guess, son, because you never will.

Since he had already made clear in such vivid symbolism that
he no longer belonged to the one side and did not yet belong to
the other, he felt he had to demonstrate where his loyalties lay;
accordingly, he began to hum, later breaking into full song: the
"Song of Masuria." It hardly mattered that the song had not yet
been composed in his time; boldly and resonantly he bridged the
centuries, fearlessly taking out musical loans against the future,
and because our people never let anyone sing alone, the audience
joined in on the chorus: "O blessed land, Mazovia's strand, long
live, long live, our dear homeland . . ."

But as Stefan Priezlav was beginning the second strophe—
"Storm-tossed the grove . . ."—a malign, copper-colored insect
shaped like a staple winged toward him, clearly not interested in
his song. And just as he was intoning the word "grove," it collided with his hard, nicotine-stained incisors. With a crack and a
snap he closed his mouth in astonishment, interrupting the song.
But no, he sang on with a sort of gurgling sound, whereupon the
insect buzzed up again and bit him painfully on the Adam's apple.
Now he really did break off his song. He squinted with narrowed, irritated eyes into the silver poplars, whose perpetual rustle aroused suspicion, squinted until the insect bit him again in the
back of his neck. Stefan Priezlav took a deep breath; rage made
his chest expand, anger swelled his veins, the rope tensed and
quivered and twisted slightly as he braced himself, and then it
gave way. It ripped into dozens of strands, not in one place, but
in many, yes, and the audience, speechless at first, burst out in
such hearty applause that Stefan Priezlav did not know which
way to turn. He hurried off the stage, accompanied by the "Song
of Masuria," which the audience believed had given him the
strength to break loose from his bonds.

Thus Conny intervened in the great moments of Masurian history, thus he lent the portentous play an unexpected turn: with a
rubber band and a handful of staples, which he sent flying in

revenge for being excluded from the play. Yes, he prevented me from reaping the applause at the end and from being present when the audience showered the actors with gifts. Prevented is perhaps not the right word; I should say, he drove me out of the play, specifically out of the great Plague Scene.

Since Lucknow had been stricken by the plague, Adam Rogalla had to devote an entire colorful scene to the pestilence, treating the subject with a frankness rare even in our part of the world. People were sitting, kneeling, standing in picturesque poses all over the stage. People at work: the cobbler at his last, the wheelwright at his frame, the peasant with his threshing flail, and there I was, crouching to one side, trying out a little flute which I had whittled out of a sprig of willow. This time I had no sister—why, only the author knew. All of us were supposed to act with utmost unawareness and not notice that a man-sized rat had slipped onto the stage, a mangy, leathery rat, yes, with large ears and whiskers stiff as a wire brush. The rat squeaked and sniggered; it darted from one person to another and peered over his shoulder, then executed a mazurka-like dance. We were not supposed to notice the dance, even though several members of the audience tried to alert us to it; we were supposed to be absorbed in our work and our play, until a burning breath singed our necks, the breath of death, the breath of the plague. Under the rat's pestilent breath most of us, not all but most, were supposed to keel forward and expire. I was one of the victims . . .

What's that?

No, no, you underestimate Adam Rogalla. It was not a foreign rat, it was a giant universal rat, death's harbinger, who was portrayed by Heinrich Henseleit, my teacher, in uncomfortably allegorical fashion. But you must hear the rest. No sooner had the rat slipped into the rushes, squeaking shrilly, than a figure appeared, all in scarlet, taking giant strides: Johann von Rogalla, my distant ancestor, the false priest, yes, accompanied by two drunken servitors toting half-filled sacks. In a voice that almost scorched the grass, this ancestor blessed the dead and put the fear of death into the living, hailed the plague as a judgment, read out a spicy list of sins, warned us, conjured up horrors, threatened doom, and offered a suggestion on how to keep the plague at bay. The only way to do this, he explained, was for people to give up everything that was dearest and most valuable to them, all their gold coin, for example. Silver was also acceptable, even worked silver if need be. And the survivors flocked to him, I must admit, and the sacks swallowed up coins and rings, chains and candlesticks.

But then, son, my stage father, a certain Dvorak who worked in our Office of Weights and Measures, took me in his arms and bore me, limp as I was, to Johann von Rogalla. On being asked what this was all about, Dvorak answered curtly, "Well, what do you expect, fellow? My dearest treasure," and deposited me at the feet of the false priest. Lying there, I looked straight at the old willow where Conny was lying in ambush, and had my eyes on the knothole, when I saw two fingers raised, a thumb and forefinger forming a V, and then it came chirping out of the dark depths, tacking a little in flight, but faster than any insect. It hit me above the cheekbone. A hot, scalding pain; no one could have stayed dead under such a sting.

Defying the rat and his pestilent breath, I leaped up, pressed one hand against my burning cheek, and raced amid the laughter of the audience toward the willow, out of which Conny now climbed or slithered. Still smarting, I chased Conny to the edge of the reeds, then through their swaying forest. There was a splattering and a squelching underfoot. He was not even fleeing in panic, but rather loping along, quite sure of himself and merely keeping a few steps ahead of me.

He ran in the direction of the tongue of land where the epochs of Masurian history were gathered; I could trace his route by the swaying rushes, and I followed him to the fallen poplar, which lay in the water, slimy and covered with algae, with leaves still on those branches that poked into the air.

Conny perched amid the branches. A plan formed in my head: to drag him down from the slippery trunk and dunk him again and again until he surrendered his rubber band and the remaining staples. With this in mind, I waded up to him. We said no word but kept our eyes on one another, refusing to be distracted by the two dragonflies buzzing around us. But just when I was going to grab him, I felt something soft underfoot, perhaps the corpse of a drowned cat. I straightened up and spread my arms to recover my balance. At that moment Conny slammed his drawn-up knee into my chin. I fell forward, my upper body over the trunk, my legs in the water . . .

Well, that was the end of my acting for that day, though I was slated to appear in two more scenes, first the printing of the Masurian Bible, then the dedication of the railroad from Königsberg to Lucknow. When I came to and found myself still sprawling in the marsh, two of my teeth were shaky and the tip of my tongue was bleeding.

Groggily I looked up and saw, not Conny in the poplar, but Edith, my barefoot stage sister, who was gazing down at me with cool curiosity. She sat there on the section of trunk that was above water, her sackcloth tunic hitched up, her feet dangling in the marsh.

The heat in the reeds, the pulsing, electric air started a miniature smithy pounding in my head. Perhaps you know the feeling and that sense of being endangered so that you must do something, anything, to save yourself. Her wet legs were very near me, and I was all set to lunge and drag her down into the water, in her brother's place, when I caught sight of the black, shiny tick already one-third into her leg and pumping away vigorously. "Look, look, your leg," I said, and she looked down without excitement, yes, she even lifted the leg to examine the tick from close up, and then she stretched her leg toward me and said imperiously, "Take care of it."

That was how she was. I clasped her leg, applied my fingers like tweezers to the tick, squeezing and pulling together. But I was not able to keep its gleaming body from breaking off. A thread of blood trickled down to her ankle bone from the dark spot where the tick's head remained drilled into her flesh. Edith watched me, her hands clinging to the branches, and when the tick broke off, she shook her head crossly. Then, as though this followed from my clumsiness, she ordered me to suck the black remnants out of her leg. "You'd better not bite," she warned.

I grasped her ankle, raised the leg to my chest, and just when she nodded commandingly, I pulled with a sudden jerk, only once, but that was enough. She landed in the water next to me. I had no trouble pressing her under, once and then again, holding her under until her coiled braids were thoroughly soaked, her sackcloth tunic sopping wet, until she lost her breath under my grasp. You should have seen her face when she staggered out of the water, dripping, her eyelashes all stuck together, her mouth wide open, and her face dazed with astonishment and fear ...

Yes, son, I could really use some tea now. If there's not enough in the little pot, ring for Nurse Margret. It's true she won't be overly gracious, but she brews a better pot of tea than you usually get in hospitals. She'll be through here in two years, by the way. She told me that she means to retire on her pension and return to Brunsholm, about twenty-five miles from here; five houses with hawthorn hedges out front, two gravestones for her deceased husbands, both of whom drowned. She can't understand my action; yesterday, while she was changing my dressings, she came down hard on me for depriving our people of the ground under their feet. Do you know what I mean? As she sees it, I meant to rob them of their right to memories. She's had her mind set against me from the very first.

But what was I starting to tell you? It had something to do with Conny's sister, right, with Edith, who was only seven days younger than I was, who verged on plumpness, but only verged, and who one day, contrary to all expectations, became my wife. Edith's dominance, at this time, came from the fact that nothing mattered to her. She felt bound by nothing, neither by a promise nor by the consequences of a deed. She would do things like tossing her ball down the dark cellar hatch of the prison at the spot where the secret passageway under Lake Lucknow was supposed to begin, and then sending me down to find it. She liked to hear how scary it was down there, in the damp passageway smelling of mushrooms. Or she would build a little fire at the foot of Castle Hill and start a kettle boiling, into which she threw toads and moths, kaddik berries, and dandelions—and dare me to drink the resultant soup. Yes, that was Conny's sister.

She was the only person allowed to enter my father's laboratory; while he did not let her play with the pans, mortars, sieves, and so on, or rummage through the sixty-eight drawers in the black chest, he had no objection to her sitting on the battered stool, her hands clamped between her thighs, delighting at the multicolored vapors rising from the crucibles and skillets ...

Pardon me? Would she faint? Even worse than I did; in fact, Edith loved these little blackouts and begged to be allowed to have them. Often she'd say to my father, "Go ahead and sulfur a bit, it's such fun to get all dizzy." She didn't even mind the vomiting that followed these episodes. And Edith hardly ever failed to get her way.

Visualize, for instance, our handsome whitewashed prison on one of those silvery summer evenings in Lucknow. Nothing was stirring, not a grain of sand shifted, the birches no longer glimmered. At most a roach splashed close to shore. Certainly there were swarms of mosquitos rising and falling; our phrase for it was "sewing in the air." An evening when one expected nothing to happen, when no phonograph music came from the boathouse, or any fire glowed out on the peninsula for thirsty woodcutters to sit around . . .

I stood in the shadow of the stone bridge, up to my knees in water, shivering although the water was warmish, and peering toward a rectangle I could just make out beyond the prison garden, the heavily ribbed door which was to open this evening, contrary to all regulations and all previous experience. Jerkily, tentatively, it had already opened a crack several times, or so it seemed to me, but I had not yet seen anyone slip out and dash noiselessly past the cabbages and tomatoes to the water, and I had already begun to doubt whether what Edith had promised would actually come to pass. She was nowhere to be seen, but I knew that she was watching the door from her favorite hiding place, the compost heap enclosed by boards. Today she was not wearing white kneesocks and buckled shoes but was barefoot like me. The lights had gone out in the prison. A single lantern hung above the entrance. No watchman was making his rounds. There were no dogs to worry about because Edith's mother could not stand barking . . .

You're quite right there, son, anything can be turned into an idyll.

In any case, Edith and I remained at our posts, and finally the heavy door was cautiously swung open, to our surprise without creaking; a head appeared, then a shoulder and a body in faded overalls, just as I had pictured the scene. The prisoner closed the door and immediately backed up against it, listening, flattened out, arms braced against the door. He seemed rather uncertain and confused, presumably by all the possibilities open to him, and stood there for a while before he made a dash for it across the vegetable beds. The pollarded willows provided dense shadow, and that was what lured him. At the shore he rolled his pant legs to the knee and peered over at the tied-up boat, but rejected that means of escape and instead waded along the shore toward the bridge, toward me. A barbed-wire fence that stretched diagonally from the prison grounds about thirty feet out into the lake separated him from the first bridge pier; he swam around it almost noiselessly, then suddenly sank out of sight. Just when I was about to step out of my hiding place, he bobbed up near a sandbar. When he stood up and peeled off his jacket to wring it out, I recognized Eugen Lavrenz.

So Edith had not promised too much after all; she had not only prevailed on the murderer and easygoing storyteller to escape; she had also kept her word and opened the door to freedom to him, with a key which must be back in the guardhouse by dawn. No, she had not promised me too much, and even before Eugen Lavrenz scrambled up the steep bank and onto the bridge, I saw her darting through the prison grounds, not along the shore, but in and out of the berry bushes and past the espaliered fruit trees, until the barbed wire blocked her way. Edith slipped through so smoothly that it seemed as though the barbed wire had been strung up for others, not for her. Then she waited for me as arranged. We merely nodded to one another, then followed Eugen Lavrenz, who was already on the bridge, leaving a trail of water as far as the lookout alcove halfway across.

On the other side of the bridge he climbed down to the boathouse, a squat wooden structure, painted dull red, with a wharf to which boats were moored at regular intervals, brown rowboats, blue and white paddleboats. He slipped into the boathouse and seemed to be rummaging through it, occasionally knocking something over. However poor a hiding place the boathouse seemed, he did find something there: a bundle of clothes, splattered with paint and stiff with varnish, which must have been the work clothes of Fahrun, who rented out boats. He also found a vest and a fur cap, which was already on his head when he stepped out onto the wharf. He ripped off his damp overalls, rid himself of his long underwear, and transformed himself before our very eyes into an innocent civilian. Eugen Lavrenz carried his prison garb to the shore. He tied knots in the sleeves and pant legs and filled the resulting pouches with sand, pieces of brick, and beer bottles, then dragged a limp, lumpy prisoner to the wharf and drowned him without a sound.

He did not wait to see the bubbles welling up, but fished a handy stake out of the water, left the boathouse, and plodded through the dusky lakeshore park toward the swimming area, the two of us still on his heels.

Don't think for a moment that he stayed at the swimming area, although he inspected each of the dressing rooms. Caution led him to the peninsula and up the hill to where, in a small enclosure, stood a massive base for a monument, its mortar still fresh. This was going to be a memorial to dreamy-eyed General von Günther, the best-loved Bosnian commander. But although the figure was already cast, the Lucknow city fathers had turned the statue down, on the grounds that the figure looked less like the general than like the sculptor, a certain Rosinski.

So Eugen Lavrenz scrambled over the iron fence, circled the base, swung himself up on it, stood there, legs apart, and gazed across the lake to the prison, which lay in brooding darkness. Then he bent down and tapped the pedestal. One side of the base bore an iron plate fastened only with wing bolts. Eugen Lavrenz loosened it, stuck his head into the cavity, looked around once more, then squeezed inside the base. The Bosnian general had his first subtenant.

Yes, that's how it was, son. I would have liked to wish him good night, but Edith beckoned me away. She did not even want to receive the thanks she so richly deserved, and as we skipped home in silence, each of us excited in a different way, she was mulling over another secret plan . . .

No, nothing to eat, no fruit, just something liquid, I'm always thirsty . . .

Do you know what I had to hear when the doctors last made their rounds? "This, gentlemen," one of them said, as they turned to go, "is typical for burns of this degree. The organism can be dying of thirst inside, while drowning in its wounds." Thank you, this Swedish mineral water is very refreshing; you ought to try it some time . . .

Yes, well, so Eugen Lavrenz slept inside the pedestal reserved

for the great Bosnian commander. The elderberry bushes on the
peninsula were full of thrushes (no nightingales in our parts, you
know), and they must have sung for him. I am sure his night was
less restless than mine. I was the first one down to breakfast,
spooned up my gruel so fast that I splashed it around, to the
satisfaction of my untalkative mother, who expressed herself
largely by gestures that said more than words. For instance, when
I sprang my request for four rolls spread with lard to take to
school, she responded with a slight fluttering of the hand that
bespoke boundless astonishment. This she followed up with a
turn of her fingers, as though she were cleaning the inside of a
glass vessel, which was her gesture for pleasure.

The sandwiches were no sooner packed away in my schoolbag
than I set out, long before my usual time, past the white prison,
over the bridge, at whose midpoint wild ducks and coots were
holding a noisy conference, and on to the swimming area. Here
I shut myself into one of the dressing rooms, after checking the
walls for knotholes. I pulled out the lard sandwiches, lifted off
the tops, and strewed the lard carefully with a coarse powder
that smelled like ammonia, my father's prescription for making
smugglers invisible. The leftover powder I scattered into the lake,
which to my amazement did not begin to boil and bubble . . .

Don't be impatient, son, just wait and see . . .

How harmless and innocent the pedestal looked in the morning
sun. I began to whistle, clambered whistling over the iron fence,
placed my schoolbag on the pedestal, and crouched down before
the removable plate. Not until I knocked did something stir inside. I heard a grunt, then a scraping sound, like a frantic rabbit
digging, and in response to a second knock, a voice actually said,
"Come in, please." The plate was slid aside, and Eugen Lavrenz's
face appeared, bleary with sleep and somewhat askew. His eyes,
with their watery irises, examined me quizzically, then quickly
scanned the landscape, but seeing no one turned back to me. "A
little early for a visit, wouldn't you say? Want to scare a body
half to death?"

I unwrapped the sandwiches and handed them through to him.
He sniffed the bread, took a bite, and chewed with eyes closed.
Then suddenly he grabbed me by the wrist and said, "If you
wanna come in, come on in." My schoolbag flew through the

opening. I dove down into the semidarkness, settled with my back against the stone, and was in seventh heaven. I watched him eat, expecting that any moment he might go up in a wisp of smoke or shrink to the size of a pea...

Pardon me? I thought you would ask. No, the powder failed in Eugen Lavrenz's case, probably because he was not a smuggler and not in dire enough straits. But perhaps you can come up with a better explanation.

In my disappointment I was hoping for a lake story at the very least, but he seemed disinclined this morning. He talked incessantly about the estate, about the old devil up there, about the rights which he meant to assert, and he spoke so heatedly that it seemed he was forcibly reminding himself of a duty. Perhaps he had to work up his courage, too, and I let him talk, because the more he talked, the more I came to understand him and his story.

It seems Eugen Lavrenz was a potter, an itinerant installer of tiled stoves; he also made plates, cups, cookware, in fact anything people ordered in that line, but his favorite assignment was tiled stoves, those huge, colorful structures reaching up to the ceiling, made of blue and green tiles which he himself etched and glazed and painted with fine brushes—in our museum we had one of these famous Masurian tiled stoves. In return for supplying the estate with dishes and keeping the stoves in good repair, he was allowed to live in the little house down by the water, its ceiling so low that a tall man could hardly stand upright. Here, in this speck of a house, under the alder trees, not far from the drinking trough, Eugen Lavrenz was permitted to live, and my grandfather also permitted a woman to move in who was not his wife.

This woman helped him in the tiny workshop he had built onto the hut; she showed gratitude because he had given her a home, but this was only at the beginning, and only when he was around. As soon as he was called away on a stove job, she also would disappear. The story was she was off visiting, but actually she moved across to Lucknow, to a sort of tavern out by the barracks where the 46th Cavalry Regiment was quartered. Eugen Lavrenz soon learned where she holed up while he was away, but he held his peace and continued to give her money from his earnings. He claimed to have said nothing, even when she left one evening and did not return until it was almost morning.

He expressed his disapproval only by keeping the windows open in all kinds of weather, saying, when she complained, that he "didn't want to go out of his skull from the stench of horses." I gathered that she often stayed away for weeks or even months on end, and that he still received her back without a word, whenever she chose to turn up.

Then one summer, when he had been away making his rounds for a number of months, he returned to see that the blue plates he had made her were missing. He noticed it from outside, through the window, and when he pushed open the door, he found a baby on the bed, a little girl with black hair and blue eyes . . .

No, no, Eugen Lavrenz was not the father, he knew that, and after he had fed the child, he went over to the tavern by the barracks, sat around there without heeding the cavalrymen's taunts, and waited for the woman. She did not appear, she never appeared again, and after a time he gave up his attempts to trace her and had the girl baptized Meta.

He kept the child with him, brought her safely through the childhood diseases, and took her along when he had jobs in distant places. He gave her lumps of clay to play with, while he himself shaped the tiles and incised designs into them. Apparently he taught her at home what she would have learned in first grade, for she could already read and write when she went to school. He fed her mostly on soup with dumplings, and she was well grown and disarmingly friendly to everyone. She called him "Master Eugen," and after school she learned to work clay like him, going at it with passion and a patience unusual in a child, yes . . .

Meta was twelve or thirteen; now young men would often come down from the estate of an evening. They sat on the lakeshore, skipped flat stones over the water, and kept looking toward the potter's house. The girl was aware of them but she did not go out, and had no answer to their shouts.

To get her to leave the house at all, Eugen Lavrenz would send her to fetch clay, or to the horse pasture to collect horsehair from the barbed wire for his paintbrushes. He would urge her to go bathing in the pool at the gravel pit. It gladdened him that she would hasten back from such outings and work with him with still greater eagerness. But once when he thought to meet her and walk back with her, he saw my grandfather ride through the gravel pit and, when the girl scurried out of the pool in alarm, rein in his horse and wait until she had slipped into her shift; then he rode up to her, spoke commandingly, and lifted her into the saddle.

Prudent in all things, Eugen Lavrenz had worked out a plan for Meta. This plan was called Wilhelm German; he was an assistant forester, lived in Little Grajevo, and had savings. Meta, who was fifteen at the time, laughed at German's way of talking, but was otherwise quite at a loss with him. All of Eugen Lavrenz's attempts to point out German's good qualities fell on deaf ears; she simply said, "He's nothing but a brute like the others." One autumn, the story went, Wilhelm German had left Little Grajevo and bought himself a train ticket from Lucknow to Rominten— not because Meta had turned him down, rumor had it, but because he had had a visit from my grandfather Alfons Rogalla.

That same fall Eugen Lavrenz was returning from the clay pit when he heard voices coming from the hut, familiar voices. This was, he said, the only time he'd ever eavesdropped, crouching under the alders. Most of the talking was done by Alfons Rogalla, my grandfather. Meta merely sobbed. First he wanted to know where it had happened, in the gravel pit or by Lake Tartar or above the stables. Then he threateningly named boys on the estate, boys who might just as well have been to blame. Then he launched into the subject of Meta's mother. Up to that point Eugen Lavrenz had listened in shock and sorrow, he said, with nothing else in mind but to hear what was said. But the girl's sobbing had become harder to bear. Finally, he picked up his shovel and stepped forward to meet Alfons Rogalla as he left the hut. Before he struck, my grandfather's plaited whip slashed across his face, so that for a moment he could not see clearly. But he struck out nevertheless. He broke my grandfather's collarbone and shattered his knee. He then stormed into the house and smashed whatever was in it with his short-handled shovel. The girl disappeared and could not be traced. But before Lake Lucknow froze up for the winter, a fisherman's net brought up a shoe and a stocking that had belonged to Meta.

In court Eugen Lavrenz did not once speak in his own defense. My grandfather Alfons Rogalla, on the other hand, had a statement to make. He testified that when lying by the hut, too hurt to move, he had heard "crazed blows and words of insane bitterness" . . .

Yes, my dear boy, that is what I heard that morning in the pedestal, instead of a lake story, but I must admit that what impressed me more than Eugen Lavrenz's confession was the appetite with which he devoured the four sandwiches and with them almost half a twist of the powder of invisibility. Then suddenly he put his ear to the stone and with a gesture ordered me to hold still.

To make a long story short, first we heard something metallic strike the pedestal, then the shouted order to come out with our hands up. At the opening they forced his arms behind his back and handcuffed him. Before I left my hiding place, I handed my schoolbag out to them; they laughed as they took it. The two constables stood me up between them, holding me in the familiar armlock, but I barely felt their grip, for at the iron fence stood Edith. No, she was not just standing there, she was hopping up and down on one leg, flushed with pleasure, one finger on her lips, her heavy coils of hair bobbing. Eugen Lavrenz looked at her in wonderment, and she returned his gaze defiantly, laughing and clapping her hands—Edith, my first wife. After an inconclusive interrogation, they released me to go to school. I hid in the elderberries until they departed: constable, prisoner, constable, and behind them, prancing along and mimicking the procession, Edith . . .

Yes, I hear the footsteps; that is Nurse Margret, probably bringing supper, but don't take that as a reason to go. You can even eat a slice of bread with me—it's insipid stuff, untoasted white bread . . . Come in, Nurse, come in; may I introduce a young friend of the family? Martin Witt, my daughter's fiancé, or should we say, fiancé-to-be . . .

Pardon me? My wife is here? Better late than never. But, of course, Nurse, I'm expecting her. I'm always ready . . .

You mustn't go now, son, especially not now; I insist that you meet my wife, you won't be in the way at all . . .

Where are you? Martin? Martin?

# 3

Down the drain, pour all the ashes down the drain and rinse them away, and please put the bag in the drawer of the bedside table. Yes, Simon Gayko sent that to me through my wife, a bag full of damp ashes, a sample of what remains of our museum—Simon with his Bosnian ways. That was his farewell present, his last sign from the old-age home where he shares a room, I heard, with a one-time crack marksman.

But as I said, my dear boy, you needn't have left so hastily. You probably passed my wife in the corridor. She didn't stay long, and most of the time she sat there in the visitor's chair without a word. Still, she relieved me of one worry: she is back in the house where she grew up, here in Schleswig. She has moved back in with her father in the narrow, half-timbered house inhabited ever since it was built by a long line of organists, all of whom tried to set the world's record for thriftiness. My father-in-law is deeply convinced that self-denial is the prerequisite of even the slightest freedom. I understand that he keeps a careful ledger in order to prove how little one needs to get by . . .

Pardon me? Oh, yes, he too is an organist, but he has been retired for a long time. So now she will be living with him again, while Simon Gayko, if I know my man, will be carving and painting his imaginary birds, whole flocks of them, beautiful, wicked, and quarrelsome. I can already see them suspended from the ceiling of his room or perched on the top of the wardrobe or preening on windowsills . . .

Ashes for farewell, a bag full of cold ashes. No, nothing more need be said, the knot has been loosened, the time of shared experience is past . . .

Simon Gayko tasted our mockery the very first day he entered our class, simply because he was short, long-armed, and bow-legged, his legs curved like Tartar swords. We used to say, "They straightened his legs over a barrel." We called him a lot of names like "Monkey," but he put up with it. He never bore a grudge, and he made no attempt to defend himself physically.

Although I, too, teased him, our personal dealings did not begin until the morning he came to class with a package, an unusually long package, wrapped in wax paper and tied with bast. He carried it very carefully up to the teacher's platform, put it down, and warned everyone not to touch it. He guarded it until our teacher, Heinrich Henseleit, entered, and Conny, the star pupil, gave his report in the style of a ship's mate: "Crew all present on deck," and so forth . . .

You are right to assume that Henseleit had served with the navy, as an imperial signaler on the cruiser *Yorck.* As a result, our class learned the Morse code and could converse in the language of the nautical flags. Now he received Conny's report, signaled us to be seated, and only then took notice of Simon Gayko and his package. Simon was permitted to untie the string, fold back the wax paper, and lift out his model of a ship, a white yacht with yellow smokestacks. Heinrich Henseleit, who could not take his eyes off its perfect proportions, stretched out his right hand to draw Simon closer, so close that in dreamlike admiration he put his arm around the boy's shoulders and murmured phrases of amazement and wonder. He ran his fingers reverently over the model, so that we could see he was checking each detail and measuring it against his recollection. But it was already obvious that we would not be having arithmetic today.

Our teacher straightened up, gave the signal for "gather around for a war conference," and arranged us in a semicircle around his platform. He praised Simon Gayko, stroking his hair, which was slicked down with sugar water and parted in the middle, and asked him to tell the class what he had built and what he had had in mind when he built it. Simon scraped the floor a bit with his right foot, blinked, and said his piece: "The imperial yacht, the aviso *Hohenzollern,* displaces 4,180 metric tons and can move at a top speed of 21.5 knots. It carries two lifeboats on each side, flies the imperial standard, and here, the bridge, is where the Emperor stands to review the fleet." More than that

Simon could not say, except that the model was done to scale, down to the anchor.

Heinrich Henseleit had already discovered that the yacht's upper deck was removable, so that one could look into the cabins and lounges, which had been furnished by Simon Gayko, not exactly to scale, but with a good deal of imagination, with sofas, chairs, and rag rugs for the Kaiser. We all clustered round, and our teacher had us imagine the Kaiser traveling on his yacht, perhaps to the Mediterranean, perhaps to the North Sea. We were also to imagine the Kaiser standing on the bridge, maybe for the opening of the North–West Canal, receiving the salute of the entire fleet . . .

Emotion? A lesson in emotion? You may call it that, but our teacher was not satisfied with that alone. Pointing out the cabins and lounges with his penholder, he asked the class what they thought the Kaiser would do in all these rooms. And the class replied: He might use the sofa for thinking over things, the lounge for giving orders to blow up enemy vessels. In the dining room he would have fish soup with beets, two helpings, and in the cabin he would rest with the Empress after all his victories.

Heinrich Henseleit approved all these answers but could not resist airing his own ideas on the subject. He showed us the room where the Kaiser consulted with his admirals, another where he was dressed for parade, and a room where he did his ruling, watching out for each and every one of us. Who knows to what lengths his enthusiasm might not have carried him if we had not suddenly heard rapid steps in the corridor. The janitor Gavlizek pulled open the door without knocking and told Herr Henseleit he was wanted in the principal's office, "real urgent and right away," and without waiting for further questions or a reproof for entering without knocking, he stumbled on to the next class-room. Henseleit gnashed his teeth in annoyance and told Conny to take over the class while he was gone.

We were still standing around the imperial model yacht; everyone wanted to inspect it for himself, and Simon, the builder, could not answer our questions fast enough, or warn us sternly enough to be careful how we handled the *Hohenzollern*. I have seldom seen Simon Gayko as happy as that day. He began revealing some of the tricks of his trade. To those who might want to make something similar, he explained special difficulties and volunteered useful tips. For the first time he was offered malt drops.

Then suddenly we heard the airplane, or rather the sound of one far away, flying high, and it was Conny who was making this noise by fluttering his lips, from the back of the room, where he stood at the window. He came down the center aisle, and the droning grew louder and more threatening. He spread his arms out like wings, as stiff as a ruffed grouse, and in his right hand there was a glint of brass. He was holding the brass pestle that belonged to one of my father's mortars; I had carried it around all summer in my schoolbag, Lord only knows why. Now Conny roared up in a curve, circled the teacher's platform playfully, and then zoomed in for the attack. The brass projectile crashed down on the yacht and smashed right through it. The smokestacks nodded to one another and flew off; the lifeboats tipped out of their davits; the hawserhole spewed out the anchor. The lounges and cabins were crushed, the bridge bent and splintered. The pestle could not possibly have delivered a more direct hit.

This may surprise you, son, but only a few members of the class were outraged. Most of them clapped, skipped for joy, and congratulated Conny on his magnificent act of destruction, yes, congratulated him and protected him against those who might have pushed and shoved him.

And Simon Gayko? He went pale, began to tremble. With one dry wail he stretched his hands toward the wreck and stroked his shattered handiwork. And still wailing, he started to gather up the pieces: smokestacks, lifeboats, what remained of the decks. He placed the fragments on the wax paper, tied it into a clumsy bundle, and headed for his desk.

I put away my pestle. I had to keep it from the others, who wanted it for all sorts of newly discovered uses. Henseleit's return put an end to the wrangling. We darted back to our seats, where we remained standing, following his progress from the door to the platform. We expected him to give the signal for us to be seated, as usual. But this time no signal came. This time he stood there rigid for a long while, and his facial muscles quivered. Then in a voice we would never have thought him capable of— he normally sounded as though he were hanging from the topgallant mast and shouting something down to the aft deck—

softly, and therefore all the more audibly, he announced, "War, we're at war. You can all go home."

After this he relaxed a little, shifted his weight to the other leg, and permitted himself something which normally would have been out of the question in class: he took a pinch of snuff. Then he went on talking, more to himself than to us. He spoke of the Kaiser, who had not wanted this, and of the Czar, who had just called his people to "armed deeds with sword in hand and the Cross over the heart." He also spoke of the Russian army, reportedly already at the borders of Masuria, of Don Cossacks and St. Petersburg Dragoons, and as he did so, he smiled confidently and alluded a number of times to our swamps, our dependable swamps.

You can imagine how fidgety we became at this news. Nothing could contain our impatience; we were determined not to miss the war on any account. Several boys were already reaching for their schoolbags when Simon Gayko gave a great moan, took up his bundle, and bore it to the platform, where he opened it in wordless accusation. Henseleit stared at the wreck, looked at the class, gnashed his teeth. Slowly but purposefully he twirled his cane: "Speak up, my fine lads, what punk is responsible for this?" Conny raised his hand immediately. He had to come to the front, and since it was my pestle which had done the deed, I also had to come to the front. No explanations were permitted. The cane whistled back and forth. First it sliced merely air because the hand jerked back, but then it hit, etched burning stripes into the fingertips, making the fingers swell up. I danced on one leg. The air resounded with the cane's humming and singing.

I don't know what kind of penalties would have occurred to Heinrich Henseleit in normal times. As it was, we had the recently declared war to thank for our receiving only a dozen lashes.

No, I must correct that. We did receive an additional punishment, Conny and I; Henseleit would not let anyone get off that easily. After he had dismissed the class, he ordered us to go home and write out one sentence one hundred and twenty times: "I must respect other people's property." Then he released us, and we pelted out into the hot, already limp midday world, in search of the promised war.

Bells were ringing from both of Lucknow's church towers, but that meant nothing to us. We forged ahead, looking for some action, down to the lake and to the bridge, hand in hand. Conny hid our schoolbags in a boat up on blocks for repairs, so that we could more easily scramble up the embankment to the bridge, where older soldiers, presumably militia, were erecting a barrier out of harrows, plows, wagon wheels, carriage shafts, and rusty pipes, everything inextricably tangled, a barrier which even twelve horses could not drag away, while at the one gap left they rolled up the front wheels of a carriage with a tree trunk laid crosswise over the axle, so that the enemy would think the bridge was defended by a ten-centimeter field howitzer. The four usable field howitzers from the Lucknow garrison headed through the gap in the direction of Dippelsee and Arys, as did our cavalry and a division of engineers with baggage train and heavy equipment, all of them in the best of spirits, flinging out words of encouragement. We began to fear that Lucknow would be spared the war.

Suddenly the bells fell silent, just murmuring a little to themselves, and no more soldiers passed by. The militiamen sat in the shade of the chestnut trees and smoked, and the lake calmly mirrored the fortified bridge; at this moment it seemed to me as though the entire town were listening with bated breath, motionless, hesitant, trying to hear its own future, yes. There was no one sitting in the boats moored down below, there were no faces at the windows, and up there in the town not a single wagon wheel creaked over the pavement—it was never this still in Lucknow . . .

I'm sorry, I didn't catch what you said, Martin Witt.

How far off was the Russian army? How large was it? Well, it was on the other side of the border, not fifteen miles from Lucknow, troops of the Army of the Vilna, Don Cossacks, Finnish artillery regiments, Orenburg Cavalry—we came to know them all. By the way, copies of their marching orders were on display in our museum.

But what was I saying? Right, the silence that reigned over the town on the white August day, when everything held its breath in anticipation. Expectation was not enough for us; we slipped through the unguarded gap, dashed past the prison and the estate, and headed for Castle Hill. Two storks were spearing toads in the bog. Far away, under the silver poplars, across the tongue of land between Lake Tartar and Lake Lucknow, soldiers were marching westward in a haze of dust; occasionally something flashed in the sunlight. The first contingents had already entered the great State Forest, far beyond the lakes. We watched them until the dust had settled. Then we went to work.

At the seven giant spruces we rolled up stones to make fortifications. We buttressed them with charred beams, took pains to leave loopholes, and the smell of scorch that lingered in the stones and the beams made us feel we already had our baptism by fire behind us.

It was a day like cellophane; there was a crackling and rustling everywhere, a flashing of light. On this day the clock hands seemed not to advance, as if it would remain noon forever, and in the warmth the bark on the spruces split and even the kaddik berries popped. The sort of day you can't help noticing, son.

Nor did we only build the fortifications; we also tried them out straightaway. We fell back into a defensive position and repelled a combined attack by Russian artillery and St. Petersburg Dragoons, with quite a few losses on our side. We were satisfied. Happy and exhausted, we stood there holding each other tightly by the hand. And then Conny drew his pocketknife and pulled out the little blade, quite solemnly. We trembled as we stood there, torsos bare, and looked deep into each other's eyes, asking the ultimate questions. I was ready. I held out my arm to him, felt the prick of the knife, saw my blood ooze out, just a few drops, into which he dipped the knife until some blood clung to it. Then he watched with curiosity as I scratched his upper arm, just under the vaccination mark. I dipped the knife into the trickle that moved jerkily down his arm, as if searching for something. Then we placed our hands on top of each other and gazed at one another, too overcome to say anything. We just stood there, under the seven spruces . . .

By the way, my son Bernhard once remarked about this incident: "There you have it; blood is the worst ink." You know, he has written to me, after a long silence. A get-well card. The nurse read it to me . . .

Pardon me? Didn't Henrike tell you that? He's a social worker,
Bernhard's a social worker in Bremen. He works with a friend
whom he's been close to since he was twelve or thirteen . . .
Thus we sealed the pact of Castle Hill, and you should have
seen us on the way home; not once did one of us remove his arm
from the other's shoulder. Our hips brushed against each other;
that's how close together we walked, happy and self-assured. First
I accompanied Conny to the prison gate, then he walked me to
our house, and finally we parted halfway between the two places
and walked backward, waving to one another. At last a change of
pace: war.

For my father, too, Jan Rogalla, the war opened up new prospects. Multicolored vapor clouds eddied continually from his
laboratory; the clouds billowed through all our rooms, and occasionally little explosions shook the floorboards. Flames darted up,
releasing smells which caused us to daydream in fabulous colors.
The moment I got home from school my father sent me out to
fish empty bottles from the lake and comb the rubbish heaps of
the Hotel Queen Luise and the Mazovia Brewery for jars and
every sort of container. I scoured them and helped him bottle the
dark, creamy, or gelatinous potions. We labored as if we had to
supply pharmaceuticals not just to our army but to all the com-
batants, and the cellar, the attic, the space under the beds, and
corners of the rooms filled up with vials full of substances that
would stop gangrene, heal saber strokes, and bring relief to punc-
ture wounds.

When my mother, suffering from the shrinking household
space, sighed skeptically, my father countered, "Think how
much they'll need when the fighting begins. With armies that size
there'll be a huge demand." In the face of this argument my
mother finally had to give up her canning jars, too, and let them
be filled with wondrous potions . . .

You've put your finger on it: a businessman who was prepared
to go all out. So far not a single Russian soldier had been seen in
Lucknow. There was no cannon fire on the horizon, and the
watchmen on the church spire had nothing to report but storks
in homeward flight. Already disbelief was becoming widespread.
My father, who had invested so much, met all these doubts with a

confidence confirmed by the principles of physics: "When you've got something over a fire," he said, "first it bubbles, then it boils, and then it boils over."

I slept through the moment when it boiled over; that is to say, I was lying in a mild faint on my bed, barefoot, with only my gym shorts on, and next to me, blissful and limp, lay Edith, who visited us chiefly for the purpose of getting "all dizzy." The heavy greenish vapors which she breathed in greedily had numbed her, and we had just managed to get her onto the bed when nausea spun me around. I vomited, being careful where it landed, staggered toward her, and reached for her hand as I fell.

As we youngsters lay there, laid out as though for a funeral that could have furnished the whole town with gossip, I seemed to hear a summer storm rumbling in the distance. First came a few short crashes, then a pelting noise like hailstones on an umbrella. I stretched cautiously, blinked, and fell back; one had to come out of these swoons gradually.

The Russians were there. After a bit of skirmishing—for so we must describe our militia's efforts to fire a few shots and then pull back into safety—the Russians took Lucknow. But what does "took" mean in this case? The great snake of an army, winding toward us from the southeast with its baggage train and a wild assortment of vehicles, could not be halted by any militia. It moved forward inexorably, swallowed us up, surrounded us, left a few units behind, which were barely missed, and pushed onward in the direction of Dippelsee and Arys.

First Siberian Artillery regiments marched over the causeway, followed by Dragoons and support troops and Pleskau militia, and we sat on the wrought-iron railing and looked them over. We examined their machine gunners, their howitzers, but also the officers riding on ahead, each of whom carried a leather map folder and interpreted every shout as a greeting deserving of a smart salute. In contrast to the poise of the officers, the soldiers displayed a sort of humble friendliness. Some of them called out German words to us, some winked at us, as if to reassure us and themselves at the same time.

Dragoons on sweaty mounts, special troops with their gear, artillery pieces drawn by horse teams filed past us, carrying out orders which had been formulated in the comfort of distant headquarters and had not even been coded, so confident were the commanders. True, the general in the white uniform jacket seemed not to share this confidence. He sat in the back seat of his open car, looking mournful, plagued by the dust and the heat. His eyelids were almost closed as he drove past us, and he seemed not to notice the four Cossack horsemen who formed his escort. After him the field kitchens clattered by, then came Finnish regiments, and finally very young soldiers in ill-fitting uniforms and new boots that obviously pinched.

My mother, who had watched the procession from the window, said glumly during lunch, "They go on and on; I just hope they don't capture our Kaiser." Father, however, ate cheerfully and with an excellent appetite . . .

Pardon me? That's true, son, nowadays one would assume that, but I can assure you that Lucknow suffered no damage from this occupation, and in those early days there were no arrests and no requisitions. They simply overwhelmed us with their sheer numbers, and as a river sends some of its water into dried-up branches as it passes, they left behind a few units of Pleskau militia and Don Cossacks to occupy our town. The policemen were allowed to keep their uniforms and remain on duty, the circuit-court courier did not have to turn in his bicycle, and the night watchman received written confirmation that his services were still needed. The occupying troops contented themselves with quarters that were already vacant. They moved into the garrison and took command of the supply office and the stables. Only the new town commandant and his staff felt they simply had to have a view of Lake Lucknow; they moved into the Hotel Queen Luise.

A change? How was it to make itself felt? Previously our world had been defined by a distant, inaccessible Kaiser. Now it was defined by an equally inaccessible Czar; both were legendary figures who inspired us with fear and reverence. And yet things did change gradually as time went on; we came to see that what we had taken for granted no longer held true. We sensed a new and unfamiliar climate, and found ourselves expecting to be called to order for this or that.

One day Cossacks rode up to the prison, an officer in the lead. They ordered the gate opened and had impatient words with Conny's father. A table and a chair were carried out into the courtyard and set up near the row of sunflowers. The officer seated himself, the seven tails of his fancily braided riding whip wound around his wrist. The shaft of the whip he used as an enormous index finger, with which he signaled that the interpreter was to stand to his left, the old prison warden to his right. How impassively the officer waited, while shouts of joy rang from inside the prison; how expressionless his face remained as individual prisoners, released from their cells by the Cossacks and sent to the courtyard, tried to thank him. A measured flick of the whip shaft and they froze and shrank back.

They had to form a column, and each, when his name was called, had to step up to the table, remove his twill cap, and stand there silently. Conny's father read out the name, the crime, and the sentence for each; and the interpreter translated it to the officer, who did not once nod or shake his head, but merely gazed at the prisoner with a stern indifference. The whip shaft quivered before he indicated his verdict. If the shaft pointed downward, the prisoner was led back to his cell; if it stood perpendicular, his imprisonment ended that very moment . . .

Like in a legend, that's right.

We stood in the courtyard feeling uneasy, as you can imagine —time and again puzzled by the officer's decisions, which often went contrary to all our expectations. We soon realized that predictions were hopeless. One fellow, in for smuggling and lèse-majesté, might be set free at once, while the next one, who had committed only lèse-majesté, would be returned to his cell. Conny and Edith and I could not grasp why an arsonist received a pardon but a fellow who stole chickens was led back to finish out his time. We could not fathom the grim judicial wisdom which released the man who had knifed someone to death but confirmed the sentence of a man who had poached on state lands.

Yes, that was true: we were in suspense principally on account of Eugen Lavrenz, who stood next to last in line. He moved forward without looking up, displaying the same indifference as the Cossack officer, and when he finally stood before the table, the interpreter had to remind him twice to remove his cap. Conny's father, blinded by the sun and drained by a rage he dared not voice, haltingly read the pertinent passages from the prison records, and the interpreter took up his words, and explained the crime and the sentence. Thereupon Conny's father unexpectedly spoke up, apparently thinking he had a right to intervene personally in this case, but all he did was arouse the officer's ire. The whip shaft flew up energetically, signaling both a decision and a reprimand, and the interpreter had to inform Eugen Lavrenz that he was free now; he could collect his belongings and go home.

Eugen Lavrenz did not say thank you like the others; he just stood there as if this acquittal were unwelcome to him, as if it thwarted a plan he had long been hatching; and later, when he vanished into the prison, I was far from sure whether he would come out again or would ask to be shut up in his cell.

But he reappeared. He stepped into the courtyard carrying a tobacco-brown bundle, at the very moment the officer was ordering Conny's father to report to the commandant's headquarters at the Hotel Queen Luise. A knotty stick in one hand, Lavrenz passed the guard without a glance, opened the unlocked door himself, and stepped quickly into the shadow of the walls. And I was already on his trail, following him along the wall and over the causeway to the stand of alders, where once his house had stood. Here he hid his bundle in the briers, scooped up some lake water to cool his face, and then headed up the hill toward the estate, yes indeed, and circled it warily. I spied him again behind the smithy, where he had a good view of the manor house. He lingered longest by the stables, standing motionless, trying to take in the features of the building and even more the habits of its tenant . . .

Don't be too impatient, dear Martin Witt. Why not let events take their course? This was the point at which my father, driving by in his smart two-horse carriage, caught sight of me, and I had to come out from behind the row of battered milk cans where I had been crouching and climb up beside him. He impressed me as unusually determined and solemn, like a salesman on his way to consummate the deal of a lifetime. His scolding was suitably mild: "Even a war, Zygmunt, is no excuse for a boy your age never being home."

He greeted the Russian sentries at the city gate in a gracious manner. A peasant cart which tried to cross the bridge before us was stopped and searched; bayonets had to be poked into the

bales of straw to test their harmlessness before the cart was allowed to enter Lucknow; but our carriage rolled past the sen-
tinels without pausing, yes indeed, although the rear of the vehicle was heaped with strange shapes under the faded tarpaulin.

We rattled across the deserted marketplace and down the
street to the railway station, which was cordoned off by Cossacks. Freight cars full of horses, artillery, and reinforcements
had pulled in, as well as a shipment of young Russian civilians, the
rawest of recruits with at most cardboard boxes for luggage, who
were having a dreadful time forming up properly on the platform. Later they were marched off to the garrison to be issued
their uniforms. We ran into them again after we had been over-
taken and ordered to turn back by the brisk mounted Cossacks.
Not that my father gave up and went home; such obstacles only
sharpened his determination, and this determination guided us
around to the back of the garrison, the back of the military
hospital. The sentry first demanded some kind of permit, but we
overcame his doubts; my father theatrically flipped back the tarpaulin, revealing his traveling pharmacy; with quiet assurance he
invited the sentry to check its contents against the inventory he
had prepared. The guard shook his head and opened the gate.

Perhaps you are smiling, dear boy, but my father was totally
confident that he was about to make the deal of his life, perhaps
with the full cooperation of a Russian military doctor. Where
imperial German military doctors had turned him down—out of
thrice-cursed stupidity—the czarist doctors would see the light;
he considered them less thick-skulled than their German coun-
terparts.

You must try to picture the contract he offered the enemy, the
144 items he had included in his inventory. The list began with
simple preparations, like salve for sore feet, cream against blisters,
syrup against coughs and fever—remedies for the ordinary troubles of any army on the march. Farther down the list the items
became bolder and more exotic. There were specifics against
shrapnel wounds, volatile essences against bayonet and lance
punctures, balm against burns, and his star product, a reasonably
priced tonic against funk on the field of battle.

Consider, dear boy, what a prospect all this might have evoked
in the mind of a commander with imagination: the possibility of

an almost invulnerable army, which would first sow astonishment among the enemy forces, then despair, so that there was nothing left for them to do but surrender.

In any case, we hitched our horses outside the military hospital, stretched our legs, and looked around for the head military doctor. All we found were two nurses. They met our question with uncomprehending stares. So we strolled down the hospital corridor, passed open doors, and nodded to the wounded men stretched out on straw mattresses. The brashness with which my father winked at this man or that did not escape me.

In one room we heard German spoken; we stepped in, and learned that the Russians had captured at least twenty German soldiers, militiamen who had been wounded near Prostken. As we left, my father nodded encouragingly to them, as if to say, Just wait, the days of your sorrows are numbered.

We continued along the corridor as the militiamen had instructed us. A signed photograph of Kaiser Wilhelm still hung on the wall. A door with milk-glass panes had two handwritten signs prohibiting something or other in German and Russian; this was the pharmacy, and here we knocked. Inside, a hummed melody broke off. Something clattered, a cupboard door banged shut, and after we had knocked several times, an irritated Wotan flung open the door. He looked exactly as I had always pictured the Thunderer, the ill-tempered boss of the gods: watery eyes, a beard the color of mist, massive neck sinews. Over his crookedly buttoned military tunic, the giant was wearing a dingy white smock. His face darkened further at the sight of us, the shaggy eyebrows drew together, and he delivered himself of a curse, which, though unintelligible to us, was sufficiently strong to make us both redden. However, this curse seemed to relieve his mind, for he beckoned two nurses, who were sitting side by side on a cot, to come to him, conferred with them in whispers, and then with a gesture in our direction indicated that we were free to say our piece. Jan Rogalla, black hat in hand, described the purpose of his visit and made his proposal while one of the nurses served as interpreter. My father spread out the lists, cited certain mysterious substances, and explained their properties, while the man in the smock stood by the window and listened, at first only amused, then with increasing interest. My father talked up the preparations, deliberately avoiding any self-praise or any allusion to the role such medicines might play in the course of the war. This discretion seemed to have made him more persuasive, for the Russian grew increasingly impatient: he wanted to see samples, proof, perhaps a little demonstration.

My father went out to the carriage to bring in the samples; I was permitted to stay behind and suck a peppermint. I saw the Russian army doctor whispering something to one of the nurses, who then also left the room. I sat down on the cot, startled at the cracking sound of my teeth finishing off the peppermint. Wotan in his doctor's smock drummed with large, blond-haired fingers on the windowsill.

Finally, Father returned, holding a basketful of his medications. Placing the basket just a touch too elegantly on a table, he lined up bottles, vials, and jars in neat formation, then passed one after the other to the army doctor. The doctor sniffed at the containers, shook them, held them up to the light, and did what he could to express his interest, a somewhat too mechanical interest—as we noticed too late.

Suddenly the door flew open and two soldiers with bayonets marched up to my father and clapped their hands on his shoulders. The military doctor took off his smock, dropped any pretense at interest, and gave vent to noises of scorn and anger. He bore down on Jan Rogalla and shouted that he was under arrest. As a saboteur. As an agent scheming to undermine the health of the entire army. They would decide at staff headquarters what to do with him. The carriage and its contents had been confiscated. He waved his hand, and the soldiers led my father away . . .

What about me? Oh, I ran along behind, down the corridor and out to the gate, where the soldiers drove me away. "Run and get Uncle Adam," my father called out to me before the soldiers hustled him off . . .

No, no tea, I'd like to try some of the grapes you brought . . . You shouldn't feel you have to bring something each time, son . . . Thank you.

So I trailed along behind, at a safe distance, of course, always hoping Father would turn around and look at me. Cowed and apparently numbed, he kept step with the soldiers, all the way to the Hotel Queen Luise. In my firm belief that he would soon be released, I waited outside by the pushcart of the woman who sold ices. But neither Father nor the soldiers emerged, so I had to go down to the river, to the great bend in the Lucknow River where Uncle Adam lived.

His narrow garden bordered on the water. The house lay farther back, on a well-planted slope, a substantial whitewashed building with a thatched roof. Uncle Adam lived there alone, carrying on animated conversations with himself; was this because he missed his wife, who had died in the first year of their marriage?

I went to the carved front door, painted in the traditional blue. I knocked and pounded, threw pebbles at the attic window—but Uncle Adam did not open up until I had shouted his name insistently several times.

Right, the passionate researcher, the mole grubbing up our past . . . No sooner had he given me a moist, poorly aimed kiss and bolted the door than he drew me across the hall and through the many rooms crowded with relics of our history to his bedchamber. The room was in turmoil. The massive bed stood awry, the rag rugs were crumpled up against the baseboards, the carved chairs were overturned, and even the painted chest, which was always kept locked, stood not in its usual place but up-ended against one wall. A trapdoor I had never seen stood open, and strewn about were weapons of bronze and iron, maps and old engravings, coins rubbed thin by anxious hands, ancient kitchen implements, brooches, distaffs, bleached animal skeletons, a glass case of charred documents—things he had excavated, chased down, begged, bought, or brought back from sentimental journeys.

I almost forgot to tell him of my mission. But when I told him what had happened, he nodded grimly, as if he had been expecting something of the sort. "Well, there we have it, boy," he said, "there we have it." Then he pondered for a moment and decided: first things first. He bounded down into the secret cellar, where by the light of a stable lantern he crouched, packing things away as I handed them down to him through the hatchway. He received each item tenderly and called it by name: "Hello there, scimitar," or "Just look at that, will you, the old mirror." And as he stowed things away, he continued to talk:

"You'll be safe here for the time being, just wait here till it's all over."

When he was done, we closed the trapdoor, laid the rag rugs over it, pushed the bed back, and heaved the chest to the foot of the bed. Now the relics of our Masurian past, the "unimpeachable witnesses," as Uncle Adam called them, were safe from pillage. He locked up the house, hid the key under the rain barrel, donned his most solemn expression, and put his arm around my shoulder. We set out for the Hotel Queen Luise, the staff headquarters.

On the way I sensed that something had changed in town. Whole brigades of men were out with their glue pails, plastering walls and trees with posters and proclamations, warnings and summonses, in German and Russian. Uncle Adam stopped and read each one we passed, and repeated to me what Commandant Vitinghoff had to say.

No signals were to be given, with lights, flags, or any other device. The fourteen militiamen who had gone underground in Lucknow were to surrender their arms. It was a punishable offense to ply Russian soldiers with alcohol. The military government could requisition horses and bicycles. The ruble was to be the standard currency. One poster actually called upon our Poles, who had been "oppressed for 150 years," to rise up and proclaim their independence.

Uncle Adam read me these texts with great bitterness, as if this, too, he had foreseen. "They're showing us their teeth, boy," he remarked, but the bitterness did not impair his historian's reflexes: he carefully peeled off a few posters and stowed them under his shirt for the collection.

He spoke fluent Polish and a little Russian, and the guards at staff headquarters let us in. Now we had our first opportunity to see the Hotel Queen Luise from the inside. It was the fanciest of Lucknow's hotels, intended for high government officials passing through, for grain merchants and sawmill owners; once the Kaiser had almost spent the night there. You can imagine, son, what outrages we witnessed: the red runners trampled by army boots, the overstuffed chairs and sofas holding a welter of staff maps and document crates, a field telephone on the grand piano, the big ornamental vases full of Cossack lances, the genteel hush broken by loud military voices.

A guard asked us what we wanted, and Uncle Adam demanded in the name of the citizenry to speak to Commandant Vitinghoff in regard to an urgent matter, namely the despotic actions of the occupying power. The words rolled off the guard like water off a duck's back; he bowed impassively and directed us up a staircase to the Johannesburg Suite—the rooms at the Queen Luise had names instead of numbers.

Yes, incredible though it may seem, we were allowed to go straight to the commandant, a correct, resigned sort of man who at his age should have enjoyed higher military rank. He sat on a green sofa and listened not without interest, toying with the cords of the lowered blinds.

Uncle Adam demanded the immediate release of Jan Rogalla and put forth compelling arguments—not only the issue of legal rights. He cleverly appealed to the commandant's better nature, suggesting that by this one deed he might win over the entire populace: "Let this dreamer go—Jan Rogalla is no saboteur, only a dreamer—and you will have many of us on your side." The commandant rose, lit a cigarette, and indicated by a gesture that he found himself in a difficult position . . .

No, no, not that. It was not a question of setting an example. Rather, the commandant was acting on orders from headquarters; because of certain wrongdoings by German troops in Kalisch, the Czar and the Czar's uncle had decreed that some of the occupied cities had to make reparations, and Lucknow happened to be one of them, that's all. Within the space of twenty-four hours thirty thousand rubles were to be collected. And to make the people view this obligation seriously, some prominent citizens had been taken into custody: Mayor Lischkohl and Police Sergeant Milevski, for example, Head Forester Blask, the sawmill owner Heyduck, Conny's father, Town Treasurer Tuchlinski, and finally, since he had practically walked into their arms, my father, Jan Rogalla. As he said, the town had twenty-four hours to ransom these citizens.

The old commandant shrugged, as if to say he did not agree with this procedure and he was sorry to have to turn down our petition. He raised the blinds and invited us to step to the window and look down at the marketplace, where our fellow townsfolk were swarming around the latest proclamation, poking one another to call attention to the large sum involved and doubtless to the consequences of not raising the tribute in time. And it seemed to me that they went their separate ways looking earnest, and hurried home doing calculations in their heads, weighing what was necessary against what was possible.

You should have seen how Uncle Adam stalked to the middle of the room, and stretched to his full height, trembling slightly, while the commandant rubbed his eyes with their prominent tear sacs. "Now," Uncle Adam announced, "now you will see what stuff Lucknow is made of." He gave a hint of a bow, and out we stalked, past the guard, past the sentries at the entrance . . .

No, I don't agree, dear Martin Witt. The sum in question was no small matter for Lucknow, for the simple reason that just before the occupation the city treasury and the city savings bank had moved their funds to safety, with the unerring instinct such institutions always display. The people of Lucknow knew that, and probably realized that the sum in question would have to be extracted from their mattresses, so to speak. Yes, that's why Uncle Adam began to speak to all the people he encountered, urging them to be generous. He took it upon himself personally to see that the money was raised; he bought lined paper, marked each line with a number, drew vertical lines: on the left would be written the name; on the right, for all to see, the pledge. He did this not out of pedantry or officiousness but because "a little pressure does wonders for people's generosity," as he remarked.

Thirty thousand rubles, or seventy thousand marks, were needed to free the hostages. We knocked at every door. We canvassed the residential streets, the shops, the workshops, and the taverns; we did not overlook the parish house, we roused the miller from his sickbed, we handed the list down to fishermen in their boats, and I remember that Uncle Adam even had the list circulate around the prison—with good results, by the way. News of our drive proceeded us wherever we went, and some people, impatient to demonstrate their patriotism, came to meet us or were waiting at their doors, ready to sign; others led us inside and instead of money offered us objects of value, which they asked us to assess—rings, clocks, silverware.

We let ourselves rest only long enough to add up our lists; we sat down on the landing pier, or on a bench in the park, and ran a pencil down the columns of figures. But the zeroes did not multiply very rapidly, and even going over the sums three times did not produce a more encouraging result. At the end of this dry, quivering day, the people of Lucknow had pledged only sixteen thousand rubles. So there was nothing to do but to continue after sundown, threatening and cajoling. Some visits had surprises in store for us; whereas, for instance, a man known throughout the town as an enemy of the mayor pledged an entire month's earnings, my grandfather, whose son, after all, was among the hostages, gave only the contents of his lean purse, more copper than silver.

Yes, that was an experience in itself, our visit to the estate. We sat there in the dusk facing each other, my grandfather with his fowling piece across his knees, looking not at us but at the window and the orchard outside; even when he answered, he did not meet our eyes but spoke to the windowpane, as if our mission held not the slightest interest for him.

Uncle Adam had laid the list of pledges on the table, with the biggest contributions on top, but my grandfather took no notice of it, and when Uncle Adam began to read the list aloud to him, with studied pauses, Alfons Rogalla merely made a face, as if he were being forced to listen to a text in a foreign tongue. How that man could sit! He simply let things bounce off him if they did not suit him. And finally he fished out his purse, shaking out the coins on the table like rain—as if to say we were blackmailing him. He skillfully caught two silver coins as they rolled away, and the rest he pushed toward us: "Go ahead, help yourselves, you magpies!"

Uncle Adam raked the coins toward himself to count them, then stood up in anger and disbelief and threw the coins down at my grandfather's feet. As I watched the coins roll away, suddenly the muzzle of the fowling piece aimed over our heads. We ducked and pressed our cheeks to the table. Grandfather was sitting there pointing the gun at a slowly moving target; he followed it by gently swerving in his seat.

He fired over our heads, through the window. The force of the explosion made my face hurt, the flash of fire was blinding. He stepped up to the window for a moment, then started out of the room, reloading as he went. We followed him down the corridor and out to the garden, where he thrashed through the currant bushes, listening, searching for traces, reconstructing trajectories. He could not admit he had missed.

"A Russian?" Uncle Adam asked. "Did you get a Russian?" My grandfather, looking out over the rye field, replied, "There's somebody here wants revenge, and he comes creeping up on a body, threatening a body, letting him know it's time to settle an old score. I don't mind settling—with gunshot."

Uncle Adam asked no further questions, but I remembered Eugen Lavrenz. In my thoughts I warned him to lie still in the field, not to set the stalks trembling, and he seemed to have heard my warning, for not a stalk rustled. And when we sat down on the warped garden bench, we did so not to wait for Eugen Lavrenz but because to the west, in the direction of Dippelsee and Arys, the horizon had begun to flicker, as with some fabulous fireworks.

Beyond the tongue of land, on the other side of the dark State Forest, there were flashes of red and yellow, pulsing up and down, and above the line of flame white stars shot up, reeled, and burst. The horizon was weaving and heaving under the hard blows, under the explosions which shot up steeply or leaped away horizontally. We sat there for a long time, feeling the vibrations and waves of heat sweeping over us, but that must have been a delusion. In any case, after a while my grandfather commented, "And all this, for Christ's sake, just at harvest time, as though there weren't any other seasons for war. But our fellows will do it, they have the upper hand because they're fighting for their homeland, yes, for their homeland."

Pardon me? A detestable word? A word with a dark history? . . . That's just what my son Bernhard said: he said this word meant nothing to him; he could not do anything with it, but when others spoke it, all he could think of was terrible things. I understand what you mean, son, I know that you, like Bernhard, see the idea of homeland as tied up with a certain kind of narrowness, with prejudices, with an ignorant, dull spirit that cannot perceive the humanity of people from other backgrounds.

Please don't misunderstand me, dear Martin Witt, I realize that the word has a bad reputation, that it has been abused, so seriously abused that one can hardly use it nowadays. And I also admit that where people live in vast concrete barracks, in cold, prefabricated boxes, such a concept has no meaning. But for that very reason, could we not try to rid the word of its bad connotations? Give it back a sort of purity?

You want to know what I have in mind? I can feel you smiling, but I would answer your smile this way: to me, the homeland is not just the place where your dead are buried; it is the place where you have your roots, where you are sheltered, in your language, in your feelings, yes, even in your silence. It is the place where you are always recognized. And that's what everyone wants, in his heart of hearts, to be recognized, to be welcomed without question . . .

But I sense you view the matter differently . . .

Pardon me? Could you speak louder, please?

The City Briefs in the local newspaper? So that is what the word homeland conjures up for you? And what else?

No, no, I won't be offended . . .

I see, a comical anecdote, told at tedious length, with idiotic complacency. You know, that doesn't surprise me; I have heard all this before, heard it long ago from Conny Karrasch, who was always wanting to prove that the homeland is the place where the most good-natured blindness prevails, the most self-righteous blindness . . .

But what did I want to tell you? Oh, yes, the war. The war suddenly heated up and came rolling down toward Lucknow. But we had just figured out when it would reach us when it took an unexpected leap toward the south and east, which left not only us but also the occupying power at a loss. A war as unpredictable as April weather. One simply could not rely on the location of the front; they dug in and scattered at the same time. At the commandant's headquarters, at any rate, they no longer knew which way to look, and one morning they simply cleared out, leaving the Queen Luise empty. They took the hostages along.

You can imagine that I had my hands full. I had to collect shell cases, grenade fragments, and uniform buttons, but my special private interest was building up my private cemetery, on Castle Hill, under the seven giant spruces.

I often flitted out there, paying scant attention to the pounding of the artillery. Fetching my shovel from its hiding place in the kaddik bushes, I sneaked up to the top of Castle Hill, where first I checked our cemeteries, outlined with pebbles. They were located side by side and were similar in size, but in Conny's there were more little sticks with slips of cardboard, little plaques describing in block letters who or what was buried there: a dove, a frog, a snail, a cat. We used the same pencil, cut the little plaques out of the same shoe box which we kept in a cave by the ravine.

Conny had stolen a march on me again, I could see that immediately. He had buried a heron, as a larger plaque made clear, one of those slim, stern birds with a lance-like beak. I had only to scratch the fine sand a bit and already I found it, the pearl-gray neck, the crest of feathers. There was no way I could match a heron. Not even the dead capon I had dragged up here from the estate could equal that.

I covered up the cadaver again and lay down, my chin on my crossed arms; down there in the flats the bog was seething with heat. A warm wind passed over me, rustling the spruces, and I read the writing on the cardboard markers and weighed the dead against each other. Only once had I outdone Conny; that was the time Ella, our adder, died, but before long he had caught up by means of a dead weasel, crushed by the hoofs of a Cossack patrol.

Do you know what counted least? Cats. We found them everywhere, drowned, killed, full of birdshot. Birds were worth considerably more, and even a rat increased the score by leaps and bounds, not to mention a polecat or a squirrel. There were points for everything, for cranes as for short-haired dachshunds, for the mole no less than for the woodpecker.

The highest points? That was for the shy and very rare black stork, which was protected, and could be found on Lake Tartar.

In any case, I was lying on Castle Hill, adding up points, while above Lake Selment, not too high, a single plane was gliding. I could make out the silhouette of the two airmen, but not the plane's insignia; presumably they were watching the columns of soldiers marching on the other side of the lake or monitoring the field howitzers sending up flags of smoke above the State Forest. From the depths of the ravine a jay swooped up with a hoarse, rusty cry of warning, but it flapped away when it noticed me. I rolled over the stone wall where Castle Hill fell off sharply, never doubting that down in the ravine, amid the matted green and the splintered tree trunks, I would see Conny. But it was not he who had disturbed the jay.

In a stand of small pines, camouflaged by all the fallen branches, sat several soldiers. They sat in a tight circle munching dry hardtack, persistently and without pleasure. The airmen and I were the only ones who could see into their hiding place. They felt safe there, five Russian soldiers, with bedrolls slung across their shoulders and their packs on the ground in front of them.

One of them stood apart, a corpulent man with his uniform properly buttoned to the neck, his saber at his side, the field glasses dangling around his neck. I recognized him as an officer by his epaulets. Several times the soldiers respectfully offered him their hardtack, but the officer waved them off or stepped out of the pine grove and gazed absentmindedly at all the shattered wood.

Whenever he left them for a moment, one of the soldiers crept after him, apparently worried for him, and once, when the airplane cast its shadow over Castle Hill, they huddled around him, as if they had to protect him. The soldiers had no weapons. They were in flight. I was of two minds as I lay there. On the one hand I wanted to report my discovery, but on the other I wanted to watch the soldiers, who, having finished their meal, lay down under the pines, all but the officer. He smoked a cigarette, leaned his back against a crooked tree trunk, emptied the contents of his map case onto the ground, read through various documents, and tore each one up after reading it. Then he drew his high-caliber army pistol, raised it, and, without the slightest faltering, shot himself in the head. His knees buckled, his body slid to one side, twisted, and tumbled to the forest floor . . .

No, son, I was not horrified, and I did not run away. Even before the soldiers jumped up, ran to him, and bent over him, my decision was firm. It was a decision reached instantly in the moment of death: I wanted to bury the Russian officer. I wanted him

in my little cemetery, where I would drive a peg into the ground
with a tablet reading simply "Russian Major," or "Major," or
even "Colonel." Let Conny decide, after his initial dumbfound-
edness, how many points that was worth. Let him bury an entire
family of black storks—after this he would not find it so easy to
catch up with me.

But for the time being the soldiers remained crouched across
the officer, touching him, tenderly cleaning the earth and moss
from his face, and apparently discussing what they should do.
There were signs of disagreement, of depression. One bearded
soldier kissed the officer on the brow. Then they carried him,
whom I already regarded as my booty, into their hiding place. I
was expecting them to bury him there among the pines, and I was
determined to dig him up as soon as they were gone. But no, they
did not bury him; instead, they shook hands over his dead body,
pledged something to one another, then felled two pine trees
about as thick as a man's arm. They sliced off the branches with
their bayonets, placed the trunks on the ground, cut a shelter half
into strips, and wove and knotted the strips around the trunks to
form a stretcher. They picked it up to test it, then put it down
again when it was clear that the strips had some give but would
hold and that the poles were long enough to rest on their shoulders. One of the soldiers, the bearded one, took command, and
the others heeded him and obeyed his gestures without objection.
They gathered up their packs, hoisted the stretcher to their
shoulders, and began to pick their way through the pines, appearing soon afterward on the edge of the bog, near Uncle Adam's
terraces . . .

That's right, that's exactly what I thought to myself. How
they must have loved that officer, or at least respected him, if
they were prepared to carry him this way, not merely to a better
gravesite but all the way to the border and home, and this in
broad daylight, with nothing to conceal their movements, in all
that hostile light. They swayed along the edge of the bog, the
bearded soldier leading the way. He pointed out swamp holes to
the bearers, as well as rotted tree stumps sticking up and quick-
sands from which gleaming bubbles welled. As they crossed the
uneven terrain, the body of the dead officer swayed on the
stretcher; his arms dangled down and bobbed to the rhythm of

the men's gait. I realized that they wanted to cross the bog and reach Lake Selment, where they planned to slip into the shelter of the forest. Because I had not yet relinquished my own plan, I followed them under cover of the kaddik bushes and the sharp swamp grass. I did not have to keep very close behind them, because they were walking upright and were easy to spot in the glimmering solitude. How solemn their procession appeared from a distance!

At the peat ponds they paused, while the bearded soldier searched for a way to get across. All he found were the two crooked tree trunks laid down to form a quaking bridge which they had to cross if they wanted to reach the lakeshore. And I remember that as they picked their way across with the stretcher, the airplane turned away from the sun and toward them; its shadow passed over the lake and the girdle of reeds, seeming to enlarge the nearer it came to the peat ponds, and as it glided over them, one of the bearers lost his balance and fell, pulling the stretcher and the man behind him down, too. The water splashed up golden brown where they slipped. The plane swooped over Castle Hill and returned to hover over the lake.

Now, I thought, the dead officer is mine, but I was mistaken. The bearers bobbed up and paddled to the poles. After rescuing the stretcher, they dived until they had found the dead man underwater and dragged him to the shore.

They poured the water out of his boots, dried his face, and combed his hair with their fingers. Then they lifted him onto the stretcher and continued on their way, along the belt of reeds toward the forest, the bearded soldier still guiding them. They plunged into the forest, never looking to the west but only forward, but still I was careful in my pursuit, dashing from bush to bush, from tree trunk to tree trunk, making use of every screen. The dense blueberry bushes slowed them down; their feet got entangled in fallen branches; they switched the stretcher from shoulder to shoulder more and more often. When they reached a knoll in the forest, they set their burden down and collapsed into the grass, all except for a very young soldier, who remained standing by the stretcher, looking down long and hard at the dead officer. Finally, he turned to the others with an explanation or a suggestion—I surmised he was suggesting they bury the officer here. After an argument which he apparently lost, he, too, lay down in the grass.

Do you know the feeling of being watched, but you don't know from what quarter? Your skin prickles, your pulse speeds up, you breathe irregularly, and you look around and listen, in vain, but the feeling persists? At any rate, I knew someone had seen me, even before I discovered who it was and where he was hiding. It took me a while to locate him, because Conny had scrambled up one of the old pine trees and was perched on a branch. It was our lookout pine, from which one could see all the way to Little Grajevo and across Lake Lucknow to the prison. His gestures were easy to interpret: he pointed at himself, then at me, and finally at the cordwood piled up along the path to Little Grajevo. I sidled backward out of my hiding place, circled the knoll where the Russians were resting, and crept over to the woodpile, where I crouched and waited for him.

I did not have to wait long. Conny drew me down onto the forest floor and made it clear, in most emphatic terms, that I was not to report the Russians. As usual he took command of the situation, and we went down to the cabins of Little Grajevo, the moss-covered cabins on whose roofs tiny birches and spiky little spruces sprouted. All the while I was thinking that the dead officer belonged to me and that I would bury him on Castle Hill under the seven giant spruces.

Little Grajevo seemed deserted. There were no pails at the well. No one was chopping wood. There were none of the usual barefoot children playing in the tarred barges. Conny shouted, but no one answered . . .

Pardon me? No, we did not mean to hide the Russian soldiers in Little Grajevo until nightfall. What Conny hoped was that one of the Polish woodsmen would act as a guide, conducting the fleeing Russians to Lake Tartar and perhaps even to the edge of the forest that stretched to the border. Conny knocked at the hut that had once belonged to Johannes Hauser, his mysterious friend, and, when no one answered, pushed the door open. Inside the stuffy single room that served as kitchen, bedroom, and living room, sat Hauser's family: his wife, children, and old parents. They sat there in their Sunday best, silent, submissive, with boxes and shopping bags around them, ready to accept whatever this war should inflict on them. Conny first greeted Anna. Anna, whom I remembered as always barefoot, cheerful, and dressed in tatters, was now wearing excessively warm kneesocks, polished white shoes, and an amber necklace. Then he turned to her brother and grandfather and explained about the Russian soldiers, who were unarmed and wanted to get to the border with their dead officer. No one was willing to serve as guide.

I sensed that they grew more frightened the more Conny urged them. They picked up their luggage and pressed the bundles to them, crowding even closer together on their stools, as if that would make it easier for them to withstand his request.

Conny did not give up. He pulled me outside and pointed to another hut, where we found another large family in their Sunday best, also humbly prepared for flight. Everywhere we met with the same silent refusal, and I saw that they breathed easier as we left the cottage. We went to the village pump and pumped water for one another. And here, at the pump, Conny suddenly said, "Well, if no one else will, I will lead them to Lake Tartar."

You must try to imagine what that meant, at a time like that, for a boy like him. He undertook to lead the enemy soldiers to the border, by paths only he knew, past the numerous guards and patrols, and he undertook it simply because no one else was available. Probably he would not have been able to state what his reasons were. Even if he would have liked me to go along, he did not insist on it. He went back to the knoll by himself, found the soldiers, and offered them his services.

Perhaps they would have left the dead officer behind if Conny had made a point of it, citing, for example, the swampy route. But he recognized how much the officer meant to them, burdensome though he was. From the shelter of the woodpile I watched as they set out; I cannot say I would have given anything to accompany them.

Don't think, son, that I had given up my plan. The space for a human body was already measured out in my cemetery, a cardboard sign had been cut out and attached to the peg, and all I needed was a fallen soldier, preferably of high military rank or from a special troop, for the higher points that would yield.

So I equipped myself with a rickety wooden cart dragged out of the nettle patch where it was rotting, and fixed it up with the help of the smith. Then I rattled off toward the war, down dusty highways and paths cracking in the dryness. The wounded soldiers I encountered told me where the most recent short, sharp clashes had taken place, these clashes that in their totality represented the battle for Masuria. I followed their pointing fingers to picturesque hills and copses or to railway underpasses and brickworks. What treasures there were for the taking: shell cases, blankets, bayonets, damaged field telephones, of course, but also canteens, staff tents, artillery pieces, mobile bakeries, even carts full of parade uniforms and horses whose saddlebags contained silver cutlery. But I found no fallen soldiers; they had already been buried. I used my cart to haul off chance booty, from horseshoes to boxes of hardtack.

One afternoon, when I had already almost given up hope, a single airplane presumed to pass over our town. It was a light Russian aircraft, which swooped down, parallel to the lakeshore, apparently intending to buzz the bridge. Simon Gayko and I were standing on the causeway watching with deep interest. It was a plane made of plywood and glue and bits of wire, with a pleasantly humming engine that drove a light-brown wooden propeller. The plane glided past the prison, threw its shadow out over Lake Lucknow, then turned and swooped at the bridge again. Now rifle fire burst out, first isolated shots that sounded like dry twigs cracking, but as the plane continued to buzz the bridge, a regular volley of explosions broke out, as though not only all the carbines and machine guns but even the reeds along the lake were participating. The shots raked the plane, chipping a piece of wing, peppering the body, tearing the canvas to shreds. But the plane held up until the stick sheared off. The plane tipped up on one wing, spun, and came crashing down on the water.

Fantastic lighting effects, as you can imagine. Fabulous waterworks with spray shooting as high as a tree. As the body of the plane bobbed and dipped in the water, it reminded me of a giant swimmer or of a huge float on a fishing line, that's right. The pilot's seat was empty.

Since my raft was a one-person affair, I had to leave Simon Gayko behind on our landing. It was a fast-moving raft, if I say so myself, made out of the door of a chicken house mounted on several large metal drums. The paddle was a stout piece of plywood. From all directions boats were hastening toward the crash site to rescue the plane or the pilot.

I was the first to arrive on the spot. There was nothing to salvage but a few scraps of the canvas that had sheathed the cabin; they would make a good birthday gift for Uncle Adam to include in his museum. After I had helped the people in the boats get a rope around the plane, I paddled into the rushes, let my raft drift, and watched them tow away the wreckage.

But now try to imagine: the sunlight among the swaying rushes, the water gurgling under the raft, and suddenly the round head of a sea lion bobs up out of Lake Lucknow; I had never before seen an airman in his flying suit, with the tightly fitting leather cap and strange goggles. The gentle little waves were not able to float the limp body toward land. I tied him to my raft, dragged him through the belt of rushes, and then into the reeds. I had not the slightest doubt that he belonged to me and would occupy the place I had already measured out . . .

His identification papers? His dog tag? Well, I was not in the least interested in those. After I had determined he had no weapons on him, I stuffed his papers, letters, and even money back into his pockets. I planned to bring him to Castle Hill by night, on my handcart, whose wheels I would muffle with rags. As soon as I could, I slipped by the estate's smithy to collect my handcart, which I kept there. Strange to say, I fell asleep in spite of all the excitement, lulled by the steady hammering in the smithy and the smell of burned hoof. At any rate, I dreamed that my grandfather had offered to let me choose the most valuable thing on the estate and call it my own.

You needn't wait in suspense, dear boy. As far as I was concerned, the most valuable thing was a vest of my grandfather's, made from the skin of his first hound dog, Hoggo. Why? Because the story was that whoever wore the vest would be warned of danger well beforehand; the fur of the vest stood on end at the approach of anything unpleasant.

But what did I want to say? Right: I was awakened by a ringing sound nearby, the sound of iron striking iron, and someone dashed through the waist-high nettles past my hiding place and pressed himself against the side of the barn, standing there as if nailed to the spot: Eugen Lavrenz. I whistled to him, but I had whistled too soon, for as he looked over toward me, Alfons Rogalla stepped out between smithy and barn, wearing only his jodhpurs and a coarse linen shirt, with a rope as a belt, his fowling piece at the ready. Presumably Eugen Lavrenz would have fled had he spotted my grandfather in time, but as he looked from me to him, he must have been thinking it was already too late. He just put up his hands and watched with narrowed eyes the man who had cornered him and was now slowly walking toward him with his characteristic limp. I was waiting for a shot. My grandfather stopped next to my wooden cart, smiled condescendingly, took his time, and I could understand perfectly why Eugen Lavrenz let his hands sink, straightened up, and said, "Come on, man, get it over with."

As he approached with torturous slowness, my grandfather appeared to have revised his original decision in favor of a new notion. For without letting Eugen Lavrenz out of his sight, he walked around my cart, tapped its sides, pushed the shaft, and set one foot on the little loading bed as if taking possession of it. "Why not?" he said, more to himself than to the man at his mercy. "Why not settle accounts? I give every wretch his due. Why shouldn't you get yours, too, buddy?"

What did you say?

No, dear boy, the other way around. My grandfather sat himself down on the bed of the cart, beckoned Eugen Lavrenz to him, bade him pick up the shaft, prodded him in the back with the barrel of his gun, and after two gee-ups, they were off.

Without my handcart I could not get my dead pilot to Castle Hill, so I postponed my plan, crept out of my hiding place, found a short staff to beat a path through the nettles, and followed the jolting conveyance, which turned by the paddock, clattered to the sandy path, and went screeching downhill, powered by Eugen Lavrenz's grinding rage. They went around the estate's outer edge to the main road, then rolled down to the causeway, giving my grandfather's steed a chance to catch his breath. Then the cart hopped and rattled over the cobblestones. Throughout the entire trip I did not hear my grandfather utter a single word, from which I deduced that Eugen Lavrenz knew perfectly well where he, not my grandfather, was being taken.

He did not once turn to look at his passenger, and perhaps that was the only way he could demonstrate his scorn. Even when poked with the barrel of the gun, he did not turn around. A stranger seeing the pair might have interpreted their relationship quite differently, thinking the man at the shaft was there of his own accord, and that the man in the cart was at his mercy. In any case, they hobbled over the causeway without attracting attention. Only a few old tramps picking baskets and cans of blueberries paused and jabbered to each other about the strange sight.

That's it, they clattered toward the whitewashed Lucknow Prison, the most beautiful jail in Masuria.

I could not stand to watch Eugen Lavrenz come through the gate, possibly to be received with catcalls, with sarcastic welcomes. As we passed my house, I gave up my pursuit.

Could you do me a favor? I would like to sit up higher; I seem to keep slipping down into the bed . . .

Careful: the best way is to grasp me under the armpits and pull me back up, that's it, while I brace myself . . .

Thank you, that feels much better . . .

By the way, I should mention that my father had gone to some trouble to concoct a balm for burns, whose base, you might be surprised to learn, was linseed oil. Had he tried the right proportions of limewater and tincture of opium instead, he would have hit on the classic burn ointment . . .

Well, so I lost my chance to see Eugen Lavrenz returned to prison. As I turned in at our house, my anger was looking for an outlet. I hurled my staff over the fence and looked at the sunflowers with the eye of an executioner—where was my footstool? To behead them properly I needed added height; our sunflowers really thrived on their chicken manure.

I scrambled up on my footstool and was measuring the green stalks with my eyes when behind the window of my father's so-called laboratory a smallish flame shot up, pale blue in the center, cardinal red around the jagged edges, immediately followed by a ball of flame shooting sparks in all directions. Even without the multicolored vapor clouds, the stench of sulfur seeping through the cracks, I knew that my father was back. I stormed into the house and into the laboratory without knocking; there stood Father, thinner, lit up by the glowing flame, his eyes sunken but gleaming with triumph.

Don't believe for a minute that he took the time to give me a fatherly hug or even to pat my head. Just back from Russian captivity, he was already so obsessed with new inspirations that the only words he had for me were, "Lookahere, it's Zygmunt," spoken as he shook a test tube so violently that a harmless-looking liquid foamed over. Still, he did not send me packing. Completely caught up in his passionate search, he assigned me the task of crushing dried Saint-John's-wort, picked at three in the morning, and grating burdock burrs—I could barely keep up with all his instructions . . .

What did you say?

You guessed right. During his short imprisonment he thought he had discovered why the Russian army was forced time and again to retreat. It was the Russian soldier's courteous nature, his inability to behave savagely toward a declared enemy. Samsonov himself, the unassuming general, provided a disastrous example of this behavior, and every last artillery man followed his lead. My father was shrewd enough to see how this weakness could serve his own interests; he was working on a drug which could be taken with the morning tea and would guarantee a glowing rage for at least twelve hours . . .

Did you say, "Rogalla's Rage Drops"? Yes, my father would have liked that name . . .

In any case, I had never seen my father work so frantically. He did not even bother to try the yeast pancakes and yoghurt served by my mother in wordless happiness to him at his workbench. Nor had he taken time to recount his experiences in the Russian commandant's headquarters or the circumstances of his release. We noticed that his absence had changed him; not only did he let us enter his laboratory, he also tolerated our presence during his mysterious researches and even tried to instruct us as to what he was up to. Instead of Basilius Valentinus, he consulted the old physician Isaak Hollandus. He boiled, cooled, and mixed according to the old fellow's instructions, made the brew bubble and foam. The tincture was hermetically dark, with a slight violet tinge if you held it up to the light. But now he needed a subject to try it out on, and since he himself had to observe the effects carefully and my mother wouldn't do because she was a woman, I was the natural choice. My mother's sighs did not move him, nor did her disturbing forecast that I might turn into a "raging Zygmunt," who would go tearing through the house like a "hammer gone wild."

I had to lie down on the threadbare sofa, close my eyes, and reverently open my mouth. The rage drops did not taste that bad, like a slightly astringent sorrel soup at first, with an aftertaste of Königsberg-style meatballs. While my mother wrung her hands under her apron, our master pharmacist counted my pulse, listened to my heartbeat, checked my pupils with a flashlight, and set various objects close by on which I might vent my fury: little mortars, cracked test tubes, a shaving mug.

You want to know how I felt? Apathetic, totally, pleasantly apathetic, with a certain heaviness of the tongue, and numbness in the legs; none of the articles he had placed there was in danger; at least for the time being, I was certainly not seeing red . . .

I realize, dear Martin Witt, that you have to get back to your seminar at the institute. I don't want to keep you. Could you speak a bit louder? . . .

Yes, I understand, you have to get back to your algae, those microscopic plantlets which will be so important someday. Henrike told me, and now I know where she learned it: how on a single field that can feed one cow they will someday grow enough algae to equal the protein produced by sixty cows.

But there is one more thing you should hear: in the middle of the experiment there came a knock, first at the window, then at the door, and since we did not open up, the visitors simply came in. It was Edith, who knew her way around our place; she had her mother with her. The poor woman extended her fleshy, limp hand to us before she had even crossed the threshold. Even I, in my torpor, noticed that the wife of the prison warden was being unduly cordial. The grownups sat down on the stools, and Edith joined me on the sofa. She instantly asked whether I was all dizzy, and started in with, "Me too, me too, I want to get dizzy, too." A word from her mother silenced her.

Since news of my father's return had already spread through the town, they had come to ask about the fate of the prison warden. They politely turned down the yeast pancakes, declined camomile tea and yoghurt. Their air of expectancy was so great that my father gave in, although this was a "more than inappropriate moment," as he said. Speaking past the well-corseted mass of Edith's mother to me, as though the information were chiefly for me, he gave a summary account of his sojourn in the Russian commandant's headquarters.

The food had been good, though overseasoned with caraway, and the beds most comfortable, even if telephone calls had often disturbed their sleep at night. A Russian military doctor had treated Mayor Lischkohl, as well as Town Treasurer Tuchlinski and the prison warden; Commandant Vitinghoff had made a point of saying good night and good morning to the hostages.

If I followed my father's story correctly, shortly before the deadline, a two-horse conveyance had rolled up to the hotel and Uncle Adam had jumped out. He threw off his rucksack and called two orderlies lounging about the premises to carry a gigantic laundry basket into the main hall of the Queen Luise. The commandant was sent for. When Vitinghoff appeared, his uniform jacket unbuttoned, Uncle Adam was sitting like a broody hen on the laundry basket. In what he considered the proper language for the occasion, he said, "Lucknow sends me to demonstrate the value we place on our fellow citizens." Thereupon he handed the commandant the rucksack full of money and waved cavalierly toward the laundry basket, which was filled with jewelry, tableware, watches, and several bars of silver. The value exceeded the demanded contribution of thirty thousand rubles, that was clear from even a hasty glance, but everything had to be precisely recorded, assessed, and totaled up. The hostages were wakened and brought to the hall, where they received wine and beer and were made to witness the procedure, to see how much their fellow citizens prized them. As the two paymasters took up their positions, the hostages stood behind them, like kibitzers at a card game . . .

No, no, there you are wrong, it was not a matter of an hour or two; on the contrary. My father noticed that the two paymasters seemed to be rivals from way back. Everything went well so long as they were counting the money, but when they got to the objects of value, every piece was contested. They were still counting when, at four in the morning, orders came for an immediate retreat to the other side of the border. Commandant Vitinghoff, my father said, appealed to the hostages to be understanding; they could not be released until the amount of the ransom had been determined, for he had to answer to higher authorities. He provided the hostages with a comfortable four-horse carriage. They were given cushions to sit on and double rations. A contingent of soldiers followed on foot. My father recognized the two paymasters in the next carriage; even during the retreat they were cultivating their enmity, lifting one piece after another out of the laundry basket and bickering over its value . . .

Pardon me?

Why should I object, dear Martin Witt? A good listener is an impatient listener, who can't wait to hear what happens next . . .

You're right: the two paymasters could not reach an agreement either before they came to the border or after they crossed it, with the consequence that the hostages had to trail along with the general retreat. Pampered by the commandant, they were present during tactical skirmishes in Poland and then found themselves in Russia, somewhere in the interior. The first we heard from them, two and a half years later, was a note from Mayor Lischkohl, mailed from a rather unexciting city in the Urals. But I am getting ahead of myself, for of course all this happened later.

In any case, my father reassured Edith's mother that her husband wanted for almost nothing, not even his gall-bladder medicine, since the commandant was all solicitude in such matters. My father himself owed his release to the commandant's concern. He had decided that the hostages would be more comfortable with one fewer man in the four-horse carriage, and therefore he had asked Jan Rogalla to stay behind—this was in Prostken, on the border—and wished him a happy return to Lucknow.

All this I heard through my torpor, and in spite of Edith's ministrations. For as she sat there beside me, she seemed to be using me for an experiment of her own. She blinded me with the flashlight, then beamed it into my ears and nostrils. She passed her hand over my numb legs, poked me, tickled me, opened my shirt and counted my ribs. For a moment I had the impulse to smash a cracked saucer down on her head, which would certainly have overjoyed the crazy scientist, but refrained. I was afraid I would not be able to lift my arm. I felt as if I had turned to jelly . . .

Yes, my friend, I realize that you have to get back to your algae. But I wanted to suggest something to you: ask Henrike about her homeland and you'll learn something surprising: the revelation that the homeland can be a place where one has never been oneself. She has made up for missing memories with imagination, imagination and the facts she has collected. Perhaps she has a purer picture than we oldsters who were born there . . .

Pardon me? You wonder about the purity?

No, you know how much I look forward to your visits.

# 4

WELL, if you really believe that the idea of homeland is a product of arrogant narrow-mindedness, my own experience suggests that it is an outgrowth of melancholy. Our sense of transitoriness makes us want to impose some sort of permanence on the traces of our own existence. And there's only one place where that can be done, our homeland . . .

But you should try a bit of pastry; it's the hospital's version of a chocolate eclair; I saved it for you . . .

The flowers? You'll be surprised to hear this, but they were sent by my son Bernhard. Moreover, he found time to dash off one of his little memos; I have the impression he works hard at developing that hectic tone. In any case, he sends his best wishes for a speedy recovery and at the same time congratulates me for destroying the museum, calling it a long-overdue act of reason. Because he assumes that his own arguments played some part in my decision, he even congratulates himself. Sons exist, he goes so far as to write, to make their fathers into sons again. I am afraid you would get along very well with Bernhard . . . A relic shack, he used to call the museum, where the fervor for one's own precious history burned so hot that no heating system was needed. He wasn't born in Lucknow either, any more than Henrike was. Just imagine, history interests him about as much as cold porridge. For instance, if anyone mentioned the name Hindenburg, he would stand up and leave the room without a word. Hindenburg . . .

A few days after the general had passed through Lucknow on his trip through the liberated villages, I was supposed to get a new sailor suit. So I washed up, put on clean underwear, and trotted along beside my mother to Struppek & Sausmikat, the best clothing and textile store in Lucknow, located in the market-place.

In the center of the marketplace, in front of the monument to the heroes of 1870–71, my mother's steps slowed as she recalled that our liberator had recently stood on this very spot, with his cropped hair and drooping eyelid, looking rather bored while festively dressed civilians gave speeches and came forward to hand him gifts, to the accompaniment of patriotic songs intoned by a mixed chorus. Among the gifts were a white and blue Masurian wall hanging, a wicker basket containing our regional hard sausages, and particularly a scroll of parchment tied with ribbon in which he was proclaimed an honorary citizen of Lucknow.

Of course, my father had made a point of appearing at the improvised victory celebration. As a good businessman he knew the importance of being on the right side in such matters. At one point in the program he simply stepped forward and handed the commander in chief, who took it all in stride, a well-polished little bottle containing a potion that both stimulated the circulation and increased beneficence. A soldierly shake of the hand, and the bottle was dispatched to join the other gifts in the general's motorcar, from which he presently delivered a short speech which more or less sounded as though he were reading off the family names from the signs over the shops around the market-place.

No, that was not my picture of a liberator, a victorious general . . .

But we were on our way to Struppek & Sausmikat for a new sailor suit; given the obstinate adoration of inlanders who live far from the sea for the nautical, it was no surprise that sailor's blue should have become the favorite dress of Lucknow's youth. Herr Struppek himself attended to us. He was not one of your obsequious salesmen; on the contrary, he acted as though he were always right. Indecisive customers aroused his scorn, but your firm-minded customer represented a challenge, simply because he wanted to have the last word as to what looked best, what would "really make a splash." I broke out in sweat when he waved to us across the whole store, and my mother's vocabulary shriveled.

It was a stroke of luck that he had already decided to make a little sailor of me. Since that corresponded to our own wishes, we merely nodded docilely and let him lead us to the children's section, where there were enough sailor suits on the racks to outfit the crew of a destroyer . . .

No, my dear boy, I told you when you first visited: I don't mind your smoking . . .

Anyway, the haberdasher had me climb up on a chair placed in the niche with the three full-sized mirrors. He stripped off my civilian garb with barely concealed contempt, poured me into a pair of sailor pants which threatened to split the first time I bent my knees, slipped on the blouse with its wide collar, and tied the knot, all the while managing to keep one hand free, which kept stroking and plucking at me in various places. Then, to my mother's delight, he enrolled me in a naval unit. This he did by selecting three bands for my cap, with the names of vessels embroidered in gold: the cruiser *Goeben*, the torpedo boat *Iltis*, and submarine number 9. As he looked me over, he seemed to be giving serious thought to where I would do the most good. He was considering whether I would make a good submarine officer when the first mortar shell exploded in the Lucknow marketplace . . .

Not in the slightest; you understood me perfectly. It was the first shot of a Russian mortar; an entire corps had moved into position to attack from the north. They were well-rested, determined troops which, encountering scant resistance, found themselves advancing far more rapidly than anticipated. With a few hard, brief strikes they were capturing our villages and towns, probably because in this case the overly scrupulous and hesitant Samsonov had left the commanding officer to follow his own instincts. Now they were just outside Lucknow, as much to their own surprise, probably, as to ours.

You must not think that Herr Struppek gave up on his sale because of the explosion. He merely stepped over to the window for a moment, looked at the column of dust, turned a bit, and gazed across Kucharzik's terrace café down to Lake Lucknow, where four jets of water shot up, slim and decorative, as if immortalized in a seascape, surrounded by a cluster of swans. Then the haberdasher came back to us, saying simply, "Looks like the second occupation is in sight," transferred me to the torpedo boat

*Iltis,* and calmly wrote up the bill; to be sure, he saw us to the door only in order to be able to close it right behind us. I was allowed to wear the sailor suit without more ado, my second sailor suit, in which they almost managed to execute me, after a heated battle near the big bridge over the Lucknow River.

And occupied we were; nothing could avert that fate, not even the battery of heavy field howitzers lined up along the lakeshore and camouflaged with willow and poplar branches. Since Conny was already there, sitting on an empty munitions crate, I had no choice but to send my mother home. She agreed to go after I had promised several times not to rampage or tussle in my new suit. Conny was already bored, since not a single shot had been fired, and the troops, with the exception of one soldier who was manning the telephone, were idling about, spooning spongy sausage out of cans. Conny beckoned to me, cunningly pointing out the cable which ran from the field telephone through the bushes, diagonally up to the linden trees, and then through the treetops toward town, a communications line that led to a secret headquarters where grave decisions were certainly being made. He did not have to urge me; we were off at once, tracing the cable, following its slack trail all the way to the massive Lucknow water tower. "Here," said Conny, "is where everything comes together." The water tower was surrounded by all kinds of posted notices prohibiting this and that. But the place was unguarded, so we slipped into the cool tower, mounted the worn circular staircase until we encountered the cable, and let it lead us up to the stout, but not very tall water tank. We encouraged each other to scale the iron ladders, then circled the tank on the catwalks, found our way back to the cable, which led over ducts and pipes and upward into the tower's many-windowed dome . . .

Precisely, dear Martin Witt, it had been turned into an artillery post. The two spotters did not hear us; one of them was looking through the telescope at the railway embankment in the direction of Milucken, which had wagon roads and copses to either side. The other was crouching by his crank box, paper and pencil at the ready. The fellow at the telescope was not a little startled when Conny plucked his sleeve and said ingratiatingly, "We've just come from down below. They're eating sausage." Thanks to this remark we were not immediately sent about our business. The two spotters exchanged glances, then the one at the crank box opened his haversack and brought out their provisions. While they sank their teeth into their ham sandwiches, Conny and I were allowed to look through the telescope, and I can still recall the amazing sharpness with which we could see what to the naked eye appeared as a mere haze: endless columns on the march toward Lucknow, machine guns on rickety carts, cannon covered with canvas, lightly armed cavalry trotting over the fields. I still remember how I swung the telescope from the orchards of the Rankow estate along Maraune Brook to the burned-over railway embankment, just as four uniform little clouds went up, dissipating even before the sound waves of the detonation reached us. Those were their mortars, shooting into Lucknow at random. I reported my observations to the spotters, who nodded casually: they already knew all about it.

That's right, that's how our second occupation began; I mentioned that already, and you should know that a second occupation is always worse than the first, or at least so it appears in retrospect . . .

But what did I want to say? When the field telephone started jingling, the two spotters gave us the remnants of their sandwiches and pointed downward with their thumbs, whereupon we climbed down one floor and took up positions at the tiny windows, perhaps twenty-five feet below the artillerymen. We were just in time to see the heavy field howitzers on the lakeshore open fire, directed by the two clever fellows above us. They wreaked havoc among the marching columns, scattering the men hither and thither, including into the beautiful Rankow orchards, where the howitzers continued to pound away at them. I must admit I felt sorry for the trees; dozens of them were hewn off at the knees or lost their crowns at a single blow. They had always borne so bountifully. And there were also our time-honored Masurian oaks being shaved to the ground, crippled, hacked, splintered!

The mortars answered the fire from the shelter of the railway embankment; we could hear the whine and roar of the shots. One well-aimed shell saw to it that the Hotel Queen Luise would not be offering suites with a lake view for the time being.

And then, dear Martin Witt, Conny stepped over to my window, and I followed his outstretched arm as he wordlessly and almost without a tremble pointed out a brisk little carriage careering down the steep wagon road to the wooden bridge over the Maraune. The madly audacious man on the box was standing, no less, urging on his horses, and was already estimating the reliability of the bridge, which had lost its railings, when there was a hit on the banks of the Maraune, not even a very powerful one, which caused muddy earth to spurt up and rain down on the bridge in great lumps. I saw the horses shy and rear in their harness, but their driver regained control of them immediately. Now he made no attempt to get them back onto the road but continued on parallel to the brook.

I realized what he had in mind; he wanted to reach the highway leading to Magrabova, in whose ditches lay our brave militiamen, their sole desire to save their munitions in the face of the advancing enemy. He kept looking for another crossing as he followed the brook in the direction of the orchards, where fountains of soil were still spurting upward and the noble trees were being leveled. But a shot that landed short, or perhaps was aimed directly at him, forced him once more to change course. Apparently a machine gun had also spotted him, for when he turned off into a plowed field, tracer bullets wove a wreath around his carriage . . .

You may be sure I knew it from the first moment, but I did not dare speak up, waiting for Conny to say it: "That's him, Zygmunt, I recognize him, that must be him." And he pointed at the man caught between the lines, who was racing his smart two-horse carriage across the disputed territory, searching for a spot where he might slip through, time and again distracted by the whining shells, turned back by burning woodland, tracing a confused pattern over the sandy fields. I saw him rattle down the path to the Maraune once more, resolved to try the bridge again —the boards were still intact, at least for the width of his wheels, and with the shots whistling around, he headed for it, reached it, and I already thought I heard the clatter of hoofs and wheels crossing when the carriage blew into smithereens.

First there was just a many-colored flash of flame, of the sort I had often seen in my father's laboratory; then a corkscrew-shaped column of smoke rose, likewise many-colored, which simply kept its form and hung over the Maraune as if anchored there. Presently, however, a seven-colored cloud formed and rose upward like a balloon loosed from its moorings—Conny assured me later that he had seen it, too,—a sort of vast bed of clouds such as the master of substances and tinctures, the lord over acids and gases, might have designed for himself. When I think back on it today, I cannot help concluding that my father's end had a certain perfection about it.

I have no doubt that Lucknow's few defenders, but also the Russian soldiers in their foxholes, puzzled a long time over this Bengal-light apotheosis. Surely a few people in the vicinity remember that after the phosphorescent end of the carriage, vapors and smells spread over the landscape, causing a gamut of reactions from simple nausea to bronchitis and laryngitis . . .

Pardon me? You want to know whether everything dissolved in flame? Whether every last shred disappeared into a seven-colored cloud? From your question I can guess you are smiling. I can report only this: Conny put an arm around my shoulder and drew me away from the window. He pushed me up the circular staircase to the room in the dome where the artillery post was functioning so efficiently. The spotters might have been in no mood to have us there, but Conny gave them his reason: "A direct hit; his father got a direct hit."

He demanded that I be allowed to look through the telescope, dragged up a crate for me to stand on. I scanned the banks of the brook for the spot where Masuria's great pharmacist had found his end. The two horses lay there, our fine grays, still crowned with the artificial flowers which had always nodded so gaily as they jogged along. The smashed front axle could also be seen, its one remaining wheel turning softly and mysteriously—but nothing else. My father and his miraculous freight, the jars, bottles, vials, and canisters were and remained vanished, annihilated in the boiling heat of the explosion, gone to join the other ethers of the universe.

This strange feeling of being neither here nor there. Although I had actually witnessed my father's end, grief did not come immediately, and pain was long in arriving. I did not even feel despair; the only sensation was a sort of fearful expectancy. My shortage of emotion may have been due to the manner of my father's death, with its highly theatrical effects. Conny gave me to understand that we had better get home at once and tell my mother, so we sped through the landscape, ignoring the new position of the field howitzers. But in front of the prison we suddenly stopped and looked back. As we watched, the smooth cylinder of the water tower exploded into many fragments, and the foot of the tower keeled over, spewing dust down toward the lake . . .

Yes, I agree with you, dear boy; bringing bad news is one of the hardest assignments. Try to picture my mother, sitting there preparing snap beans, with an enamel bowl in her lap and her quick little knife flitting back and forth, just grazing her thumb. Her first worry on seeing me was that my fine blue suit might have already had its baptism by dirt. That is how it was: she raised her eyes from the beans, looked me over sharply, and in this state of mind was met with news which struck in such abbreviated form that she could not draw any sense out of it: an accident—a direct hit—just a flame shooting up—as he was driving—his medicines exploded with him—a column of smoke like a corkscrew—a seven-colored cloud that blew away and vanished—gone to heaven—simply went up in the air . . .

The more excitedly we talked, the greater her confusion. When Conny summed it up, saying, "As I see it, ma'am, it was a sort of ascension," glowing certainty suffused her face and she replied, "Yes, lad, that's what it must have been, a sort of ascension." She simply refused to credit the grim fact. She could not and would not accept her husband's death. Rather, she considered the occurrence some kind of special enchantment, a dazzling open-air experiment. At any rate, our report did not plunge her into immediate grief or pain. She cooled our excitement with buttermilk, no, with refreshing mushroom water, which she ladled out of an old stone crock, its bottom a sediment of brown, ragged fungus which lent the water a pleasant, tangy taste.

You could see how sure she was of my father's eventual return from the fact that she continued to set a place for him at table, washed, ironed, and folded his clothing, and when a small commission appeared several days after Lucknow's reoccupation to register all of the town's male inhabitants, she reported that her husband was off on a business trip, helping to conquer certain diseases. After all, he had often been away on such expeditions.

For at least a week she went around filled with this idea. To prove her devotion, she scrubbed out all the mortars, crucibles, and test tubes in his laboratory, but gradually an uneasiness stole over her. Her breathing would suddenly quicken and her neck break out in spots. Dishes dropped from her usually steady grip. I caught her brooding; she would sit there, hands clasped, nodding as she went over various possibilities, weighing them indecisively. Each time she seemed to come to the same bleak conclusion, to which she responded with angry shakes of her head, whereupon she would stand up, go to the window, and take a deep breath. Finally, those hypotheses became unbearable to her; she recognized that something had to be done.

We set out for the estate, where the occupation forces were once more on a requisitioning binge: hay, beets, and potatoes, but also cheese rounds as big as wagon wheels, smoked hams, and cattle, which they simply hitched to their carts. An officer was going from cart to cart, taking inventory of the loads, converting the sums to rubles, and sternly handing receipts for the same to the head milker: "Hang on to this, documents, good as cash." One of these invoices, by the way, stamped and signed, was in our museum.

My grandfather was nowhere to be seen. He kept out of the way, perhaps because he could not answer for his self-control. We found him alone in the woodshed by the wobbly sawbuck, one hand pressing down the log, the other guiding a Swedish saw. He did not look up or return our greetings. When the saw blade caught, he hobbled past us without a word to find the steel wedge, which he drove into the groove with a sledgehammer. Then he grimly continued his work. He had this way of totally ignoring you; faced with such treatment, most people would have shrugged and taken themselves off. But my mother had always set her own standards for feeling insulted, especially with my grandfather. She decided we would see who could wait the longest. We just stood there, darkening the entrance.

After the requisitioning unit had cleared out, with shouts and much cracking of whips, Grandfather looked up and had to acknowledge our presence. His mood at the moment was hardly generous.

"If it's provisions you're after, go elsewhere. Like you see, they take the leather off our shoes." Mother's posture, the toss of her head, repudiated any such intention. It was not a question of potatoes or flour, and certainly not of smoked ham. No, this time she had something far more important in mind. My grandfather heaved a heavy log onto the sawbuck, resumed his furious sawing, cursed at an obstructing knot, and waited to hear our petition . . .

That's what I'm getting to, dear Martin; we had planned our strategy carefully. First we wanted to ask whether we might owe him the rent for a while, for our small whitewashed house by the lakeside belonged to the estate, and before we had taken it, hired hands had lived there. At this he grew pensive. It seemed he had just engaged a new overseer and had offered him the cottage, on the supposition that it was now vacant, since Jan had, as he put it, "gone up in smoke."

This was bad news. My mother asked for three months' grace. He couldn't do it. The new man was urgently needed, had five children, required suitable quarters. My mother then asked for some alternative—perhaps the rooms of the two milkers who were serving with the Corps of Engineers in Lötzen. Grandfather refused. He was counting on a quick victory, so the milkers might be back any day. Sawing doggedly, he advised us to apply at the Lucknow residents' registration office; after all, all kinds of residents had fled at the last moment, with and without their furniture, people who had reason to get out. We might do very well, better our circumstances . . .

Why did we take this so meekly? you ask. My dear young man, what else could we have done, especially in times like those, when everyone was at the mercy of chance. You should have seen us following up the recommendations of the registration office, inspecting apartments in town, the former residences of businessmen or higher officials. The surprise and embarrassment each time, the bitter taste in our mouths, when we entered the place, tried out the chairs, tested the view from the windows, or opened doors of abandoned wardrobes—there was not a single apartment where we felt at ease. Such places were not for the likes of us, with their polished floors, rich wallpaper, and alien furniture.

On loan. These places would just be on loan, my mother exclaimed, and she sorrowfully handed back the occupancy permit she had received at the registration office. I suspect she had known even before we began our search that it would be all in vain, simply because we could not live on such a temporary basis, and she had gone through the process only not to have to sit around idle during the two-week grace period we had been given.

No chance of my grandfather's retracting his word. He prided himself, above all else, on being consistent. For us, especially for me, the consequences were far-reaching. You, too, may eventually conclude that I would not have destroyed our Masurian museum if we had been allowed to stay on in our little whitewashed house by the lake.

But they came, the very morning our time ran out: my grandfather, the new overseer with his family, two farmhands, and a wagon loaded with furniture that would replace our own. The day they came, it was also clear that Samsonov's divisions were beaten, and Rennenkampf's First Army began a retreat. So that Grandfather's little party was intermingled with sections of the cavalry. Grandfather headed for the little house, where we were cowering. He pushed the door open with his boot, came up to us threateningly, and gestured to the two burly farmhands who stood by as if they were being buffeted by a cutting wind. They carried our things, down to the smallest item, to the edge of the road and left them all in a heap. The overseer took no part in this; he crouched on his wagon and stared with neither ill will nor pity as the house was emptied, while his children were already wrangling over anything they could carry, even my footstool.

I could not get it away from them. I sat down on our piled possessions and defended them against the retreating soldiers. As they passed, they reached for a picture here, a sofa cushion there; while one distracted me, others snatched up jars of preserves. Dragoons reached out with the tips of their lances for towels, earmuffs, and boots. Their interests, however, were more than utilitarian, and they made selections from the contents of the laboratory: folio volumes, kettles, mortars, and crucibles, which would do as souvenirs.

I still remember that as the heap of our possessions melted, as my mother sat on the bench among the sunflowers and tied knots in her handkerchief, as my grandfather urged the two farmhands to hurry, suddenly some disturbance seemed to afflict the column of soldiers; it slowed, wavered, and many of the men peered about to discover what was causing all this confusion.

It was a little farm wagon which was struggling against the military movement, an icebreaker forging against the current. The driver was Uncle Adam, who kept up a continual shrill whistle. By the time he had fought his way to us, he was dripping with sweat and could not get out a word.

I handed things up to him as he loaded the wagon. First came the more unwieldy items; then we filled chests and laundry baskets with modest objects. My mother might have helped us here, but she still sat as if numbed among the sunflowers. We heaved up the crates with the laboratory equipment, and by our combined efforts finally maneuvered my mother onto the cart; this proved more difficult than all the rest, since her legs seemed to have lost all sensation and she was about as easy to budge as two hundred pounds of potatoes in a wet burlap bag. Only then did Uncle Adam go up to my grandfather, and in a voice the overseer and the two farmhands could not help hearing, he said, "You cur, you foul-smelling cur, you." . . .

I wonder at certain of your reactions. The expletives, the curses? The richness of our invectives interests you? This may surprise you, but some of these expressions could also be used as endearments, endearments only we would recognize as such, I admit. With us it is often hard to draw the line . . .

What did you just say? I find that almost incredible. You have the impression Henrike is once more trying to put together her index of Masurian colloquialisms? How is she going about it—do you have any idea?

If true, this is a significant bit of news to me. It could mean the beginning of something, or a response to something we don't yet have a name for.

But what was I telling you? The move, right. How Uncle

Adam reached us with the farm cart, fighting against the whole length of the retreating army, how he moved us to his thatch-roofed habitation on the great bend in the Lucknow River. And not just temporarily, but, as he put it, "As long as one stone rests upon the other, and no crack can be found through which to peep in at us."

So we moved into our rooms, both looking out over the river and somewhat cramped, it must be admitted, for the entire house was filled with the relics and remains Uncle Adam gathered with such passion. Whatever we could not fit into our quarters we stored away, partly in the shed, partly in the attic. I had to adjust to the collection of old Masurian wedding costumes in my room, threadbare, limp garments slightly fragrant of camphor, which hung with their sleeves lifted a little, so that many a bad night I imagined they were reaching out to grab me. I must not forget the bed, with its stout spherical feet, or the painted blanket chest, or the carved washboards and mangles stacked in corners, while a shelf over my bed held historic kitchen implements: cabbage slicers, herb crushers, wooden molds shaped like blossoms or six-pointed stars . . .

Have you ever slept in a museum, or lived in one?

So there!

But I got used to plate and spoon racks, even made friends with the wooden clogs, with their uppers of incised leather, lined up on a shelf like bulky model barges. I sat as a matter of course on a venerable chair with a carved back. The only articles I found troublesome were the old flat irons, whose shapes reminded me of dog snouts with bared teeth.

The stuff in my room was naturally only a small portion of Uncle Adam's collection. The prize pieces were kept in the front hall and the broad but unfortunately poorly lit corridor; they filled the roomy parlor, the workshop, the kitchen, where we also took our meals, and last but not least the secret cellar. You may well assume, dear boy, that every bit of the place was given over to relics, so much so that when you took a swallow of buttermilk, you might be drinking out of a Sudauese funerary urn.

So we moved in, and tried to make ourselves at home . . .

What would you like to know? How we spent our first day? Well, if it interests you: my mother unpacked, put things away

as best she could, explored the kitchen, and sat for a long time
alone by the river, watching the water flow by. I headed straight
for the workshop, where Uncle Adam sat ensconced by the window, a grimy, once-blue apron around his middle, his steel-
rimmed glasses assisting his ever-astonished blue eyes as he puzzled over shards, murmuring to himself all the while, or delicately
restored bits of wood and leather. He glued, sanded, and polished; no one could scrape more gently or hammer more tenderly
than he, and when he was not at this activity he was writing
labels: a description of the object, where and when it had been
found, its probable age. Although he was usually silent with me—
no, that's not quite true, he did once point to his worktable and
comment, "Past times, generous times"—I had the feeling I was
welcome in the shop, so long as I did not get in the way.

There was one occasion, though, when he reproved me. That
was when he had reassembled a huge painted plate, from which
a whole family could have eaten its fill. He had fitted and glued
all the shards together and mended it so skillfully that, once he
had touched up the colors, I could not find the cracks. I clapped
for joy. At this he gave me a somber look and shook his head; but
that was all.

Whereas earlier, when we used to go out digging in the bog
below Castle Hill, I had tired rapidly and just hacked away list-
lessly with my shovel, here in the workshop I was gripped with a
new excitement. Perhaps I already sensed that this part of the
game was going to affect me still further; perhaps I was beginning to recognize that Uncle Adam was engaged in a contest with
time, with limp oblivion and silent decay. What he wanted of
these particles of the past was testimony, "unimpeachable testimony," as he called it, whose purpose was to sustain us in difficult
times, as well as to strengthen our desire for something lasting.
But that was not all; he hoped the viewer would develop a personal relationship to the objects, a sense that they were his, too,
and would realize: that was how we used to live.

Would you wonder that on that first night I was so excited
that I could not sleep? I sat in the dark on the antique chair. The
window was hooked open, and I could keep watch on the farther
side of the Lucknow River, where a unit of enemy cavalry was
bivouacked in a green field. The sentries passed among the smol-

dering fires, making the rounds from the trees on the bank to the clump of alders where the animals were tethered. In the direction of Arys and Dippelsee there was activity as usual: they were firing signal flares, which, however, did not call forth the usual artillery response. Knowing I might get hungry during the night, I had stowed a rutabaga under my bed; I had just cut a slice and was standing by the window to eat it when I spotted the two soldiers down in the garden. One of them tapped on a window, the other hammered on the garden gate. When no one opened up and no lights appeared, the second soldier rejoined his comrade, who sent him around to the main entrance, where he could soon be heard pounding and shouting and kicking at the locked door. I flitted across the dark corridor to the workshop, groped my way past the tables and benches to the alcove where Uncle Adam slept on a sort of trundle bed. He was awake and already pulling on his trousers. "Russians?" he asked. I nodded. In view of this information, he put on his stiff collar, slipped into his vest, and donned a black jacket . . .

No, no, it was not a house search. The soldier was only looking for a billet for his ailing staff captain. The soldier seemed delighted when Uncle Adam opened the door and asked him in, as well as the officer in question. Lights were turned on in the front hall, in the corridor, in the parlor. The captain came in first, with a polite bow to Uncle Adam. He appeared despondent and weary and was shivering in spite of the warm night. As he passed me, he pressed a coin into my hand. And behind him, grinning under a load consisting of several bundles and a wooden trunk, came his orderly, surprisingly advanced in years for the role. The captain's dragging, unmilitary gait became even more so at the sight of our collection. He paused to examine the early weapons, bent over a glass case of ancient coins, read the labels on the straw, wood, and rag dolls, and tapped the chain-mail tunic of a Crusader. He shook his head thoughtfully at the sight of the two oldest Masurian spinning wheels and glanced condescendingly at the handsomely displayed array of historic tools . . .

Pardon me?

Oh, yes, the orderly had taken care of the formalities even before they entered, had asked how many people were in the house, and seemed glad to hear there was a woman present.

So Uncle Adam ushered the captain into the parlor, dominated by painted wall cupboards and peasant wardrobes. They sat there in silence, while the orderly and I, positioned behind their chairs, winked at each other encouragingly. Upon a wave of the hand, the orderly placed a cloth on the round table, whisked glasses and a bottle of red wine out of his pack, and poured. The officer and Uncle Adam drank. The officer lit his meerschaum pipe, leaned back wearily, and followed the smoke with his eyes as it curled around the antique tiled stove.

They scarcely spoke, and their silence apparently fed their interest in each other. Finally, the captain inquired what motive a man could have for collecting all these reminders of past defeats and short-lived glories. It was then that I heard Uncle Adam's own explanation. He had, he said, received a call. In a dream he had been instructed to reconstruct the strange, twisted world of Masuria, to gather the relics that testified to our special way of being, to show the rest of us that we were links in a chain reaching far back in time. Uncle Adam even named the emissary from whom he had received the call: it was the legendary Prudeno, a brother of Waidewut, who in the beginning had probably been a fairly good mediator between gods and working folk; at any rate, Prudeno had styled himself a *kriwe*, or supreme priest, who spent most of his days listening, simply because the truth was revealed to him in the blossoming of flowers, in the lightning, in the drifting ice. As proof of their fondness for him, our people had called themselves Pruzzi, that is, sons of Prudeno . . .

A nice story, you say? You think this dream of Uncle Adam's was a literary invention? Not at all, dear Martin Witt. He had really dreamed it. That much I had to believe; also, that he was in frequent communication with Prudeno, by way of dreams of this sort. He would receive praise, blame, or advice, and at times he even quarreled with the *kriwe*.

But you should have seen how the captain's spirits rose, how he emptied his glass and promptly had it filled again. You should have seen the mild irony with which he listened to Uncle Adam's tale—this obviously ill man, who, by the way, wore a distinguished medal for bravery, the St. George's Cross.

"Imagination," he said, with a wave of his hand, "all well-meaning, high-flown imagination. We see, more and more each day, that everything points up the necessity of taking leave of the past. But this collection of yours maintains the fiction of permanence and recurrence."

And now you must try to picture Uncle Adam as he pushed back his glass, glanced meaningfully at the clock, crossed his legs, and smiled to himself with a touch of smugness. He would not argue with his guest, he remarked, but one point surely had to be emphasized: from the fields of Catalonia to Borodino, when the chips were down, victory had gone to the idea of the homeland, the burning, determined, perhaps even fanatical love for one's native land. That love would certainly prove victorious in Masuria as well, and not by gradual degrees, either. When the moment came, it would be unmistakable. The staff captain might as well prepare himself for that. And to hammer the point home, Uncle Adam said, "You will be defeated soon, in at most a year, because Masuria is against you, the land itself: our sand, our pines, our wells and treetops, the bogs, fields, and swamps; all are against you."

Oddly enough, after these words the staff captain drank to Uncle Adam. He told him his name—I recall something like Plechanov—and mentioned that he himself came from Latvia. Yes, he drank to Uncle Adam, too histrionically, perhaps, and he said regretfully, "We will help you throw off these happy illusions. We will show you just how much your faith in your native land is worth. You will see that the sand does not belong to you but will support anyone who walks on it. And this will be for your own good. If we care at all for brotherhood, for international understanding, we must eliminate the fetish of regional idylls and sacred traditions, the petty creed based on the concept of love for one's native land."

Yes, I could have expected you to say that, dear boy; this staff captain's arguments sounded just like those my son Bernhard put forward years later . . .

Anyway, they drank their last glass standing up, and I was already thinking that the evening was over when the officer unbuckled his holster with the army pistol and laid it on the table, a bulky pistol, which he stared down at stolidly while he asked Uncle Adam to show him the most valuable document in the collection. Uncle Adam hesitated. Every item was valuable in its own way, he said; ranking them was impossible. Well, the oldest item, then, the captain replied, and after a moment's thought Uncle Adam brought him the oldest document, mounted under glass, a donation according to "Magdeburg Common Law," issued by Grand Master Heinrich von Plauen, in the year 1411. The staff captain bent over the document, inspecting it. He asked to have several sentences read aloud: "Herewith we do confer upon thee to hold so long as . . ." and so forth. The officer picked up his pistol, smashed the glass with one blow, pried out the document, and handed it to his orderly with the words, "Pjotr, my pipe is not burning well."

I held tight to the seat of my chair and kept my eye on Uncle Adam. He did not move, did not tremble, just watched attentively as the officer's man with unsteady fingers folded the document, twisting it into a spill. Uncle Adam did not interfere or even protest when the man took his lighter, set fire to the document, and held the flame over the bowl of the captain's pipe. The captain drew rapidly and hard on its stem; we could hear the smacking of his lips. Then he took the remains of the spill and tossed them into an ashtray, where they burned themselves out. And as if regretting that such a demonstration was necessary, he asked Uncle Adam, "Do you see what your precious relics are good for?"

"Yes," said Uncle Adam with equanimity, "I see that even such an old piece of paper can still strike a bit of terror. When it flared up, your hand began to shake."

Pardon me?

No, you are mistaken; he still had every intention of lodging with us. Uncle led them to my room. The orderly swooped the sheets off my straw mattress and made up the bed anew for his master, while for himself he spread his greatcoat on the floor and put down one of his packs as a pillow. We wished one another "Good night"—yes, we did.

Uncle Adam had gone on ahead. I groped my way along the dark corridor, listened at the door of my mother's room, but since only a dry, mechanical sobbing came from there, I went on to the workshop and asked in the dark, "Where should I sleep, Uncle Adam?" "Here with me," he said, I groped my way to the alcove, crawled under my uncle's coverlet, and wiggled myself into a comfortable position. I felt his hard knee against my calf and heard his remarkably calm breathing behind my ear. One time he reached over me to make sure I was properly tucked in; his chin touched my cheek, and he whispered, "That was a lesson: the really valuable things have to be kept hidden. For the public a copy does just as well." I turned over quickly, and he guessed what I wanted to ask. "I'll tell you all about it; now go to sleep," he said.

You guessed it, young man: the originals of the documents were all stowed away in a metal trunk in the cellar; that's where they were always kept, even in uneventful times, when they seemed to be in no danger. As Uncle Adam reasoned, "If the original comes to grief, then the past it stands for is lost."

Time and again he drew me into his secret cellar, especially when our artillery and the Russians' were fighting it out over Lucknow, when shells went hurtling through the air and the earth shuddered as if from distant earthquakes. While others listened for hits, I listened to Uncle Adam's explanations. He set me the task of interpreting various finds. "Everything, but everything depends on the interpretation," he said. I loved to hear the stories connected with each piece in the collection. Uncle Adam had as many legends and anecdotes as Eugen Lavrenz had lake stories, and then there were the "tales with a moral," which had clearly acquired rings like a tree in the telling. Unless the item was unwieldy, I would hold it in my hand during the story.

Naturally, dear boy, each piece had a double story, the story of its origins and the story of how it had been acquired. You may rightly infer that a number of documents and other significant items had been obtained in a somewhat dubious fashion, not to say stolen. Far from Uncle Adam's feeling remorse about such episodes, he rather gloried in them. His idea was that things with great testimonial significance "should be expropriated, since they belong to the people as a whole."

In any case, during those days he extracted the utmost from his witnesses, took me back to the earliest beginnings, lifted the mists from this spare land. By now I felt at home in Masuria's ancient times, and I must admit I felt curiously sheltered in those eras, yes, sheltered. More and more I felt myself a link in this long chain of history, and during the days when the wild ducks were taken by surprise and frozen into the lake, when the winter battle of Masuria won its name and fame, I became Uncle Adam's confidant and assistant in his Masurian museum . . .

Pardon me? What was the first find I made on my own? Well, I remember that I decided to collect buttons: uniform buttons from the various units that occupied Lucknow that winter—Pleskau militia, Siberian riflemen, Dragoons, and a squadron of Tartars.

I remember we were in the midst of a snowstorm when old Pivko came over from the estate, not with bacon or flour, as we had hoped, but only with buckwheat, two sacks of groats, which my grandfather had doled out with much grumbling. We took the sacks from him and steered the old braggart into the kitchen, where he downed his meschkinnes with a grimace before he pulled off his water-logged boots, then unwound his soaking foot wrappings and wrung them out. He draped the foot wrappings over a line around the iron stove and rested his cold-mottled feet on the woodbox. He had come across the frozen lake, which had cracked under his weight near the mouth of the river, fortunately by the sandbank, where the water was only knee-deep. He had taken the path over the ice because, as he said, in town "the devil was on the rooftops," spraying with bullets anyone who showed his face outdoors. Even out on the ice some bullets had come "moseying" after him.

While we all sat down to soup with dumplings, the snow let up, and the great bend in the river emerged clear and black in the twilight. Then my mother and Uncle Adam went off to their chores, while Pivko and I watched from the window as a battle took place on the other side of the river, complete with howitzers, heavy machine guns, shrapnel, and other weaponry. The Russians had taken up a defensive position on the cemetery hill, which dominated the river and the surrounding area, but especially access to the bridge.

The snow was granular, the access road sheer ice; it glittered as the tracer bullets whirled down. As long as I had known old Pivko, he had always ground his teeth after eating, and this time, too, he was grinding them as we huddled close together waiting for the Mecklenburgers and the Hanseatic militia who, we had heard, had mounted such a determined siege at Thalussen and Woszellen that the Russians had finally been forced to retreat.

Finally, they came, flitted almost stealthily over the bridge while their grenades raked the mound of the cemetery, took one section after the other of riverbank, and finally assaulted the cemetery wall in several waves.

Our position at the window was not without danger, but we only realized that afterward, when we noted the scars and bullet holes in the door. In any case, the din of what would probably be Lucknow's last battle for a good while died away, drifted off to the south, where the highway led into the forests along the border, the wintry forests . . .

Which brings me back to my concern with the museum. Old Pivko wrapped his dried foot wrappings around his ankles and climbed into his boots, whose uppers had separated from the soles. He stamped several times to make the obstinate leather obey, while looking out the window at the abandoned battlefield. Speaking more to himself than to me, he remarked, "Those guys over there, they were issued some fine boots and now they ain't got no use for them. But the likes of us, who've got to keep going, ain't nobody issuing us nothing." He was setting out for that tramp to the estate. Peering through the window he muttered, "Jes' a little detour, and who knows what nice boots you could find, a-lying there in the snow and no use to no one." "Well, why not?" I encouraged him, and he replied, still somewhat hesitant, "Better if someone else came along."

I slipped out and waited for him while he took leave of Uncle Adam. In my right glove I was holding the jackknife Conny had given me; I was jiggling it, already excited at the thought of the trophies awaiting me out there—uniform buttons which, later, polished up and properly labeled, would tell the tale of Lucknow's occupation . . .

No, not over the bridge, where they were already busy loading bodies onto a sleigh. We poled ourselves across the ice-choked river in Uncle Adam's skiff, then scrambled up the snowy hill. We spotted the first ones, small heaps in battlefield gray. We ran from one to the other; most were lying with one cheek in the snow, knees drawn up, arms rigid against their bodies; some lay on their backs, with a thin thread of blood in the corner of the mouth, their fingers frozen in a plucking gesture; one of them had burrowed his head into the snow, and another lay there with limbs spread as if he had been caught in the middle of a breast-stroke.

Old Pivko was checking their boots, feeling the tops, examining heels and soles as if he were in a shoe store. And was he choosy! Springing from one to the next, he cursed in disappointment. No pair seemed good enough. For in spite of the large selection, these were all boots which had just slogged several thousand miles over the roughest terrain in Masuria, in forced marches intended to fool the enemy as to the size of the forces.

We continued our search. A smell of burning hung over the battlefield, and we heard a dull moaning in the snow, a feeble call for help, but we did not stop. We were still after our booty. Suddenly I heard Pivko whistle sharply; apparently he had found an officer with some high-class footgear, the sort he had been looking for. Lying before me were an artillery crew. Their bodies had been hurled together by a shell. One of them had his forehead torn open. It was from this man's tunic that I cut my first button. Old Pivko was not far off. He was cursing, furious because he could not get the boot off the officer's foot. As if the officer owed him the boot, as if he were wresting back his own property, old Pivko pulled at the leg, tweaked, pressed the boot between his thighs, dragged the body through the snow, even spun it around in a half circle. Finally, the boot seemed to give, and with one more tug the old fellow held it up for me to see . . .

What was I thinking?

You mean you find it hard to imagine what crossed my mind as I hustled from one corpse to the other, cutting the buttons from coats and tunics? I thought I was doing something remarkably useful, salvaging tokens of history. Thanks to my buttons, the battle would become unforgettable. That is what occupied my mind, and I simply overlooked the smashed faces, the twisted bodies. After a while my pockets jangled pleasantly, and I could imagine how Uncle Adam would first frown at the risk I'd run, before gloating over these newest treasures.

I was just bending down to cut off another when two men grabbed me from behind, knocking the knife out of my hand.

They were huge men with rifles; no use squirming or struggling. One of them struck me in the back with his rifle butt. I staggered against the cemetery wall and collapsed, right by the gap through which several other men were pushing old Pivko. They were whipping him. I heard the blows and his muffled cries of protest. He had put up his hands to protect the back of his neck. I did not understand what they meant to do with us and did not grasp why old Pivko reached for my hand, pressed it hard, and ground his teeth. I was looking up at him when a flash burst from a gun barrel; I felt the impact on my forehead, like a stone, that's right, and that was all . . .

If it weren't for these bandages, dear boy, I could show you the scar, the souvenir of the execution that failed. A piece of burning timber hit me on almost the same spot during the recent fire, when I went back in to rescue Sonja Turk's legacy . . .

Old Pivko? He is supposed to have grabbed me and shielded me with his body as he fell. But I cannot vouch for that. In any case, when I came to, I was in bed in the old military hospital, with my class standing around me. Our teacher Henseleit was there, conducting them in the patriotic song: "Proud waves the banner black-white-red from our vessel's mast." They sang loud enough to waken the dead, or someone who had been in a coma for forty days, not a mere four like me. I had scarcely opened my eyes, and the applause of the wounded militiamen who filled the ward had scarcely subsided, when they struck up another: "We kept watch by the boilers and engines," and through a sort of underwater dimness I saw Henseleit's face glide closer, with a wig of seaweed, and thin kelp on his chest, a gentle Neptune who placed a small bouquet on my blanket, stepped back, and gave the flag signal for "Welcome on board." I recognized Conny's face and the face of Simon Gayko, also Lojevski and sickly Masuch. They filed past me, shook hands hurriedly, and deposited little gifts on my bedside table. What Conny gave me was that very knife I'd had in the cemetery—he had gone back and recovered it. Before leaving, the class sang the Masurian song "Wild Storms the Lake"—all three verses of it.

The buttons? They had all disappeared from my pockets, nor did I find any scattered at the spot by the cemetery wall. I kept the whole episode to myself. Even Uncle Adam never learned why I had been out there, and since old Pivko would never be able to give his explanation, the assumption was that the sad incident had simply been one of those "mistakes" that occur so often in wartime.

I must say I enjoyed the first six weeks in the military hospital. The militiamen spoiled me with spoonfuls of jam and combat stories, the nurses made a great pet of me. The visitor's chair barely had a chance to cool off, since in addition to my mother, Edith's mother also sat there, and my schoolmates came in a steady stream, presumably by prearrangement. Edith came too, and Heinrich Henseleit, and my sorely shaken Uncle Adam. I witnessed how the two men, who seemed less than keen about each other, reached an agreement across my bed: once I was better, the teacher would bring our class to visit Uncle Adam's museum, for educational reasons, of course.

The presents that came in added to my importance. Most amazing of all was the vest sent by my grandfather, along with his wishes for a rapid recovery. It was the famous garment made from the skin of his favorite hound, Hoggo, whose fur was supposed to stand up to warn of impending danger. One of his burly farmhands dropped off the gift, and when its rare properties became known around the ward, a skeptical militiaman from Altona mocked me until I let him try out its magic for himself . . .

Yes, I knew you would ask that, and I can assure you that the vest proved its worth. Whenever the fellow shut himself up in the medicine cubicle with a nurse, he was never caught by a doctor or an orderly. So he offered to give me a pocket watch for the vest, and on the day of my release made an even more extreme offer. But I waved it away; the vest was not for sale.

In spite of all the pleasure and excitement, I could barely wait for the day I would be going home. I was filled with a prickling sort of joy, such as I had never felt before. When I finally found myself standing in Uncle Adam's workshop, I realized that it was connected with all the objects among which we lived. Before we sat down to a heap of yeast pancakes, I had to go down the corridor and through all the rooms and the spaces under the eaves, simply to reassure myself that the old musical instruments were still in their places, the battered toys, the shelf with the ancient kitchen implements, and even those menacing flat irons.

I was reassured to discover that they were all there, calm and communicative in their stillness. I was happy and felt that I belonged here, had chosen to be here. That was it: it was a voluntary bond.

When you try to review it all and understand my reasons for finally destroying our museum in Egenlund, you must not leave this out of the account. Way back then I discovered the satisfaction of belonging. Everything was familiar, yet nothing was dull, or lacking in mystery. And when I contributed my first item to the museum, the first find of my very own, which Uncle Adam exhibited in a place of honor, I felt I had passed a final examination . . .

What was it?

A straw crown, which I found in old Pivko's room. Apparently he had woven it himself from wheat straws of differing lengths, held together by string. You must imagine it as a four-sided pyramid; that sort of thing was a gift a young man made to a girl. It was supposed to hang in her room, to turn in the slightest breeze, and through its gentle movement ward off evil. As I said, the straw crown was still hanging in his own room; apparently he had never found the girl to whom to present it.

It goes without saying that my passionate sense of belonging had to make things different, and this became obvious when Henseleit turned up with the entire class for the guided tour of the museum. It was a première, in the sense that Uncle Adam had never before shown his private collection to such a crowd.

I stood there waiting at the window as the class approached, Henseleit in the lead. They were pushing and shoving one another in their usual unruly way, a bunch of schoolboys without a serious thought in their heads.

As he greeted the class, Uncle Adam gazed dreamily up at the ceiling, speaking of the "well of the past," whose depths held evidence of life in far-off epochs. I did not join in with the ruckus of the class, did not even respond to their grins, but as they were about to start the tour, I gave Lojevski a warning kick in the shins and snatched away Masuch's favorite plaything, a box of safety matches. As they stepped into the hall, Henseleit assumed an expression of earnest attentiveness. I knew that expression; it meant he had already drawn his conclusions about this expedition: it won't do much good, but it can't hurt, either. His behavior toward Uncle Adam was also somewhat too correct.

I needn't describe my classmates to you, my boy. They were just like your classmates, just like everybody's—the same pranks, the same junk in their pockets, the same schoolboy smell, the same tendency to lose interest the moment anyone stood in front of them and spoke for more than ten seconds. You can imagine how the twenty-two of them fidgeted as Uncle Adam gave his introduction, summarizing facts they should know from the "well of the Masurian past."

He was not more moved by his subject than usual; his recital was fairly cut-and-dried. First of all, there was the explanation of how our homeland had come into being. He took them back into bleak prehistoric times, described massive glaciers moving in from the Vistula, creeping forward, forward, until the sun struck their lips and the great thaw began, the thaw whose waters carried off all the loam and clay, leaving us Masurians with nothing but sand, on top of a layer of glacial rock. Sand for fir forests and for military parade grounds. Then he painted in lakes, those 3,300 Masurian lakes, unique geographic features which formed a natural habitat for cranes and kites, black storks and fish eagles.

I was well acquainted with his abbreviated Masurian Genesis, and was waiting for the appearance of the first Pruzzi huntsman, who, scantily armed but with his simple gods in tow, was to take possession of the land.

At that moment an alarm clock went off, muffled, as if from inside a closet. The class exploded in laughter. And since the noise seemed to wander up and down the hall, the guffawing and pummeling also went on forever. I looked in horror at Uncle Adam. His gaze had narrowed, his breathing was rapid, his face twitched. At least Henseleit knew what his job as schoolmaster called for; he pushed his way through the crowd of boys, and nabbed a shoe box that was making the rounds, in which an old kitchen timer was rattling away. Shaking his head, he brought the carton to Uncle Adam, who did not accept it, did not even deign to look inside. He stood there trembling. Heinrich Henseleit perceived the gravity of the situation. Stepping back among the boys, he freely distributed boxes on the ears, cuffs, wallops, and, for a climax, banged two offenders' heads together . . .

Did I make it clear how much I had been looking forward to my class's visit? I had been so sure that they would be as interested as I was in the museum. I had imagined leading them through, with Uncle Adam giving explanations, while I myself added a few details to his stories, making a big thing of the straw crown.

Matters seemed to improve when Uncle Adam finally picked up the thread of his story, somewhat hesitantly, to be sure, somewhat more softly than at the beginning. He now populated our land, described Galindian honey gatherers and Sudauese fishermen living together in harmony, protected by the very wilds which gave them sustenance. No one but I noticed how much he was abridging his history, which was always concise in any case. He had the Teutonic Order triumph too quickly and then lose; the Polish colonists, the Mazovians, adjusted too soon to their new surroundings. Our name evolved too smoothly from Mazovia to Masauer to Masuria—a recent term, by the way, appearing for the first time in the administrative reports of the previous century. But all the while he was hurt, disappointed, and embittered, and omitted the expansive jokes with which he usually garnished his recital, as well as the expressive proverbs he liked to toss in.

Now the actual tour of the museum began. He called the boys' attention to wood carvings, to old weapons, tools, and ancient jewelry, and while he expounded, I circulated among the rascals on the edges, the ones whose boredom seemed incurable. I scolded, cuffed, collected playing cards and rubber bands, made sure they were at least conscious of where they were. All this had to be done discreetly, without creating a scene or an interruption.

I had especially to keep check on my enemy, Albin Jakubzik, the beanpole, who could cause a wave of titters to spread through the whole party. But all the while I felt real pain; it was not only that they refused to show any interest in Uncle Adam but also that they seemed unaffected by the objects; nothing touched them, nothing caught their imagination. It was all a waste.

Uncle Adam appeared to have recovered from the first incident. He was speaking with increasing energy. His aim, apparently, was to win them over by freely dispensing his knowledge, and he did capture their attention by the somewhat cheap trick of demonstrating the musical instruments. Yes, one could achieve something with noise, but as they crowded around to hear, they were not taking in a word of Uncle Adam's explanations about our traditional carnival music.

Suddenly I went weak in the knees. From the corner where Conny was stationed emerged, to the catchy rhythm of the devil's fiddle, a festive couple, a Masurian wedding couple: the beanpole Jakubzik as the lanky bride and puny Masuch, who reached only to the other's chest, as a fancily dressed, somewhat sickly groom. Surreptitiously they had put on the costumes, and now, as my classmates made way for them, hooting with pleasure, they launched into their version of a Krakoviak dance. The instruments made an uproar, the wooden floor creaked. Old dust eddied out of cracks and crannies. I watched the dancers, my stomach curdled with a boundless hatred . . .

Why? What do you mean, why?

I'll tell you why, my boy; even though these were old, threadbare costumes, they were being dishonored, it seemed to me, robbed of their magic, degraded to comical trappings. Also, the people who had once scrimped and saved so hard to pay for these festive garments seemed to be held up to ridicule. But Uncle Adam, strangely enough, was amused. At first he just stood there speechless, and there was no saying how he would react. But contrary to my expectations, he began to laugh, then gestured to the boys to dance faster and faster. Henseleit stepped over to Uncle Adam and offered him a cigar. He, too, found the incongruous wedding couple amusing.

I did not find the scene amusing in the least, and I despised the dolts from my class who, when they were shown the "native fauna," pried at the already cracked incisors of the stuffed beaver, broke off the tip of the lynx's tail, and were impressed by the mounted specimen of the European bison only because its pelt was full of mothballs, which they threw at one another. Even the Sudauese funerary urns awakened no solemn feelings; the boys took some down from the shelf and mooed or whistled into them.

Precisely, Martin. I could hardly understand how Uncle Adam put up with the noise and the levity. He let them touch whatever they liked, uttering not a single stern word. For my part, I could hardly wait for the tour to be over. We had made the rounds of the house and were standing before the workshop again. I was already looking forward to having the place to ourselves again when a piercing cry came from Uncle Adam. He was pointing to the shelves where fragile items were displayed. There were painted warming bottles, pottery plates and jugs, but also early blown glass, irregular in shape, sparkling with innumerable tiny bubbles. My uncle was pointing at one of these bottles, the only one which was not empty. It held a cloudy, amber-colored liquid topped with a bit of fresh foam. The label read, *Masurian medicine bottle, mid-eighteenth century, found near Aulaken.* Someone had scribbled over this in pencil: *Pee Liqueur, 200 proof.*

"Who did that?" Uncle Adam demanded in a terrible voice. "Who did that?"

Naturally no one came forward, although the question was repeated several times. I worried about Uncle Adam. I hated the class. And suddenly I heard myself saying, "Jakubzik did it, I saw him myself." In fact, he could not possibly have been the culprit, because he had been lurking around the coin collection. But I had made my accusation. Uncle Adam gestured to the beanpole, who shook his head, put on a show of puzzlement, and sighed reluctantly. Uncle Adam waved him up close, very close, then struck out with all the strength lent him by fury, so hard that Jakubzik's head jerked back and his body, usually slightly hunched forward, straightened out and flipped backward. Henseleit caught him as he fell. Henseleit loaded his pupil, whose legs seemed to have given way completely, onto his shoulders and looked in utter shock at Uncle Adam, who stood there swallowing hard and grimacing. The class, too, seemed in a state of shock.

Henseleit felt called upon to make two statements: one, that Uncle Adam had definitely gone too far, and two, that there would be repercussions. To which Uncle Adam replied, blinking agitatedly, "Get out of here! Quick! Out!"

Since Henseleit was lugging the gangling Jakubzik, he could not give the nautical signal for marching out two by two. But he led the way, leaving without any goodbye, drawing the class after him. Most of them sent hostile messages in my direction, which I returned. I had never slammed a door shut so quickly as I did behind my departing classmates; I then ran back to aid Uncle

Adam. He was not in the living room, nor in any of the other rooms I rushed past. I finally found him in his sleeping alcove, lying on the bed with his face to the wall. His shoulders were shaking. He was sobbing. I perched on the side of the bed, reached out my hand to him, then drew it back. After a while I went into the workshop, sat down at his cluttered workbench, and decided to wait for him. Lying in front of me was . . .

Pardon me, what did you say?

Oh, it's a pity you have to go, but if you must, you must . . .

Yes, you see, dear Martin Witt, our early experiences never leave us . . . I hope these bandages are coming off soon . . . I'm eager to see how you really look, as it compares with the picture I have formed of you in my temporary darkness . . . If it is true that Henrike has been working on her word collection again . . .

Perhaps you can tell me more about it next time . . .

Thank you, there's nothing I need, you're very kind . . . Or rather, I have a big favor to ask: I still haven't heard from Marian Jeromin, the master weaver Jeromin, who was once my favorite pupil. If anyone knows where he is, Henrike will. Marian is the sort of person one has to go on worrying about, our child prodigy, now himself getting on in years . . .

Yes, yes, he is also from Lucknow. He started out as a child prodigy with me, and he stayed on . . .

Ironic? You think that sounds ironic? Marian simply realized the worst fear of Sonja Turk, the greatest of our Masurian weavers, to whom I owe almost everything. When I showed her Marian's first design—she was already half paralyzed and had to depend on us for help—when I showed her the diagram of the clover pattern and the paired birds, she looked at it long and hard and then made her pronouncement: "Right you are, Zygmunt, my dear; little Marian is a prodigy. Let's hope he carries through, because being a prodigy is only good for the beginning."

Yes, I know you have to go, and I'm going to try to sleep a little . . .

But that interests me, tell me about it before you go . . .

No, don't feel you have to spare me . . .

Oh, I see. You think we would all be better off concentrating on the world rather than on our homeland. I don't know how much stock you put in other people's experience, but I have met quite a few people who have believed with all their hearts in international understanding, only to find their way, by and by, back to the homeland and its values. Perhaps we ought to recognize that knowing the world always comes back to knowing one's homeland, and can never be anything else. In any case, I'm looking forward to your visit tomorrow.

# 5

Today I can give you a bit of a jolt: I haven't left this bed; yet I know that your father was a veterinarian and that you often helped him in his practice. I also know that your father had the reputation for having "hypnotic eyes," with which he could subdue the most difficult animal, and that you have two older brothers, both of whom are pharmacists, and—what else? Oh, yes, I also know that there was a serious accident out there in the bay, and then . . .

Pardon me?

Well, I did not learn it directly; the sunken boat was mentioned, as well as your father's suicide, but nothing was said about insurance fraud. The head doctor here seems to have known your father; he noticed you leaving after your last visit and asked if you weren't the "young Witt." That's how I came by all this information.

You shouldn't spoil me this way, dear boy, although I admit I could drink tea and juice by the bucket; would you pour some into that cup? They are satisfied with my progress; the skin grafts seem to be taking well. Might I ask you to help me sit up higher? I'll brace myself—there, that's better. No proper Masurian would have put up with such a miserable bed; you may smile, but only the French have beds as good as a Masurian has. The reason is that we stripped our feathers off the quills by hand, rather than cutting them with shears. So a bit of tissue came away, too, and the feather immediately curled up, a tight little spring that lasted forever. By the way, this whole business of feather stripping was what got Edith, my first wife, the reputation of being possessed . . .

Was there any truth to it? That I leave to you to decide . . .

It must have been fall when Conny invited me to go out in the patrol boat with him and the fishing commissioner, Albert Dudei. Since the death of their mother—she had come down with blood poisoning—Conny and Edith had been living with the family of the fishing commissioner, who was a cousin of our still-absent prison warden. Dudei, among whose liabilities were three unmarried daughters, was a fair and good-natured person, which did not make his life any easier for him. His territory included Lakes Lucknow, Selment, and Sunovo, as well as several miles of the Lucknow River. He was in charge of setting fishing quotas, supervising the hunting of water birds, restocking the lakes, and confiscating illegal fishing gear such as eel traps, snares, and the like. He performed this latter duty without enthusiasm, storing the confiscated stuff in a lakeside shed which he often forgot to lock up, probably because he hoped the owners would break in and retrieve their property.

But what was I telling you about? Oh, yes, the patrol. On my way to join Conny and the fishing commissioner in their boat, I had to pass their house, whitewashed like our own. As I approached, I heard singing from the corner room, whose windows overlooking the lake were open. I had to pause and listen, for these were hymns they were singing. I peeked through the window; on a bench around the stove, surrounded by tubs containing various sorts of feathers, sat the three Dudei girls, who sang while they stripped the feathers. Across from them, in her armchair, Frau Dudei set the tone and likewise stripped feathers, though somewhat less energetically. If a gust of wind had swept through the room, the resulting storm would have made a blizzard look mild by comparison . . .

Too many feathers, you think? If you only knew, dear boy, what significance feather beds had in those days! We had a rhyme which summed up the main preoccupation of a Masurian girl as she neared marriageable age: "With down of geese/full fifty head/the bride must stuff/her bridal bed." Once she had collected enough feathers for her mattress, pillows, and a great mountain of a comforter, she had to begin on the feathers for the guest bed, for the children she counted on having, perhaps for her brother, and finally for the old parents, whose beds would have to be replaced eventually. So working up feathers was anything but frivolous in a place where in event of fire people would rescue their beds before they went after their money box.

In any case, the Dudei daughters—Lisbeth, Elsbeth, and Julie— were singing and stripping feathers under the supervision of their stern-featured mother, and although I peeped through the window several times, I could not see any sign of Edith—Edith, who had been taken in by this family and should certainly have shown her gratitude. No, she was not there. I listened to the singing a while longer, then tiptoed past the house and bounded down the path through the reeds which led to the shed and the dock.

The water fowl were making their usual clatter. There by the dock, moored with heavy ropes, the *Albatross II* floated on the dark waters, with three seats and the wood-encased motor in the middle. Two little gulls swooped up from the motor casing, splattering their chalky droppings. The shed was closed tightly, and there was that look about its door which suggested that someone had double-checked the lock to make sure it would hold. The platform around the shed rocked at every step, and I was jouncing along it when someone called to me, not by name, but in such a conspiratorial way that I stopped and put my ear to the wall of the shed.

It was Edith whimpering inside and asking timidly whether someone was there. "Conny, is that you?" she asked. "Conny, why don't you say something? Conny?" I looked about to make sure no one was nearby before I answered. As soon as she heard who it was, her voice became firmer, more authoritative; she did not ask, she ordered me to pry a certain board loose. "Hurry up!" she said, "I've got to get out of here." I pushed in a knot, directed Edith to the hole, and caught a glimpse of her eye, her mouth, and her ear. She repeated impatiently, "Well, hurry up, what are you waiting for?"

Why had she been locked up in the shed, I wanted to know. She replied with her usual imperiousness, "Get me out of here, or you'll be sorry." I would have done what she asked, as always, but as I started loosening the board she had indicated, Conny appeared, pulled me back, put a finger to his lips, and nodded toward the dock. Ignoring Edith's supplications, we left her in her prison. We scrambled into the boat and squatted down on the bottom. Then Conny told me why Edith had been locked up . . .

To punish her, you're right, Martin, and it was not the first time, either. Edith refused to strip feathers. The moment the tubs and scoops were brought into the room, Edith began to tremble and to edge toward the door. If they begged and cajoled enough, she would sit on the bench by the stove, but her hand never dipped into the tubs. It would jerk back if one of the Dudei girls laughingly sprinkled a few feathers on it, and Edith leaped up and seemed short of breath the moment a strainer of feathers was set in her lap. She closed her eyes and refused to touch a single feather.

And just as nothing could persuade Edith to join in the work, she would not join in the singing, either, although she knew an extraordinary number of songs, patriotic songs and soldiers' songs, and usually liked singing them. The commissioner's wife, a woman of narrow piety, thought she understood what the matter was and what must be done about it. Since devils can be driven out only by means of a combination of punishments, Edith was first denied food, then, when that did not help, forbidden to talk. When she remained obstinate, the fishing commissioner had to give her a caning. When even that did not bring her around, several punishments were applied simultaneously. So Edith was denied food and locked into the shed, which reeked of tar and dried algae ...

You wonder why Conny did not set her free. I don't know; perhaps even then he was thinking of drastic solutions. He had had his fill of Lucknow and was placing all his hopes on Haparanda, Haparanda in Sweden, that's right, which he probably knew from a picture. It was the location of the most northerly lighthouse in the country.

In any case, I decided Edith had been mistreated, and I had just resolved to help her when the fishing commissioner turned up, looked through the peephole I had made, and called in some words of cheer. He started up the motor, casually took the rudder, and off we chugged to patrol the lake.

We had almost completed our rounds when we skimmed along the edge of the estate, then steered for the inlet on which Little Grajevo was located ...

When did all this happen? It must have been in 1917 or 1918 during the third or last year of the war; you could have rutabagas cooked in any of twenty-four different ways, and the cows were already dead set against giving milk—as my grandfather commented. In any case, you had to be both clever and lucky if you wanted not just to eat but to eat a varied diet.

At the time the thought did not cross my mind, but nowadays I wonder how the people of Little Grajevo got through the war, the Gutkelches and the Hausers, whom one saw less and less of the longer the war lasted.

In any case, we headed into the inlet, which had become choked with reeds, and tied up at the main dock. On shore the only sign of human presence was a woman in a head scarf, kneading, rubbing, and rinsing her laundry. The shouts from the distant Borek Forest made it clear why no children came running to meet us; they were all off picking blueberries. No dogs barked. The usual small armadas of ducks and geese gazing at their own reflections in the water were nowhere to be seen. The woman with the head scarf did not even look up as we scrambled out of the boat, checked over the lines that stretched out from the landing like rays, and pulled in the first line, to which was attached a wooden fish trap.

The fishing commissioner opened the slippery, algae-covered trap; all it contained was one scrawny carp, which he returned to the water. Working in consort, we pulled in one trap after the next, but left it to the commissioner to open the perforated containers and throw the fish back into the lake—there were just a few bony specimens, no pike, and certainly no eels or zander, and the traps out in the deeper water were empty.

The fishing commissioner was visibly disappointed. He seemed unable to believe that the traps contained so little in the way of fish, and he was brooding as he let the traps slide back into the water, brooding as he climbed into the boat and ordered Conny to start the motor. But this time the motor, usually so reliable, would not start, not even when the commissioner tried it. It just sputtered dryly and refused to turn over. There was no help for it. Conny and I had to head into town on foot to fetch Buttkus, the mechanic . . .

You're right; we were not exactly wild about the assignment, but since we had no choice, we set out, passing the woman at her washing, who pushed back her scarf and greeted Conny in surprisingly friendly fashion, then up the hill through the village, where doors opened a crack and snapping fingers tried to catch our attention. Here and there Conny shook someone's hand, whispered something, shook his head regretfully, and drew me on. I did not catch much of what was said, but whenever a door opened, I got a whiff of fish—dry, baked pike, perch frying in hot fat, brace marinated with onions and vinegar, poached zander, carp stuffed with dried fruit, and last but not least, jellied eel. Gradually I realized that they were inviting us in to taste all these delectable dishes.

No, we could not stop; we had to continue up the hill to the edge of Borek Forest, along the sandy path lined by widely spaced spruce trees, gigantic ones, whose roots crossed the path in great ridges. As we so often did, we put our arms around each other; that made it harder to walk, but it felt good, and we continued this way until we came to a large reforested area with its young trees in neat rows. There we took out our homemade balls, which consisted simply of pieces of fabric stitched together and filled with sand. As we walked along, we practiced hitting targets or seeing who could throw the farthest.

And I still remember that on one throw, when I gathered all my strength, my aim was so wild that the ball flew crookedly in the wrong direction, over the dense young trees, and fell noiselessly to the forest floor. If Conny had not said, "Go on, get it, I'll wait for you," I would probably not have ventured into the new stand of trees to find it. The hard grasses scratched me, the fir twigs whipped my face, and the underbrush clawed at my skin. But because of Conny, I put one arm over my eyes, took note of the direction, and went crashing through the spruce trees. Soon the white sand of the path I had left could no longer be seen for all the green. Here the wind seemed to have been turned off. There was a rustling and a crackling of undetermined origin. Although only one woodpecker was hammering away ahead of me, the whole section of the forest seemed filled with woodpeckers. By a dead tree trunk lay an adder, patterned like our Ella; I gave her a wide berth and began to search systematically . . .

Yes, something like that, my dear boy: as if one were searching for a bunch of keys one had lost overboard when sailing; I assume you never did find them, any more than I found my ball.

In any case, as I was searching, I suddenly heard muffled applause from not far away. I went down on my knees, reconnoitered on all fours, making larger and larger circles, that's right, and then I saw them in a clearing: Hugo Bandilla, king of the Masurian smugglers, and all around him, sitting with their backs against knapsacks, a select band of his people.

But the reason for their merriment was that Hugo Bandilla, who had stripped down to his baggy underpants, was now opening a cardboard box and taking out a genuine border guard's cap, which he saluted sarcastically before donning it. The smugglers clapped, and wanted to see more, whereupon Hugo Bandilla took out a neatly folded uniform jacket, which he first showed around the circle. Then, rising to his toes, he pressed it to his chest and waltzed it gracefully around the clearing. The smugglers slapped the ground in delight, and the merrier they became, the grimmer seemed Hugo Bandilla. The trousers fit him, the military belt might have been made to order for him, and when he buckled on his side arm, put his left hand behind his back, and stuck his right hand into the flap over his chest, some of the smugglers jumped up in pure rapture at the idea that one of their own could play a border guard more convincingly than any border guard they knew.

Suddenly Conny was lying beside me. He winked at me, and was just murmuring something admiring about Hugo Bandilla, when a hand closed over my throat and two thighs straddled my back, pinning me to the ground. And it was simply not enough when Conny attacked the man from the rear and—without thinking of his own safety—tried to wrestle him to the ground. He had to flee; for those in the clearing had heard the sound of our scuffle, and came to the assistance of the man who had overpowered me; I had to lie there with my face to the ground until Hugo Bandilla after a moment's deliberation reached a decision. They pushed me into their circle, where Bandilla interrogated me. He wanted to know everything, especially which Rogalla I was; my father's name seemed a good recommendation: apparently they had had close dealings of a satisfactory nature . . .

Don't be so impatient, I was just getting to that. Hugo Bandilla snatched a bottle from the mouth of one of the smugglers, looked at what was left in it, glanced at me to measure how much my physique could take, then gave me the quarter-full bottle and ordered me to drink up. "Sip by sip," he advised. I had no choice; under Bandilla's scrutiny I drank the golden brandy, smelling of honey, while the other smugglers seemed to be preparing to depart. One of them frantically dug up something he had buried, another was sewing coins into his jacket lining. They rolled up their coats, girded themselves, redistributed the contents of their knapsacks . . .

What sort of things did they smuggle? Well, cloth, tobacco, spices, but also soap and medications, and when they opened their knapsacks and passed the stuff back and forth, you can imagine the medley of scents in the clearing.

First the brandy made my legs rubbery, then it made the tips of the branches spin, then it turned the clearing into an inclined plane, then it wound wire around my temples, then it pressed me down to the floor of the forest, then it made the smugglers swim before my eyes and the clearing itself roll as if in heavy seas. The men shouldered their knapsacks as easily as if they were huge balloons, and upon Bandilla's orders, the file glided past me and disappeared into the thicket . . .

No, not quite; I had not quite emptied the bottle, but I had drunk more than enough to give me my first experience with our meschkinnes, which concurrently sharpens the hearing and makes you numb, so that you could catch the slightest mistake in a birdsong but would hardly notice if a finger were amputated. In any case, to this day I am convinced that two crows led me back to Lake Lucknow, two crows who fluttered to the ground rather awkwardly, just eyeing me at first and circling around me in their crow's gait, which included odd little hops, and came up so close that I was tempted to reach out and grab them; I followed them across the clearing, crashed my way through the plantation of young trees, while they flew ahead from spruce to spruce, and I saw them hopping down the sandy path ahead of me as I let the last branches snap back. The meschkinnes was clamoring in the back of my head, and I could feel every one of my hair roots. I did not give up the idea of seizing one of the crows, even leaped at them a few times, but they eluded me, of course. They piloted me past Little Grajevo to the wild pear tree, and there they alighted and peered down at me, watched me slither down the clay bank and wade into the lake, where I washed my burning face and the back of my neck before I continued in the shallow water, toward the estate . . .

The fishing commissioner, you mean? You wonder whether the *Albatross II* was already tied up at the landing dock?

No, precisely because they had not yet returned—from the wild pear tree I could see the channel through the rushes—I decided to approach the shed from the lakeside, the shed where Edith was imprisoned in punishment for her "perverse refusal" to strip feathers. I did not knock timidly on the wall of the shed; no, this time I pounded on the wood so demandingly that Edith's eye instantly appeared at the knothole, and without any urging on her part, I crept under the shed, found the board that could be loosened, squeezed through the opening, and pulled myself up to stand by the heap of confiscated nets and fish traps. "Come along," I said, "what are you waiting for?" She looked at me with something like incomprehension, sank down in the little hollow where she had been sitting, and clutched the nets as if for dear life. I promised what lay within my power: that I would get her out of here, and then to Borek Forest or the big barn on the estate. But Edith no longer had flight on her mind, at least not with me. She wanted to wait for Conny, who had indicated that he would not leave for Haparanda and the most northerly light-house without her.

The meschkinnes made the shed roll and pitch like a freighter in a gale; I had to go down on all fours; I dragged myself, holding on to Edith's legs, up onto the nets, lay beside her, and rocked for a while in the deep troughs of the waves. Then I asked her whether she had some notion where Haparanda was, how they would get there, and what they would live on at the start. In lieu of answering, she scrambled onto a cable reel, reached into a hiding place between the beams, and produced a purse, which she opened close to my face . . .

Not marbles, there you are wrong, dear boy; her purse was full of silver talers and golden ten- and twenty-mark pieces, which Edith drew out with a serious expression and allowed to rain back into the purse, slowly, so that I could appreciate how the dream of Haparanda might be paid for. It was money she had taken out of her mother's legacy on the sly; neither the fishing commissioner's family nor Conny knew a thing about it. No, not even Conny; because she was afraid her brother might leave without her, she showed me her wealth to make the point that she was indispensable to the success of the venture. And then, slinking back into the half darkness of the shed, she spirited her purse away and lay down beside me again, probably wanting me to make various pledges, give her my word of honor, and so on. But under the influence of the meschkinnes, I had only one wish, to die as quickly as possible and be buried by a wave. While I was longing for relief from my heaving stomach, I heard her at what seemed a great distance going on and on about Haparanda, what was there and what was not there; she kept conjuring up images for me: the white lighthouse, the redwood houses mirrored in the calm water, tame seagulls and sailboats. I heard her saying that in Haparanda there was no soup with dumplings, that you went to school when you felt like it, but especially that girls in Haparanda were used for sorting fish and not for stripping feathers. I had no wish to contradict her, nor could I; with my face pressed into the nets, I fell asleep . . .

Pardon me? Not at all. I didn't know Edith well enough yet. I woke up, not only tangled in the nets, but also with my wrists bound fast with twine, and I was lying there like that when Conny slipped into the shed. While he undid the tight double knots, Edith crouched beside him, fearfully making him repeat again and again that if we set out for Haparanda at all it would not be without her. Not until Conny ceremoniously shook her hand and repeated the vow did she seem satisfied, and then we sat there and conferred in whispers about the best time to set out. Since the meschkinnes had set a little spinning wheel a-whirring in my head, I agreed with whatever was suggested, down to the day in the spring, right after our confirmation and the end of school . . .

Thank you, I'll have an apple now. How juicy this one is, how fragrant, quite unlike the fruit they raise nowadays, which appeals only to the eye. I daresay this is an old variety, not much to look at, maybe even scabby. Perhaps the tree is all contorted . . .

In an old schoolyard, you say? Aha, in the yard of the abandoned village schoolhouse in Pudby, and you picked it yourself, with Henrike? . . .

Marian Jeromin? Well, well, well: so Marian has opened up his own weaving studio: our aged child prodigy has taken the plunge, my most outstanding pupil, that's right, who once charged me with having stifled his talent by insisting on rigid adherence to the rules of the craft. So the hobbled genius has freed himself from his guardian, and I assume he has recruited my last weaving pupils, the girls, not to initiate them into the discipline of the craft, but to awaken the sleeping originality and talent in each one . . . Five of them . . . Well, didn't I say so? . . . Take my word for it: the former village schoolhouse in Pudby, which he has just rented, will be the last way station for master weaver Jeromin. That is where he will come to see that "being a prodigy is only good for the beginning," as Sonja Turk remarked, and that in the end what counts is attention to detail and perseverance. At any rate, I now know where my people are, even if they are through with me; it's better to recognize that one's bridges have burned than to remain in suspense . . .

Haparanda? You want to know whether we really ran away to Haparanda? I'm sure you realize that the more firmly one commits oneself to some vision of the future, the less likely one is to accomplish it. And in our minds we had already so tasted all the joys of Haparanda that there was no need to go there anymore— but that was not the real reason we never laid eyes on that most northerly lighthouse.

Shortly before I graduated, in the spring, when it was already warm enough to go barefoot, my mother was sitting in Uncle Adam's workshop, and while he repaired a splint basket, they were discussing my prospects, going over my inclinations and talents, and testing out the idea of various professions. I was standing outside, eavesdropping through the crack in the door, and hearing for the first time what they really thought of me. I also discovered for the first time what rung on the ladder of life they expected me to attain. My mother was thinking along the lines of a "position of influence," while Uncle Adam saw me engaged in some form of "service." "The ideal profession," my mother said, "would be that of a policeman, because then our Zygmunt would be able to supervise everything." Uncle Adam gave the matter thought and objected, "I'd rather see him a furrier; he has an eye for fabrics and pelts; he could make fur boas and muffs and robes, which are things people always need." Fearing this might involve only seasonal work, my mother suggested that I be apprenticed to Struppek, of Struppek & Sausmikat, as a salesman for coats, trousers, and sailor suits, because "then Zygmunt could learn how to outfit every little scamp in Lucknow to look his best." "I'd rather see him become a cabinetmaker," Uncle Adam remarked; "the smell of glue and wood is healthier than the smell of textiles, and besides, he wouldn't have to see half of Lucknow in their underwear." As they talked on, proposing to apprentice me as a planer at the plywood factory on the outskirts of town, I could take it no longer. I slipped past the workshop door, groped my way to the hall, and dashed through the garden down to the river. I was not ready to accept the various fates they were so well-meaningly mapping out for me.

Our river was at flood stage, tugging at the willows that hung down over it. Great logs floated on the dark water, coming from Poland, headed toward the mouth of the river, some of them having blundered into little inlets along the way. At the mouth of the river, where a wire was stretched across to catch them, hundreds of logs were piling up, logs destined for the plywood factory. Simon was already there waiting for me, and after exchanging a few words we set out to join the others, who were far out on the logs, balancing precariously as they made them bob and rotate. There was nothing we watched for more eagerly every spring than those felled forests from Poland which came swimming down the river and were dammed up at its mouth, before an old-fashioned tug towed them to the factory.

Try to imagine yourself out there, dear Martin Witt, balancing on those swimming forest giants, which could easily bear the weight of five men without noticeably settling lower in the water, and bouncing on the young logs, which could just about take the weight of a child, making them roll over, faster and faster, until to save yourself you had to leap to another log. Our game went this way: when the leader gave the word, we made the logs spin under our feet, so rapidly that water sprayed up at the edges; it was like treading a devil's wheel, never gaining distance, and the logs swayed and seesawed, while we tried to keep our balance, waving our arms wildly, twisting our bodies this way and that. Simon Gayko, who was crooked to begin with, could keep his footing the longest; he would still be upright when the others had leaped off or were sitting astride the logs, up to their thighs in water. We were all somewhat tired of his feats, for which reason one of the boys—probably Conny—suggested a race over the logs, over the treacherous surface of the floating wood, from the bridge over to the old drinking trough. The logs did not stay in orderly formation; depending on how the current caught them, they floated parallel to one another, at right angles, and in all sorts of crazy patterns, with open water between them.

You should have seen us flitting and flying barefoot across the logs; we barely skimmed the thinner logs, while we came storming down on the thicker ones. Rapidly estimated leaps carried us over the open spots.

I miscalculated on one leap, not getting enough impetus when I sprang; as I flew through the air, I already knew I was not going to make it, and spread my arms so as not to plunge in too deep. The swirling current seized hold of me; I felt the pressure more than the coldness of the water; it was a compelling force which would not let me come to the surface, but carried me along underneath the logs, in the darkness, which was pierced now and then by a strip of light . . .

In addition, the pressure of the current was forcing the logs together. I tried, but could not widen a gap between two logs and work my way up. I was swept along under the logs, peeping up, on the lookout for a wider strip of open water. I remembered the fish that we saw float belly up to the surface of the ice when we went ice fishing. Driven by the need for oxygen and numbed by the pounding in my head, I gathered all my strength for a final thrust to the surface. In that moment I collided with a log. I still remember the brief pain, and the feeling of dim relaxation that spread over me as I collapsed, a release from all physical sensation. An eddy twirled me as if in slow motion, let me float like an uprooted water plant, and turned me over to the current, which swept me away toward the old drinking trough.

I did not actually see the forked branch which reached toward me in the water, but grabbed it without realizing what I was doing, and as she pulled me to land, more under the water than on top of it, I did not hear either her voice or Conny's . . .

Where were the others? In view of my accident, they had

stopped their game, and after a brief, hasty search, they had run away, except for Conny. In response to his shouts, Sonja Turk plucked up her skirts and waded into the water, waded down from her drying meadow, where she had been turning the glowing skeins of wool.

Sonja Turk: I came to on her meadow, and the first thing my water-logged eyes rested on was her expressive face under the straight middle part, her mysterious gaze, which called forth confessions, her lips, whose curves revealed stubbornness and wisdom. There was no telling her age. She did not smile and showed no satisfaction at my rescue; in an irritable tone she sent Conny to my family, and pulled me to my feet and led me to the simple wooden house near the mouth of the river where she lived alone. When she walked one could not see where the movement began or distinguish the individual footsteps; her stocky body seemed rather to be driven by a constant wind, like an overladen sloop.

Once in the kitchen she reached for a long towel of stiff linen, looked reprovingly at the trail of drops and the little puddles I was leaving on the floor, and told me curtly to take off my wet things and hang them on a clothesline by the iron stove. She rubbed me dry. The stiff fabric reddened my skin, produced tingling heat. I held still in amazement when, after setting my back aflame, she simply rotated me and rubbed my chest and stomach and everything, including the toes, which she looked at and wiggled in amusement. Then she put me into warmed house slippers, popped me into an oversized shirt, wrapped me in a goat-hair blanket, and compensated me for all the rubbing by letting me watch as she changed her drenched skirt, her petticoat, and her black kneesocks. She brewed some linden tea, which we drank in her spacious workroom . . .

What did you say? In the inner sanctum? Let's say, rather, in the workroom of the greatest Masurian weaver, between the two old-fashioned looms. The walls were hung with rugs which were never for sale: the solemn, portentous *kuddrä*, for which the wool could never be hard enough, the soft, festive *kotz*; in addition the double-weave pagan rug, said to be the donation of the witch Bianca, which was supposed to stop illness. What colors! What telling figures, scenes, and symbols! While Sonja Turk suddenly sat down at her loom as though she had to make up for lost time—I believe she was binding off the last threads of a marriage hanging—I wandered about from wall to wall in my warm wrappings, dazed by all the symbols and echoes, the hopes and vivid spells woven into the rugs. I could not tear myself away from the woven *kuddräs* and the knotted *kotzes*, whose patterns and motifs filled me with excitement, with the rapture of recognition, ah yes. Although I was acquainted with some of the symbols from Uncle Adam's collection, only now did they open themselves up to me, in clearest blue, red, and brown, held in a spell by warp and weft. All of a sudden I realized that the trefoil meant something to me, and the fertility cross with the nine points. I trusted the eight-pointed star to protect households and the magic knot to keep misfortune at bay. The staring eye was proof of the presence of a companion, and the odal rune of the longing to escape from the dark depths. But the sun cross also had something to say to me, and the white hind, not to mention Wotan's white horse and the bird that accompanies the soul on its journey . . .

You're right there; pagan symbols, rich in vitality, which applied to our life . . .

The rugs glowed along the rough wooden walls; I thought I could sense all the tangles of experience that had been worked into them; I thought I could recognize the fear which was kept in bounds by woven magical charms. But above all I understood that as long as the twelve-pointed hind stood under the six-pointed star and the tree of life, we did not need to give up hope. I could no longer loiter around. With Sonja Turk's broad back in clear view, I sat down on the floor in the midst of the brilliant snippets of many-colored yarn, found myself a pair of scissors and a piece of stiff paper, and without further ado began to cut out ornaments and animals. The bite of the steel jaws, which were releasing from the innocent paper suns and cows, lozenges and leaf-work, did not seem to catch Sonja Turk's ear. She did not once turn around to see what I was up to. She seemed utterly absorbed in her own work and produced humming, groaning sounds as she worked—a barrier of noise protecting her from the outside. In any case, sitting there among the brilliant-colored scraps, all aglow myself, cutting out the motifs and patterns of our life, I discovered that I wanted for nothing, that I was happy, and wished only that Sonja Turk would turn around just once and say a few words of praise.

She did not take time for that. She did not interrupt her work even when a tanned man in a leather jacket came in, whip in hand, a prosperous farmer from Stradaunen who held out a limp banknote to her and ordered a rug with a special power. Could she do it fast? After glancing up at him briefly, she wanted to know his name—he was called Franz Narutsch—had him explain his family circumstances—married twelve years, no children, two hundred and fifty acres of land—and working without interruption, she listened to the client's specifications for the rug. It was to have the fertility cross in blue on a white ground, two brown lozenges on a red ground, and four red pairs of birds on a black ground . . . That's right, my dear boy, that says it all. As far as its measurements went, the rug was to serve as a bed cover, without hanging over the edges.

Sonja Turk listened attentively, apparently thinking over the artistic possibilities. I was expecting her to relieve him of the limp banknote, when she shook her head and said, "Franz Narutsch from Stradaunen, take your money and go; I won't be able to do a *kuddrä* for you, because the sight of you doesn't inspire me a bit." The prosperous farmer looked at her in dismay; the last thing he had expected was such a refusal. "How the devil do you need to be inspired to do me a rug like that?"

"A certain feeling," Sonja Turk replied, "that is, the feeling that I am also making the rug for myself, that I need it, too." Well, whom did she make rugs for, Narutsch wanted to know. She said calmly, "I don't make my rugs for this person or that; I make them against something, and if you care to know what that is, it is the fleetingness of life. Yes, that is what my weavings are all about." The farmer asked if he might return in a year, whereupon the weaver shrugged almost imperceptibly.

But what did I want to tell you? Oh, yes, my cut-out patterns, right, all the motifs and shapes I had cut out of paper: I laid them out on a table, grouping them, creating relationships among them, even suggesting a development from the heathen sun star to the Christian Tree of Knowledge. But even now Sonja Turk seemed to pay no attention to what I was doing. I needed color. I asked her where in the house I might find colors, and she said, "Well, where do you think? In the dye room, boy." Still wrapped in the blanket, I went into the corridor, listened, tiptoed past seven closed doors without opening them, went up a staircase, and was startled to find myself in the weaver's bedroom, a dusky room almost filled by an enormous bed; gnarled branches extending from the wall held an array of owls, so real that they seemed about to swoop: the snowy owl, the great horned owl, the tawny owl, all with glowing, russet eyes, and I actually held up my elbow to protect my face. Later I gave the stuffed birds names and liked to ruffle their dry feathers. Next to the bedroom were two storage rooms, one containing a jumbled library thick with cobwebs, the other, among other things, a number of pale mannequins, which lay there, their limbs intertwined, their eye sockets hollow, seemingly waiting for their moment of glory.

There was no help for it; I had to go back downstairs and open the doors along the corridor, heavy doors, all of whose latches seemed stuck; they yielded only to determined pressure. You can imagine that I anticipated a wealth of discoveries. First I entered the room where Sonja Turk kept the raw materials from which she extracted her dyes: hanging in bunches, or laid out on sheets of tin or paper, were sheaves of kaddik, dyer's camomile, and the madderwort, a little of which goes a long way. There were stacks of bark and strips of pale bast. I still remember how expressive the materials seemed, how everything began to rustle and creak as I entered, and I recall the uneasiness that seized me. At the next door I listened before entering: a narrow room, furnished with only a table and a chair and an iron stove. On the table lay a book, thicker and more mysterious than the oldest folio volumes in my father's laboratory. The book lay open, and I went up to it cautiously and found an assortment of colored symbols and ornaments, and in a hand which later on I came to read as fluently as its author, the tested recipe was described.

What sort of things? They were rhymes in Masurian dialect, with nicknames given to the different symbols and colors.

I did not dare rummage through the book, the handwritten and illustrated compendium of the Masurian art of weaving, Sonja Turk's most precious possession. Flies clustered at the stove were roused, circled around me, crashed crazily into the window. I had to find the dye room, and after looking into two more rooms—

one of them had a table set for three persons—I found it right next to the weaving studio, a small room one could barely edge one's way into, because the entire floor was littered with cans and pots, tubes and bottles, with daubs of color running down their sides. I pierced dried skins of color, rubbed off wrinkled layers of pigment to get at the true colors underneath, and returned to the weaving studio with containers of brown, red, and blue. My patterns and motifs were waiting for me on the table, and now I gave them what they needed to awaken them to life and significance. Sonja Turk was still paying no attention as I colored my cows and lozenges, my fishes, runes, and long-necked geese, and the color gave them the desired powers. With the color everything was intensified; the shapes had some sort of magic. I was carried away with joy, sensing that I had found my place. And that was not all: I suddenly realized what I wanted to be . . .

You're right, Martin Witt. I, too, had been found, discovered. But my apprenticeship did not begin all that easily, without any obstacles . . .

As soon as my Uncle Adam appeared to fetch me—he came by himself, my mother being laid up with her spring flu—when he formally thanked Sonja Turk from the doorway, I sensed that it was some old reservation or bias that made him so stiff and abrupt. On Mother's urging he had brought along three jars of honey in gratitude for my rescue. He deposited them on the windowsill, immediately retreated backward to the door, and from there made the unavoidable inquiries as to health, business, and so on, without seeming interested in the replies. The weaver smiled at the ostentatious coolness of his good manners, and continued to smile when he remarked, in response to her own queries, that his Masurian museum would soon be ready to be opened to the public. Regular visiting hours, entrance fees at the visitors' discretion. His reluctance to converse was palpable.

He kept on hurrying me to dress, and would not let me dawdle. Sonja Turk pressed him to come in and look at her most recent rugs, but he replied in a forced, insincere manner. He was not in the right mood, he said; he was still upset over my accident. He gestured tellingly in the region of his stomach: "No more time, Zygmunt. Let's get going." All this formality and prickliness indicated that there were hidden elements to the relationship. I could not penetrate the mystery, but I had a faint idea.

In any case, after I had pulled on my clothes, which were still far from dry, I went over to Sonja Turk's loom, thanked her, and gave her my hand. Only then did I dislodge her from her bench, draw her over to the table, and nod down at my work: "There, look: what do you say?" She eyed my figures and symbols, obviously considering their relative positions, and the color effects. What she murmured fell far short of my expectations: "Well, just look at that; not bad for a beginner." She stroked my head with her hand. She suggested that I come back and pick up my shapes another time—"But come on foot, not by water, you scamp." Then she invited Uncle Adam to come over to the table and have a look at my colored designs; but Uncle Adam refused. One hand was already on the latch, he was snorting with impatience. The main thing was that I was permitted to come again; I might enter the weaving studio when I pleased; that was Sonja's parting promise, and that was all I needed to make me happy . . .

Punishment? You wonder whether Uncle Adam punished me for my accident on the logs? Of course. But it was a curiously delayed punishment—perhaps he was already showing traces of the tragic forgetfulness which later befell him. We had already walked a good way along the river, and had crossed the wooden bridge, when he suddenly stopped, cleared his throat, and gave me a slap with his flat hand across my cheek and mouth. It only tingled slightly. Then he continued on his way, satisfied that he had taken care of the unpleasant business.

We passed through the park along the river, and were almost home when he turned off and had me climb into his tarred boat. He himself scrambled in after me, clumsily, very clumsily. Sitting across from me on the rickety bench, he hesitated a while, gazed at the weeping willows that hung down over the water and the drifting logs, and out of sheer embarrassment fished out his carving knife and whittled a sap-filled branch into a little pipe, after gently stripping off the bark. And as he worked, the words came. I had almost known what he was going to say. He was opposed to my visiting Sonja Turk, the rug stringer, as he called her. He would not forbid me to, but I should know that he disapproved. "She's nothing for you," he said. "Don't hang around with her, it might rub off. If you look at her carefully, she has the split goat's eye . . ."

You can imagine how I felt after this warning, but I did not give up so easily. I could not simply turn my back on an experience which had so excited me. To test how seriously he meant it, I replied, "I don't want to become a furrier, and certainly not a policeman. If I must become something, then let me be a rugmaker, and I can do my apprenticeship with her, with Sonja Turk."

Uncle Adam looked at me, sadly and suspiciously, yes, perhaps because he feared I had already come under the spell of the weaver. He brought the blade of his knife down hard on the pipe and shook his head vigorously. Apparently my condition seemed suspect to him—the determination, the clarity of my wishes—and he was resolved to save me before it was too late . . .

How? Very simply, my dear boy: he described my future teacher to me, painted dark spots into her life, hinted at matters that could not be explained, alluded to dark, mysterious pacts, spoke riddles, and finally alluded to grim threats and dangers. There in his rickety boat, surrounded by the burbling of the dammed-up water, I learned that Sonja Turk's house stood on the site which had once been Bianca's house. Bianca had earned her living less from weaving and knotting than from making magic spells to cure animals no veterinarian could help.

Back in the old days, the Gypsies used to assemble once a year at Bianca's house, parking their caravans on the drying meadow, and for three days they celebrated a festival whose meaning only they knew. Sonja Turk is supposed to have come with the Gypsies one fall, sitting as if in a trance on one of the caravans, a thirteen-year-old girl not herself of Gypsy blood. Still in a trance she sat by the fire, and danced, and she is supposed to have spoken not a word, even when Bianca gave her a necklace, an amber necklace. Bianca alone knew why Sonja Turk was missing when the Gypsies went on their way.

After the Gypsies had moved on—to Narbonne and Andalusia —Bianca took Sonja Turk into her house. She gave her a pillow filled with the down of young wild ducks, and a dress with rare fish-scale embroidery—tendrils on a background of black velvet —and fed her nourishing stews until the girl recovered from her curious state of apathy. From Bianca, Sonja Turk learned weaving and knotting, cross-stitch and beadwork. When Bianca was called to distant parts to use her arts for healing sick horses and cows, she took the girl along as an assistant, and soon Sonja became familiar with all the ways of reading cards and extracting signs from ashes and urine. Together they collected feathers and harvested chokecherries; they went everywhere arm in arm, always in good spirits. It was said that Sonja Turk wanted Bianca to be her mother.

When the Gypsies returned in the autumn, Sonja Turk disappeared for the duration of the festival. No sooner had their caravans rumbled off again than Sonja Turk reappeared, with strings of drying mushrooms over her shoulders. Her clothing exuded the faintly musty odor of a hollow tree trunk. Even when the Gypsies were temporarily forbidden to enter Lucknow, Sonja took off for the critical five days. The story went that one of those times when she went into hiding, she brought back a little *kotz*, a knotted rug of such subdued yet glowing beauty that even Bianca was astonished. A landowner from Pupinnen paid a collector's price for it, and laid down the sum a second time when his wife, who had lost the power of speech, began to speak again at the sight of the rug.

Yes, Martin, all this I learned, and more. There had been a time when master weavers came from afar, even from foreign lands, and found various pretexts to enter the house above the old drinking trough. Enraptured by what they saw, they made extraordinary offers to Sonja Turk. Since Sonja turned them all down, the disappointed suitors were bent on winning revenge. Or perhaps they only spread word about things they actually experienced in their dealings with the two women. In any case, there was talk of happenings which horrified many residents of Lucknow.

Uncle Adam's voice trembled as he told me these stories, though, to be sure, he also mentioned that, one day after she reached her majority, Sonja Turk took her examination for master weaver. The examining commission was confused and most unwilling, but she was given the highest grade without even a vote's being taken. On the night when Bianca died, having shown no sign of illness, a bush of daphne, waist-high, is supposed to have sprung up close to the front door. Sonja Turk hung colorful ribbons from it and swathed it in an old curtain to protect it during the winter.

Sonja Turk had no need to worry about selling her works. Customers came from as far away as Königsberg and Kaunas to give her commissions, for which they were prepared to wait a year and more. Some of them had to turn back with no hopes of owning a rug, because they did not "inspire" the weaving master, that's right. Folks said that Sonja Turk lived on goat's milk, honey, and fish which a fisherman brought her twice a week— until the man began to suffer from insomnia and had to give up fishing. Rumor had it that she was engaged to Konrad Segatz for a while. Son of the richest cattle dealer in Lucknow, Segatz had returned from Chicago after the death of his father to take over the considerable family fortune. He not only commissioned her to make him six rugs; he also gave her a loom. But it was not in return for this gift that he was allowed to watch Sonja as she worked; rather, he earned this right by coming to her house during the most bitter days of January and trudging around in the snow until she finally called him inside. But his visits came to an end after he, too, began to suffer from insomnia . . .

And what else did my uncle tell me? Right, that the house had been struck by lightning and burned to the ground before the Lucknow fire brigade could get there. They found Sonja Turk sitting calmly by the unharmed daphne bush, with Bianca's pagan rug around her shoulders and in her lap the book on the art of Masurian weaving, which she had already begun to write. The earth was still warm from the fire when a troupe of Gypsies—not the old familiar ones, but a group nobody recognized—drove up and unloaded beams and boards for a new house, which was constructed on the same spot. This was a larger house than the one it replaced, with a windowless room facing east, from which duck hunters passing in the white dawn claimed to have heard cries for help. Finally, Uncle Adam emphasized, after he had painted a thoroughly sinister picture of Sonja's life, the master weaver had never taken on an apprentice, neither one of the talented girls whom ambitious mothers brought to her nor one of the two brothers who offered to work for her without pay for five years if she would only teach them the craft . . .

Prediction? What prediction do you want to make? I'm curious . . .

Perfect, my dear boy. I can see you are listening your way into our world. For that is exactly what happened: after telling me all this, Uncle Adam assumed that I had given up my plan. He tried out the willow pipe—it produced only one note, a sort of querulous whistle—handed it to me, and climbed contentedly out of the boat. As we approached the house, Uncle Adam put an arm around my shoulders, as if he wanted to make amends for divesting me of the wish that was dear to me.

Four weeks later, after finishing school, I turned up with cropped hair and washed hands at seven in the morning for my first day of apprenticeship at the house above the old drinking trough, as Sonja Turk's first and only apprentice . . .

No, no, go ahead and interrupt. You have every right to ask, for I'm just telling you all this from the vantage point of my experience, unfolding it from my point of view . . .

The book, oh, I see, you want to hear about the language in which the manual on the art of Masurian weaving was written . . .

Absolutely, I already know what you mean . . . You imagined it in some foreign language, a special Masurian tongue. Well, I must tell you that there was no special Masurian language, never has been . . . individual words, yes; private usages full of connotations which only we understood—many loan words from the Polish, pagan and old Germanic expressions which had remained in use, even distorted French words which had arrived with the Huguenots, who came to our parts fleeing religious persecution—but, as I said, there was no special Masurian language. Henrike—if it is true that Henrike is trying to reconstruct her glossary—will back me up on that.

I assume she still does not know whom you have been visiting the past few afternoons, right? I find that most painful of all, that Henrike does not know the reasons that forced me to act as I did. Perhaps she could come to terms with the loss if she knew more, if I could make her understand my dilemma . . .

By the way, she met Conny Karrasch and often talked with him when he visited in Egenlund. The last time she could not shake hands with him, because she had just been fixing her bicycle and her hands were all greasy. Afterward she spoke with amusement of the "well-groomed old boy in flannels." Conny, oh, yes . . .

What did he do after graduation? The same week Sonja Turk took me on as apprentice, Conny became a printing apprentice with the *Lucknow News* under the supervision of Master Weinknecht. That was not to be his final profession, but in any case, his working there had the effect of separating us. Perhaps—I'm not sure—he was equally puzzled at the changes I was undergoing, but perhaps it was not a question of our changing but simply the fact that we were coming to be more and more ourselves and recognized our differences as we grew older.

Anyway, in July of 1920 it became clear how much we had grown apart. It was the time of the great plebiscite. Jaunty Bersaglieri occupied Lucknow, sent in by the victorious Allies to make certain that every Masurian could decide, without fear or favor, whether Masuria should become German or Polish.

In our big house on the bend in the river, the better part of the Homeland Association sat around constructing so-called triumphal arches, painting posters with patriotic slogans, weaving garlands to take down to the railway station, where people were arriving in droves from distant parts in order to vote as native Masurians. What an atmosphere! Everyone, musical or not, felt compelled to sing. Arms linked, Lucknow's men marched twelve abreast over the rough cobblestones of our marketplace. Down by the lake, woodpiles were built for the victory fires. Our statues, whether of cast iron, bronze, or stone, were decked out with wreaths.

Uncle Adam, guardian of our heritage, was one of the most effective propagandists, coming up with historical documents which provided themes for daily articles in the *Lucknow News*, accompanied by striking photographs. Reading Uncle Adam's column, you would learn that even a carved rolling pin testified for Germany. One almost pitied the Polish Party, which was trying to persuade us to go over to Warsaw. They printed their slogans on red and white posters in such small lettering that it hurt the eyes to read them, and offered vague promises to the effect that the family of Slavic peoples was willing to forgive and forget.

But a few members of the Lucknow Homeland Association fell

speechless when, shortly before the plebiscite, posters appeared which were not only highly legible but also remarkable for their boldness of tone and the clarity and force of their arguments. Our old teacher Henseleit was thunderstruck, Fishing Commissioner Dudei enraged, Uncle Adam dumbfounded when one of these posters, peeled off a wall, was spread before them and read aloud. It was so unlike everything the Polish side had previously come up with. There were allusions to the chronic German lust for war, to the German hangover after defeat; Versailles was mentioned and its consequences spelled out, so that no great reasoning powers were required to see the vast economic advantages which would follow from belonging to a peaceable country like Poland, especially now, after another lost war.

These readers reacted even more touchily to historical arguments which the poster recalled in concise and cogent terms, for instance, that after 1410, that is, after the Battle of Tannenberg, the entire country had surrendered to the Polish king, Wladislaus Jagiello, who was probably himself surprised at how quickly the bishops, cities, and landed aristocracy threw themselves at his feet. Further mention was made of the precautionary homage offered by the Pomeranian duke Bogislav VIII and the so-called Hunger War, in which seven German princes fought on the Polish side against the Teutonic Order. Finally, the poster also demanded why the sagacious Council of Constance had ignored the Order's complaints against Poland.

At first the members of the Homeland Association wanted to take drastic action against the perpetrators of the Polish posters, but soon their anger was deflected. Uncle Adam had dug up a document showing that no Poles could possibly have lived in the territory ruled by the Order, because the authorities had not permitted them to. His hand trembled as he held the coarse, brownish piece of paper, and I recall that the document trembled in my hand, too, from involuntary respect; I sensed that though this decree was ancient, it represented telling evidence of our inalienable rights.

I had never seen Uncle Adam in such excitement as during those days before the plebiscite. He himself was surprised by the importance his museum suddenly acquired, and he ransacked his collection for still more testimony to his side's claims.

Every second day Uncle Adam sent me through the streets, where now the tough, spirited little Bersaglieri lorded it over the town, to the *Lucknow News* building, with galley proofs of his articles. I waved the proofs in greeting as I passed the two sentries posted before the building, ran up to the second floor and through the rabbit warren of passages to the room between the classified-ads office and the morgue, where Managing Editor Kukielka could be found. Room is too fine a word—it was a cubbyhole formed by walls of filing cabinets and heaps of newspapers where we could find, behind forever-closed windows, the man who was not only the oldest but also the most genial editor in the world—or so he struck me at the time.

The moment he caught sight of a visitor he offered him his own wicker chair, proffered his snuff box, and invited him to have a drop of buttermilk from his streaked cup, while he himself leaned modestly against one of the cabinets and skimmed the manuscript he had just been brought. He was seldom less than highly pleased with it. Whether one handed him a report on poultry stealing, a description of a train derailment, or a mood piece on All Souls' Day, he considered the items equally significant and at first held every piece of writing as reverently in his hands as if it were the Ems Dispatch.

And without modifying his admiration, he leaned over the table and began to edit, tentatively suggesting a cut here, shyly proposing one adjective to replace three others, and still full of admiration rewrote the piece completely, until finally, clicking his tongue in admiration, he came up with a new ending. Ernst Kukielka, the senior editor of our Lucknow paper . . .

That was true: I only brought him the proofs, which Uncle Adam had already checked over, and which Kukielka for his part admiringly corrected all over again. The cord of his pince-nez dangled, his sleeve protectors swept impatiently over the table. He murmured certain formulations with pleasure before he cut them. Then he modestly scribbled his initials on each galley, the sign that they were ready for the printer, and although he knew that I knew the way to the presses, he never failed to accompany me out into the corridor and to the spiral staircase.

I slithered down to the printing presses, but before bringing the proofs to Master Weinknecht, who sat there in the dim light setting the headlines, I flitted unnoticed to the toilet in the cellar. It was plugged up, as usual, and I grabbed the handy wire snake, which was bent into a hook at one end, pushed it through, and kept plunging it, but the hook repeatedly hauled back damp paper. I was about to give up when something red and white swam up in the water, expanded, and revealed German and Polish letters. To disguise my find, I threw pieces of the *Lucknow News* on top of it, went whistling into the press area, and delivered the galleys to Master Weinknecht, who without a word hung them on a meathook. He signaled to Conny, busy tidying up the type cases, by holding a half-empty beer bottle in his direction.

Conny understood the signal, which meant that some time during the next hour he would have to go out for another bottle of Mazovia beer. Like the other typesetters and printers, Conny was wearing a smock over his clothing; his was still a little stiff and gleaming with newness, but already displayed a good assortment of promising ink stains. He beckoned to me, and we took shelter behind a high table, where with a grin he handed me a little packet full of notices he had printed himself—birth and wedding announcements, obituaries, his first secret exercises, in boldface and semi-boldface—and all of them in my name. They were more or less of this tenor: Today the rug weaver Zygmunt Rogalla passed away, after a long itching attack. Or: Found: in a dressing room of the public swimming pool, two glass eyes. Owner should apply to Zygmunt Rogalla. He explained all the different typefaces to me—most of which I promptly forgot, but I do remember the hammer uncial, because in this type Conny had printed an engagement announcement: Edith Karrasch and Zygmunt Rogalla, both presently residing in Haparanda, announce their engagement. Pursuit pointless. Before his master called him, I had given Conny his first private commission: to print up labels for our museum; I would provide a list of our holdings. As far as price went, I was willing to go as high as two marks, payable in installments . . .

The nurse is coming? That's no reason for you to leave, my dear boy, no, stay a while longer; Nurse Margret is probably just bringing me my medication . . .

Thank you, Nurse. You've met Martin Witt, my most faithful visitor. As long as he is here, I feel better . . .

You want to know if the dressing is too tight? Not a bit, Nurse, not in the slightest . . . I no longer feel the bandages any more than one feels a sweater . . . When you bring my tea, would you be kind enough to bring a second cup for my visitor?

She's gone already. You see, you can tell by the way she bustles in and out what a bad opinion she has of me, her problem patient.

No, she doesn't approve of what I did. Last night she actually accused me of robbing people of their chance of going home. As long as our museum was there, she said, our people could go home—even if only in their imagination; and now that was gone . . . But where were we?

Right, we were talking about the plebiscite. The opportunity for all of us in Lucknow to show the world our feelings and our wishes, our sense of commonality, our wish to belong. There was hardly anyone who did not greet the occasion with joy. So you will understand that I had to tell Uncle Adam what I had discovered in the toilet at the printing plant. He received the news incredulously but immediately passed it on to the members of the Homeland Association. It was the day before the plebiscite. They discussed the matter intensively; I did not hear everything they said, but I could infer a good deal from words here and there, facial expressions, and gestures. When our former teacher Henseleit and the former naval artillery man set out, I slipped away, too, trotted along the lake, since I knew their destination, and arrived at the newspaper building long before them. I squatted behind some lumber in the courtyard and peeked through the ground-level windows into the printing plant, where the printers cast great shadows as they worked by artificial light. Yes, I had had to tell Uncle Adam, because, after all, I shared his confident expectation of victory, and his form of education had long since converted me to his goals.

The two watchers, who were watched by me, arrived after a while in the same courtyard. They moved cautiously, finally hiding out behind a sand sifter as tall as a man. One of them lit a cigarette. When the two Bersaglieri were relieved, I heard denigrating remarks, and the navy artillery man seemed to be aping the Italians' marching style. It was, as I said, the evening before the plebiscite, a dry, flammable July evening. Singing male voices wafted from the marketplace; rowboats decked out with Chinese lanterns plied the lake, and from most of the windows hung flags. The flags were limp, many of them run up in a hurry at home on sewing machines. Over by the silted-up inlet of Little Grajevo almost all the huts lay in darkness; only a single torch moved searchingly back and forth across the slope. The tension, the excitement: the whole town seemed to be living in front of a gigantic theater curtain, waiting feverishly for its folds to open and let us see a play which would confirm each of us in his expectations. Yes, that was what we wanted above all: confirmation.

Presently I saw the little glowing point made by a cigarette tossed into the sand, and looked toward the side door of the newspaper building. Two men were standing there, with a bicycle between them: Conny and Master Weinknecht. A guard called out to them; they stepped under the street light, letting the greenish light fall on their faces, and called something to the guard. Then they both climbed onto the bicycle and pedaled off, toward the marketplace, past male choruses and the illuminated public buildings with their ropings of pine boughs. Master Weinknecht pedaled, and Conny sat on the handlebars. As long as they were maneuvering across the crowded marketplace, their pursuers had no trouble keeping up with them, but suddenly they turned off toward the lake, picked up more and more speed on steep Carpenters' Street, shot down into the park along the shore —the pursuers and I began to run, struggling through the same evergreen hedges and arriving at the pagoda-like quarters of the Lucknow Rowing Club . . .

And now imagine you are standing behind us, watching the beam of a flashlight straying over the wine-red wooden side of the clubhouse, skipping over something red and white, coming back to it, and finally resting on it. Near the entrance, at eye level, hung the first poster, held in place by bubbly glue; Henseleit and his companion peeled it off like sunburned skin. Then they removed all the other posters with which the clubhouse was plastered, a whole ring of posters, that's right, which even shouted out the Polish message over to where the boats tied up. The pursuers seemed to know which direction the poster brigade had taken; they sped over to the Mazovia Brewery and to the board fence protecting the blocks of ice buried in sawdust. There they were again, those red and white posters, their glue still wet. Apparently the poster brigade actually believed they could still influence people out for early walks on the day of the plebiscite, perhaps on their way to vote. The pursuers pulled down all the posters they found, cursing because the gluey paper stuck so to their fingers. They were hard on the heels of the two poster hangers. It was at the beach that the two groups converged, collided.

They were just decking the dressing rooms and the ever-rustling silver poplars with posters: Conny was holding the bicycle, from whose handlebars the pail of glue hung, when Henseleit and the former navy artillery man crept up on Master Weinknecht. One well-aimed punch, and he keeled over and slumped into the warm sand by a poplar trunk. They did not bother with him after that, just leaped with a shout to one side and stopped Conny, who was trying to flee with the bicycle but could not make speed because of the deep, loose sand. One of them dumped the half-filled pail of glue over Conny's head from behind. Then they turned him around and around like a spinning top until he staggered and fell . . .

Don't ask, dear boy, how Conny looked from close up. Later on, by the river, I helped him wash the glue out of his hair and off his skin, and got a good look at the gummed-up eyelashes, the dull walrus gleam of his back, the eyebrows with little globules clinging to them; yes, even his toes had glue between them, which in its half-dried state formed a film in a duck's webbed feet . . .

Conny's eyes were burning. He could barely hear and was terribly dizzy. He was not vomiting, but spit kept gathering at the corners of his mouth. We scrubbed away at his clothes in silence, then slipped along the bank, Conny dressed only in his wet gym shorts, and approached the house where Uncle Adam was still sitting with the members of the Homeland Association, contemplating a colored wall map of Masuria, marked all over with mysterious circles, dots, and crosses. We climbed into the house through a window, tiptoed to my room, and spread Con-

ny's things on the windowsill to dry. I pushed him down onto
my bed and lay down beside him. "You can stay here, Conny," I
said, "till early tomorrow morning." He drew a damp towel over
his face, and then, talking into the cloth, began blaming himself
for not sticking by his master but leaving him there in the sand
under the poplars . . .

Pardon me? But of course, that interested me immensely, and I
didn't even have to ask him. He himself started to talk about it
during the night, while I was wetting the towel for him in my
water pitcher. I had never heard him speak with such bitterness
and such clearheadedness; it was a borrowed clearheadedness, to
be sure, and even then I had the sense that his positions were one
size too big for him, that he still had to grow into them. At any
rate, he despised the simpleminded worship for the native sod
which members of the Homeland Association expressed in their
very eyes if, for instance, they gazed at a Masurian birch tree.
They were creating a new religion out of the idea of the homeland, and the time would come, he feared, when they would treat
foreigners as unbelievers. But what disgusted him most was the
prevailing borderland mentality. Here they were, making so
much of their being "German" in order to compensate for their
own disappointments and shortcomings, and in such an atmosphere minorities were sure to have a rough time. I asked him for
what cause he had put up the posters, and he replied melodramati-
cally, "For Reason." The point, apparently, was that our terrible
history gave everyone the right to live here.

Suddenly he leaped up and wanted to go back to the beach to
help Master Weinknecht, to whom he had attached himself from
the first day of his apprenticeship, whom he worshipped and
imitated even down to the smallest gestures. I had a hard time
quieting him. I applied the wet towel to his face and told him
what from my point of view simply had to be said: that I placed
great value on the homeland; that it was our strength and our
shield. He peeled off the towel, looked at me pityingly. "You've
forgotten something, Zygmunt," he said. "You've forgotten all
the hatred that grows out of this homeland business. Look what
they've just done to Master Weinknecht. And he's not even a
Pole. He doesn't even want Lucknow to become Polish. He simply wants to underline the fact that no one group has any sacred

claim to these lakes and forests. That no one can say, 'It's our homeland, not yours.' That anyone who lives here has the right to call it his homeland."

No, of course not, dear Martin Witt, go ahead and ask . . .

Whether Conny suspected anything? Oh, yes, he had some thoughts on that. The next morning we went back to the place where his master had been struck down. We followed the track of the bicycle to the bridge and sat underneath, dangling our feet in the water and munching my lard sandwiches. There Conny expressed the suspicion that someone must have denounced them. He thought he knew who. He left it at that, ate with gusto, and washed it down with river water. Over our heads the heavy planks of the bridge jounced and jiggled, and sand came trickling down on us. There was a general air of festivity, and I would have liked to be in several places at once.

Since Conny was still plagued with dizziness, I took him out to see Sonja Turk. My teacher met us in a dress decorated with rare and wonderful fish-scale embroidery—that old gift of Bianca's, which she had altered several times to fit her maturing figure. Her hair was gathered in a bun, and the bun itself was fastened with a dozen different hairpins, including short knitting needles. A bulging pocketbook and a black crocheted shawl lying nearby were signs that Sonja had been about to leave the house. She was just dashing down to Lucknow to "toss her vote in the box," but she postponed this errand to take care of Conny, who had to steady himself on my shoulder as he admired the wall hangings. Sonja Turk made me describe Conny's mishap. She appeared neither surprised nor outraged, simply nodded as I talked. Then she donned an apron, poured warm water into a bowl, and brought out a bar of black soap, from which she shaved fine slivers that dissolved in the water. She sat Conny on a chair with his hands behind his back and directed me to tie him down. As she examined her patient, she went into her reasons for taking part in the plebiscite. Ah, you should have heard the considerations which impelled this great artist of the loom to go to the ballot box . . .

Unequivocal? Hardly so! Sonja Turk proved once more that she was an uneasy spirit: "If my vote helps the Poles to win," she began, "then life in Lucknow will have style, but it will be disorganized. If we stick with the Reich, we'll keep thrift and brown gravies. A little Polish liveliness wouldn't hurt us—so long as the Reich looks out for the trains and the potato supply."

Calmly examining Conny's throat, eyes, and ears, she commented on the special talent of the Poles for hearing heavenly music everywhere. "There's no one can read between the lines of life like the Poles," she said, "but what would become of our Lucknow if its citizenry was entirely made up of artist types?" She tossed the question back and forth, weighed each side against the other, giving all sorts of examples. When I asked her if she felt clear enough in her mind to vote, she admitted, "I'm going to vote for both—for one side out of conviction, for the other side out of politeness."

She tossed that off as she drew one of the knitting needles out of her bun, wrapped a bit of cotton wool around the end, and gently inserted it into Conny's ear. She listened, pushed it a bit deeper, and still deeper, until I feared it would come out the other ear any moment. She turned the needle, pulled it out, sniffed the cotton wool, and apparently found an idea confirmed. She then cut a tiny bamboo rod to shape, sucked up the soap solution, and blew it with the strength of a gale into the ear. She repeated this six or seven times. Conny swayed. The soap solution was dripping out of his mouth and ears. He jerked at his bonds, but I did not untie him until Sonja Turk gave me leave.

It is not saying too much to assert that the treatment did Conny all kinds of good. Not only was his sense of balance completely restored; he also felt light, as if he could fly, and eager for new experiences. Sonja Turk secured the house by sprinkling clear water in a half circle by the entrance—no locks, bolts, or chains could provide better protection, to her thinking. Then with Conny and me on either side of her, she set out for Lucknow, to the heart of the plebiscite.

Any adult Masurian had the right to vote either at the boys' high school or the girls' high school, both of which were guarded by Bersaglieri. In front of each stood a so-called triumphal arch, woven of pine and birch branches. Everyone who voted for Germany and wanted to proclaim the fact entered through these arches. A goodly crowd who already had the business behind them were hanging around the schoolyards, standing in groups, smoking, chatting, but keeping a sharp watch on those who were just going in to vote.

Sonja Turk, who had decided on the boys' school, went up to the triumphal arch, plucked out a birch twig, and with a rapid evasive maneuver went around the arch rather than through it. She had almost reached the entrance when to our amazement Uncle Adam blocked her path. He wanted to know whether she realized what she had expressed by what she had just done. Had she not gone under the arch because she had decided to throw her vote away on the Poles? And finally—but this was something only the initiate could understand—he asked whether her private ambiguities were to be extended to the political realm.

My teacher looked at him blankly, then smiled sadly, her smile suggesting a knowledge based on common experience. She then retraced her steps, went under the arch, and entered the school building without hindrance. That was her second vote.

No, we were not allowed to follow her in. We wandered down to the meadow by the river, past the booths selling doughnuts, past the field kitchens dispensing little dumplings. We ate several helpings, then wandered on, past the musicians, the folk dancers, the brewery cart, where a roast ox was being carved, and on through the crowds. Suddenly the word spread through the tents and booths and stands: "The Poles are coming! The Polacks from Little Grajevo!"

Yes, you might think, Martin, that the people of Little Grajevo would have tried to reach the polling place as quickly and incon-spicuously as possible, considering their memory for past humilia-tions and hopeless resistance. I, too, expected them to pass with lowered heads. But there they came, two by two, their children holding hands and going on before them. Some of the girls were wearing their First Communion dresses and had meadow flowers in their hair, some of the boys had on white shirts, with handker-chiefs showing in their breast pockets. The adults were also wear-ing their Sunday best. They walked along, not exactly solemnly, but thoughtfully, their heads held high, apparently determined not to let themselves be either distracted or provoked. Amaze-ment drew people out of the booths and tents when the file of Poles appeared at the schoolyard. We massed together, dividing

down the middle to form a passage, a passage of scorn, or menace. But the Poles did not turn aside. The folk dancers ceased
their capers. The champion eaters' jaws went slack. The Bersaglieri reminded themselves of their duty and tore themselves
away from the light-blue eyes of our Lucknow maidens. Can you
imagine the tension?

Then one of the high-school students began to sing, a song of
protest and triumph: "I have surrendered . . .", the anthem with
which the students had once marched straight toward the mouths
of the machine guns at Langemarck. Now we were singing our
song into the teeth of the Polish demands, and we more or less
expected that the people of Little Grajevo would turn around
and give up their right to vote.

But they refused to let themselves be intimidated. They walked
down the passage toward the schoolhouse, turning aside to avoid
the triumphal arch, which was not for them. Singing along with
the others, I barely noticed what some of the older high-school
students were doing to Conny, who was not joining the chorus.
They were kicking him in the back of the knees and prodding
him with their elbows. Suddenly he gave a groan, ducked, and
tore free from the crowd, who sent a shower of curses after him.
I stayed where I was, spellbound by the people of Little Grajevo,
and remained until they had cast their votes, rejoined their children, and turned back, this time watched in silence by the bystanders. As far as I could see, there was no expression of hope
or satisfaction on their faces—at most relief, and to this day I
do not know why we began to clap once the Poles were out of
earshot.

That's the way it was, my dear boy; after that the celebration
could continue. None of us doubted that the German side would
win; it was only a question of the percentage. I searched all over
for Conny, first by the river, then by the carousels and the shooting galleries. He was not in the crowd listening to the drunken
accordion player, nor in the square in front of the railroad station, where a cheerless bear was lumbering through a dance for
its trainer. By the ice-cream cart hung with pennants I ran into
Edith, surrounded by a flock of boys begging her for ice cream.
Some of them were little snotnoses, others of her own age, and
these she finally obliged, in return for their performing certain

tasks she set for them: one of them had to scramble up the linden tree, another had to polish her sandals. In return she gave each a single cone in the flavor of his choice.

She, too, had been hunting for Conny, in order to take him home, where they had been anxious about him since the previous day. Now she joined me, and together we roamed through the feverish town as far as the new water tower, but in vain. Then we circled the lakeshore, where she finally lured me out to the peninsula, then up to the monument of the Bosnian commander von Günther, where I had not been since the episode with Eugen Lavrenz.

"Here?" I asked. Only then did Edith reveal that a few weeks earlier Conny had decided that he needed a hideout. Naturally he had thought of the monument, and had begun equipping it for the purpose. We looked around cautiously, then clambered over the sharp-pointed wrought-iron fence. First we knocked on the removable plaque and called out his name, then pried it off and squirmed our way into the pedestal, quickly replacing the plaque from the inside. I groped from side to side, and wherever I felt, there was Edith. The small space was filled with her rapid breathing. "Feel this," she said, and took my hand and moved it along the ground. Guided this way, my hand wandered around the little lair until I found something dry and soft which rustled: Conny's bed of leaves. Edith did not release my wrist. She seemed to be kneeling as she helped me see in the dark. "Here, this tin box has St.-John's-bread, don't take any. Those are dried apple rings in that pouch. Over here is his bottle of kerosene; he doesn't have a lantern yet."

Under her guidance I touched a rope, a supply of matches, a wooden toolbox, and a bag of assorted nails. As you can well imagine, I did not feel particularly at ease. Obviously Conny would not be overjoyed to find us rummaging through his secret supplies, and I kept urging Edith that if we did wait for her brother, we should do so outside. She paid no attention, seeming not to be the slightest concerned about how Conny would take this. She persistently and at times impatiently guided my hand, making me guess what each thing was.

Excuse me if I interrupt my story for a moment; the injection is wearing off, I feel the pain coming back. Would you mind giving me those two pills, the little yellow ones, and a drink from the cup . . . Thank you, that will help . . . This pain—sometimes it seems to be replaying the way it all happened: it sends licking flames over my body and showers of sparks down my back . . .

No, no, I'll tell you when I want you to leave. There's still a bit more to today's story.

So, anyway, we were there inside the pedestal when suddenly we heard voices. We crept into a corner and cowered there, lowering our heads so as not to be blinded by the light when they opened the plaque.

At first I could make out three voices; then, after a pause, only one man was speaking. From the sound of it, he was ranting and raving and uttering all kinds of threats. Edith clung to me in her terror, whispering, "They're going to wipe us out, Zygmunt, maybe with dynamite." I could cower there no longer. I scrambled up into the statue, forcing my way upward by bracing my legs against the sides and hauling myself up by my arms until my head was inside the general's and I lent the glitter of my living eyes to his lifeless, dreamy ones. I looked down over the peninsula and recognized five men standing by the iron fence, members of the Homeland Association dressed in black with top hats, carnations in their lapels. One was carrying a great wreath, which he awkwardly hung on the fence after completing his speech. When he had rejoined his companions, they came out with a ragged but mighty "Long live the general!" which startled several crows from nearby trees. I waited for the five to straggle away, then climbed down to Edith, comforted her, cuddled her, let down her coiled braids, pressed her onto Conny's bed to relax her, and did various things, until she remarked fretfully that she didn't want to be pawed . . .

No, that was by no means the high point of the plebiscite celebration, nor its end. Conny did not turn up, and although conditions inside the pedestal were certainly pleasant, we felt we were missing something. Back in town, we let ourselves be carried along by the crowds. Toward evening smallish groups formed and gravitated toward the marketplace, where the ballots were being counted and the result would be announced. I still recall how the euphoria gradually died down, and how in the quiet that followed, torches began to appear. I can still see the people of Lucknow waiting by torchlight, murmuring among themselves. I expected the people of Little Grajevo might also be there to hear the outcome, but I did not see a single one of them.

Finally, the glass doors on the Queen Luise's balcony opened, and the so-called supervisor of the plebiscite stepped out, followed by half a dozen assistants and witnesses, among them Alfons Rogalla, my grandfather. His triumphant grin gave the result away: it had to be an all-out victory. Yet none of those waiting below had counted on such an overwhelming landslide: 9,813 votes for Germany, 17 votes for Poland.

The supervisor of the plebiscite, a certain Snopinski, waved aside the applause; that is, he accepted it with an appropriate gesture and returned it to us: This is your vote, clap for yourselves. Then there were three cheers for love of the homeland, and crates full of torches were carried out of the hotel. I grabbed three for myself, and the crowd formed a torchlight procession, which apparently moved so undecidedly because people did not know where they should go with their joy and emotion. The procession drifted past the official buildings, went by the churches in embarrassment, circled the modern public toilets on the marketplace—not triumphantly, as I said, but troubledly, needing to find someone or something to pay tribute to. It was already late when someone mentioned old General von Zenker. The procession moved more briskly now toward the sparsely lit house of the general, not far from the barracks.

We climbed over the wrought-iron chains, pushed our way into the narrow front garden, spread ourselves around the house, and watched lights going on in the modest dwelling. If you were close enough, you could see old General von Zenker inside being dressed and brushed into shape by a sporty young orderly. The gouty old fellow had not won his fame in local battles, but in far-off China, during the Boxer Rebellion. Supported by his orderly, the general tottered out onto the veranda, put his hand to his cap at the sight of the torches, and forgot to lower it again. Some men from the procession came forward and respectfully reported the result of the plebiscite, whereupon the general nodded solemnly, pulled himself up, as if meaning to launch into a speech, only to suddenly reach for his orderly and cling to his arm. We sang, "Now all give praise to God," the general listening with apparent pleasure. In the middle of the second verse I spotted Conny; he was with a cluster of other boys, straddling the statue of the equestrian knight. Conny was not singing along, just looking at me sardonically, and when I made a sign to him, he slid down from the horse and disappeared.

Yes, dear boy, that's as far as I'm going to go today, you can see how hard it is for me . . .

Questions? I'll answer them next time, don't worry . . .

No, no special requests . . . except that you come again soon, that's right . . .

# 6

A crisis, I know; the doctors hinted as much. My memory, usually so dependable, has retained nothing of the critical days. At most, low-voiced consultations at my bedside, people in white flitting around. They say I was talking in my fever . . .

Pardon me? They did not let you in? That's too bad; I would not have minded your hearing whatever I said in my fever . . . Presumably a number of things would have been confirmed. Excuse me, Martin, I didn't mean to use the familiar mode of address: it just comes naturally after all we have shared. It doesn't offend you? I think I will just continue this way. All right?

Ah, these memories, how much simpler if one could simply suppress them, the way it happened to Uncle Adam when his memory suddenly began to fail—a process there was no reversing, not by any medicine. I say suddenly because, as I recall it, an incident preceded the lapse, a visit, a discovery, a confrontation, yes, in Sonja Turk's house, there above the old drinking trough.

Yes, I remember I was sitting at my loom, struggling with a piece of double weave which I was supposed to do for practice, while Sonja Turk was puttering in the dye room, by the caldron with the steaming dye stew, in which the wool had to cook until it reached the right brilliance. How easily I could have completed the assignment if only my teacher had consented to give me the benefit of her expertise. But her method was to leave me to myself, because she believed that was the way to awaken a person's dormant powers. I was having a terrible time, when I suddenly realized that two parts had been removed from the loom, the cylinder and a lever. I went to the shed, found some bits of wood, which I whittled to shape and inserted, and the pattern was just beginning to emerge when Sonja Turk looked in to see how I was doing. Without a word of praise for my resourceful-ness, she went into her bedroom, fetched the missing pieces, and replaced my crude substitutes.

With a glance she invited me to come into the dye room, where she first threw my improvised parts in the fire under the caldron, then pulled a tin canister down from a shelf. It was filled with marzipan, and Sonja Turk broke off a sizable piece for me—her way of showing approval.

Yes, we were standing there eating marzipan and looking down into the dye kettle when someone came into the house without even knocking. It was Uncle Adam, who seemed agitated, drenched in sweat, his face drawn up in a grimace. In one hand he was carrying a package wrapped in gray paper and tied with a much knotted string. He tramped around the dye pot several times without explaining himself, then stopped in front of Sonja Turk and with a look of helplessness laid the package at her feet. At a sign from her I opened it and unfolded a wall hanging, a double weave of methodical beauty which I immediately recog-nized as my teacher's work. In the corners, in pale green on a light gray ground, was the trefoil motif; the middle was indigo blue accented by red stripes, and at the very center was a motif I had never seen in her work before, a stylized eye, grave and merci-lessly calm. I had the feeling that this eye recognized me and was examining me. It was an eye that had seen everything and could be surprised by nothing. It rested upon me with cold curiosity and did not release me even when I stepped back and out of its range. This rose-red eye with its black iris seemed able to reach every-thing in the room . . .

Don't be impatient, I was just getting to that. Sonja Turk merely looked at the piece, which I draped over a rod on the wall, while Uncle Adam tried to stammer out an explanation, describe an old dilemma, some incomprehensible difficulty. I re-call that he avoided looking at the weaving. So he had returned it, after many years, purportedly because he could no longer toler-ate it. In order to escape from the eye, he had banished the rug to the attic, to the cupboard, and finally to the secret cellar. But nothing had helped. He could not escape the feeling that he was being observed.

I myself had never seen the hanging in his house, but this was the story I pieced together: in the first years he had kept it in his sleeping alcove, where the eye, he claimed, even winked at him, but without disturbing his sleep. But after my mother and I had moved in, the eye had become more troublesome. He could no longer sleep under the hanging, and put it away in the workshop. But here, too, he felt under scrutiny, and moved the weaving to the living room, in an out-of-the-way place between the two huge wardrobes. Nevertheless, the eye remained vigilant and fastened itself on him whenever he so much as passed the door to the living room. And things did not improve when he banished the hanging first to the cupboard and then to the cellar. Indeed, his nervousness grew, since he felt he was being spied on from those hidden places. It was a prickling, piercing, imprisoning sensation, in the long run unendurable.

And then Uncle Adam asked the master weaver, who had listened in silence, to take her present back, after all these years, the present that had been woven especially for him, with hidden wishes, secret implications. Sonja Turk turned to him. How slowly she raised her eyes to gaze at him. She touched the nap of the piece lightly, as if she were dusting it off. Then slowly she returned to her dyeing, gently pressing the mass of wool deep into the kettle with her stirring stick. Finally, she removed her splattered smock and quickly ran her fingers through her rumpled hair; she had come to a decision. She left the dye room and went up to the second floor. Uncle Adam did not notice my presence. He was breathing hard, completely in the grip of his agitation . . .

You're right, dear boy. I, too, began to grasp something, and I understood still more when she returned, unwrapped a little black cloth, lifted the lid of a tiny cardboard box, and held out to Uncle Adam a simple little ring on the flat of her palm. Since he had returned the hanging, she wanted him to take back the ring. The gifts were interconnected, and could not both remain with one person. His gaze wandered from the ring to the wall hanging and back again. I sensed how tortured he was, but the eye in the center of the hanging forbade any change of heart. Neither solemnly nor overdelicately did he take back the ring; he scooped it up quickly and left with heavy tread. At least he managed to say goodbye as he went.

I hurried to the window to watch him cross the drying meadow. He stormed along, following the riverbank, and that was the final audit of a transaction that apparently had never produced much in the way of profit.

Meanwhile, Sonja Turk took down her hanging and with considerable emotion carried it over to the light. She seemed to be still satisfied with her work, after all these years. Yet it was not displayed in the weaving studio with the other pieces. It was placed in a lined cardboard box and entombed in one of the dusky storage areas next to the bedroom.

All this occurred in early summer. A short while later—it was the time of the great crab catch—we had our first experience with Uncle Adam's forgetfulness. It happened one evening when the Homeland Association was meeting. The session began with a feast of crabs, where anything was permitted: cracking, sucking, slurping, snapping, crunching. Piles of empty shells and claws were everywhere. The plates had puddles on them, the napkins were drenched through. You should also picture pieces of nibbled bread and a few overturned glasses. Now it was time to elect a new chairman and a new vice chairman, not by secret ballot, but by a simple show of hands. The election went without a hitch: Uncle Adam became chairman, and Bilitza, who had smoothly reverted to the land registry office from his tank turret, became vice chairman. The membership congratulated themselves on the election, toasted the new officers, then sat up straighter in their chairs to listen as attentively as possible to the customary acceptance speeches.

Uncle Adam heaved himself to his feet, threw his head back, seeming to be receiving inspiration from on high. His air of dignity was unusual. I was not the only one expecting a disquisition on the remote past that would lead into mystic territory. But apparently he had something else in mind this time. First he thanked everyone for the confidence they had expressed in him by electing him their president. Then he paid tribute to the outgoing chairman, and while the applause for Arthur Ruchartz was still vigorous, he went on to give thanks for the "silvery blessing" of the local waters which they had just enjoyed, for the incomparably delicate whitefish. Someone called out jestingly, "Since when does the whitefish have claws," whereupon Uncle Adam shook his head at his own mistake, shifted to the other leg, and forged ahead with his speech. He briefly reviewed the tradition and the financial status of the Homeland Association, then discussed its present objectives. As he viewed it, recent developments required the association to assume the role of watchman, protector, and defender.

He saw the homeland threatened, the sense of homeland wavering, the pride in homeland vanishing. He saw the menace wherever he turned, one particularly dire example being the great border highway slated to run from Lötzen to Poland via Lucknow, a "poisonous, root-destroying band of asphalt." He painted dreadful pictures for his listeners: dying forests, homeless wildlife, unappetizing mushrooms. But the worst of it all was that the highway was to cut through the bog, so rich in archaeological material, the bog at the bottom of Castle Hill, where the shy kite brooded, and the rare black stork. True, he did not mention the black stork. He had named the kite, and now apparently wanted to add the black stork. Instead, he started, looked around in confusion, as if begging for help, struggled to capture the name he had always known, which had now slipped from him. Little bubbles of spit burst between his lips. He raised his right hand in supplication. But the name did not come to him, until his predecessor, speaking in matter-of-fact tones, supplied it: "You must mean the black stork."

The rest of the speech went off well; Uncle Adam showered us as usual with a wealth of dates and facts, and to judge by the applause, no one felt there had been anything amiss.

But the very next morning, at breakfast, this seemingly harmless lapse revealed itself as the onset of a serious affliction which demanded more of us than we felt able to give at the time. Imagine: we were sitting at the table, and my mother had just poured some sour milk into her bowl, into which she stirred crumbled brown bread. Uncle Adam wanted to ask for the pitcher of sour milk, was already holding out his hand for it, but in the midst of the motion a shiver went through him, his lips parted violently, and the word would not come. He silently took the pitcher, obviously embarrassed, and helped himself, while my mother and I exchanged troubled glances and secretly watched him. But all we could see was Uncle Adam eating with his usual moderation. At the same meal we witnessed the fact that a person can totally forget the words for "fork" and "salt." And I still remember that when we supplied the words for him, he repeated them uncertainly, as if he had never spoken them himself.

More and more words slipped from him, words for the simplest things. He would sit at his workbench staring helplessly at his hammer, and only after I had named it for him, would he pick it up and go to work. But it was worse than that. One day when I was leaving for work, he unexpectedly put his arm around my shoulder, pressed me to him, and looked at me with brooding tenderness, digging so hard in his memory that tears came to his eyes. With a start I realized what he was looking for, and said, "Zygmunt, Uncle Adam, I'm Zygmunt," after which he nodded and whispered, "Yes, my boy, Zygmunt. Now take good care of yourself."

He forgot my mother's name only twice. After that she put on a name tag, and when he looked at her with a tortured expression she simply tapped the name tag, where IDA was written in large, black letters. He forgot appointments, plans, projects. How often I saw him setting out purposefully for somewhere or sitting down to his workbench, only to lose track of his aim and remain there, straining to recapture it. The two Lucknow doctors who examined him could not help him. The world around him became nameless, a strange, white world he could no longer possess because he could no longer name it. Several times neighbors brought him home—he had forgotten where he lived. After that I always put bits of paper with his name and address into his pockets. And just as we had once made labels for all the items in the museum, I now went about labeling the most common objects. Sometimes it seemed to me as though we lived in a world which had to be spelled out anew each day, as in a child's first reader . . .

Pardon me? You want to know if the process was irreversible? That was the strange part. Sometimes he would remember a name out of the blue, like an island emerging from the waves with volcanic force, and when that happened, he repeated the word happily as if he wanted to hold on to it forever . . .

But what was I about to tell you? Right: along with the names the significance of the objects left him. I had taken over the tours of the museum and one time conducted a flock of eighteen girls from the Lucknow School of Household Arts through our collection, with Uncle Adam at my side. He went along, not to keep an eye on me, but only to be able to read the labels on the objects again and again. I lectured on, ignoring the girls' giggling or inattention; I felt superior to all that, secure in my alliance with the objects, from which I had already learned that resisting distractions is a condition of continuity.

But after the tour I slipped away and went to my room to puzzle out why the girls had seemed so much more interested in my knickerbockers than in the Sudauese jewelry and why they giggled at the names of our old gods, Perkunos, Potrimpos, and Pikollos. I was ruminating over all this when my mother rushed in and dragged me into the entry hall, where Uncle Adam was distributing farewell presents to the girls: household objects from our collection. I stood there dumbfounded, until I saw him giving away a two-hundred-year-old bridal dress. Then I knew what I had to do.

I rushed from the house, caught up with the teacher, and explained what was happening. Together we relieved the girls of their gifts; the whole experience was still a joke to them. Uncle Adam seemed not the least annoyed when I returned with the objects; he offered to help me put them back in their places, did as I said, read the words "coffee cup" from one of the labels, thought this over, and commented, "There's nothing like a good cup of coffee, is there?"

A threat, that's it; Uncle Adam became a threat to the museum. Things reached a point where we had to lock him into his workshop during the tours. And I realized what a heavy responsibility rested on me, now that we could no longer count on Uncle Adam.

There came the night I was lying in bed, with everyone else asleep, when I suddenly spied the largest column of ants I had ever seen. They were black ants, creeping out of their villages in the old wall and swarming into my room from under the loose baseboard, heading straight for their goal in the icy moonlight. Each had his own destination, one heading for a historic flour sifter, others swarming over rolling pins, mangles, straw crowns, even bridal dresses: black armies of highly disciplined ants. They took booty, hauling away threads and scraps and crumbs. I watched them for a long time at their business and visualized how much they could destroy, how many tokens of past existence, and with the tokens also the meaning and significance they contained. That is a point, by the way, on which Conny often argued with me later. He maintained we did not need to give our existence significance; for him existence had its own meaning, and he considered any attempt to embody significance in objects a conceited error of the provincial spirit.

In the course of that night I once more came to the conclusion that all the threatened objects belonged to the meaningful continuity of the past. They had helped overcome the transitory quality of life. They had given happiness. They must not be allowed to perish. We were under obligation to preserve this past from total oblivion.

Why? Because the past was what had led up to us. Because we owed all our experience to it, including the experience that everything eventually passes on. There is only one way to combat the sorrow for things past: to give them significance.

I suppose you see it differently. But let me tell you what I did: I got up, stepped over the rampaging hordes of ants, groped out to the shed, filled a battered old milk can with water, and crumbled lime into it. I carried the bubbling mixture back to my room and turned on the light. The army took to its heels, rushing back along its trail of scent, back to the cracks in the walls. I was able to pry loose the baseboard. Using a funnel, I poured the seething lime water into the hidden labyrinth of ant homes. It bubbled and hissed as it trickled over the cracked mortar, and I heard stirrings inside the wall. The ants did not emerge . . .

All right. Now, would you plump my pillow and help me sit up higher, I keep sliding down into the hollow . . .

There, that's better; I can talk better this way . . .

Uncle Adam continued to function as president of the Homeland Association. He had to sign petitions, make decisions, rally the membership to various drives and projects. He had to be available to the members, hear their grievances, deal with their indignations. My mother often transcribed the proceedings for him or pressed him to make notes for himself. We did what we could to conceal his illness, which is what we considered it.

We managed fairly well, too, until the fateful Sunday on which certain members of the Homeland Association gathered on Castle Hill, at dusk, beneath the seven giant spruces. They were all boys or men, all armed with hidden metal stakes, light crowbars, wooden slats. I observed that, and observed how their interest focused on a figure in a black coat, the only girl there, Edith, of course, who stood there stiffly beside the fishing commissioner, looking self-possessed and unapproachable. She did not respond to any greetings, and showed neither fear nor impatience, although the worst was still to come. Several times Uncle Adam stepped up to her, whispered something to her, apparently comforting her, but she did not answer even him.

I sat behind her on the low stone wall I myself had built in the days of our cemetery games. I was unarmed, and I looked at her and tried to imagine what had happened to her the previous evening in Little Grajevo when she passed the Mushroom Cellar, which was the name of their little tavern. I imagined her passing on her way home, hearing music and stopping to listen, peeking in the window of the tavern, so absorbed that she did not notice the two boys sneaking up behind her. And I pictured what followed: how they dragged Edith to the beach by our old amphitheater and pushed her into the reeds. And there it happened, or so I imagined it, on the spit of land where the actors in our Masurian pageant had been costumed.

Yes, I tried to imagine it, as we waited there for darkness, a group of about twelve silent men and boys. Not Uncle Adam but Fishing Commissioner Dudei gave the signal to set out. First we hastened toward Borek Forest, working our way along the edge of the woods where the trees were not so close-set. Now I, too, had a club. Where the forest dipped toward the bay of Little Grajevo, we separated. I stayed in the same group with Edith, Uncle Adam, and the fishing commissioner, who made no effort to creep up cautiously. They strode along to the Mushroom Cellar, full of righteous desire for revenge.

Picture the tavern as a building of roughly hewn logs, slightly larger than an ordinary house; it was, in fact, a former stable. On its roof grew moss, sod, little birches. There were rough flower boxes at the windows. In its front yard was a well with a wooden housing and a number of battered milk cans. Without pausing to check the lay of the land, we crossed the front yard, counting on our fellows to be blocking avenues of escape, and pushed through the door, freezing there shoulder to shoulder as if posing for the photographer.

Even though we still kept our weapons hidden, our posture was sufficiently menacing for the seven or eight people drinking their Mazovia beer in the low, smoky room to stand up slowly from their benches, back away, and seek safety in huddling together. The only person I recognized was Anna Hauser, the one girl there. She stared at me in shock, as if she expected me to explain, but I had nothing to say in this situation. That was up to Uncle Adam and the fishing commissioner, especially to the latter, who seemed pleased with the fear we inspired in the group and in no hurry to allay it. When he finally stepped into the middle of the room, I thought he would first send Anna away, but he instructed everyone to stand up, backs to the wall, the girl, too. They obeyed. They let go of each other and lined up along the wall, beneath a picture showing a deserted bridge over the Vistula. A breeze swept through the room, and Edith stepped over to the fishing commissioner, looking discomfited, her eyes cast down. He forced her to look up, forced up her chin with the end of his wooden slat, and ordered her to look at each face carefully, going down the line. As Edith scrutinized every face, I did the same. For me every one of them was suspect.

Edith went from face to face, even staring silently at Anna Hauser. I had the feeling that the two girls looked at each other mercilessly. She turned away and shrugged indecisively. "Who was it?" the fishing commissioner demanded. "Who?" "Don't know," said Edith, and wanted to rejoin us. But the fishing commissioner would not have that. He directed her to look at the faces again and search her memory. "That kind of thing you don't forget. It stays with you for the rest of your life." Edith shaded her eyes with one hand, as though she were blinded by light or were trying to see something far away, then blurted out, "That one, maybe that one." She pointed at Heini Hauser, standing beside his sister, a gangling youth, who returned Edith's gaze scornfully. "Are you quite sure?" the fishing commissioner asked. Edith replied, "It might have been him; if it was any of these, then him." You should have seen the way Heini Hauser ducked, gathered all his forces, and leaped over Dzietko, the tavernkeeper, who was standing at the rear. He kicked open the door and flew out into the dark, so startling us that we could scarcely have stopped two or three others if they had followed him. But the others stayed, paralyzed by fear and long experience.

After all of this, we had to take some action. I don't know who delivered the first blow, since we advanced across the room in a body, but once it had fallen and had called forth a moan, every one of us seemed released from the tension, and we let loose in the violent desire for further release. That was not a moment in which to watch oneself in action. Too much fury had built up, and anyone there seemed fair game. We struck out at random.

We beat them into a tangle of bodies, and were not satisfied to leave them lying there groaning. We dragged them out to the well and emptied bucket after bucket over them; even Anna was not spared. Then we left them to pick themselves up as best they could while we went back into the tavern and sat down on the benches and chairs . . .

Where was Edith during this time? She did not go out to the front yard. She had stood by, watching us wielding our weapons, but without showing any sign of satisfaction, rather with pure interest. She seemed to feel no emotion and had nothing to say about what had happened; even when the fishing commissioner came over and asked her if that hadn't been too much for her, she merely shrugged. And by the way, his question was not asked solicitously; I had already noticed that the fishing commissioner regarded Edith with untempered bitterness, and had heard him remark to Uncle Adam, "When that kind of thing happens to a girl, you can be sure she brought it on herself."

In any case, we took over the tavern, had Dzietko bring us drinks and listened with strong emotion to former officer Bilitza, who brought out in jerky phrases what everyone wanted to hear: sometimes national differences had to be underlined again . . . teaching people a lesson, however rough, was a necessity . . . Even if we'd gotten used to them, that didn't mean we liked having the Polacks here. If you meant to be the master of the house, you had to make things clear . . . We nodded our approval.

And listen to this: Bilitza had just done proposing a plan for tracking down Heini Hauser that very night when Uncle Adam came out of the back room carrying a stack of checkers sets he had apparently found there. He cheerfully put down the boxes, went from table to table distributing the boards, and seemed not to notice the others' hissed disapproval. Nor were they only irritated; I saw that our Homelanders were also distressed and startled. Bilitza sat there as if staggered, while Uncle Adam tranquilly passed out the sets and then prepared to speak.

He seemed to think we were the members of the Lucknow checkers club, and welcomed us as such, gathered here to play a checkers tournament. Then he held forth on the game itself, its ancient origins, the symbolic significance of jumping the pieces over squares and over each other. By this time I had to intervene; I dragged him over to my table, forced him down on the bench, and tried to distract him. Suddenly the room was full of incomprehension, mistrust, whispering, and sidelong glances. Then Bilitza came over to our table, sat down diffidently, and looked frankly into Uncle Adam's face, before asking when he had thought up this strange scene. Uncle Adam did not understand; he rattled on about the Greek origins of the game, and whenever he addressed Bilitza in particular, he called him "my dear Waschulzik." He seemed in no way aware that anything was wrong. He ordered a brandy, with it smoked bacon, and then a bowl of lentil soup. A number of the others did the same.

Conny appeared just as Dzietko was collecting the dirty dishes. He stood in the doorway, apparently surveying our condition. He stood there, looking scornful, breathing hard, not acknowledging my wave. Then he went past the other tables to Edith, stared down at her until she stood up and asked him irately, "What is it? What do you want?" "Come along," he said. She followed her brother and like him paid no attention to what was called out to her. She calmly pushed aside an arm that reached out to hold her back, and together they left the tavern. I followed.

They stayed in the front yard, by the well, with the wooden spout between them, standing there for a long time, facing each other in silence. Someone who did not know better might have thought they were lovers who could not bear to part. Perhaps you are expecting what I was expecting: a violent argument, recriminations, self-justification. Nothing of the sort. After a while they even took each other's hand and sat down on the edge of the well. Conny spoke quietly and patiently to his sister; he seemed to be repeating himself, since she kept shaking her head in the same manner, refusing to accept or admit to something. I lay there, pressed into the moss on the tavern roof, and watched an Edith who expressed herself without words, just nodding or shaking her head. After Conny had apparently persuaded her, she started whimpering . . .

Convinced her of what? I'm coming to that, son, I'm coming to that . . .

He stroked her arm and tickled her cheek. He spoke insistently to her and led her back into the tavern.

Conversations ceased as they entered; everyone could see that something had happened. Conny made Edith stand there and carry out her promise. He had foreseen her qualms, how hard it would be for her, and he put an arm around her and drew her to him, gently reminding her of some compact, despite the distrust and open hostility of the fishing commissioner.

The first words she said were almost inaudible. She had to repeat that she had made a mistake. It had not been Heini Hauser, or in fact any of the boys of Little Grajevo, as she had at first presumed, in her state of shock. Now that she was calmer she could remember better. With Conny's encouragement, she confessed jerkily that it had been Hugo Bandilla who had lain in wait for her in Borek Forest, had invited her into his underground lair, and, when she refused, had taken her there forcibly. Edith sobbed dry sobs, almost mechanically. I saw her glance up to see the impression her confession was making, and as she did so, the fishing commissioner stood up, climbed over his bench, pulled Edith roughly toward him, and struck her full in the face. He pushed her to the door, came back, pointed at Conny, and said, "You—we'll take care of you later." . . .

Pardon me? Embarrassment? No, you're wrong there. There was not a moment's embarrassment. Just thirst. All of a sudden most of us felt overcome by thirst. The Homelanders sent Dzietko running back and forth, stumbling over himself to bring one round after another to the tables. No one said another word about Edith, at least not directly, but everyone was thinking of her as Bilitza gave voice to a plan which the Homeland Association should propose to the city government for solving the problem of the ethnic minorities once and for all.

His idea was to turn the northern part of the Borek, together with the inlet of Little Grajevo, into a nature preserve. Since people were prohibited from living in such preserves, we would be rid of the unwelcome villagers. We could insist on the nature preserve because we would be losing our bog to the new highway. He asked how this struck us, and everyone seemed to back him, except, of course, for Conny, who fidgeted on his bench, sighing and rolling his eyes but not saying a word. After he had finally managed to fish a drowned fly out of his beer, he tossed down the rest at one swig, poked me, and proposed I go home with him.

I went along, tortured by a guilty conscience and an unfamiliar itch which manifested itself as we left the Mushroom Cellar under the critical eyes of the Homelanders. But when Conny beckoned, I had to join him, although, as I was coming to realize, he seldom had more to offer than opposition.

We sat there under the old wild pear tree, in the whitish night of that time of year, dangling our feet in the water. "You'll see," Conny said, "pretty soon they'll be calling Little Grajevo a disgrace and branding every foreign resident a disturber of the peace. Jealously clinging to their past, they'll raise the cry for racial purity, and that's dangerous: talk about purity, and you start eliminating the impure." And I knew who was speaking out of him or speaking with him when he said, "Purity is one of those watchwords for people who feel they've got the raw end of the deal."

I was hardly listening to him. I had to think of Edith, of the way she had calmly accused Heini Hauser, of her readiness to take it all back after some prodding from Conny, and I pictured the scene when she and the fishing commissioner came home, while the Dudei girls eavesdropped behind the door.

"How will they treat her, do you think?" Conny shrugged. "They might send her to Neidenburg," he said. "They're always threatening to send her there, to the brickworks that a brother of the fishing commissioner owns. They've decided she's to learn a trade; they make stoneware there, along with bricks." When Conny said that, it crossed my mind for the first time that we ought to take Edith in with us; she could care for Uncle Adam and help my mother. It crossed my mind, but I did not mention it. Although I thought she deserved to have her knuckles rapped, I felt sorry for her.

We stood up without another word and went to my house at a leisurely pace. We both wanted to prolong the leave-taking, and when I suggested that he come up to my room for a moment, he accepted as happily as if he had had the same idea and had hesitated to propose it only because of the lateness of the hour. And this may make you smile, but we let ourselves give way to emotion, and when we were in my room, standing at the open window, we found ourselves shaking hands without premeditation, only to express what could not be said in words.

But what did I want to tell you? Ah, yes, the disclosure Conny made there in my room. He told me he meant to take part in the competition being sponsored by the *Lucknow News.* The topic was "Faces of the Homeland," and he had already finished his piece, with the encouragement of Master Weinknecht.

Conny fished a lined notebook out of his shirt, looked at me, smoothed it out on his knees, shone a flashlight onto the pages, and read his piece to me in a whisper . . .

Pardon me?

Why, of course, I remember his story—if one can call it that . . .

All right, if you insist . . .

"Daily Gifts" was the title he had chosen for his piece, yes, daily gifts . . .

All right, here goes: a public lecture was announced in Lucknow with considerable fanfare. A researcher called Goliass was to report on the results of a six-month study during which he had traveled the length and breadth of Masuria to investigate the Masurians' concept of happiness. But not only that; as the announcements for the lecture indicated, he had succeeded in finding someone who was indisputably the happiest Masurian, and this man was willing to appear in public and reveal the factors that had made his exemplary happiness possible. Long before the presentation began, the doors of the hall had to be closed because every seat was filled.

Goliass spoke first, explaining in somewhat too much detail the nature of the task he had set himself, surveying the many possible interpretations of happiness, and developing a definition of the Masurian concept, which he illustrated with his recently acquired insights. Apparently he had found the most durable happiness among beekeepers, broommakers, and loggers. He calmly overlooked the audience's restlessness. They were there to see the happiest Masurian, but Goliass dwelt on each station of his journey, set forth his research methods, and then offered a blow-by-blow account of how he had come upon Paul Plaga, who, as he himself testified and his family and neighbors confirmed, had been happy every day of his life.

Finally, Goliass summoned Paul Plaga; an ancient, stooped little man in a threadbare suit got up from the first row. He mounted the podium and gazed earnestly at the researcher, who was giving a few biographical details and sketching in the circumstances under which his happy man passed his days.

He was a cottager, seventy-eight years old, who had raised six children. Speaking a little louder, the social scientist asked if it was true that he, Paul Plaga, had been happy all his life, every single day? The old man nodded in confirmation: yes, every single day. The researcher then asked whether this remarkable feat had been achieved by any particular method, and the old man nodded again and said, "Can't get nowhere without a method." Now the researcher asked whether he, Paul Plaga, might be willing to reveal this method to the audience, whereupon the old man reached into his breast pocket and pulled out a piece of paper, which he unfolded with great solemnity.

The sheet of paper looked like a schedule. Across the top of the page the days of the week were written in seven different colors, and beneath them a text in many short paragraphs like the text of a law book. The paper itself was very old, a brownish, rough-textured paper whose edges showed traces of rust from nails Paul Plaga had carried in his pocket. The researcher asked where this paper came from, and Paul Plaga reported that his great-great-grandfather, a peat worker, had received it from Masurian bog folk, in gratitude for his inventing a wooden peat spade.

Now the researcher asked the old man to explain the significance of this document. And Paul Plaga explained that it contained the sum of all experience with the seven days of the week.
The many people before him who had collected and transmitted
this experience had come to recognize that every day had its own
character, and they were convinced that each of the seven days
of the week exercised its peculiar power over everyone. Since
resistance was futile, the important thing was to get on the days'
right side, and that meant doing what they specifically required
and avoiding what they frowned upon. In his view, accumulated
experience indicated that a sinister rivalry existed among the
different days; they carried on their struggle by contradicting
one another's recommendations and prohibitions; thus, the best
course was to conform strictly to the demands of each day as it
came.

And then Paul Plaga said that as long as he could remember,
this table of accumulated wisdom had hung on the inside of the
door of his house in Kerwixen; no one could help seeing it as he
left the house. And the whole family made it a habit to study
each day's individual characteristics before setting about a task.
And because they took such care to do what the individual days
required, all seven days looked upon them with favor and treated
them well. Not only did they send them happiness; they also let
them understand why they were happy. "In the long run," Paul
Plaga said, "the only people in Masuria who will find happiness
will be those who go according to the daily gifts."

He disregarded the whispers and smiles in the audience; secure
in his wisdom, he stepped down from the podium and tacked the
paper to the front of the lectern, and glanced over at the researcher, who nodded to him. Without changing his tone of
voice, Paul Plaga set forth the factors on which happiness depended.

"MONDAY does not like it if wood is sawed or chopped first
thing in the morning; someone you know might have an accident.
Anyone who takes on a new job will find the year too long.
Anyone who slaughters a chicken will have to slaughter three
chickens, for company will come and stay the whole week. Anyone who accepts a gift from a woman must fast in the evening.

Anyone who hires a person on Blue Monday to do work in the house must expect to be robbed. Anyone who gives away honey or syrup will be helped when he needs it.

"On TUESDAY anyone who eats meat—roasted or boiled—must be prepared to need false teeth in a year's time. But anyone who drives his livestock out to pasture will be rewarded, for it will fatten up nicely. Any person who cannot find any other day on which to marry will have a marriage full of strife; he should also brace himself for some act of violence. Anyone who puts a broody hen on a nest will multiply his flock of layers. If a boy child is born around vespers, it is to be feared he will become an arsonist. Anyone who sets out for market will not be disappointed. Anyone who sneezes repeatedly in the morning is in for a serious illness. If herons fly over the house and do not return before nightfall, a burial is in the offing. No bread will burn in the oven.

"WEDNESDAY is no day and no evening; anyone who moves on this day will never have to leave his new house. Anyone who sows beets and wheat will receive his due. Anyone who publishes his banns will have nothing to regret. If someone counts the money he has put by, he may find he has more than he started with. Anyone who cuts leather will have hardly any left over. If you don't pamper an unexpected visitor, you will lose an inheritance. If you have swept away all the cobwebs while cleaning the parlor, you should bring your neighbor some yeast pancakes. Anything that is repaired will not break again. Anyone who catches a disease will be a long time in bed.

"THURSDAY gives and takes like no other day. Anyone who brushes his hair in the evening or does the washing and dumps the water out the kitchen door will have nightmares in the house. Someone who uses the spinning wheel will suffer from insomnia. Anyone who digs something up before dawn will walk in darkness for a long time to come. Anyone who does not feed his horses before supper risks having the colic come in the night. Anyone who gives birth should place the baby under the table at once, lest it become a person with second sight. If you have a sick animal, have the hands laid on it today. Anything round must be covered with a cloth. Anyone who complains of pains should take baths before daybreak and should repeat these on the next two Thursdays. Anyone who meets a man with thick lips will do well to lay his traps and his nets. If the farm dog begins to bark without a reason, one should drink linden tea.

"FRIDAY wants to be a wedding day. Anyone who sings as he is getting up will not be able to make gelatin stiffen. Anyone caught by fog in the peat bog should make seven more piles before knocking off. If someone manages without salt, he will be honored in an unexpected way. If someone has to change bandages, it is advisable to give away dried fruit beforehand. Anyone driving to his wedding in a coach should secretly place a straw doll under the box; horseshoes one finds must be spat on three times before one throws them behind one. Anyone who takes on a new job will find the year short. Anyone who weaves baskets, binds brooms, goes gleaning in the fields, or saws boards will find lost tools in the evening.

"SATURDAY wants to smell of soap. Anyone who spins will soon find maggots in the bacon; anyone who begins something new must prepare to lose his poultry. If no sand has been scattered in the front hall, the windows may not be opened. Anyone who finds only necks in the blood pudding must watch his purse. If you shear sheep in the afternoon, your toes will get chilblains in the winter. If a woman's petticoat shows under her skirt, the Saturday will be longer than the Sunday. Anyone who has not 'attended to' anything in the afternoon will find his eyes tearing. Anyone who does not get a piece of soap thrown in free by the grocer will soon suffer a plague of mice. Only by the fence does one meet pleasant company.

"SUNDAY does not want doors, cupboards, or graves to be open. If a dead person is not buried, soon another relative will die. Anyone who touches the threshing flail will find the milk turning sour as it comes from the cow. Anyone who has fed the animals need only wait for the ringing of the bells. Visitors will bring along their own food, and if you offer them elderberry juice, they will leave substantial supplies behind. Anyone who is baptized on Sunday might well develop the ability to 'see the dead.' Anyone who gathers mushrooms must not carry a knife; anyone who goes into the blueberries must not follow the magpie. Anyone who starts a peat fire on an empty stomach need not blow on it . . ."

It was striking that the longer and more willingly Paul Plaga read and expanded upon the recommendations and prohibitions of the separate days, the quieter and more attentive the audience became. At the end of his explanation, the researcher urged them to ask questions, but no one spoke up. The audience sat there in silence, until the old man folded up his table of wisdom and put it away. Then someone asked if he might copy the chart, but Paul Plaga shook his head and refused even when many people stood up and begged him; someone even offered him money. He seemed a bit tremulous and was obviously in a hurry to get away. When the researcher was asked whether he planned to repeat this lecture here or elsewhere, Paul Plaga answered quickly for him: "No, it won't be given again."

I should add, Martin, that this is only a brief summary of Conny's story—or his contribution; but I wanted you to have some idea of the piece he entered in the competition sponsored by the *Lucknow News*.

He sent in his piece and was more surprised than anyone when the results of the contest were announced on the anniversary of the Battle of Tannenberg: the second prize went to him—with more than sixty entries. The prize was a fourteen-day cruise around the Baltic, with stopovers in five harbors, plus one hundred marks for pocket money ...

Pardon me? Yes, that actually happened: Haparanda was one of those harbors, and Conny had a chance to see whether our childhood dream had any basis. All he could tell us later about "our city" was that they tied up in a cold rain and dashed from house to house in the downpour. Drenched to the skin, they were asked into the house of a railroad employee, where they were treated to herring prepared nine different ways. After the meal their host saw them back to the ship under a tarpaulin . . . Haparanda ...

But a more important result of the contest was that Conny was called in by the newspaper's senior editor. Yes, none other than Ernst Kukielka invited the young printer to his cubbyhole and went over the prize-winning piece with him word for word. The lavish praise was accompanied by merciless editing; then Conny's article was marked "Ready for the printer," and appeared in the paper's weekend supplement. Our museum in Egenlund owned

half a dozen copies, though visitors were apt to pay more attention to the quaint ads than to the text. Conny, the printer, was
invited to write for the paper. I recall he wrote articles about the
big horse fair, the storks in Masuria, and some of our Christmas
customs. His articles were all very popular, so much so that the
newspaper owner, Friedrich Maruhn, asked Conny to his office
and proposed that he drop his apprenticeship as a printer and
become a cub reporter, working under Ernst Kukielka.

Conny hesitated. He waited until his master, Weinknecht, was
out of the hospital, and after talking it over with him, he accepted the offer and moved from the cellar to the second floor of
the *Lucknow News*, and exchanged his smudged smock for a
linen jacket with sleeve guards.

I remember as though it were yesterday the evening he and I
went to the Hotel Queen Luise to celebrate his promotion and
ordered the best of everything, just like the sawmill owners and
high government officials. How could we afford it, you wonder.
Just listen: Conny paid from a leather purse which seemed somehow familiar. It was Edith's purse, which she had given him of
her own free will—at least that was what he claimed—with the
request that he get the money to the Hausers. She had apparently
tried to give the purse to Anna, who had only turned away
bitterly every time she saw Edith approaching. And Conny had
accepted the assignment, with a modest commission for himself.
Although Heini Hauser had given him to understand that it was
no use—they would not be bought off; no sum in the world
could efface the memory of what had been done to them. But
Conny seemed determined. He was resolved to get the money to
them, and together we thought out various schemes.

You will never guess what we came up with. No, don't even
try; it was something only Conny could have cooked up, and we
were so excited that we did not walk across the bridge but skipped.
We skipped all the way to the inlet of Little Grajevo. In the
willows we slipped out of our clothes, then waded into the water,
and dove as soon as it came up to our thighs. We swam over to
the private landing docks and untied the ropes mooring the
Hausers' fish traps, took the lines over our backs, and towed the
traps to the willows on the bank.

The traps were full of wild carp, leather carp, brace, even a few zander. I grabbed the fish one by one, held them by the neck so that their bony mouths opened involuntarily, while Conny stood by, ready to force a coin into each fish's throat, pushing it past the ring-shaped diaphragm. The fish thrashed about and flapped their tails, but there was no help for it; they had to swallow the coins. Only the ones stuffed with silver were allowed back into the traps, where they lay for a moment as if numbed. I stroked their glistening undersides, massaging the coins toward their stomachs. Afterward we towed the traps back to their mooring place. The fish seemed to be in good shape once they were back in the water. At least none was floating belly up as we fastened the traps to the landing dock.

If we had any further wish for that evening, it was to see the Hausers' reaction when they went to clean the fish and found the coins inside. But though Conny kept alert for any clue, no word was ever said about the matter. Neither Anna nor Heini appeared in new shoes or with a shiny new bicycle. They did not even replace the fly-specked candles in front of their picture of the Virgin with proper votive lights. We did not learn what they had done with the money until the following winter, on New Year's Day, the day when the race of the iceboats took place on Lake Lucknow.

But I should mention that it was after our adventure with the coins that I began to weave a friendship rug for Conny, with a red that would safeguard affection, a blue that would prevent misunderstandings, and a motif of trees of life, under which would stand the two Biblical spies, Joshua and Caleb.

On the day of the ice race, an unpatched red sail could be seen heading for the starting line. As we looked over the slim, varnished boat with its custom-made runners and greeted Heini Hauser, who was steering the boat in pilot's cap and goggles, Conny and I were finally sure that the coins had reached their intended recipient. The two-seater was called the *Stormbird*, and next to Heini sat Anna, she, too, in goggles and wearing the longest woolen scarf I had ever seen . . .

What a sensation the smart vehicle created; no one gave much thought to his own chances, not even Simon Gayko, who had turned up in an elaborate boat of his own devising. Conny asked

Heini Hauser how long it had taken him to make his iceboat and received only an evasive reply: "As long as necessary."

You should have seen how this armada went flying across the gray-blue mirror. Runners crackled, whistled, and sang, while the captains tugged at the lanyards, and the wind carried the iceboats along so fast that they were sweeping by on one runner, diagonally across the ice, held down only by the weight of their crews, who braced themselves or lay down on their padded seats. It wasn't long before the armada was thinning out along the course, with the finest sails ahead of the pack, then the billowing rag sails, and finally the sails made of potato sacks. It did not surprise us that a red sail took the lead, flying along proudly in front of its pursuers, rigid and trembling with tension. But right behind Heini Hauser came the gray sail belonging to Simon Gayko's complicated invention. It refused to be shaken off, and headed straight for the buoy frozen into the ice, as if intending to ram it, while Heini Hauser was apparently determined to execute a great swoop around it. As if they had agreed on their positions beforehand, they stormed toward the turn marker, and it was only in the middle and last groups that there was any maneuvering, with warning shouts or shouts of triumph, inconsistent with the gravity that could be observed among the leaders, who had their minds fixed on victory.

And then something began to happen at the turn marker. Conny had no need to point it out to me. I had my eyes glued on Simon Gayko, who crouched on his boat as if rooted to it, let out his lanyard, and with whipping sail turned into the wind and skittered around the buoy in the tightest turn imaginable. No sooner had he accomplished the maneuver than he pulled the lanyard tight. A gust of wind lifted the boat and thrust it forward. Heini Hauser appeared to have ruined his chances, for he approached the buoy too fast and swung far out on the turn, although he braked so hard that a cloud of ice chips flew up around him. But he tacked skillfully, picked up speed, and signaled to his sister that she should lean over the side as he was doing. They were in hot pursuit of Simon, refusing to give up . . .

No, if you're interested, I can certainly tell you. They must have been doing close to sixty-five miles an hour, that's how fast those iceboats could go with a tailwind . . .

Anna's shawl trailed along the ice. They straightened the sleigh by leaning audaciously over the side, and were steadily gaining on Simon, fired by the cheers of the rest of the pack, which had not yet reached the turn. The Hausers noted that Simon Gayko kept turning to look at them, estimating the gap that remained between them. He, too, was leaning over the side, but only with the upper part of his body, not bracing himself as they were. Far ahead the referees were waiting at the goal, apparently expecting a tight finish. The flag which would herald the winner was already unfurled. Although there was the impression that Simon lost his momentum on the last stretch, braked by the dull surface of the thawing ice, his iceboat crossed the finish line first and at once turned into the wind, while the red sail, freed of all weights and restraints, flew not only past the goal line but onward with unabated speed in the direction of the bridge. He'll turn aside any minute now, we thought, but the boat careened on, straight toward one of the bridge's arches.

From a distance, from our gently gliding boat, the whole business looked scarcely dangerous at all, almost like a toy race in which a toy catastrophe was about to occur. Then everything happened so quickly. It was as if the boat were made of matchsticks; the mast smashed into the arch of the bridge, splintered, and tipped onto the boat, which still had so much inertia that it went shooting under the bridge and began to skid wildly on the other side, like an insect that had lost its balance.

We were not the first to reach the stranded *Stormbird*. Some members of the awards committee were there, men on skates who hoisted off the mast, pulled Anna from her seat, and laid her down on the ice with utmost care. As we rode up, we saw Heini Hauser being helped out. He had one hand to his collarbone, but he could walk by himself, and moving stiffly, numb with pain, he first went to Anna and knelt down beside her . . .

That's right, Martin, he had been relying on his brake to the very last, but the brake line had snapped without his knowledge as he rounded the buoy. He crossed the finish line at full speed and could no longer bring the sleigh under control when he reached the bridge.

In any case, Anna lay unconscious on the ice, bleeding from a slash at her hairline. When Conny saw her on the bare ice, he left it to me to slow our boat, himself jumping off and slithering toward Anna. With the ice so slippery, he had trouble stopping. He quickly took in the situation, exchanged a few words with Heini Hauser, then bent over Anna. After a moment he straightened up and told me, "Undo the foresail, Zygmunt." Together we unhitched the sail of the *Stormbird*, laid Anna on the canvas, and lifted her onto our boat, whose seating was broad and even, a better fit for transport than the *Stormbird*. We furled our own sail, and Conny attached a rope to the front of the runners, with which he could tow the boat. Heini Hauser and I followed behind, for as long as the boat was on the ice, it required more steering than pulling. We let Conny lead the way. We passed the whitewashed prison and followed the causeway for some distance. Heini held his collarbone and groaned, but when we had to climb the causeway by the old drinking trough, Heini was able to put his shoulder to the task, and the three of us brought the boat out on the road, which was packed hard with snow . . .

So Conny had decided to take Anna to the estate, and not simply because she had been working there since finishing school and even had her own room, but because my grandfather, Alfons Rogalla, had a telephone. As we came through the gate, the dogs set up a furious barking, all four straining at their chains and snapping. They did not recognize me or obey me, it had been that long since I had been at the estate. Regina Ziemek, now long since known as Regina Pravdzik, rushed from the hen house with a wire egg basket on her hip, hastened toward us full of curiosity, and pointed at Anna, saying, "Drowned?" Heini Hauser kept her from touching Anna; he explained what had happened and crouched down by the iceboat. At that moment my grandfather appeared at the window and scowled down at us.

But Conny was not waiting for a by-your-leave. He pulled open the door to the manor house, whereupon my grandfather came to the door, hobbling on a homemade crutch. "What's up? What are you doing here?" As he listened to Conny's story, he was staring unabashedly at me. "You're Zygmunt, huh?" he demanded. "You've put on a lot of growth from all that food I let you have."

Then he hobbled down two steps, pointed his crutch at Anna, and growled that she could not be brought to her room in that condition. No one here had time to look after her. We had better take her home, to Little Grajevo. Since I knew better than anyone that when he spoke that way there was no appealing to him, I asked if Conny might at least use his telephone to call a doctor. That much he allowed, but went along to make sure we put the money for the call in the metal box by the telephone . . .

All right, now you can give me something to drink again, yes, from the feeding cup . . . If there's nothing left, Nurse Margret will bring more tea, you need only press the bell . . . By the way, she's been more friendly lately, probably because you brought her those flowers in my name . . .

You even chatted with her? There, I guessed something had softened her heart . . . Thank you, thank you, dear boy . . .

Where were we? Right, we took Anna home on the sleigh. In the cabin on the mountainside we found no one in the main room and no one in the kitchen, but there was a peat fire smoldering in the iron stove. We carried Anna into the house and settled her on the cot under a little window. Heini Hauser knew where to find his mother. He left us alone with the girl, and the two of us stood there, our arms dangling uselessly, staring down at her broad-cheeked, tranquil face and the dried trickle of blood by her ear. While Conny went to the stove to put on more peat, I looked around the room and was amazed at the quantity of numbered and labeled boxes everywhere—under the bed and stacked in the corners. *Angel's Hair* was written on one, *Healing Herbs* on another. Just as Conny was closing the stove door, Anna sighed and opened her eyes for a moment. Conny quickly came to her bedside, but she seemed not to recognize him.

When Heini Hauser returned, he was accompanied not only by his mother but also by a vigorous, bulky old woman wrapped in a black crocheted shawl. She walked past us as if we were not there, sat down by the cot, and looked searchingly at the girl, undistracted by the mother's sobs. The old woman placed her hand on Anna's forehead, eyes, and mouth; then nodded to herself and called out something to Heini, who fetched a salt container, went up to each of us, and poured a spoonful of salt into our hands or pockets, as if this were something he had done many times before. I saw the mother creeping toward the cot, then backing off—she was plainly longing to touch Anna. Now the old woman issued another order, and the mother went into the kitchen and returned with a breadboard and a sieve and a flour canister. The peat fire smoked, the air in the cottage grew sweet and dense. I can still see how the old woman beckoned Heini to her, to whisper to him. The boy came over to me and told me I had to leave. He himself held the door and waited with lowered gaze until I was outside . . .

Don't ask, Martin, I don't know why I was sent away, when Conny was tolerated there. I decided to wait for him to emerge, even if it meant hanging around till dusk. When he finally came, he told me nothing. But before we parted on the bridge, under the gas lantern, he handed me a sheet of paper, saying, "Read this." It was the first anonymous threat I had ever seen, only three or four sentences in block letters, addressed not to the Hausers but to the Gutkelch family of Little Grajevo, reminding the family of their native land and recommending that they go back there as quickly as possible, or some surprises would be in store for them. I read the letter several times, not sure of what I ought to respond. Then I handed it back to Conny, and as he folded it with the tips of his fingers, as if hating to touch it, he commented, "Just wait and see. In no time the Teutonic exterminators will be here, teaching us cleanliness and hygiene and flushing out all the non-German vermin." He shook my hand briefly, turned, and headed for the dimly lit house of the fishing commissioner. He was dragging his iceboat behind him, and it kept skittering off the path, as though it wanted to go somewhere else . . .

Pardon me?

No, no, you shouldn't take that back; you're perfectly right. Conny was certainly prescient, more alert to what was going on, and he had more inside information, although I could often too easily tell where his opinions came from. But I've said that already. And although these convictions of his seemed not always to fit him, he was growing into them and making them his own so successfully that gradually one forgot their origin . . .

But I must tell you what news awaited me at home, in our museum on the bend in the river . . .

No, not a break-in; Uncle Adam had disappeared, or at least he had gone for a walk and had not returned. It had been fourteen hours already, longer than he had ever been gone before, and my mother no longer trusted that he would be rescued by some stranger who found his address in his pockets. The ice on the lake was crackling and a howling northeaster was sweeping everyone inside.

We hung out a lantern, bundled up, and ventured out to search up and down the lakeshore and along the river. We checked the railroad station and combed the deserted streets, until finally we turned to the police, who took down all sorts of intimate particulars but could not give us any lead. We did not sleep much that first night for thinking of the terrible things that might have happened to Uncle Adam. We could not believe he might have left us on purpose. Nevertheless, the following morning we began hunting around for a letter or some sort of a will. All we found was an old paper, written in the form of an affidavit and dating back to the day we had moved in. It stated that he had taken us in for an unlimited period and that I was to become an assistant in the museum.

Uncle Adam did not come back, and at last we had to report him missing. From that moment on, we lived in constant fear that we would be notified we had to leave the house, which would revert to his legal heirs. I still remember that we avoided the living room and the workshop and withdrew to our own rooms. My mother packed our belongings, and even the canned goods to which we were entitled were put on a separate shelf. We did not speak of our impending departure, but we were prepared. I thought of it every morning as I set out for Sonja Turk's, and as I hurried home at the end of the day, I tried to steel myself for bad news. But for the interval we remained in uncertainty . . .

No, no, not without a trace, just wait and see. It was spring, at least after the ice thawed, when I learned from Sonja Turk that the famous giant smelt of Nikolaiken had been stolen. This was a wooden fish, three or four yards in length, which had been chained under the bridge there, the king of the fish, half sturgeon, half perch, with an eight-pointed crown on its back just before the tail fin. Legend had it that the fish had landed in some fishermen's net, and had promised them good catches forever and ever if they would return it to the water. The fishermen consulted the town council and agreed, but it seemed prudent to chain the giant smelt to the bridge piling. No one had ever imagined that the fish might be stolen, but now it had happened. Sonja Turk made no secret of the person she suspected: "When the giant smelt disappears, can Adam be far away? A crazy relic like that would be the very thing for his museum . . ."

Mother and I were on the point of leaving for Nikolaiken when we learned from Sonja Turk that the fish had just turned up. The villagers had discovered a trail of something being dragged across fields and sandy paths into a pine forest. There they found the wooden fish suspended between two mighty trees, with two vagabonds asleep on its back. The fellows swore up and down that they had nothing to do with the fish's being there. No one believed them, and they were given stiff jail sentences for purloining the ancient Mazovian symbol of the good catch. But I had not the slightest doubt that Uncle Adam was behind the incident.

Not long afterward we received another clue as to his whereabouts. A crate was delivered at our house. It had come by rail and was so heavy that the men had to roll it off the wagon on skids. They lingered, curious to see what was in this box, which had caused them so much trouble. But since I had already looked at the bill of lading and recognized Uncle Adam's handwriting, I waited until they had gone before opening the crate with a crowbar.

Here was proof that Uncle had moved on from Nikolaiken to Neuenburg. For what he had sent in his demented passion for collecting was neither more nor less than the granite ball from the Neuenburg Tartar Rock, a monument commemorating the siege of 1656, in which the leader of the Tartars had been killed. There was no question of rolling the ball into the museum; too many people would have recognized it. So I buried it that evening in a secluded spot along the riverbank and planted a willow . . .

Pardon me?

No, not any longer; today it is at the bottom of the Baltic, where it will never be found. But I will tell you how that came about, just wait.

Then we lost track of Uncle Adam for several years. We had gradually grown accustomed to his absence and no longer tried to imagine under what name and by what manner he was living, when the cartographer arrived, sent to us by Sonja Turk. He was a pensive man, rather distant in bearing, who had commissioned a wall hanging. He went through our museum without manifesting a single emotion. I recall that he paid with a banknote that was three times the usual entrance fee and waved me off when I wanted to make change. At the end of the tour he asked whether the museum's founder had been Alexander Helenden and whether we had a photograph of him. I pointed out Uncle Adam's picture in the hallway. The cartographer nodded; he had come to the right place.

He had met Uncle Adam, who was apparently calling himself Alexander Helenden and had offered his services to a group of cartographers mapping the swampy outlet of the Memel River. The cartographers quickly realized that he was not to be depended on. He forgot their orders or did only part of what they had assigned him. Yet they kept the old fellow on and were touched by his generosity. He made them gifts of local bobbin lace or carved and painted finials from the masts of fishing boats. He spent about a week with the cartographers. Then came his accident.

I will describe the incident as it was described to me. You must picture the mouth of the Memel—a green delta choked with reeds and swamp grass growing in a stagnant lagoon, impassable without a boat. Since the vegetation made rowing difficult, the cartographers used poles to push themselves along. On the fateful day, Uncle Adam was approaching from the lagoon and sailing toward the dead arm of the river, where the cartographers were waiting. From time to time they observed his progress through their telescope. They were not sure whose path crossed whose, that of the boat or that of the swimming elk. At any rate, they suddenly spotted the elk's antlers alongside the boat. Uncle Adam, in what seemed a sudden decision, threw out a rope, lassoed the antlers, and pulled the rope taut, disturbing the animal's quiet rhythm and drawing the elk closer toward the boat. The elk puffed and tossed its head, and a moment later was submerged up to its eyes as the rope tightened. The elk began to struggle, its hoofs raked the water, and it threw back its head until the antlers almost dipped toward the lagoon. As Uncle

Adam continued to tow the animal along behind him, it grew quieter and followed almost docilely for a while. At moments there was even some slack in the towline . . .

But, of course, elk are excellent swimmers. Some would swim all the way across the lagoon . . .

In any case, Uncle Adam wound the end of the rope around his waist and was sailing along with his prey in tow toward the dead arm of the river, when the elk suddenly felt ground under its feet, scrambled onto a sandbank, dripping and draped with water plants—like some prehistoric creature, as the cartographer expressed it. Once on firm ground, the elk had only to toss his head to drag Uncle Adam out of the boat. The elk did not stay on the sandbank, nor did it change its course. It calmly cut across the sandbank, sinking into the soft ground, apparently without noticing the weight of the body it was dragging behind it, then plunged into the water and swam toward the dead arm of the river. The cartographers jumped into a boat and steered toward the elk, which changed course, heading for the reeds. It crashed into their midst before the men were able to block its passage.

The rope held. They saw it stretched tightly back from the elk's antlers as the animal pushed through the reeds, frightened less by the men's approach than by the weight which it could not shake off. The men followed the elk along the path it had broken through the reeds to a stand of alders on the bank. There the beast stood, almost submissively, its antlers lowered, pawing the ground with its front hoof. The animal could go no farther because Uncle Adam's body had become wedged between two trees, or rather, was jammed at right angles to two tree trunks, forming a barrier. The cartographers severed the rope and drove the elk away with the pole they used for the boat. They carried Uncle Adam to the boat. He died on the way to Tilsit.

This was the story the cartographer told us. As I said, although we had become accustomed to my uncle's being gone, we had not been prepared for such an end. Nor had we come to terms with Uncle Adam's disappearance as definitive. My mother went into her room and cried, longer and more bitterly than I would have expected. I went into my uncle's bedroom, took up the rag rugs, raised the trapdoor, and climbed down into the secret cellar, for the first time since his departure. Although in the meantime we had been declared his official heirs, I had still not felt it was suitable to claim as my own the prize documents and rarest finds sequestered in the cellar.

So I lit the kerosene lantern and shut myself into the cellar. You must not imagine that some sort of *unio mystica* took place. I simply took possession of my inheritance. I looked through everything—documents, tools, weapons—and familiarized myself with them by rearranging them in my own order. I deciphered the documents, handled the tools, and felt the weapons until I could tell one from the other in the dark . . .

You want to know what I learned from them. Well, I learned that these were not simply objects, worn out and cast aside. They were there for purposes of comparison, for us to test our possibilities against. I sensed, Martin, that the more one learns about others, the more one learns about oneself . . .

But what did I want to tell you? Right: after I had promised Uncle Adam in my heart that I would dedicate myself to the museum, I instituted a policy that was to have grave consequences. My mother and our regular visitors did not notice anything, but I secretly moved the copies and imitations into the secret cellar and brought out the originals. I knew I was exposing them to danger, but I was acting from the conviction that even irreplaceable things should run risks. Moreover, I thought the originals would be more effective. It gave me real satisfaction when I conducted my Sunday tours to be able to say that all these items were originals.

My tours! I wish you could have heard me shepherding people through the collection. I leaned more on anecdotes than on dates. I was cheerful in spite of all my gravity, dreamy in spite of all my enthusiasm, and always tried to make the past come alive, so that visitors would apprehend it as something more than merely historic. I spoke of the Sudauese as members of our own family, and I would not hesitate to let certain female visitors wear the oldest necklaces for the duration of the tour. I cast aside Uncle Adam's rule that nothing was to be touched. School classes were allowed to play the devil's fiddles and the humming pot. Whoever wished could try out the old weights and measures. Visitors could slip into the chain-mail tunic of a knight of the Teutonic Order, could twirl the spinning wheel, crawl into the skeleton of a

Masurian bear, sip water out of a wooden dipper. Only the old coins remained under glass. I don't know; possibly it had to do with the style of my tours, but by and by the Homeland Association awarded our museum a yearly subsidy of 175 marks . . .

Pardon me? Is it really that late already? No, no, Martin, I realize you have to go. You have your work to do, while I have to lie still, so the islands of skin can heal . . .

You're right, we will have many more opportunities. No one wants to hazard how much longer I'll be here. You see how much evidence I have piled up. If you really want to know why I burned the museum, you'll have to listen for a long time . . . And how about Henrike? Is there any reason not to tell her you were here today? . . .

She has moved in with her mother? You see, that's what I was afraid of. Now they'll form an alliance against me . . . Duck your head when you enter the organist's house; everything sags there. And don't be surprised if you find Marian Jeromin with them, before I have had a chance to tell you what you need to know about him. Marian, my so-called favorite pupil. He and Carola discovered early on that they—how should I put it—that they had a special understanding; such things are supposed to happen . . .

How hard your hand is, as if you worked with tools . . . Tomorrow again? Splendid. All right, until tomorrow at the same time . . .

# 7

SUDDENLY I started receiving letters, first a short, noncommittal note which revealed the effort that had gone into the writing; then, after I had replied, a new letter three days later, this time more communicative. I was just acknowledging it when I saw our mailman, Karpowitz, toiling up the path with a pale-blue envelope which contained so many words that I had to pay for extra postage. Up to then I had received hardly any mail—who was there to write to me?—but now I was in for a regular flood of letters, as if lost time had to be made up for.

Edith wrote from Neidenburg, where the fishing commissioner had sent her to learn how to "work." She wrote that I was the only one she could confide in, as well as the only one who cared about the kind of person she was and had sympathy for her odd thirst for knowledge and her changeable moods. Something occurred that would probably not have come about had Edith stayed in Lucknow. Separated, exchanging letters, we discovered one another at a distance, had more and more to say, were ready to make confessions which would have been inconceivable in a face-to-face situation. And the more openly and trustfully we exchanged these confidences, the more astonished we were to realize that we missed each other.

We wrote to each other about all sorts of things, and our correspondence became more and more extensive as time went by, simply because we had a great deal to tell each other and assumed that whatever affected one of us or happened to one of us was worth telling to the other.

Well, to give you some idea of what went into the letters: I still remember her writing that she had cut off her corn-colored coils of hair once and for all, and I composed many pages considering all the imaginable hairstyles and recommending the one that would be most becoming to her. And once I wrote to her that a stone ax had been found in a field belonging to the estate, whereupon she replied that she knew for a fact that Hugo Bandilla buried the profits from his smuggling business in earthen jars in the forests and hills around Lucknow. Moreover, she gave a clever survey of the most likely sites for these caches. She wrote that now that she had learned to use the potter's wheel, she wanted to make me a hot-water bottle. She would also be glazing it, so she asked what my favorite colors were, and I devoted a longish letter to explaining why blue, white, and green were my favorites and why I cared for red only at certain times. I wrote that I had been out picking mushrooms with Sonja Turk, whereupon she sent me a table identifying all the local varieties, and added recipes for preparing three tasty kinds. This was the nature of our correspondence, but we also described our emotions, our moods, and our hopes, and traded candid observations about people around us. Something was being born; I felt that keenly on the evenings when I withdrew to my room to sort out the day's events and try to find the language to express my thoughts and emotions.

During this time I was working on my friendship rug for Conny, weaving whenever I found time. I hoped to show the piece at the first weaving exhibit the Lucknow Homeland Association was sponsoring. The show was to be held in our museum. Sonja Turk was cooperating, but without enthusiasm. Sometimes she would stand by my loom, studying the emerging pattern, only to turn away the moment I started to explain what I was doing. When I asked whether she could envision the effect I was aiming at, she replied, "If it's good, nothing need be said, I'll find the meaning myself."

I stayed at the loom after hours, weaving a cluster of trees of life into a background framed in white, blue, and red. Stepping out of the shade of those solemn trees were the two Biblical spies, Joshua and Caleb, holding bunches of grapes. I was not quite finished when Sonja came over and gave me a piece of marzipan. After being laconic for so long, she surprised me with a flood of advice: "Remember, Zygmunt, to let the material speak for itself. You can't match the warmth and softness of wool. So let the material have its say before you try to fancy it up with color. Let the wool soak up the light and give off light, and that'll create the space for you. Don't try to imitate painting, and don't hide what the warp and the weft bring forth on their own . . ."

That's weaver's talk, dear boy; you know how the threads cross each other at right angles to form surface and pattern . . .

In any case, Sonja Turk agreed to let my rug appear in the show. She contributed certain pieces of her own, but grudgingly, and only after being repeatedly solicited by Bilitza and Henseleit, speaking for the Homeland Association. I did not understand her reluctance. All that mattered to me was my pride in appearing in the same show as my teacher.

The first person to hear the news was Edith. After I had mailed the letter, I cut out a little label of white cardboard and painstakingly lettered the words, *Not for sale. Friendship gift to Konrad Karrasch, Lucknow.* When the exhibit was finally mounted, it turned out that nineteen of the twenty-two entries were not for sale, either because they had been lent by their owners, or because they were Sonja Turk's, and she was not parting with any of hers. Twenty-two pieces altogether, and you cannot imagine how the colors and forms competed with and complemented one another, and how the contents—for our rugs were full of symbols—spoke of our history. Even the ornamentation was eloquent about our special character. I need not tell you how time seemed to crawl before the show's opening.

The great day came, a Sunday in September. Almost the entire membership of the Homeland Association turned up, as well as the deputy mayor, the district administrator's wife, the church superintendent, the Catholic priest, and the owner of the Hotel Queen Luise, two woebegone Lucknow artists, the smartly dressed pawnbroker, and, to my surprise, Herr Struppek of Struppek & Sausmikat, who had brought along a group of business associates, whose discomfort was plain to see. And who else? Conny, of course, accompanying senior editor Kukielka. Conny had his notebook in his jacket pocket, and was thus there in his official capacity.

Sonja Turk and I were at the window watching the guests arrive when an elegant, old-fashioned, four-horse carriage drew up to the museum. The coachman jumped down from the box, ran around the carriage, and helped out its passenger, who, if he had not mistaken the address, had certainly mistaken the time of year. The massive body that heaved itself out of the carriage was swaddled in an open coat of fox fur. The short but agile legs were protected by costly knee-high boots. He waited until the coachman had given the horses their oat bags and lifted a wicker trunk from the carriage. He then jerked his slipping trousers up over his paunch, buttoned the shirt under his double chin, snapped his fingers lordlily, and ambled toward the entrance. He bowed to the people he passed with the space-saving grace of the fat man. "Do you know who that is?" I asked Sonja Turk. "How should I?" she answered. "But he's unhappy, that's for sure. Yes, not a happy man."

The crowd was ushered into the entry hall. Bilitza, president of the Homeland Association, stationed himself on the second step of the staircase, with Sonja and me behind him on the third looking down at his gleaming bald pate. Conny and I winked at each other. Bilitza called for quiet, first with a few gestures, then with a hiss, which because of a gap between his teeth almost turned into a whistle. He wanted to say a few words concerning the exhibition, the first of its kind to be held in our town.

He would not dwell on all the difficulties involved in organizing such a show. Suffice it to say that without the aid of the great weaving artist Sonja Turk the exhibition could never have come into being. With a slight turn of his head he guided the applause toward Sonja.

He thereupon unfolded a manuscript and launched into a disquisition on the Masurian rug-weaving art, which to his mind had to be viewed as a "folk art," based as it was on ancient symbols which led back to the source of the sense of community. True, there was some controversy over the origins of this art. Some maintained that captive Mazovians had learned rug weaving among the Tartars in southern Russia after 1656. Others held that the art had been propagated by the Tartars who had remained in Mazovia after the campaign. All this was beside the point. It was a fact, and the archives of the Teutonic Order confirmed it, that several centuries earlier Mazovians had already been weaving and knotting. Bilitza waxed almost indignant as he repudiated any relationship between our weaving and Oriental traditions. His voice quivered as he stated categorically that our peasant rugs showed a clear kinship to the technique and design of the Swedish rya rugs. He might also point out that the floor rug was considered a sacred relic only in a Germanic house . . .

Louder, Martin, could you please speak a bit louder . . .

You'd like certain words banned forever?

Like the word "origin"? I'm afraid you'd have to muzzle a great many speakers, me included. Believe me; I know all about the arrogance that goes along with the idea of "origin," but you can't suppress an idea simply because it has been abused and falsified. On the contrary, you should try to purify the idea and make sure it is used properly. But enough of that . . .

Bilitza was still holding forth. He went on to describe the two great periods in the history of Masurian weaving: one at the beginning of the eighteenth century, and a second, perhaps more significant period, in which one name was prominent, that of Sonja Turk. Here he again turned toward my teacher and applauded, his manuscript held between his teeth, so that the spectators had to do likewise. I was burning for the moment when the visitors could finally proceed into the exhibit area, but the manuscript still appeared lengthy. Bilitza went on and on about the creation of a rug, from the first intimation of the motifs to the achievement of the miracle of texture and colors. He felt he had to "interpret" the motifs. Nor did he spare us what he never spared any audience: his exposition on the meaning of custom, as he understood it.

I don't know how often I had had to listen to his declamations, but I always felt profoundly uneasy when he hailed folk customs as an "experience of the blood," or a "law of the soul." Whether it was the ritual of driving the cows to the summer pastures or feather stripping or Easter customs, Bilitza saw in these a magic power, because such folk customs created a bond with our ancestors, and to him ancestors were sacred. We could look to them for lessons on how to use the powers of the soul to counter the threat of foreign influence.

There was scattered applause, and finally he led us into the exhibit—Struppek's friends plainly felt out of place. I leaped up the stairs and waited for Conny, who walked in calmly, accompanied by Kukielka. Conny was all attentiveness, trying not to miss a word the old man was saying. Conny greeted me in a friendly but not effusive manner. He gave me to understand that he was here on duty and had to conduct himself accordingly. I contented myself with following him and the others around. The crowd did not disperse itself through the rooms, but remained bunched up, so that everyone had to peer over and around others to see the rugs.

I noticed how Conny was studying the rugs, not letting his gaze wander over the assortment on the walls, but looking at each one for itself and evaluating it, which for us is a sign of expertise. Now and then he jotted down a few notes, without looking at what he was writing. I had never before seen him absorbed in his work this way, observing and judging, and the closer he came to the piece which had his name under it, the more anxious I became. I was sorry now I had not given him the friendship rug earlier, in private.

There he was, standing before the two spies, scanning the entire rug with his eyes, taking it in with no more haste or acuteness than any of the others. His pencil jotted something carelessly onto the paper, and he was already on the point of moving on when Kukielka placed his stiff old finger on the little sign with the dedication. Conny read it several times, looked up at the two figures, looked down again at the sign, shook his head in something like bewilderment, and only after a moment saw my wave and returned it hesitantly.

I forced my way through the crowd, stood expectantly before him. "It's for you, Conny," I said. "I made it for you; do you like it?" He avoided my eyes. Apparently he had to think before he spoke. "Did you make it all by yourself?" he asked edgily. "Seven weeks," I said, "it took me seven weeks to weave it."

Yes, as you say, an unwelcome present, a friendship gift that upset him rather than pleased him. I felt perplexity, disappointment, and bitterness like a weight on my stomach, pressing so hard I thought I would have to vomit. "You'll accept it, won't you?" I asked. He replied, "Let's talk about it later."

They both nodded to me and moved on. I crept into the workshop, pushed open the window, and sat down on a crate where I could catch the breeze. I sat there, my eyes closed, listening to the footsteps and the murmur of the visitors.

Sonja Turk found me there. I should be out looking after matters, she reminded me, and pushed me across the hall and into the room where my friendship rug hung. In front of my piece stood the heavy man in the fox coat. He was stroking the wool, tracing lines between the figures and the symbols, obviously guessing at or perceiving relationships, and searching for something, making measurements which would confirm his guess. Others had gathered around him on flimsy pretexts, watching with curiosity or amusement. The great hulk of a man, whose gaze was at once calculating and dreamy, seemed not to mind. Sonja Turk led me up to him, told him my name, and remarked that my rug was in every respect an independent piece of work. He shook my hand and congratulated me, with far more solemnity than mere politeness would have warranted. He snapped his fingers, and the coachman stepped up briskly, carrying the heavy wicker trunk. He placed himself where he and the fat man could communicate with their eyes without turning their heads. It was preparation for a game which they had played many times before and at which they were accustomed to win . . .

Don't be so impatient, Martin, just wait a bit . . .

So the hulking man stood there with both thumbs hooked into his vest pockets and announced in his curiously high-pitched voice that he planned to buy the friendship rug. No matter that it was dedicated to a particular person. What it represented was universal. He glanced over at the coachman, who opened the wicker trunk and counted out 380 marks to me, but instead of handing me the money, he tucked it under the rug itself, against the baseboard. I was startled, for that was the very sum Sonja Turk had mentioned when I had asked what the rug would be worth if I had to sell it. I shook my head and tapped the dedication plaque. Sonja Turk seemed to have disappeared, or perhaps she was still there, only screened by the visitors. As though word had flown about the place that something was afoot, everyone had flocked into the room. Conny, too, appeared behind the coachman.

After another exchange of looks, the coachman opened the trunk again and counted out twenty marks in silver. The coins jingled as they were piled up to form a little tower. I can still hear the murmur that went through the crowd as we reached five hundred. The visitors formed a close circle around us, craning their necks and watching in silence as the coachman, undeterred by my gestures of refusal, piled up the towers of hard coin beside each other . . .

That's right, Martin. You should know that Sonja Turk paid me two hundred marks a month in those days. To be sure, I ate two of my meals with her.

I don't know what came over me. I simply could not refuse forcefully enough. I was no match for them, and could not play at this game, which some people there took for a test of nerve. These folk were probably the most disappointed when I suddenly quit the field. I made a dive for the door, and called back that the rug no longer belonged to me, so I could not accept any offers. Then off I went and shut myself into my room.

I lay down on my bed and was not going to let anyone in. But when Conny knocked, of course I changed my mind. Still, I did not offer him a chair or any of the apples ripening on the windowsill. I simply went back to my bed and lay there in silence.

He went slowly over to the window and looked down at the bend in the river. He picked up an apple, sniffed it, and put it back. What care he takes with his clothes, I thought, as I compared the two bows on his knickerbockers, which were perfectly equal in size and crisply tied. He turned around, trying to look composed, but it was clear he had something on his mind. He came over to the bed and looked down sternly at me, until I had to ask, "Well, what is it, Conny, what's bothering you?"

His voice quivered a little as he demanded, "Show me your iron rod." "My what?" I asked. He persisted: "Your iron rod. Don't pretend with me." "I don't know what you mean," I answered. "Zygmunt," he said gravely, "someone saw you with an iron rod, and saw you use it." Now I realized what he meant and jumped up . . .

No, no, Martin. You remember the fracas in the Mushroom Cellar that time, when we beat up the fellows of Little Grajevo in their tavern. The only girl there was Anna. I admit that our blows fell at random, in our muddled desire for revenge. Now I learned that I was supposed to have been one of the more savage of the lot, and not only that; someone had seen the iron rod in my hand and had felt its blows: Anna.

Conny told me this not so much to accuse me as to dispel a doubt that had long been gnawing at him. He himself had seen the scar on Anna's shoulder. What more could I do than volunteer to go out to Little Grajevo with Conny that very day, though Conny did not think that would make much difference. Anna would stick by her story, and what way would I have of clearing myself? But he drew so close to me that I could feel his breath. He reminded me of the seven giant spruces, and I saw us standing there in the wind, our arms bare. Then he asked about the knife, and I was able to produce it, the pocketknife we had used that day, which I had lost once and then recovered. Once again he threw the question of the iron rod at me, and once more I gave him my word that I had never had one.

He took my hand. He looked about for some way to show his relief, and I can still see how he seized an apple, bit into it, and made a face at its tartness. Then he fired the apple out the window, straight into the four-horse carriage . . .

Did he accept the rug? Well, what do you think? But the exhibit itself, and Bilitza's speech in particular, had disturbed him. Once more he had become aware of the basically antirational quality of the folk cult. He did not put it exactly that way; he called all that folk business ideological tatting for people who fancy themselves superior in some way. Nor had he any love for the language of symbols. He considered such language arrogant, a way of escaping the responsibilities of thought. Not that he had anything against Masurian weaving; he simply wanted to keep it in its place.

Later we went back to the exhibition, where we learned that the hulk in the fox coat had bought up the three rugs that were for sale. It made me happy that Conny lingered in the room where his rug hung. Once, when I noticed him stroking the wool with his fingertips, I felt as if I myself were being caressed.

But do you know how he headed the article that appeared in the next issue of the *Lucknow News*, which Sonja Turk clipped and placed on my loom? The title was catchy enough, of course: "Art and Blood Pudding," that's right. You have to remember that blood pudding was a Masurian specialty, a black, granular soup with blood as its base, aswim with dumplings and duck giblets and plums and duck necks and duck feet wrapped in tripe.

Sonja Turk came over and stood by my loom. She wanted to hear my reaction—I could tell what hers was, for I could see her outward display of indignation and her secret assent. All right, here we go. First he gave the full name and title of all the participants. Then the setting was described, and finally each individual rug drawn in appreciatively and acutely, so that the reader not only saw the rug before him but understood its content. Conny rewove them in his own medium, with their multiplicity of meanings, their various styles, their imaginative use of personal allusions. Up to there the article was uncontroversial.

But the tone changed when Conny summarized Bilitza's speech, which he called "profound" and "origin-conscious," and from which he quoted extensively, chiefly sentences containing the words "blood" or "soul." He was equally fulsome in describing the dinner given by the Lucknow Homeland Association. The main dish had been blood pudding, which Conny lauded with the naïve enthusiasm of someone who has discovered a dish for the first time. He went on and on about the various giblets and other ingredients, and concluded that what really made the dish was the quality of the blood. Even if Kukielka had helped him, and he probably had, Conny's article was a masterpiece of satire. Or so it seemed to me, at any rate.

But Sonja Turk seemed to take the article as a personal affront. She muttered angrily at this passage and that, and saw the whole piece as a totally destructive polemic. Conny had failed to distinguish between the weaving per se and Bilitza's ridiculous speech and had thus given the impression that weavers were concerned with so-called blood feelings and with paying tribute to the "Germanic soul." "Anyone who reads that article will form a completely wrong impression of what we stand for," she insisted...

Marian? What did he explain to you?

There, you see, I said you would find him with my wife, with Carola...

Oh, yes, you don't have to tell me anything more; I know all about the opinions of my former favorite pupil. He never would rest content with the peasant tradition of rugmaking. As far as he was concerned, that hampered his "art," or at least lowered it to "folk art." Heaven forbid that you should remind him that our first Mazovian rugs were simply rough blankets—they became prized for their decorative qualities only later. You see, Marian has to feel miles above the artisan, the weaver, the knotter . . .

By the way, my wife was here this morning. She has spoken with our insurance agent. Apparently the company regards the whole matter as a case of felonious arson, because when I destroyed the museum I should have taken the danger to the house into account. So this, too, remains shrouded in uncertainty, like so many issues in my life, like almost everything. But at least one thing seems clear: tomorrow they are going to remove my head bandages, and for the first time I will see my surroundings, the people who have helped me, and you, too, Martin; I will see you in a new way . . .

Henrike, you said? What is this plan she and I are supposed to have, when I don't have a ghost of a plan for myself yet? All I know is that when they release me I will be facing my third new beginning, and possibly I will be more dependent on Henrike than she is on me. I hope she manages to find a foothold, to become sturdier than she has been, and generally come down to earth. No doubt she has that from Carola, that disdain for all the mundane necessities, that indifference to petty, everyday obligations. Just try talking to her about money! When I was happy over a payment for a rug, she would look at me, sometimes surprised, sometimes repelled. When Carola and I discussed how we were going to pay our bills, she merely listened, shaking her head, unable to see how this could be a matter worth taking seriously. My Henrike: for so long, I did everything in my power so that she would not have to worry her pretty head about these things . . .

Pardon me?

Yes, that doesn't surprise me; the two of them always were congenial. I have to admit that in the beginning Marian looked out for Henrike more than I did or had the time to. She was even closer to him than to Bernhard. He was her playmate, protector, and father confessor all at once. When she was six or seven, she decided that she would marry Marian someday. But we'll be getting to his story in a little while. First I have to tell you how we came to have a lodger who turned out to be a tremendous help in the museum. He saw his work as a kind of service, and continually amazed us with his conscientiousness.

I found him, or rather rediscovered him, at an amusement fair which was held twice a year on the other side of the river. He was standing by one of the booths, had apparently just been hired, for the proprietor led him behind a partition, where he was made up for his role with broad red eyebrows, blue laugh lines, and a huge heart-shaped mouth. In this guise he poked his head up in the booth, balancing three battered tin cans on his head, one on top of the other.

People paid their money and were given soft cloth balls to pitch at him. The first throw usually knocked off the two upper cans, while the third can held steady as if glued to his head. In the attempt to dislodge the third one, some of the pitchers inevitably hit the man's face, to the pitcher's glee, but to the even greater glee of the children standing around. The balls bounced off his skull, nose, and chin, and the man grimaced and grinned each time but made no effort to avoid the missiles.

I recognized him even under the makeup: it was Eugen Lavrenz, the itinerant stovemaker, the man with the ninety-two lake stories. They had reduced his prison sentence for good behavior. He had just been released the day before.

After he had washed off the clown face and pocketed his pay, I accosted him. He looked at me amiably but without recognition. I reminded him of certain encounters, but his expression revealed that he could not place me. The look on his face had changed; it no longer had the hard, forbidding, inscrutable quality I recalled from our first meeting. Now it showed a sort of humorous tranquillity. An air of contentment and indifference surrounded him, as if he were armored against everything, even against insults.

In any case, he listened agreeably to what I had to say, then picked up his short-handled Engineer's spade, thanked me, and sauntered off with his bundle through the amusement fair, a patient spectator. Without quite knowing why, I followed until I lost sight of him among the little tents around the edge of the fairgrounds.

But on the way home I came upon him again. It was late, and

rain had driven away the last fairgoers. I walked home along the lakeshore, because I wanted to check on the fishing line I had stretched across the river, fastening it to two trees and weighting it in the middle with lead. He was lying there all huddled up in a boat, his head under the middle bench, his torso skimpily covered with the cloth in which he had had his belongings wrapped. Eugen Lavrenz was sleeping so soundly that he did not wake until I shined the flashlight directly into his face. Then he sat up grumpily, blinking. You mustn't think he accepted my proposal immediately. Before he followed me to the house, I had to point out to him that the boat was slowly but steadily taking on water. But finally he came along, and I showed him into the workshop, where we placed a mattress on the floor. He was stretched out even before I came back with a pillow and blankets. I don't know if he really fell asleep at once or only pretended to. At any rate, he made it clear that he was not in the mood for talking and that the mattress suited him just fine . . .

On the contrary, Martin; the next day we were awakened by sounds of rattling and banging. Eugen Lavrenz had gone to work on the valuable old monster of a tiled stove that stood in our museum. He had removed the doors and grates and was lining the firebox with material he had found in the workshop. He was wearing Uncle Adam's old work apron. Even if the stove was only a museum piece, Eugen Lavrenz was determined that it should be in perfect working order. He explained that he wanted to "work off" his bed for the night. I had to call him to breakfast, where he stared at the hot porridge with the same unconcealed greed with which he had once attacked my lard sandwiches in the pedestal.

To their surprise, my mother and Eugen Lavrenz discovered that they had gone to the same village schools, first in Rosinsko, then in Oratzko. After this revelation they could not get enough of asking each other, "Do you remember So-and-so?" and "What was his name again?" and "I'm sure you recall her." They named names and dug up old stories, and every person they mentioned caused laughter. Presumably they were still sitting there trading memories long after I had set out for work, and so he stayed for lunch and then worked on the stove, and we could not bring ourselves to put him out in the rain when night came on. With

Eugen Lavrenz things just fell into place without any need for formal arrangements.

And so he stayed for the time being, partly because there were a number of things in urgent need of repair, partly because he had not yet decided where he should go after his release. He often sat in the museum examining the objects and how they were put together. If you spoke to him there, he answered only in whispers and drew you out into the corridor. He never lost his reverence for old tools and weapons. When he was working in the shop, he would explain what he was doing without your asking and give you a good reason for it, even if it was only sharpening the edge of his spade.

We were just getting used to having him there when it became obvious that his previous life had not yet been buried, that he could not simply put it all behind him. But I must say that we were more pained and astonished by the incident than he was. On the evening in question he acted as though he had been expecting the shadow to catch up with him sooner or later. The three of us were sitting in the workshop when steps approached from the hall. Eugen Lavrenz simply stayed at the workbench and did not get up when Alfons Rogalla appeared in the doorway, bareheaded, his hair dripping, his crutch already halfway inside the door. Eugen Lavrenz did not pause in his work for a moment; he was oiling his spade to keep it from rusting, and he gazed calmly at my grandfather, who seemed not to notice him but turned coldly and menacingly toward my mother and me, after glancing over the contents of the room. He did not come in. He said his piece from the threshold in that rasping voice of his, which brooked no interruptions or objections, not even a question.

Just imagine, he had come to remind us that he had not claimed his share of the inheritance when we had received Uncle Adam's house and the collection and the land leading down to the river; he had renounced his share out of generosity, he explained, but now he was thinking better of it because we had seen fit to harbor a jailbird, a killer, who belonged behind bars for life. All this while he steadfastly ignored Eugen Lavrenz, directing all his venom at us and warning us of the dire consequences if we went against his wishes. And when he had delivered himself of this threat, he turned, deliberately striking the door frame with his crutch, and hobbled across the hall toward the door: Alfons Rogalla, my grandfather, who had never yet seen reason to curb any one of his feelings.

We were still struggling with our confusion when Eugen Lavrenz stood up, picked up his spade, and spread out his cloth, into which he dropped his belongings: broommaker's knives and paintbrushes for making tiles, a wooden bowl and woolen underwear, and a little tin box which served as a sewing kit. He collected all this without a word, knotted his bundle, and said, "Well, off we go again."

You know, son, I think I would have let him go, but my mother stood up, not a bit less resolute than he, took his bundle from him, carried it to the sleeping alcove, and announced only after her return, "You're staying right here. *He* has nothing to say about what happens in this house." Eugen Lavrenz had to sit down and try the currant wine my mother poured us. As she urged us to drink up, her words rang like a declaration of war. We did not shape any plan or strategy; we simply pledged ourselves to resist his claims now and forever.

Eugen Lavrenz stayed. The only thing he asked for was an old blanket, which he draped across the window when darkness fell, on hooks which he himself screwed in. After he had lighted the lamp, he would go outside and quietly circle the house, to check on whether anyone could see into the workshop. We could only wait, and the longer Alfons Rogalla left us alone, the more we worried that his case was going so well that he could dispense with further threats ...

Would you give me a peach, Martin? No, don't bother to peel it, just rub off the fuzz, there we go. What did you say? ...

That's right; he did not return, either to threaten us again or to gloat over a legal victory. But at that time we had no idea what turn his own situation had taken.

No, things began to change for him when one day a tall man arrived by train, checked his luggage at the station—his bags were plastered with stickers from foreign hotels—and, following a map someone had drawn for him, strolled through town, across the bridge, and along the causeway to the estate. He was a laconic, self-assured man of about thirty-five, who bore the same name as the bedridden woman in Königsberg, she who demanded an annual accounting from my grandfather and would send back her corrected versions of the accounts along with some sarcastic comments on his recordkeeping.

The man was called Toni Lettkow. He entered the estate grounds as if they were familiar, said hello as he passed the smithy, and glanced into the barn and the stables before proceeding to the house. There Alfons Rogalla received him gruffly, but quickly asked him in when he recognized the writing on the letter which the stranger handed him.

From this moment on, he treated the newcomer obsequiously —as the people on the estate had never dreamed my grandfather could behave. He himself took charge of the luggage and set the maids to cleaning the large unoccupied room that looked out over the garden. He gave orders to make up the bed, to prepare a special, ample breakfast. He bustled and fussed around, while the stranger calmly observed all the tumult his arrival had caused.

The people on the estate did not learn immediately how extensive the newcomer's rights were, but they drew certain conclusions when my grandfather gave instructions for a horse to be kept ready for the visitor. They had similar thoughts when they saw Toni Lettkow in the storeroom or in the equipment shed or the gravel pit, almost always accompanied by Alfons Rogalla, who, they noticed, did more talking than circumstances seemed to require. The gentleman never asked questions; apparently he had no need to, since Alfons Rogalla would start speaking the moment the visitor's gaze rested on anything a trifle longer than usual. The gentleman demonstrated his knowledge of agricultural matters from the first day on. Nor was he shy of lending a hand where necessary, a trait that earned him the hired men's respect, if not their instant liking. He spent not a single evening with my grandfather; after they had taken their meal together, the younger man withdrew to his quarters, to go over the books of previous years. He seemed not in the least perturbed that the servants saw him at this activity.

Although my grandfather tried to drive them off, the servants would keep gathering outside the window to watch Toni Lettkow, trying to interpret his actions. Some reported that he wrote down many things in a brown notebook; they even asserted that in a single evening he had used up a quarter of the book. The man's presence filled the people on the estate with a new feeling, a sense of uncertainty they had never before experienced. Everything that had previously seemed stable and lasting now began to waver. Suddenly they feared they had to expect changes which would affect not only life on the estate but their personal lives as well. I don't know, Martin, and I can't say whether their foreboding was greater than their anticipation.

In any case, everyone sensed that the information Toni Lettkow was gathering was assuming an ominous cast. You will not be surprised to hear that many hurled themselves into their work, simply to avoid being questioned on any score. But he seemed prepared for that. After some days he was out watching the men logging. It was the general rule that no two trees would be felled simultaneously, but when the warning cry of "Timber!" rang out and Toni Lettkow jumped aside, he found himself in the path of a second falling tree. The crown brushed past him, the needles whipped his face, branches scratched him, and there was a crashing and splintering around him, but he himself did not fall. No, he just put one hand to his neck, scrambled out of the way, and dusted himself off. He mounted his mare and rode away; presumably he never learned that the people spoke of the incident as "a sort of warning."

Another time he was injured by the straw machine. He had barely thrown in the first bundle of barley when the drum with its sharp blades began to rotate, grinding not slowly as it usually did on the first few turns but hard and fast. It was sheer good luck that the machine only took off the tip of his finger. Alfons Rogalla hitched up the hunting wagon to take him to the doctor and later made a big to-do about finding out who had left the guard off the machine. But the carelessness could not be traced to anyone in particular.

Don't think for a moment that the accident affected Toni Lettkow's investigations. That same evening he was back at the books, his bandaged hand lying on the pages to weigh them down, the brown notebook near the base of the lamp.

Finally, it became clear what Toni Lettkow's untiring efforts were all about. Many had already suspected the truth. Alfons Rogalla, who had so long ruled with an iron hand, on whom they had all been so dependent, was himself dependent on someone else. It was enough to see the manner in which Toni Lettkow called my grandfather into the room, beckoned to him to approach the desk, sat down, and pointed with his pen to an entry in one of the ledgers. As he pointed, he looked icily and challengingly at the grizzled bailiff. Alfons Rogalla glanced hastily at the book, shook his head, and tried to brush aside the silent reproach with a wave of his hand. But Toni Lettkow flipped over a few more pages and made Alfons Rogalla read another entry. When the old man shrugged truculently, the younger man opened his brown notebook and began to read aloud, without looking up. The servants watching outside the windows waited for the bailiff to interrupt, to set the record straight. They were amazed at the passive way in which he listened to what was clearly an indictment. He just stood there, his eyes glazed. An expression of bitterness and scorn played around his mouth, while his hands groped for each other as if he wanted to wring them. One of the servants later related that he had twisted his stubby pipe in his hands until suddenly the mouthpiece broke off.

The younger man terminated the lecture. He handed the notebook to my grandfather. Alfons Rogalla merely weighed the little book in his hand and threw it down on the table with contempt. He made for the door. He paused as he pressed the latch, turned around, and, apparently following a sudden impulse, went back to the ,desk, dragged up an armchair, sat down without being invited to, and expressed by his very posture his low opinion of what he had been put through . . .

Understand him, you say? You wonder whether I ever tried to understand Alfons Rogalla? No, Martin, I never did, for the simple reason that it seemed unnecessary in his case to look into the source of his arrogance and his ruthlessness. I suppose I also had no desire to penetrate his motives—if indeed there were any— since I did not want to find myself in the embarrassing position of having to excuse him. But enough of that.

And now the servants listening at the door were in a better position than those watching from the darkness of the lawn, for they got to hear the bailiff's refutation. He had recovered enough spirit to present his own account and to play what cards he had left. When I think back on it today, it seems only natural to me that he should have revealed what linked him to the ailing, greedy woman in Königsberg, who had sent her son to look into Rogalla's administration of the estate.

He supposed that Toni Lettkow had no idea how the gravel and clay pits and the ponds that went with them had come into the possession of the estate. Sparing neither himself nor the woman in Königsberg, he described a swindle, plain and simple: how they had made a secret compact with the owner of the United Brick and Ceramic Works of Lucknow; how they had conspired to put such a squeeze on the stubborn old owner of the gravel and clay pits that he had to sell; how they had concluded a seven-year contract highly profitable to both sides.

I need not tell you what ulterior motive led the old man to bring up these matters. The conspiratorial manner, as well as the pleasure and even glee with which he retraced the business, spoke for themselves. I can thus comprehend his chagrin when Toni Lettkow responded to the story with the simple words, "She has been declared mentally incompetent. We had to have my mother declared mentally incompetent." Then Lettkow stood up, looking over Rogalla's head, and asked him to leave the room. He stood there until Alfons Rogalla was gone, and those watching from the lawn saw that he sat down and without taking even a moment to collect himself began to write on special stationery, which he produced from his suitcase. There was no need to see more. The following day my grandfather received a letter saying that his administrator's contract had been terminated. It was a contract that had remained in force for twenty-eight years, and had been renewed repeatedly on the same terms, so automatically that he had forgotten such a contract existed . . .

Pardon me?

That's exactly the way they felt, Martin: as if God had been demoted, as if the world were suddenly without its ruler. I would have liked to be there to see my grandfather's fury. All that day no one on the estate needed to ask where he was; he made his whereabouts known, growling and muttering to himself, his voice occasionally squawking with rage. Several times he read the letter aloud for his own benefit, with no regard for those who chanced to overhear. What particularly smarted was the passage questioning his qualities as an estate administrator. He ignored the reasons cited. He had crushed and smoothed out the letter so many times that it could hardly be deciphered. People gave him a wide berth.

As the midday sun beat down, he abruptly had his horse saddled and rode off in the direction of Borek Forest. He did not reappear until the iron wheel was struck to signal quitting time and all the hired hands congregated in the big rutted courtyard of the estate, on orders from Toni Lettkow. It looked as though Grandfather, too, had been summoned by the resounding blows. A nervous stableboy helped him off his mount and led the animal away, its flanks black with sweat. When he returned, the stableboy handed my grandfather his crutch and scurried off to join the others.

How often I have pictured this scene to myself: evening on the estate, not the slightest breeze stirring, a smell of burned hoof, and over there in loose groups the smiths and the milkers, the maids and the field hands, the feed masters and the stableboys. And the two contenders for supremacy. The men looked at each other sidelong, each behaving as though the presence of the other meant little to him. Toni Lettkow stood there watching the people assemble, while my grandfather kept pounding his crutch into the ground and muttering. Now and then he cackled scornfully to himself.

After they were all there, Toni Lettkow clasped his hands behind his back and haltingly but calmly announced that he had been obliged to cancel Herr Rogalla's bailiff's contract. He himself, as owner of the estate, gave everyone the choice of staying on. For the present he had no intention of making far-reaching reforms. He was looking forward to working with each of them, and he asked the foremen, the head milkers, and the feed masters to come to his room after supper. That was all: no expression of thanks to my grandfather, no farewells with praise and the usual tributes, but also no reason given for this dismissal after twenty-eight years.

The people were dumbfounded. They were not ready to disperse; apparently they had expected more in the way of explanation, and Alfons Rogalla noted their mood and tried to turn it to his own advantage. He managed to get their attention, to force them all to look his way. "Listen here, folks, all of you," he shouted. He pointed toward the lake with his crutch, down to the paddock where the old horses were put out to pasture. "Look," he roared, "look down there. That's how we've done it all these years. Anyone who gave his strength for us could count on not being let down." He paused, seeming to realize that his analogy was not an apt one, or would not get his message across effectively. He dug his crutch irritably into the ground and started again: "You took your orders from me for a long time, some of you for a long, long time. Together we farmed this estate that was given to us to take care of, and I bore the responsibility for your mistakes—for twenty-eight years. And now it turns out that some of these mistakes are unforgivable. And to pay for them someone has to pack his bags and go. Me. I'm supposed to pack my bags and go, after twenty-eight years. Me. After all that time. You know me, as I know you. I judged your work, and you judged mine. And now I'm being shown the door; you can't just stand there and gawk. You must have something to say, some reply!"

They looked at him uncertainly. Perhaps they recognized what he hoped to achieve, what he was demanding of them in this situation, but their inertia or old memories held them back. No, not one of them raised his voice to question Lettkow, not one of them stepped forward to take the old man's part. Even when he laid it on thick, asking shrilly whether they thought he had earned this treatment, no one spoke up in his favor or so much as expressed regret. Finally, the bailiff gave up and hobbled away without another word. He went into the austerely furnished house and began to pack. He left the estate without taking leave of anyone.

No, no, just be patient, I'm coming to that. Well, first he tried to foist himself on his friends, or those he thought were his friends—Fishing Commissioner Dudei; Heyduck, the sawmill owner; but also Bilitza of the Homeland Association—but all these people already had long-term guests or were living in cramped quarters themselves, so that if they could take him in, it was only for two or three nights. They shrugged their shoulders and sent him on his way. When the situation became clear to him, he went and had himself announced to the owner of the Hotel Queen Luise, dickered with him, and rented a double room at Lucknow's best hotel for an indefinite period, with permission to bring along his own easy chair and hassock. In the restaurant he had a table reserved for himself at the window that looked out over the street. A well-filled cigar box was placed on the table the moment he took his seat. Word went around in Lucknow that my grandfather had the means to pay for his room not only one month in advance but for half a year. But word also went around that he did not set foot outside the hotel, because he was determined to get every penny's worth by making full use of all the services offered . . .

Pardon me, Martin, what did you just say?

Photographs? You want to know whether there were photographs in our museum? No, never, neither in Lucknow nor in Egenlund; no portraits, no pictures of buildings and public squares, not even of landscapes. They simply did not mean anything to me. There was an itinerant photographer named Bandulewitz, who for a time made the estate and my grandfather his favorite subjects: Alfons Rogalla out duck hunting, resting in a clearing; Alfons Rogalla on horseback against a Lucknow sunset; and then the seasons on the estate, with their characteristic chores: the plowman, the sower, the smith, the mower with his scythe, the shepherd—all perfectly fine photographs. Bandulewitz made me a present of the whole series. Nevertheless, I could not persuade myself to mount them in the museum. My feeling was that they captured a landscape or a face too definitively, too much once and for all. Uncle Adam would have said, "Photographs do not constitute testimony"—that kind of testimony a tool or a weapon or a toy held for him. I think he was right, for something was trapped in the objects, like a fly in amber, which could not be described with perfect clarity. What this secret thing was eluded me. Sometimes, in a despondent mood, I wondered whether what the object enclosed was not a sense of futility.

On the other hand, when I remember the wife of the old toymaker—he lay on his bier in the parlor and Edith and I were in the kitchen spooning up milk soup and sourdough bread—I had to agree with the half-blind old woman when she said, "What a person has brought into the world, that stays in the world, even if it was only fussin' and fumin', like with him, my Wilhelm . . ."

But that's something else I have to tell you about, Martin, my first trip with Edith, a business trip to Sokolken, to the house of the old toymaker, where I hoped to acquire rare Masurian toys for our collection. I got the tip from Sonja Turk; just as she always knew everything that happened in and around Lucknow before anyone else, she was the first to hear of the death of the toymaker Wilhelm Rattay in Sokolken, and she gave me the time off and lent me her knapsack and urged me to hurry. She herself wanted a toy spinning wheel of rosewood, if such a thing was still available, with rosettes made of bone. That meant I was practically forced to set out on this, my first expedition, which was to take me to a place not even Eugen Lavrenz had visited in his wide wanderings. According to the map, Sokolken was located at the mouth of a river. It looked out over a narrow lake which was naturally linked with other lakes, all of them surrounded by forest. There was no railway station, but you could depend on a ferry and motorboats. Eugen Lavrenz laid out the trip for me, noting where I had to leave the train and walk, then take the ferry, and when I looked closer at the map, I discovered that Sokolken lay halfway to Neidenburg . . .

Right, my dear boy, halfway to Edith. The thought of seeing her struck me at once, for I was filled with an eagerness inspired by her flood of letters, a desire that had been growing and growing the longer our correspondence continued. Before making the other arrangements, I sent her a night letter: "Must go to Sokolken on urgent business Friday; will wait for you that afternoon by the ferry; tell you the rest when I see you; looking forward very much." Then I packed provisions for the journey—bread and dried fruits mostly—drew thirty marks from the museum's funds for the purchase of toys and other items, and set out on a Thursday, by the first train.

I did not stick it out on the train for long. Alone in the compartment with a war veteran, who dropped off to sleep after telling me where he was bound, I gazed out the window at the quiet, uncommunicative landscape, looking through the soft contours of my reflection at the sandy fields and barely ruffled lakes. Winding sandy roads led to farmhouses huddled under great roofs, storks swooped down on swampy meadows, the forest went on and on, with an open hilltop sometimes crowned by a monument, sometimes by a clearing punctuated by a forester's lodge. Down by the lake, nets dangled from leaning poles, a herd of cattle stood up to their udders in the murky water, rafts drifted down a long river. The landscape seemed curiously untouched. It was gentle and full of mystery. Gypsies sat outside their encampment of caravans, a shepherd stood in a field silhouetted in black like a charred tree; a horse-drawn wagon toiled over a hill, the driver asleep; everything one saw testified to the generous supplies of time and patience without which life here became impossible, yes, impossible.

At the second stop I got out, turned in my ticket, and had the unused portion of the trip refunded. I set out in the direction of Sokolken, first on a sunny cobbled road, later on overgrown paths which did not show on my map. I was so happy I did not even feel the weight of the knapsack.

Edith's image accompanied me all the way. As I walked, I reread those of her letters I had liked best. I already knew certain passages by heart. In view of all that had passed between us in letters, I kept trying to imagine our meeting by the ferry, even working out alternate versions without deciding for one or the other. By the way, Conny knew I was on my way to Sokolken, but he did not know that I had a rendezvous with his sister.

As I walked along through this peaceful countryside, I understood at last why Eugen Lavrenz had never wanted to set up shop properly; that would have put an end to his journeyings. I took off my shoes and waded across a shallow lake, just as he would have done, and continued barefoot along narrow paths by the shore and sandy roads through the forest. When thirst came upon me, I approached a farm and asked for water, whereupon the farmer's wife silently placed a pitcher of buttermilk before me. The second time I got thirsty, in the afternoon, I went up to another farm, and the farmer made me sit at the rough trestle table and share his barley coffee and yeast pancakes with him. He refused to take any money for the meal; he just wanted me to tell him about Lucknow; he had heard we had wonderful pharmacies.

Outside of Jetossen a man gave me a ride on his wagon as far as Milacken. I spent the night on a farm where I came upon the farmer tending his bees, working quietly without smoke or protective gear. He sent me into the house, and his wife came in from the barn; that is, she emerged from the family bedroom, which opened directly upon the barn. The door was wide open and for a moment I caught sight of the black and white backs of the cows and the glow of cats' eyes in the hayloft. When the woman heard that her husband had sent me in, she set out a crock of farmer's cheese flavored with caraway, bread, and a pitcher of mushroom water, and I had barely begun to eat when the children's pet hen fluttered up to the windowsill and perched there, looking down at my plate. A goat thrust its forelegs into the room and stared at me. From the dark hayloft darted several orange cats. They jumped up onto the bench around the stove and watched my every movement, and the children besieged me from both sides, laughing and chortling, taking delight in a stranger.

We did not stay up long. The man asked my name and my destination, nodded at both pieces of information, then rolled out a rag rug in the bedroom and placed a horse blanket over it and shook hands to say good night. He and his wife donned their nightshirts, huge garments with sleeves like wings, made of an off-yellow material so stiff that they might have spent the day standing in a corner. The children slept on padded wooden ledges along the wall, or were supposed to sleep there, but I did not say a word when first the little girl, then the little boy slipped under my blanket and cuddled up to me. From the barn came the rattling of chains when one of the animals tossed its head. There was a crackling and rustling, a hoof scraped the ground, a piglet scratched its back against a board. When I awoke, the children were standing looking down at me, hopping up and down and putting me to shame, for they had long since breakfasted. I drank a cup of malt coffee; then the farmer accompanied me several miles over the hill and along a river until we came to a sign pointing to Sokolken. In farewell all he said was, "All right," and headed back.

Both of us turned again and again to wave to each other, until he disappeared beyond the hills.

Now I walked more rapidly, so rapidly that I reached Sokolken by noon. Half the town was on one side of the river, half on the other, with approximately the same number of wooden ramps for doing laundry. Just before the mouth of the river was the ferry, which ran along a rope and was poled by the ferryman.

Flotillas of ducks kept crossing and recrossing the river on the diagonal.

When I asked the ferryman if he by any chance had a message for me, he wanted to know my name, my place of birth, my most recent domicile, my destination, and even the purpose of my journey, only to inform me blankly that he had no message at all. He knew the house of the toymaker Wilhelm Rattay—he gestured across the lake, but suggested I might want to reconsider laying out money for the crossing, since the old hothead, as he called him, was probably "long since with the folks down there."

I decided to wait for Edith; indeed, I had to. I unstrapped my knapsack, dug myself a little hollow on the sloping riverbank, and watched the sluggish river traffic for a while. Later I reread Edith's letters again. She did not come and she did not come. Soon I knew entire letters by heart. Although I could see who got on the ferry on the other side, I went down to the landing each time it came in and looked the passengers over from close up, as if it were a question of discovering Edith under a disguise. After I had helped the ferryman several times with mooring the boat, he let me cross for free. I poled with the extra pole, trying to pole away the time, but although the willows were already casting their shadows over the river, Edith was nowhere to be seen. When darkness fell, the ferryman hitched his nameless craft to a stationary anchor. In parting, all he said was, "You know, there's many a one has planned to come and then didn't come after all." . . .

No, no, you'll hear in a minute. I did not give up and didn't dare leave, even after night had fallen. I lay next to my knapsack in the fine sand, which retained the heat; the moon shed enough light. Perhaps I had fallen asleep and was dreaming of a sharp whistle which agitated the ducks. In any case, I started up when a whistle sounded piercingly across the water, and there she stood in her flimsy little dress, her cardboard suitcase in one hand, and pointed to the river that separated us, which was a good sixty feet wide at that point and not very deep. I saw no other choice: I undressed, stuffed clothes and shoes and leather wallet into my knapsack, adjusted the straps so that it sat higher on my back—at times I carried it on my head—and then I slipped into the river, parting the reeds with my hands. I had to make only a few swimming motions, for my feet touched bottom most of the time, and the gentle current did not pull me down even once . . .

You are a good listener, Martin. You remember that I had waded through water like this once before, through muddy, weed-ridden water. For a moment I found myself thinking of that episode, too, as I labored across, toward the yellow dress which flitted up and down the bank. She wanted to help me out of the water and was still looking for a spot where she could get through the reeds and rushes and weeping-willow branches when I was already on land. My first words were to ask her to turn away while I put on some clothes. As I was dressing, I began to hiccup, first just a few bothersome little hics which seemed almost amusing. And Edith did seem amused, as when we finally shook hands, prepared for something we had both imagined but which did not come about because my hiccups cut off my words and forced my chin down toward my chest.

It was all hopeless: although we quickly looked each other over covertly to see how the reality compared with our memories and our imaginings, nothing came of it, for my hiccups determined the form of our reunion and dictated the style of our greeting.

We walked into Sokolken, announced by the barking of the dogs. We walked hand in hand in silence, I trying desperately to hold my breath and count so as to banish the hiccups, which were intensifying and making me jerk so violently that Edith's hand jerked, too, as if an electric shock were passing through it. I had to let go of her hand. I did not dare say another word. I watched her and saw that after her initial smiles she was sighing at each hiccup and occasionally stopped in vexation. All she said was that she was tired and hungry. We did not spend the night under one of the barges up on blocks for repairs farther downriver; before I could steer her in that direction, the ferryman called to us from the bench outside his cottage and advised us not to be out hiking at this time of night. "There's all kinds of no-good types lurking in the reeds," he said, and Edith asked him if he had anything for us to eat. He warmed up a peppery fish soup for us, and sliced beets into it. I kicked Edith under the table to urge that we be on our way. She understood my signals but ignored them. Instead, she looked at me expressionlessly and asked the ferryman if we might spend the night at his house.

When the man agreed, she picked up her little cardboard suitcase and had him show her the small spare bedroom; from the wall General Ludendorff's glassy eyes glazed down on the plump straw mattress. I slept in the loft, surrounded by ropes and old oars, with a faded sail to lie on. My disappointment so engrossed me that I did not even notice when my hiccups subsided. In any case, our reunion had turned out differently from the way I had pictured it.

Don't ask about the following morning; I had long since said goodbye to the ferryman and was sitting on a barge waiting for Edith. Now and then I walked past her window whistling, or pounded on the porch railing, but Edith was calmly sleeping the morning away. When she finally came out, blinking in the sun and plucking at her dress to straighten it, all I could muster was a silent nod. To hide my irritation at all the wasted time, I went on ahead on the damp path, without regard for any difficulty she might have following, giving no thought to the reeds that snapped back in her face. I acted as if we had to hurry to make up for all the hours she had slept away.

To think that we could remain silent so long. That neither one of us broke the silence, when there was so much to be said! It was painful. I felt the way she toiled to keep up, and felt how hard it was for her to suppress all the questions that had accumulated during our long separation.

We walked on in silence until we came to the house of the toymaker. It was a wood house with patches of moss on it, shaded by fir trees and surrounded by a rustling hedge. An ancient, stiff-legged dog greeted us at the gate and accompanied us, growling, into the kitchen. Edith groped for my hand, and I found a pretext for withdrawing it: I put down my knapsack and knocked on the door to the living room. After several knocks a woman's voice called out, "Who's there?" I opened the door and there was the toymaker's wife, sitting beside her husband, who was laid out on his bier. She was filling a little sachet with dried rose petals; when it was full, she began to sew up the opening with tiny stitches. She gestured to us to enter. She pointed at her husband and spoke quite freely of his hard life, which she had shared for forty years or more. Before her sight had begun to fail, she had made the rounds, delivering the toys to their customers. She seemed to be at peace, to take it for granted that a man should have had to struggle as her husband had, that he had not wished his life to be any different, and even that he had now died. "It would be bad if there were nothing left from a man's life," she said, "not a trace, not a mark. But what a person has brought into the world, that stays in the world, even if it was only fussin' and fumin', like with him, my Wilhelm."

She made that remark later, as we were spooning up the milk soup she served us in the kitchen. She told us that her husband had often brooded over all the forgotten toys in attics around Sokolken, toys he had made over the past forty years. "You could fill the museums with them toys that are up in the attics," she said. She led us into the workshop, where her husband had done his stint up to the last day of his life. On the workbench stood a duck on wheels, with the toymaker's wire-rimmed glasses dangling from its beak. Shelves reaching from floor to ceiling were filled with wonderful old dolls, with peacocks spreading their tails, with forest animals on rollers. Several dollhouses contained frozen tableaux of great tenderness. There was even a miniature workshop, with objects strewn about in artful disorder. It was called the "toymaker's workshop." And there was the rosewood spinning wheel Sonja Turk wanted to have, and on a folding table by the window two of the famous "Sokolken boxes," which were not for sale; their entire contents were made of turned beechwood and bones: tiny chairs, mortars, jugs, rolls of yarn, baskets, plates, butter crocks—a whole household in miniature.

Quite involuntarily I spoke more softly and stepped more lightly in this house. Whatever I touched or handled, I patted once more as if in apology, in contrast to the half-blind woman, who seemed to accept everything, including talk of prices in a house where someone lay dead. She agreed with all my choices, took the objects from the shelves, and carried them into the kitchen, and congratulated me on my purchases, quite without reservation. As I was selecting delicate little sets of bowling pins, dolls, yarn winders, and carved animals, I was already planning to set up a special section in our museum. I would move into Uncle Adam's sleeping alcove and devote my room exclusively to native playthings.

While the woman was adding up the bill, Edith suddenly began to cry. She was sitting at the folding table, where she had opened one of the Sokolken boxes and arranged its delicate contents on the tabletop so that it looked as though tiny beings might come along any minute and put them to use. Sitting there, lost in the sight of these appealing and vulnerable tiny objects, Edith wept. She could not give a reason, neither now nor later, why just looking at those miniature containers and cups and mangles made her burst into tears; not until the woman with quiet decisiveness repacked the finely turned objects in the box did Edith recover her composure . . .

What did you say, Martin? Just wait, you're in for a surprise.

We bowed toward the dead toymaker and left the house, but we had barely reached the hedge when the woman called Edith back, took the cardboard suitcase from her, and placed a Sokolken box inside. Only now did I become aware that Edith had come from Neidenburg with an almost empty suitcase. A helpless look and two stammered phrases were all the thanks she could muster; she curtseyed to the woman and dashed back to me, anxious to get outside the gate.

She did not fit the image I had constructed of her. But then I should admit that Edith had not contributed in any way to my delusions, to the self-delusions without which I could hardly have held up my end of that extravagant correspondence. I was unwilling to reconcile myself to her having moved so far from the picture I had formed of her—and this picture was a product not of my memories but of her letters. In my disappointment I noticed things I would otherwise certainly have overlooked, for instance, that one of the shoulder straps on her yellow dress was held together by a safety pin and that the soles of her oxfords were almost worn through. At the time, these observations only strengthened my disillusionment.

In any case, I had accomplished my mission and we had time to kill. We trailed along the lakeshore in single file to the pier where the old paddlewheel steamer tied up several times a day; it carried both passengers and freight across the lake: milk cans, crates of fruit and smoked fish, mail. By common accord, we went to the foredeck, where we could be alone. We sat down next to the anchor chain. I placed my hands on hers, and we turned our faces into the gentle breeze caused by the boat's motion. We still did not manage to talk, or at least in no sense as freely and openly as we had done in our letters. Every sentence we spoke sounded as though it had been thought out beforehand. I listened to a long explanation of how she had acquired an almost invisible scar on her cheekbone, and she dragged out this account of her bicycle accident almost beyond endurance—you know how it is. We got off in Sokolken; the ferryman who poled us across the river favored us with one of his self-coined proverbs, something in praise of persistence, a sentiment that was hardly worth discussing but which we belabored endlessly as we walked along the wood road that led to Spunken, where the nearest railroad station was located. I asked her whether the dark spot on her dress which looked like grease might come from her bicycle accident; she replied that that was possible.

We ran into some woodsmen who were apparently having a small celebration. They invited us to share their beer and sausage, and when they asked whether we were brother and sister, I let Edith answer. She told them we were indeed brother and sister, on our way to Neidenburg to collect an inheritance, a huge brickworks with an attached ceramics factory. I felt a slight stab at this account, which she delivered so convincingly that the woodsmen believed every word.

We stopped at one point so that she could disappear into the underbrush, and I could not resist looking into her suitcase; I had to find out what she carried about with her. I saw the corn-colored braids, wrapped carelessly in a piece of newspaper. Later, when we had already been married for several years, she told me that she had wanted to give me one of the braids and had not done so because she had not found "the right moment" and besides, everything "was going wrong." What unreasonable expectations we had, both of us. Each of us had assumed that the other would never change. But enough of that.

When we reached the station in Spunken, it was deserted. We walked across the rails in the dusk and inspected the building, which smelled of carbolic. No one was at the ticket counter, and we could easily have supplied ourselves with tickets to Königsberg or Tilsit or Elbing, but we contented ourselves with going into the waiting room, which was occupied by a stocky woman in black, a figure to be encountered in every Masurian railroad station. She had two baskets on the bench beside her, with young goslings peeping inside. We assured her that trains did go in the direction of Neidenburg from Spunken, whereupon she was visibly relieved and returned to her abstraction. There was no refreshment stand at the station, so we shared our last apple. Edith suddenly asked me if I could lend her the money for a ticket; she was totally broke. This request did not do much to improve my feelings about this reunion. I gave her the money, but only the exact amount she needed, two marks forty-five. My disapproval, expressed in my counting out the sum, passed her by. In gratitude she moved close to me, rubbed her face against my arm, and whispered: "Just listen to those goslings, how cute they're peeping."

I now could hardly wait for her departure. I invented several pretexts to go out on the platform and listen for the train. I sauntered over to the modest freight section, where two men were piling up boxes of smoked whitefish; I watched them, simply not to have to spend all the remaining time with Edith. What baffled me was that she apparently was suffering from no such disappointment. She seemed unperturbed by all that had happened and acted as though no problems existed between us as a result of this botched encounter.

You needn't tell me anything about my behavior; I have learned since that it was a common mistake of mine to see the future as all mapped out. My train arrived first, and Edith took my hand as we ran out onto the platform. She was cheerful and apparently satisfied with the meeting, and repeated again and again that she would write, as soon as she got back, a good, long letter. I hoisted my knapsack into the compartment, and instead of jumping back down onto the platform, I stood on the step, since the conductor already had his whistle in his mouth. So our farewell had a formal cast to it; the difference in levels made that unavoidable. And what a startled and pitiful look she gave me as the train jerked into motion. She ran along beside the train, looking up at my compartment, not waving, just hoping for some gesture of confirmation. And this was the picture of her I carried home with me: Edith standing at the end of the platform with her arms spread in the milky light, motionless in expectation.

As soon as I was back home I wrote to her, had to write to her, not least because of the surprise I had received when I unpacked. On top of everything else in my rucksack lay the Sokolken box with its contents of beechwood and bone, the most valuable item in the special section I set up for Masurian toys...

Sorrow, you say? You wonder whether I feel sorrow for all those things lost forever in the fire? I admit, Martin, that I sometimes think I went too far in my purge; but at the time I had no choice. How would I have decided what to save, before everything went up in flames? What sorts of reasons could I have found for rescuing some items and not others? No, it was all or nothing, and perhaps you will understand when you have heard the whole story. I know only too well how many precious objects turned to ashes; in addition, all the catalogues were destroyed, the catalogues which listed and explained every single item. The thought becomes more difficult to bear with every day that passes, but thus far I have managed to dispel all the doubts that present themselves...

Pardon me? Is it that late already? Well, I have no choice; I have to accept that ... But do take the apples, Martin; I receive so much fruit here...

Certainly, go ahead and tell me, what is it you've noticed?

Oh, the many moods I have preserved in my memories. You'll see, moods and the feel of situations are our most reliable possessions in the long run ... Did you take the apples? Good ... Moods help me bring back memories ... Tomorrow, I hope ... Oh, yes, would you send the nurse in?

# 8

Can you guess the first person I saw when they took off the bandages? My son, Bernhard. In a rush, as usual, and as usual he had not had time to let me know he was coming. Suddenly there he stood at the foot of my bed, trying to catch my attention. He was there between two trains, on his way to Copenhagen to participate in an international congress about recent developments in penology. He took about half a minute to determine that my condition was no longer cause for concern—"You look pretty damned good, old boy, a bit more battered, but none the worse for wear." The remaining nineteen minutes of his visit he spent lecturing me on the crucial issue of our times: the rehabilitation of criminals. Lying there defenseless as his words cascaded over me, I gathered that our society had only one way to make amends to those it had wronged: to let prisoners put on plays, attend sporting events, and be exposed to poetry readings. By the way, his boss will be delivering a speech in Copenhagen which could never have been written without Bernhard's experience in this field. Before he hurried off, he wanted to hear how much remained of the Masurian "relic shack," and when I held out my empty hands, he patted me on the shoulder and comforted me: "The present can be glorified just as well as the past, old boy. You might try that for a change . . ."

Yes, yes, a visit from Bernhard . . .

Pardon me? Oh, I am, too, I'm sorry you did not have a chance to meet Bernhard. I'm sure the two of you would have got on splendidly, cynics that you are. You both wear the same faded blue jeans, the same desert boots—yes, yes, I know one can't go by that.

Yes, for a time Conny and I wore the same windbreakers and

the traditional carpenter's trousers of wide-waled corduroy; we were the first in Lucknow to give up neckties in favor of extra-long shoelaces, tied in a graceful bow. Although externally we proclaimed solidarity, in our convictions we were moving further and further apart. Yes, we no longer agreed on the connotations of certain words or on analyses of what was happening. I need only think of the events around the time of the spring thaw . . .

I'd be glad to, Martin . . .

Well, the great thaw was not yet past when they moved in with steam shovels, rollers, and trucks. They came down from the north and settled in on the spit of land between the lakes. From Castle Hill it looked as though they were corking the spit of land like a bottle. On the very first day they felled the silver poplars for firewood. This was the army that would push the great highway down toward the Polish border, across the Lucknow bog.

When our thaw came, there would be a dripping and pouring of water all around you for weeks on end. It fell from the roofs and the branches, it beat out a rhythm as you awoke, it splashed frigidly into your face, pounded in your thoughts, and outside, the remaining snow and the drenched earth became pitted. Crevasses appeared, as though made by dynamite blasts, and where the ground sloped, the melting snow formed rivulets that rushed down into the lakes, where gray, porous ice floes drifted. The sky was clear at this time of year, as if swept clean. The east wind brushed through the tops of the fir trees, plucking off the older needles.

From Castle Hill you could make out the trails which their chain saws had carved through the forest, sharp-edged trails which soon ran sand-yellow through the blue-green woods. Our bog could not halt them; their trucks brought in brush, stone and gravel, and mounds of fill to make the embankment on which the highway would run. Two field kitchens proved barely sufficient to feed the road crew, which included Poles, Lithuanians, and Gypsies. What preparations were taking place there by the spit of land! What clouds of smoke went up from the stoves and caldrons!

When Conny came to fetch me, I did not know that he had been assigned to write a report for the *Lucknow News*, not only on the construction project, but also on an attempt by the Homeland Association to fend off this tremendous force of strange men and their machines from our bog, one of the last spots to be left inviolate. I jumped on his motorcycle, and we rattled past the prison and the estate, causing consternation among the poultry, which scattered in all directions. Conny enjoyed the speed. He seemed refreshed after every such ride. We parked the motorcycle by the construction-company trailers and asked to be directed to the project engineer. The engineer, who was wearing a leather cap with a visor and a three-quarter-length leather coat, invited us into his cabin. It was a warm, roomy cabin furnished with a card table and an army cot. Through its long, narrow window we could see the bog and the first part of the embankment. The engineer earnestly and expertly explained the course the project would take, at all of which Conny nodded attentively: the special difficulties of laying the roadbed, the materials needed, the estimated cost. I still remember my amazement at the way Conny seemed to take all this for granted, as well as at the engineer's manner of answering Conny's questions. He spoke as if called upon to justify himself, as if obligated to give Conny the information. He offered us hot coffee in tin cups and drew us over to the window. On the packed-down sand of the future embankment stood a tent, an olive-green pup tent. "They are still holding out," the engineer remarked. "The Homeland Association still believes it can hold us back." . . .

Yes, that's right, Martin, even in those days they had nothing but a condescending smile for anyone who tried to defend the land against their encroachments. They regarded people of this kind as silly malcontents, eccentric saints, folks who had a few screws missing, to be treated with forbearance.

The engineer, too, smiled as he gazed at the tent, that pathetic barrier the Lucknow Homeland Association had placed in the way of the project. He pointed to men who, following his instructions, were wielding their picks and shovels close to the tent, as though they could not possibly take the obstacle seriously.

Conny suggested that we walk over, and the engineer led us along the edge of the embankment and actually looked into the tent to wish the occupants good morning. After a while the canvas billowed and flapped, and our old teacher Henseleit, vice president of the association, stepped out. He blinked at us, rubbing the back of his neck. He responded curtly to our greeting, but apparently Conny's visit came at a welcome time. I must confess his statements sounded like a broken phonograph record: he was convinced he could turn back the chain saws, bulldozers, and steam rollers, convinced we had a sacred duty to protect the wilderness. "The land has its own laws. When we force our human will upon it, we destroy its underlying life," he orated. "Once in our presumption we have subjugated the entire earth, we will reap the consequences." He borrowed a match from the engineer to light his pipe, and pointed silently to two hawks gliding over Castle Hill without a single wing beat and suddenly swooping down toward the lake.

Conny listened as calmly to Henseleit's account as to the engineer's. He took no notes, just nodded slightly. An occasional faraway look in his eyes told me he was weighing the two stories against one another. The engineer took leave of us on the pretext he was needed in the project office. I expected to have a more intimate talk with Henseleit now, but he had apparently said his piece and contented himself with staring in outrage at the long band of grayish gravel, crisscrossed by tracks.

As we were standing there, a truck roared up, going much too fast. It carried a load of sand, and its windshield was almost opaque with dust and dried mud. None of us could understand why the driver honked his horn—perhaps he was trying to call attention to how hard he was working. He came bearing down on us, seeming to enjoy the way we leaped to either side in alarm. In a maneuver which did not exactly spare the shock absorbers, he backed up toward the tent. With a cheerful wave he climbed out of the cab, a Lithuanian in a close-fitting fur jacket. Grinning, he went around to the body of the truck, released two hooks and let down the tailgate. Sand poured out on top of the tent. Workers sauntered over and watched with obvious satisfaction as the Lithuanian jumped back into the cab and activated the hydraulic tilt mechanism, whereupon the rest of the sand began to slide and flattened out half the tent and buried it . . .

No, no, not Henseleit; it was old Blask who took action, the stiff-limbed old forester, who had been lying inside the tent and now could only escape by slitting open its side. The old man doggedly worked his way through the slit and stood there for a moment quite dazed before stomping up to the truck's radiator. In order to dispose of the last bit of sand, the Lithuanian raised the truck body until it stood almost vertical, and drove slowly forward, drove right toward old Blask, who did not budge and would not give way before the advancing radiator. I can still see the dim, expressionless gaze of the old man, his pinched mouth; I see him standing there in a posture of stubborn refusal, defying the huge weight that was slowly rolling toward him. Shortly before the bumper touched him and knocked him down, he raised his rifle and shot directly into the windshield. Bird shot and glass flew in all directions, and a wild web of fine lines spread outward from the jagged hole in the windshield. The door of the cab was pushed open. The Lithuanian tried to crawl out on all fours but could not control his limbs. He rolled over and fell into the sand.

As you can imagine, some of the workers hurled themselves at old Blask, disarmed him, and forced his hands behind his back, as if he were still dangerous. The old forester only groaned as they tightened their grip. He gazed vacantly into the distance and did not even turn his head when Henseleit appealed to Conny to act as a witness: "You saw that it was self-defense. You must testify to that."

After they had carried the Lithuanian away, the engineer reappeared. He did not ask for details. Standing on the heap of sand that covered part of the tent, he put the full blame for the incident on Henseleit. In fighting a project launched by the government, he had created a climate of hostility which was bound to produce violence.

We did not wait for the police; we mounted the motorcycle and rode back to Lucknow, to the newspaper offices, where Conny immediately sat down at his venerable Remington, while Kukielka, in an expansive mood, invited me to help him file the hate mail which had come pouring in. As he read through the letters, and sorted them in alphabetical order, the editor could not refrain from making certain stylistic improvements . . .

On the contrary, Martin; it was something else entirely that had provoked these letters to the newspaper. What it was about was soldier songs, a collection of soldier songs whose content he had presumed to review critically in the weekend supplement.

But what was I getting to? Oh, yes, to Conny's report, of course, to my perplexity and his certainty, to the discrepancy between his reading of the event and mine. He portrayed the engineer as a man of wide experience associated with a project that would serve the cause of international understanding, a project whose fulfillment was dear to his heart. Yes, Conny's report actually began with a portrait of a man whom I, at least, could not recall meeting, a practical-minded idealist whose highway would open up the Masurian land and rescue its inhabitants from an isolation not of their own choosing—that was the gist of it. A man of the future, bold and enduring: that was Conny's picture of the man. Whereas I had seen only a competent construction engineer, plodding rather than passionate, interested in the technical side of the project, not in any grand ideas.

Conny's description of the work site so mystified me that I read it through several times. That scene of organized confusion was wrapped, for him, in an aura of high-spirited resolve. He had found workmen who viewed the project as a "peacetime call to battle," and several who prided themselves on having a role in the opening up of Lucknow's bog.

I need hardly tell you the image he created of the men from the Homeland Association who had tried to save our landscape from destruction. He mocked them gently as complacent muddleheads, obsolete champions of nature, who loved narrowness for its own sake, and were blind to the more important task. Conny put the question in the simplest terms: the preservation of breeding places for the black stork versus a vital link between peoples that could be kept open all winter. He admitted that the Homelanders were bent on conserving a heritage, but came down severely on them for refusing to open themselves to the wider world. With the picture already so slanted, the shooting incident itself was reported with a certain bias. The Lithuanian who had dumped the load of sand on the tent was a busy truck driver who in the press of his work had miscalculated by a few feet. Of course, he had had no intention of running down the old forester.

Blask's action, however, had been quite senseless. Conny saw him as the victim of a campaign which, in the final analysis, was directed against rationality itself. As I said, I read Conny's piece through several times and found myself wondering whether I had actually been out there with him. I asked him whether this was what would go into the newspaper, at which Conny assumed an air of astonishment. "But the facts—" I protested, and Conny replied with a statement that remains with me to this day: "Oh, facts; they are only replacement parts for our political convictions." ...

Pardon me? No, go ahead and say what you want to ...

Well, if I understand you correctly, you are on Conny's side because you feel that solutions on the local level are not adequate. But you see, I believe that everything we can settle in the local sphere benefits the whole; one does not exclude the other. You make another point: that the idea of homeland implies the notion of uniqueness. In response to that, I would like to ask what we ought to aim for—to become nameless and completely homogeneous? Do you really believe we will be happier if we let ourselves be swallowed up?

You will be surprised to hear what Conny's dream led to later on. But enough of that; we still have a lot of ground to cover. Right now you must hear how Conny and I became kinfolk, that's right, kith and kin ...

Your guess is right, Martin: our correspondence prepared the way, our wild correspondence, which did not stop after our ill-starred rendezvous, and in which we tried to outdo one another in baring our souls.

But listen to this: I was up half the night composing my letter to Edith about the circumstances leading to my master's examination and then the examination itself. I started out with a long preamble, since that is the only way I know to tell a story. I told her how I had worked out the design for a blue and white wedding rug and had begun weaving it, a piece whose center was a black star, black as night, black as outer space, with a suggestion of floating fish forms around it and trees with crowns shaped like antlered deer heads. I told her how after weeks I had asked Sonja Turk to look at the rug and to give me her opinion, and how my teacher looked the rug up and down, softly whistling and hissing to herself, and finally said, "Well, Zygmunt boy, you have what it takes to be a master, but don't let me catch you laying back, you knucklehead, because a person only shows what he can do after the examination." Then I described how Sonja Turk without another word fetched down the canister, pinched off a good chunk of marzipan for me, then sat down beside me and discussed the various points of my master's examination, staring unabashedly at my rug all the while. I could barely keep my mind on what she was saying.

Edith received a full account of the weather on the day of my examination—it was a typical dry midsummer day. She learned that my teacher had invited me to breakfast and had coached me before the examiners arrived, two tired-looking men and a jolly woman in handwoven garments who kept up a constant humming. "At the examination," Sonja Turk said, "it doesn't do a bit of harm if you sometimes seem sort of shaky and shy. It's only the dummies that think they know everything." And she also said, "A gap here and there warms the cockles of the heart."

I don't know whether I merely imagined it, but it seemed to me that the fish soup Sonja Turk offered the examiners when they arrived—made of zander with beets and thyme—heightened my nervousness, put me in a sweat, in fact undermined me completely.

Naturally I was aware what a credit, but also what an additional responsibility it was to be the one and only pupil of Sonja Turk, the great rug weaver.

At any rate, I described to Edith the almost ceremonial procession to the weaving studio, where the examiners took their places in the upholstered chairs, while my teacher stood behind them by the window. I sat at my loom, which suddenly seemed like a totally strange instrument to me. I could barely remember the significance of warp and weft. I had the feeling I was being asked to perform something I had never done before, like a person forced to guide an airplane into the air without ever having sat at the controls. How cold and unyielding the loom felt! The most everyday techniques seemed to have abandoned me, experience fled, and into this vacuum the examiners tossed their questions.

I outlined for Edith not only the exact order of the questions but also my helplessness when I was supposed to describe basic procedures like stringing the loom and binding off the edges. A pleading look in the direction of Sonja Turk proved in vain; she just stood by the window and smiled. When they asked me how a pattern came into being, I had no idea what a simple answer they expected; I tried desperately to provide complete directions for achieving honeycomb weave, reversible weave, and open-work, but the cheerful woman broke in to ask how, for instance, a rib weave was done. I could hardly believe that all she wanted me to say was: by changing the way you thread the loom. But I said just that, and was surprised at the contented air with which she leaned back in her chair. There was not even need for me to add that color and texture played their part in the creation of a pattern. I had never seemed so idiotic to myself as at my master's examination; at moments I felt as if my memory had failed, like after an accident, with the result that I had painfully to reconstruct piecemeal all I had once known. Sonja Turk continued to smile; even when I could not come forth with the shrinkage factor of hemp and jute, she smiled as if the examination were going completely to her liking. At last, when my explanations grew so sketchy that the examiners were staring at the floor in embarrassment, my teacher suggested we take a break. She served tea, and I, too, received a cup of the brew, in which swam bright-red berries which popped the moment they touched your lips and released a bracing, astringent juice.

Yes, and I went on to tell Edith how after the tea break they questioned me on the history of the pictorial rugs. The questions were gentle and tentative, presumably because the examiners wanted to spare the feelings of Sonja Turk. But now my performance was less disappointing. I started off with Justinian, who had introduced silk weaving into Byzantium, then mentioned the early Nordic pictorial rugs, which imitated Byzantine motifs in wool. I compared the products of the Paris weaving studios with the masterworks of the Dutch workshops, which by far surpassed all other weaving in the sixteenth century. There was hardly anything I did not touch upon: the pleasure-garden rugs and the Swedish peasant rugs, and so on, up the historical ladder, tracing the styles and traditions of pictorial weaving right up to the First World War.

The examiners turned toward Sonja Turk and winked. Then they probed my knowledge of colors, asked me to estimate how much yarn would be needed for a hypothetical project, and to top it off wanted me to explain weaving with swords. I handled their questions so competently that the examiners almost apologetically waved their hands to indicate that that was quite sufficient. They rose from their chairs and stepped over to the wall where my blue and white wedding rug hung behind a canvas, waiting to be judged as my master's project. It was not I but Sonja Turk who drew aside the canvas. Since our rugs all have a story to tell, I was not surprised at first that the examiners just stood there looking, but grew uneasy when their evaluation seemed to be stretching well beyond the usual time.

I told Edith how the examiners sent me out of the room, apparently to deliberate on their verdict, and how I sat outside on the garden bench and looked out over the Lucknow River, soothed by the scent of the shrubs and plants surrounding the house. I felt a strange, comfortable indifference creeping over me; no matter what the verdict, I was reconciled to it and would take it serenely, without self-reproach.

Then they beckoned to me from the window, and I unhurriedly went into the house, to the weaving room, where the examiners were awaiting me with inscrutable, solemn expressions. After a short speech, of which I retained not a word, they handed me the master's diploma, already signed, and congratulated me. Someone brushed a hand over my head from behind; it was Sonja Turk. My attempt to hug her misfired, since she grabbed my outstretched arm and pulled me over to the blue and white wedding rug. She pointed to my initials, Z.R., and said, "Signing your name that way, child, is only for those who need to; you've no need to parade that way so people will recognize you."

I also let Edith know that my master's diploma was lettered in gold, that I had framed it in cherry wood and hung it in the entrance hall of our house, at eye level . . .

Disappointment? You mean that when one writes such letters, any actual encounter cannot help being a disappointment? Well, I don't think that's necessarily true, at least not in every case . . .

But I see you're anticipating: sure enough, four days after my examination, Edith turned up in Lucknow, without prior warning. Suddenly she was there in the hallway, holding her cardboard suitcase and reading my master's diploma. Her face was glowing, and she was all sweaty. Around her neck she wore an amber necklace made particularly valuable by the seventeen insects embedded in big golden chunks.

We embraced wordlessly. She opened her suitcase and lifted out a wooden hanging candelabrum, cruciform in shape, with bright painted spikes for the candles. From the arms dangled wire spirals to which painted birds were attached, fantastical birds which seemed to be trying to snap the little metal rhomboids which danced in the draft, catching the light and refracting it in hundreds of tiny lightning flashes. "For the master," she said, and bent down and pulled one of her golden braids out of its newspaper wrapping: "So, and here's something you should have had long ago, and that's all I've got for you." She picked up her suitcase as if her visit were already over, but I could see how pleased she was at my pleasure, and how calm and steady her emotion seemed.

I called Eugen Lavrenz and my mother. They both admired the candelabrum and wanted to install it in the living room then and there. Together Edith and I scrambled up and mounted it above the seldom-used dining table. Edith stayed for supper; we lit the candles, and the metal pieces twisted and turned constantly, setting the cocoa and even the farmer's cheese to sparkling ...

My mother? You wonder what my mother had to say about Edith? Not all that much; later she commented, "She's a healthy girl, nice-mannered and probably able enough, but when she sits there, there's no need for everyone to see she's got black gym shorts on."

But what did I want to tell you? Conny, right. As soon as we had eaten, we set out, since Conny was supposedly expecting her; I took the cardboard suitcase, and hand in hand we walked through the grass along the bank of the river, with a trail of June bugs behind us. It was a moonlit evening, and out on the lake drifted the boats of the night fishermen, while in the boathouse belonging to the rowing club they were playing the same phonograph record again and again, some sentimental song about Lake Constance.

What we had to say to one another was pure repetition; it had already been said in our letters more intensely. If Conny had actually been expecting Edith urgently, we should have gone by way of the big wooden bridge, but we passed the bridge without stopping and strolled toward the peninsula, as if we had agreed on our destination without having to say a word. Before we knew it, we were standing beneath the monument to the Bosnian commander; ivy wound its way up the pedestal, and when we touched the iron bars of the fence, chips of rust broke off.

"Remember?" "Yes, I remember." I scaled the fence, knocked on the pedestal until I found the iron plate, which could still be lifted out, although the ivy had taken hold so firmly that I had to rip it away. Arms first, I squeezed through the opening. An odor of fungus wafted toward me. I carefully let myself down, listening and groping, and when Edith asked, "Should I come in?", I said, "Yes, come," and I took hold of her arms and drew her in close to me . . .

No, Conny's supplies were no longer there, but his bed was, or at any rate, its remains, which rustled as I felt about; with every motion something crumbled. Edith wanted me to replace the plate over the opening. We sat there silently in total darkness for a while, just sat and listened to each other's breathing, and for a long time neither of us dared reach for the other's hand. High above us, probably in the Bosnian commander's breast cavity, whirred the June bugs that had got in through the eye openings; their confused and frantic buzzing seemed to set the bronze to resonating. I looked up and thought I could see their little armored bodies shining and their wings glowing, but that was probably an optical illusion. Then, as if on signal, our hands met in the darkness, we slid onto Conny's bed and stretched out, and we were not long growing accustomed to the rustling and crackling, ah, yes.

When I woke up—we had both fallen asleep and awakened several times—well, one time I climbed barefoot up into the bronze statue, toiling upward, bracing myself against the sides, up through his stomach and torso. I started when I saw a thin ray of light shining through the Bosnian commander's eyes; I squeezed in behind them and looked out; fast-moving islands of morning fog hung over Lake Lucknow, and beyond the bay of Little Grajevo the sun was rising, its reflection blazing in the windows

of the prison. Over by the mouth of the river, two men were
hauling in eel lines.

I quickly scrambled down, loosened the plate, and let morning
light into the pedestal. I had to replace it at once, for Edith sat up
and protested; she insisted on getting dressed in the dark, and not
only that: she asked me "not to listen" as she pulled on her gym
shorts and the red-and-white-checked dress. And later, when we
waded into the lake to wash, she ordered me "not to look," with
the result that the splashing and puffing she caused only gave me
a strange impression. At that time I did not yet realize that Edith
always made such noises when she washed up. When she was
done, she filled her mouth with water and spewed it out in a great
arc. Since she wished it that way, we avoided each other's gaze,
but that did not prevent us from returning hand in hand. As we
passed the monument, our colossal fellow conspirator with the
empty eyes stood there bathed in reddish sunlight. This time we
crossed the wooden bridge. As we leaned over its side, trying to
hit floating sticks and bits of bark with pebbles, some of our
lightheartedness returned.

Conny lived in a little one-story house on the lake which belonged to his former master, Weinknecht. Since Edith did not
dare knock at such an early hour, I pushed open the unbolted
casement window and snapped my fingers until Conny, who was
sleeping with his head buried in the pillow, woke up and stared at
us in perplexity and disbelief. Our good spirits made him suspi-
cious, as did the fact that we had turned up together at so early
an hour. "Well, come in, but try to be quiet." He opened the
door for us, and we slipped into his room, where we helped him
make his bed and sat there shoulder to shoulder while he shaved,
smoking a cigarette as he did so, which he skillfully shifted from
one side of his mouth to the other. I noticed he was watching us
in the mirror.

"Zygmunt," he said, "let's not have any news before breakfast." He tossed me the latest edition of the *Lucknow News*,
where he had planted an item about my passing the master's
examination. Then he slipped into the kitchen, put water on to
boil, and prepared breakfast for the three of us, while we looked
over his room, silently noting his sparse furniture, the strict tidi-

ness and order in his closet, the photograph of Heinrich Mann he had pinned to the wall beside his desk. On his desk stood the glass case I had given him for his birthday. It contained rare Masurian plants—club moss, cankerroot, rockrose—pressed and mounted on pink paper. On the wall behind the desk hung the friendship rug . . .

Well, anyway, we breakfasted together, he sitting there between us, looking amused; he did not even need to be particularly clever to sense that something had changed in my relationship with his sister. And then suddenly I heard myself asking, "What would you think of Edith and me getting married?" And as if the question struck me as too tentative, I added, "Everything seems to favor it." How little surprised Edith was; she merely drew her shoulders together, placed both hands firmly around her coffee cup, and looked at Conny, who this time did not put out his cigarette the way he usually did, by simply rubbing out the little glowing stub; this time he pressed the butt almost mercilessly into the ashtray, so hard that the wrapping burst. He stood up and went into the kitchen, where we heard him whispering something. When he came back, he pulled us up from our chairs and gently pressed us together, so that our faces were close, then moved close, too, and standing there with us in a conspiratorial knot, he kissed both of us and said, "Oh, I'm so happy. Nothing has ever made me so happy . . ."

Then the Weinknechts knocked and came in, bringing plates heaped with cocoa cookies and honey cake, and a beverage which they described as their specialty—a tea and brandy punch. Master Weinknecht gave a toast and promised to print up the grandest wedding announcements for us, free of charge. I was amazed to see the composure with which Edith decided what had to be done. She wanted Conny and Sonja Turk for witnesses, and by the time our hosts left for work, all the plans had been made.

Even if you have seen pictures or heard accounts, I must tell you about the preliminaries, which for us in Masuria are considered almost as significant as the wedding itself. The most crucial ceremony involved a head of cabbage, by which the prospective bride affirmed her assent. I bought a cabbage at the Lucknow market, let a horse nibble it, and had Eugen Lavrenz go to Edith and hand her the cabbage, with the formula, "In our garden, if you please, someone nibbled on this cabbage, and the tracks led straight to your house." Edith received the cabbage in silent embarrassment, as was required, and so there was no doubt that she accepted me.

The next step was to send out the wedding bidder. Simon Gayko agreed to serve in this capacity. We decked him out in scarves, streamers, and artificial flowers. We covered his gloomy Bosnian visage with powder, fastened a bunch of rosemary to his lapel, and gave him the leather pouch with the invitations. Before handing one out, he had to repeat the traditional verses:

> *Pears and phlox and thyme*
> *Grow in Zygmunt's garden patch.*
> *Because his Edith's sweet and sour,*
> *He'll no more delay the match.*

Eugen Lavrenz decorated the door frame with greenery, spread fine sand in the entrance hall, collected all our shoes in a sack, which was hidden in the secret cellar, and gathered all the hats and hung them on a many-armed rack which he had nailed together . . .

Excuse me, Martin, I did not catch what you said . . .

Oh, you wonder why the shoes were hidden and the hats were put on display. Pure superstition. We Masurians believed that if you stumbled over shoes, it meant that partings were in the offing. Whereas hats were a symbol of a long life together.

But I must tell you about the day itself, the wedding day, when I awoke before dawn and, carrying out my mother's instructions, soaked bread in brandy to feed to the horses, so they would be all fired up as they drew the carriage. I would thus be able to show off my skill in handling horses. I stood by the gate waiting for the rented carriage, which was delivered by the disabled veteran who usually acted as coachman, an impertinent fellow whose talk consisted entirely of indecent allusions. As soon as he had gone into the house to throw himself upon the complimentary breakfast, I stepped up to the two brown mares, stroked them, and held out my palm with the alcohol-drenched bread, which they gobbled appreciatively. They so enjoyed the tidbit that they began sniffing each other eagerly and snapped at me, almost ripping open my pocket. For safety's sake I fastened the reins to the fence with a double knot.

With the blue and white wedding rug as luggage, strengthened by a second breakfast, cheered on by Eugen Lavrenz, and with my mother giving my best suit its final brushing, I set out alone to fetch Sonja Turk, my witness. The mares trotted along briskly; only once did they break into a gallop, but I easily forced them back into their former gait. We reached the house, where Sonja Turk rose from the wooden bench in a saffron-colored blouse and shimmering velvet skirt. I helped her onto the box, and she smilingly tucked a little bag of dried herbs into my pocket. As she tied her bonnet strings tightly under her chin, she remarked, "With these herbs on you, nothing can go wrong. Now let's giddap."

Something was afoot in town; there were crowds streaming toward the center of Lucknow, columns of men in black uniforms with runes on their collars. The air was crackling with a sense of explosive forces. On the broad main road I managed to maneuver by, and in order to escape the commotion completely, I turned into a cross street, with the idea of reaching the church by back ways. But suddenly we found ourselves on the parade route; they were lined up on either side of the street, all the way to the railroad station—men with leather straps across their chests, their faces inscrutable as they stood in formation behind their leaders. The horses were still trotting along sedately. As we passed, I looked into the men's faces, and to my amazement recognized a number of former classmates, sickly Masuch, for example, and Albin Jakubzik, the beanpole. But I also recognized some of their leaders: Bilitza and Henseleit and even Struppek of Struppek & Sausmikat, with a loop of gold braid on his tunic and a pistol at his side.

One of the leaders apparently took exception to our presence; perhaps he felt we were introducing a frivolous note into this scene of deadly earnest. At any rate, he leaped into our path with arms outstretched, determined to halt us and turn us back. The mares reared up, their front legs raking the air. The carriage began to sway. I braced myself against the narrow footboard, wrapped the reins around my wrist, and dragged so hard on the hot leather that the horses threw back their heads, snorting and blowing saliva into the air. The iron-rimmed wheels thundered on the cobblestones; I saw the old chestnut trees along the roadside rushing toward us; I caught a flash of saffron reflected in a dark display window, but above all, I saw the line of uniforms yield before us; first the leaders jumped back, then the men behind them leaped onto the sidewalk, out of harm's way, sheltered by trees and house steps. We hurtled down the street like a storm gust, sweeping aside the crowd, destroying the neat lineup, endangering men and shop windows, and as we tore along, sowing panic as we went, pursued by angry cries of command, I could not help thinking of my father, of his last ride amid fountains of earth, before the grenade hit his miraculous wares and he went up in a multicolored cloud. I do not even like to contemplate how our wild ride would have ended if—but then I caught sight of the car.

It was a big, heavy car, and it was coming toward us, a black car full of people and with six or eight headlights on its prow. One simply had to make way for a vehicle like that, and I tugged at the reins with my remaining strength, but the mares did not obey; the alcohol had gone to their heads, and they were enjoying the alarm they had caused.

Disaster was already staring us in the face when someone ran toward us from the side of the road, a tall man in a black uniform. With a leap, he grabbed at the harness. The horses were in full gallop, and his body swung and whipped back and forth, up and down, but the mares could not shake him off. They angrily laid back their ears and tried to rear up—one even snapped at him—but to no avail. Using his weight and steadily pulling on the bridles, the man forced their heads down. They yielded and stood there almost indifferently, their tails switching and their flanks dark with sweat.

The man who brought our horses to a halt just in front of the automobile was Toni Lettkow, owner of the estate; he had four stars on his collar patches, twice as many as Struppek, whose windows no longer displayed sailor suits but only black and brown uniforms . . .

In a moment, Martin, I'm getting to that. My teacher sat beside me with eyes closed and a hand on her heart. I jumped down from the box and went over to Toni Lettkow, who was standing by the horses. He was breathing hard and scratching both their foreheads at once. He raised his eyes only as far as the bunch of myrtle pinned to my lapel and, before I could thank him, said, "There, you see what can happen, you marrying types. The beasts are of finer stuff than you fellows and can't take cheap liquor. But we'll teach you, just wait and see."

Behind Toni Lettkow a car door swung open, and over his shoulder I saw a man in uniform step out, who in addition to four stars also had silver trimming on his collar patches. It was Reschat, the Statthalter of Lucknow, who held himself very stiffly and had the appearance of an ill-natured schoolmaster, with his pinched mouth, the narrow brush above his upper lip, and the thick, sparkling pince-nez which concealed the color of his eyes. Later on there were many pictures of him around, in barracks, schools, and offices, and his insignia by that time consisted of bunches of oak leaves. Reschat, who seemed remarkably young for his high rank, whispered with Toni Lettkow. I can still see the long, bluish dueling scars on his face. He came toward me. In one hand he held a pair of suede gloves, which he playfully slapped against his jodhpur-style trousers. "Come on, Zygmunt, it's getting late," called Sonja Turk. I looked up at her, and at this moment Reschat struck me in the face with his gloves, once, twice. Then he strolled casually back to the car and tapped the chauffeur on the back. The car started up and rolled on slowly along the lineup, which had regrouped.

"Rotten bastards," Sonja Turk said, with a fury I had never before witnessed in her. "Thrice-cursed rotten bastards."

Toni Lettkow cleared a path, and we left Railway Street and clip-clopped along quiet back streets to St. Elizabeth's, the oldest church in Lucknow, whose weathered brick walls were studded with Swedish, Polish, and Tartar cannon balls, held by ancient mortar. There were also old iron rings, from the days when folks came to church on horseback. To one of these I hitched the horses. Then I lifted Sonja Turk from the box. She stroked my burning cheek and muttered something, then drew signs in the air, conjuring signs, cursing signs.

During the processional I forgot all the insults and threats, for the organist, a lover of the middle octaves, carried us over dark, rippling waters on whose surface blossoms floated. A familiar, reassuring force encompassed us, flute sounds drew us on, a sudden plunge into the bass struck awe to our hearts, and Pastor Naguschevski, who was waiting for us at the altar, appeared like a friendly black bird poised for a current of air that would waft him into the sky. He had let me spread my blue and white wedding rug before the altar, and he led Edith onto the black star that formed its center. This was the same Pastor Naguschevski of whom it was whispered that when he was alone in his drafty lodgings he liked to listen to waltz music and tipple cheap red wine.

He was to marry us, and in order to give Edith and me something substantial to take away with us, he had chosen the passage from James which says, "By works a man is justified and not by faith only." He had just begun to define what good works consist of—I remember he was citing the example of a man who fails, not in the face of the enemy, but in the face of his friend's need—when singing began in the Lucknow marketplace, more than six hundred male voices lifted in the chorale of Langemarck: "I have surrendered . . ."

Pastor Naguschevski looked up startled, listened for a moment, and asked for the windows to be closed, whereupon Sonja Turk rustled down the side aisle and closed them, with the long pole meant for that purpose. The singing was not entirely shut out, but was muted enough so that the pastor could be heard once more.

How simply he began! He described the works by which the coal dealer, the "true master of the Masurian winter," could justify himself, and what the baker might do, and the prison warden, and the doctor, and the pawnbroker. Pastor Naguschevski's answer in all these cases was the same: "Mercy, simple mercy, for that involves sacrifice, and sacrifice makes one just, and he who is just is also justified"—that was the tenor of it.

Suddenly a voice chimed in, an emphatic, impatient voice booming out of a dozen loudspeakers mounted in the trees and echoing back and forth. Edith leaned against me, looked at me with startled eyes, and began to tremble. Despite the closed windows, we could all make out what the voice was demanding; something about honor and loyalty, about an oath and unconditional obedience. Pastor Naguschevski tried once to drown out the orator, but only by way of experiment. He gave in when the highly amplified voice called for us all to acknowledge him as the leader, to follow him, if need be, to offer up to him all that was dearest to us, and so on.

Pastor Naguschevski stepped up close to us, standing half on the blue and white wedding rug. "My children," he said in smiling despair, "my dear children," and now I could smell the wine on his breath and see the wine spots on his surplice. Without any hope of making himself heard, he moved his lips, shaping the questions, the old formulas, and strange though it may sound, we managed to hear his inaudible language, reading each word from his lips, even without the help of the accompanying gestures. And while outside more than six hundred men were repeating a text which the speaker read out to them sentence by sentence, Pastor Naguschevski smiled at us and declared us man and wife. For the recessional the organist unleashed all the voices and registers, and for a moment the organ triumphed over the loudspeakers...

Come in, Nurse, come on in, you're never in the way. You already know Herr Witt ... How nice of you to bring a second cup ...

Exhaustion? You think this talking wears me out? On the contrary, Nurse Margret; the more I get off my chest, the lighter and more bearable my burden becomes; I have the feeling I am dividing myself up, redistributing parts of myself to all those who have made me what I am; at the same time, I am getting to know myself better and better.

No, leave the window open—now I know, by the way, where that sound is coming from, that sound as if someone were gently tearing a piece of silk: it is the sound of tires on the wet pavement.

No, thank you, Nurse, no requests for the moment ...

Have some tea, Martin, here, drink up.

But what did I want to tell you? The wedding, right, our silent wedding. After the ceremony we distributed ourselves among the carriages and drove home, where my mother and Eugen Lavrenz surprised us with a wedding feast in the garden. For a while no one wanted to sit down; our twenty-two guests first had to circle the table, taking everything in, admiring, praising, and certainly also secretly comparing, while Eugen Lavrenz had much to say about each of the special dishes . . .

As I watched our guests, I suddenly became aware of a quiet strength within me. It was like that day when Conny and I had pricked our arms with the tip of his knife, up there on Castle Hill, by the seven giant spruces. It was a kind of daze, a breathless daze of joy, you might call it. I did not even notice that Conny was missing from the table, and had not time to be amazed when he suddenly emerged from the house, hurried toward me, and drew me over to the alders. "Master Weinknecht," he whispered, "the secret police arrested him, but he managed to escape by jumping out of the truck." After delivering this piece of news, he asked to be excused for his hasty departure.

We sat down at the tables, which had been pushed together, and ate for a good three hours, sampling and testing all the dishes. Finally, a huge baking sheet with streusel and poppyseed cake was brought in, accompanied by coffee, prepared in great quantities in borrowed coffee pots; and then we sat there longer, eating and drinking until suppertime, when we responded with interest to platters of pike grilled with bacon and fried eel. Paper lanterns were strung up on lines stretched across the lawn, and in the light of these paper moons, which swayed gently in the evening breeze, guests rose one by one to present something "for your pleasure": one sang a song, another recited a poem. Fishing Commissioner Dudei teased the "Song of Masuria" out of his fiddle, and Eugen Lavrenz treated us to one of his ninety-two lake stories.

Edith was freezing all day, on this, our wedding day. In spite of the warm air, she was shaking and shivering. Even when we led off the dancing, on the grass, down by the river, I felt the way she trembled and snuggled against me, and that did not change, even when Conny returned late in the evening and wrapped a jacket over her shoulders. Conny swung her around several times to the music of the phonograph, but that did not warm her up either, or calm her nerves. No sooner was she back with me than she seized my hand and whispered: "I'm freezing, can you feel how I'm freezing?" Finally, I had no choice but to put her to bed, unobtrusively, without her having said goodbye to the guests, and later, when she was lying under the winter feather quilt, she called me to her and wanted me to tell her what was wrong with her and why she was trembling this way. I did not know what to say; all I could do was reassure her over and over again: "You'll be happy, Edith, you'll be happy."

And I remember what happened the next day; we were sitting there eating leftovers and recalling the celebration, ten of us in the kitchen, each calling up the previous evening's experiences, perceptions, observations, things which had significance only for those who had been there. Suddenly the doorbell rang, and Conny got up, sighing, since he imagined it would just be someone delivering a bouquet a day late. The rest of us went on eating and talking, pleasantly tired and relaxed by the laughter which Simon Gayko set going with his priceless imitations of this person or that. But the laughter broke off when Conny reappeared, whistling through his teeth and shaking one hand as if he had burned it. It was obvious he had something unusual to report. He quietly stepped into our midst and in a low voice announced that Bilitza had come to the house, and with him a high-ranking, a very high-ranking officer in a black uniform, with oak leaves and a star on his collar patches, who introduced himself as brigade commander. I asked Conny to come with me when I went to see what was up.

As I stepped into the hall, they greeted me with that salute of theirs. The man with Bilitza was lean, with a bony face. He apologized for the interruption and proffered his congratulations. Bilitza explained that Brigade Commander Professor Melzer-Tapiau had come to Lucknow from the capital, Königsberg, just for the day, that he had heard about the rare collection in the local museum, and that the distinguished guest would be sorry to leave town without having laid eyes on the "eloquent relics of the Masurian soil." Remembering the subsidies which the Homeland Association sent our way, I was prepared to give them a tour.

Although Bilitza clearly was irked by Conny's presence, I urged him to accompany us, and we set out on a second-class tour, the kind I had worked up for those occasions when I was tired or not in the mood. My commentary would have been superfluous in any case, for Bilitza missed no opportunity to whisper names, dates, and other cues to his brigade commander. He did know the lore; he even recited passages from certain documents by heart. At first the brigade commander gave no sign of being impressed; he looked at all the objects with an unchanging expression, thoughtfully, as though he was measuring them against established norms and patterns. But when we got to the Masurian musical instruments, the humming pot and the devil's fiddle, he allowed himself a grin, and even cracked a thin smile for the "fauna of the homeland," the carved kitchen implements, and my toy collection, which a number of previous visitors had extolled as the richest and most significant collection in the entire southwest. The professor was pleased by the contents of the Sokolken box, and admired an example of beadwork. Bilitza, with his two stars on his collar patches, seconded all his words and was quick to light his cigarettes for him.

Melzer-Tapiau nodded as he inspected the weapons collection, took a lance socket and a dagger down from the wall, turned them around in the light, and identified them: "Iron artifacts from a Vandal warrior's grave, one hundred years before the Christian era." In the tool collection he noted the age of a wooden plow and set a spinning wheel in motion; after that he wanted a brandy. He drank it down with no apparent enjoyment. He avoided looking at Conny or me; everything he had to say was directed at Bilitza, who, it was obvious, had suggested this visit, with God knows what hopes in mind. From the course of the tour, you would have imagined it was Bilitza, not I, who owned and administered this museum. There were even hints that he had been giving thought to the future of our collection.

In any case, the professor seemed to feel some verdict was called for, and, speaking again only to Bilitza, remarked, "Not suitable for official support." So our museum did not meet his criteria.

Bilitza seemed to grasp at once what this judgment signified. He made a gesture expressing regret, but also resignation. Conny, as was his way, did not simply swallow the answer but asked rather heatedly for what reason our museum had become worthless all of a sudden.

The brigade commander shook his head and said, "Not worthless, but also not worthy of support in our sense." And when Conny asked further, with a show of hurt feelings, how our museum fell short, the brigade commander referred to the "touchingly random quality" of our collections, the "disregard for political implications" in our treatment of history.

After downing his second brandy, he continued in this vein: "What good does it do when one find after another is simply deposited in the collection? The objects receive their significance only through the manner in which they are organized, and that means when they are put in the service of an idea, a great ideal. Everyone knows that our ancestors worked, fought, and developed their rituals and traditions; it is almost superfluous to collect evidence for that. What is important is that the collection be arranged to demonstrate that the Masurian has always seen himself as the advance guard of the Germanic spirit in the East. The relics must speak for a cause." The professor gave an example: "When weapons and peasant tools are arranged properly, they evidence the vital link between defense of the homeland and connection with the soil." Bilitza asked sedulously whether he might interpret this remark as a suggestion; he was told that he might, and he gestured to me as if to say, "We'll discuss this later." He turned to the professor and asked whether official support might not be forthcoming if certain changes were made. The professor allowed that it might, but his manner was not exactly effusive.

We accompanied them to the entrance hall, and before they took their leave with that salute of theirs, Bilitza announced that he would call on me soon, in order, as he said, to remold the museum "in the spirit of the new times." I must have winced at this, for after the uniformed visitors had left, Conny stepped up close to me and said, "You should see your face, Zygmunt!"

Instead of returning to the kitchen, where they were still laughing and going over yesterday's party, we both went into the workshop. Conny closed the door and offered me a cheap cigar. Putting his arm around me and speaking with careful pauses, he warned me against opening my museum to the new riders to the East, the self-appointed advance guard, whose ideology called for making everything into a battle and every battle a show of their own strength. Bilitza and his crowd would turn our museum into an aggressive display, a shrine to glorify defense of the homeland and pride of race. Conny drew a brochure out of his pocket, the *Lucknow Homeland Yearbook* for 1933, and showed me the photographs: laughing plowmen, smiling fishermen, and Work Corps members. Work had been pronounced sacred, and every worker a soldier who plunged into battle joyfully, with the sound of trumpets resounding in his ears. Every worker helped to man the front, whether in the forest, at the brickworks, in the potato fields, or out on the lake. They chalked up victories for the country's future. But victories were also being achieved in the realm of the past. The mounds of ages past were being excavated, and under every hillock were found relics of German folkways and Germanic culture.

And Conny read me statements by the "Masters of the New Time" declaring their aims: they wanted to advance boldly into the storm, the Eastern storm, the universal storm, and certain of their strength, they promised to create conditions such as had never before been seen. They would plant the country with so-called cells of destiny, which would join to form a new Community of Race. Conny was afraid that one day they would make me into an ally, and he reminded me how the Lucknow Homeland Association had fallen prey to the new spirit. It was clear that his warning was well-founded.

But enough of that, my dear boy. Let me tell you how our jollities came to an end: Edith again complained of being cold, feeling numb all over, and even before the lamps were lit, I took her upstairs to the bedroom, where the trembling and teeth-chattering still did not stop when she was tucked in under the winter feather quilt in an ankle-length linen nightgown. In her embarrassment and nervousness she pathetically begged me to forgive her. Finally I asked Sonja Turk what she would suggest, and my good teacher advised me reproachfully, as if I should have thought of it myself, to expose Edith to the beneficial influence of the blue and white wedding rug. I rolled her up in it and tied the rug around her, making an Egyptian queen of her, rigid and majestic, and had her drink a tea Sonja Turk had brewed. Then I sat beside her and waited for the promised effect.

As I sat there, she asked out of the blue, "What will happen, Zygmunt, what will happen?" I was so taken aback at her earnestness that at first I could only answer in the most general terms: "We'll be happy, that's how I see it." She sat there brooding; my answer did not satisfy her. She looked as though she had been condemned to something, some feeling or attitude, or as though from now on I had some sway over her—I don't really know. She was looking for something like certainty, groping for a thread that would lead her to that end. That must have been it. After a while she repeated with fresh concern, "Tell me what will happen, tell me."

I found myself conjuring up images of summer, scenes of contented domesticity. I boldly cast myself into our future and held out to her what she needed. But what she longed to hear were the details: "Tell me how we will live," and I mounted flower boxes at the windows, hung curtains to blow in the breeze, and spread the floors with rugs which I had woven according to her specifications. That was not enough for her. I summoned up winter, heaped split wood by the door, buckled skates onto Edith and myself, and in the pale-gray winter air we glided with singing blades over the lakes, to the cries of the ice fishermen hallooing back and forth.

"But here in the house," she asked, "what will our life in this house be like? Tell me, Zygmunt." There was no help for it; I had to plot out a whole day, from the moment of waking to the moment of bedtime, a day blessed with friendliness and crowned by the evening hours when we sat together and described what had happened while we were apart. I told her about my day at the weaving studio, and she told me about the Gypsies, and how she had given them a loaf of bread, fresh from the oven. "But why," she asked, "why did I give them the bread?" And I replied, without hesitation, "Because you wanted to be rid of them; you did not want them to read your palm."

Whenever I began to flag, she begged me, "Go on, go on, tell me about the children." "All right," I said. "Let me tell you about Paulie first." And I described his growing up in the garden by the river, barefoot, brown, with light-colored eyes, a little reconnoiterer and path stalker who knew every bird call and wild animal track. I saw him through the childhood diseases and made him a short-spoken but excellent pupil, and Edith listened breathlessly to all of this, apparently satisfied with the names and destinies I invented. But when I made Paul my apprentice and wanted to train him as a rugmaker, she expressed doubts and said,

"A potter, you mean; Paul cannot possibly be anything but a potter."

My head was humming. There was a whistling and twittering as if I were standing under a telephone pole or were one of those weatherbeaten poles myself, supporting the lines over which voices traveled from a distant source to a distant destination. Edith wanted me to go on, but before I had brought Paulie to his twentieth year, she noticed with surprise that the cold had left her and she was no longer shivering . . .

Excuse me, Martin, but could we stop here for today? The skin grafts cause a certain tightness, and I haven't been sleeping all that well. Besides, I feel a memory coming on which I cannot face just now. You know how one has to be in the right frame of mind for certain memories . . .

No, no, I'll be better, I'll surely be feeling better next time you come . . .

# 9

You're surprised to find me at this, are you? Just open that umbrella and set it in the sink to dry. Yes, I thought it would give you a jolt to see me sitting up in bed with a writing pad on my lap. I felt it was time to start getting it down, Sonja Turk's manual, I mean, her book on the art of Masurian weaving, which I once knew by heart. As you see, my memory is still reliable: the first chapter, on colors, is almost finished, with all the curious errors my teacher made:

> *Blue and yellow wed for life*
> *Firmly tie to home the wife.*
> *Bright green meadow, bright green wood*
> *Luck and milk will come right soon.*

Later; I'll go on with it later, when I'm alone again. Say that again, Martin . . . Gloom? Ancient superstition? That's not what I'd call it, but what did persist from our earliest times into the present was the old Sudauese cult of the gods. We had this almost unspoken veneration of heroes, and the black- and brown-uniformed riders to the East by no means tried to suppress it. On the contrary, they fostered it for their own purposes. Let me tell you about the celebration at the Krupischk altar, an old festival of thanksgiving. But at the same time I must tell you about Conny's trip to Kapice, to the famous horse market in Kapice, where he was sent by the *Lucknow News*.

The sacrifice altar: you must picture a weathered granite slab, about nine by fifteen, massive and uneven, blackened in the middle by seven fires, standing knee-high on a slope above Maraune Brook, with thirteen pitch oaks in a semicircle about it. We clambered up there in the dusk, the owlish dusk, thirty or even thirty-five men, members of the Homeland Association and a few guests, all of them invited by Bilitza, who was wearing the black uniform of the SS.

A number of the others were wearing uniforms, too, black ones or brown, and those who did not belong to the SS or SA were at least dressed in blue, the favored color of Curchos, the generous Sudauese god who blessed the beekeepers with honey, the fishermen with whitefish and smelt, the hunters with game. In an exalted and festive mood, we stepped under the trees, which in spite of the assaults of time and lightning were still full of sap. As we passed, we placed offerings on the granite slab—a little bag of grain, a jar of honey, a silvery fish, a rabbit's paw. Although there was no wind, the crowns of the oaks rustled. There was the sense of something awakening, shaking off the sleep of centuries: our Masurian past was being roused to transmit its lessons to the men gathered around—grown-up men, all of them married and respected in their professions.

And now let us stand there in the reverent attitude fitting to that spot, while we follow Conny over the border to Poland, to Kapice, in whose meadows they held a horse market, a market that drew people from far and near: Lithuanians, Gypsies, even Belgians and Dutchmen. There were peasants and soldiers and representatives of the great mines, who bought up dozens of those shaggy ponies, rugged little beasts fated to spend the rest of their lives pulling the coal carts down there in the dark. Breeders and stable owners came, folk who set much store by a horse's pedigree, and many a seller, along with his nag, also brought his oldest daughter, both of them decked out to show to their best advantage, and for the same reason.

Conny sauntered past the tents and booths. He listened while the market superintendents explained that this year there were fewer horses for sale than the previous year, three thousand eight hundred, to be exact. Then he strolled over to the corrals and rings where men in fur jackets, their hats pushed far back on their heads, examined the horses' teeth and their gaits and usually responded to the first price mentioned by saying, "Oh, no, you don't, you old fox." Mocking laughter and feigned indignation issued from one of the rings, where two men were making a deal for an East Prussian gray and apparently putting on a good show for the spectators. A crowd had gathered, and spurred by the laughter and applause, the men dragged out their negotiations. The grumbling buyer kept ambling around the ring, counting the horse's ribs as he ascribed every imaginable defect to the beast, while the owner sat on a railing, toying with his whip and uttering an endless stream of insults, including colorful Polish invectives, which Conny jotted down with relish.

While Conny is there gathering material for his article, we can return to our place under the oaks with the members of the Homeland Association, who were gazing not ecstatically but at least respectfully into the west, where the sunset flaunted its ribbons of red, black, and gold. And believe it or not, standing there together we all felt a secret current move through us. Awe brushed us like a welcome breath of frost, and we were prepared to receive a judgment.

And then Bilitza stepped forward, Squad Leader Bilitza; he fished a sheet of paper out of his sleeve, quickly glanced over the text, and then, looking over us or through us in the direction of Bialystok or Smolensk, he recited a poem called something like "German Faith," which bristled with threats and apostrophes. Then we sang. Then one of the men stepped over to the sacrifice altar, pulled out a little bag of briquets, laid them out to form a circle around the sacrificial offerings, poured lighter fluid over them, and at Bilitza's signal set fire to the little heap. In the darting flames the offerings came to life, shriveling up, bursting, melting into each other and lending color to the fire. Curchos was well disposed; the ancient Prussian god of generosity accepted the offerings brought him by the Lucknow Homeland Association—men experienced in their trades, as I mentioned, who had conceived this notion of creating a bridge between pre-Christian times and the present, in the process overlooking the lamb, the sacred lamb of the Knights of the Teutonic Order. We all moved in closer to watch the slow, spasmodic melting and merging of the offerings. No one ventured to speak.

And now let us return to Conny at the horse ring, where he reveled in the cheerful hurly-burly. He heard the duel of curses to its end, at which point the buyer agreed to stand the cost of the *magrietsch*, the free round of drinks without which no business deal was considered valid in our parts. Amid rousing applause the buyer and seller shook hands, the new owner slapped and tickled the horse and pulled a lead tag out of its mane, the customs tag, then led the animal away from the ring, or at least tried to lead it past the crowd of horses and men who were waiting their turn. Suddenly the animal shied, whinnied irritably, and tried to bite a dapple gray. The dapple gray reared up and came crashing down, splintering the bottom railing of the fence. Conny never did discover whether it was the hoof of the East Prussian or the dapple gray that struck him in the thigh, not with full force, but still so hard that he fell, rolled over, and remained on the ground for a moment. The seller, a sturdy man with gray hair, helped him up, and, as though taking responsibility for the accident, led Conny to a trailer, which was as roomy as those of the Gypsies camped by themselves in a corner of the meadow, and far less rickety.

The man pressed Conny down on his homemade bunk, examined the thigh, prodding it with his hard brown fingers, while Conny looked past him at a shelf on which stood a photograph in an oval frame. As the man was winding a cold compress around his leg, Conny asked after the boy in the photograph. The man replied that the boy was his brother, who had loved to follow the brooks and rivers and had one day disappeared into the waves, presumably washed away to the north by those same waters. Conny commented that the boy reminded him of an acquaintance of his called Bilitza. Thereupon the Lithuanian horse dealer, who was just tying the ends of the bandage, looked up in astonishment, for his own name was Andrej Bilitza, after his father.

Don't ask what thoughts passed through each man's mind as the sacrificial offering on the slab gurgled and merged into a bubbling, multicolored mass, a toothsome meal for Curchos, who graciously accepted it. The men stared fixedly into the fire. Most of them remained motionless, legs slightly spread, their hands loosely fisted. Then Bilitza summoned us to the oaks. It had grown dark. He spoke, with many a pregnant pause, and much cold passion, of the dangers he foresaw, and his images overpowered us, even those of us who were almost too tired to listen.

He conjured up storms and floods issuing from the East, a tossing sea of ice, made up of bodies surging toward our border.

He could already hear the waves pounding in the distance, the roar in the air. He called on us to gather all the strength of our arms into one mighty arm, the protective German arm—and so forth. We must each be a barrier, a little border fortress, just as our Masurian forebears, the Sudauese, had been. We were to be the watchmen, the guardians of the border, who would not give ground even at high tide. He spoke without a qualm of "the rebirth of our race" and "returning to ancestral sources," and in this new language of his promised that the "good German sword" would cut out all that was sick and rotten. He then proposed a song, during which we all linked hands, a moment of meditating on ancient heroes—there suddenly came to my mind that bit in the old play, where Wadoles had cut my throat with his dagger, out of love—and finally we celebrated the night with a dozen fiery wheels which we hurled down the slope. They were made of old wagon wheels wrapped with rags and doused with kerosene, then lit and spun in the air before they were launched down the hill. They drew a wild train of fire behind them as they raced down the slope, bounced into the air when they reached the bank, and plunged hissing into the brook.

And now back to Conny, as he leans on the helpful Lithuanian horse dealer and attempts a few steps in the caravan. It turned out that he could walk on the injured leg with only a slight increase in pain. The man asked several times about the person in Lucknow who went by his name, but Conny was evasive; he felt potential trouble here.

The horse dealer would not let Conny go without their first drinking a cup of coffee together. Beneath the picture of the black Madonna, he described a time when he had been the foremost horse dealer in the swampy Narew region. His father, too, had been a horse dealer, and he told Conny a story out of his own youth which had changed his life in a certain sense.

One day his father had sent Andrej and his brother, eight and nine years old, into the town of Ruda, where they were to collect the final payment on a horse. One behind the other in the saddle, they crossed seven fords and found their way to Ruda. Their father's debtor paid with a single gold piece, which the older boy put not into his pocket or wallet but into his mouth for safekeeping. The weather turned bad on their return journey, the trees were storm-tossed, and they miscalculated at a ford, so that the horse stumbled into deep water. Hanging on to the horse's mane, they reached the other side, but the gold piece was gone, lost when the older boy opened his mouth to shout a warning to his brother. Dreading to return without the money, the older boy began diving, with his brother looking on and giving advice. He dove again and again, fully clothed, groping among the stones and gravel of the river bottom until he ran out of breath and had to use his last strength to return to the bank. Still, he did not dare give up. He wanted to dive down one more time, nearer the rapids, and trembling with cold and fear, he let go of the drift-wood he was clutching and threw himself into the current. That was the last Andrej Bilitza ever saw of his brother, and although a detachment of Engineers on their way home from maneuvers searched the river for a distance of seven miles, the boy was never found.

And now let us return to the sacrificial slab under the oaks, where a small fire still smoldered. Upon a signal from Bilitza, we threw ourselves down around the altar to Curchos and dug into the contents of our knapsacks, eating with frank voracity in the manner of our forefathers. We traded food with one another—cutlets, drumsticks, and fried fish; we drank, not, to be sure, mead out of horns or skulls, but our own honey brandy, which we slurped out of enameled cups; it gave us a sense of what those prehistoric drinking bouts must have been like. To properly carry out the old Prussia freedom cult, we should have recited heroic tales after the meal. But groggy from the meschkinnes, we found ourselves swapping anecdotes, recalling our first loves, clacking our tongues to offset our sleepiness.

Finally, the sky brightened in the east, and the dawn which we were pledged to wait for got underway on the horizon. We rose, greeted the sun with a song, collected our refuse, and set out for home. On the way I found Bilitza beside me; pleased with himself and with the night's doings, he sketched out a plan which appar-ently went beyond the proposal made by Professor Melzer-Tapiau. He wanted to create a borderland museum, the Great Borderland Museum, as he called it, which should testify to the "invincible will" of the population between the Pissa and the Pissek Rivers to withstand foreign domination. Visitors should be able to descend into the world of our fathers and be edified by their example. Numerous models of historic scenes were to aid this act of imagination—for instance, the protracted border negotiations between Duke Albrecht and the Polish king Sigismund August, which ended with their erecting a twelve-foot-high border marker decorated with the crests of their respective countries.

But the main stress would be on scenes of land taking, colonization, martial struggle. He wanted to know whether I was willing to put myself at the service of this grand plan—that is, would I let my "jolly hodgepodge," as he expressed it, be integrated into the projected borderland museum. For the time being, the only ruse I could think of was to feign indecisiveness.

All right, now we shift to the crowded newsroom, where Conny banged out his impressions of the horse market on his trusty old Remington. He reeled off page after page of his feature article, revised the manuscript by hand, and dropped it on the desk of Senior Editor Kukielka. Kukielka put on his usual act of enthusiasm, but at a certain point in his reading let the manuscript fall out of his hands. His shoulders slumped, and he shook his head gravely. Conny stepped up behind him and glanced down at the page, but he could not detect what might have caused such a reaction.

It was, of course, the passage bearing on Bilitza's origins. Together Conny and Kukielka mulled over the text, looking for some more subtle way to convey the information. Finally, Kukielka insisted that they take the article to Friedrich Maruhn, owner of the *Lucknow News*, for his blessing. But Maruhn was in Königsberg again, and after Conny had insisted that he would take sole responsibility for the piece, Kukielka gave the go-ahead and himself brought the pages to the typesetter.

Do you want to hear what happened with me and Bilitza? He had announced that he was coming by, in order to look over our collection and list those items worthy of being transferred to his planned borderland museum. I was waiting at the window, watching for him. Suddenly I spied Edith on the road, with a basket on her arm and her head scarf all awry. She was breathing hard and staggering from tree to tree. Before I could rush out, a motorcycle came roaring along, screeched to a stop, turned, and moved slowly back to Edith. It was Conny, and he brought her home.

He helped her into the house, where my mother quickly took charge of her, with tender concern. Conny and I went into the workshop to wait for Bilitza. I still remember how Conny sat on the workbench, his legs dangling, and lectured me, calmly and emphatically, with that self-assurance of his. I can still hear his warnings: "Don't get mixed up in this, Zygmunt. Let them find their own stuff, if they can. There are some things that cannot remain innocent, and one of them is a museum of local history. At its best, it fosters sentimental stupidity. At its worst, it plays straight into the hands of the ethnic-purity boys." Conny grew more and more bitter as he spoke. His heels pounded the leg of the workbench; his sentences became shorter, fiercer, and more helpless. I was amazed at the fury which he felt for the idea of the borderland museum. "A temple of prejudices. A declaration of war by means of historic relics. A total submersion in the cult of the past—which all too soon becomes an attack on the present." ...

I knew you would say that, Martin. It is spoken from the heart, I can tell ...

So anyway, Conny begged me not to support Bilitza's plan in any way. Bilitza was more than an hour late, and Conny was due at the town hall, where a competition for "the most beautiful town in Germany's eastern provinces" was to open. He had some ironic suggestions for Lucknow: we could deck out all our swans with the Iron Cross; black, white, and red curtains might billow from every window in town; the pets should be taught to do the Hitler salute, and all our monuments be turned toward the east.

Let us now move to the town hall, where an enthusiastic audience had gathered in the smaller council chamber to hear Bilitza announce the terms of the contest. He had forgotten the visit to the museum. He was in an expansive mood, sure that Lucknow would capture the prize, but sure also of the happy effect the competition would have on the life of the towns participating. Buildings would be hung with pennants and bunting, tulip beds would spring up around dreary railroad stations, twig brooms would sweep the drafty marketplaces clean, doors and window frames would sparkle with new coats of paint—all this and much more to point up the difference between these towns and those on the other side of the border. He was imparting this vision to everyone present when Conny came into the room. He gestured apologetically to the speaker and was heading for an empty chair when two men stood up and not only blocked his path but gave him to understand that his presence was unwelcome. Conny showed them his invitation, but they remained unimpressed. They shoved Conny toward the door, pushed him out into the corridor, and shook their fists at him.

Bilitza paused in his speech and looked questioningly at the men. They consulted with one another in whispers, after which one of them walked up to the podium and showed Bilitza a copy of the *Lucknow News*, with a paragraph that someone had circled. Bilitza pushed the newspaper aside, as though this was no time to look at it, but as he did so, his own name caught his eye and he began to read, ignoring the audience, who stared at him expectantly. Later, some claimed that his face had turned white as chalk and his lips began trembling.

At any rate, he read the passage several times, then attempted to speak, but words failed him—all the audience heard were a few inarticulate groans. He put on his cap as if in a trance, saluted, and stumbled toward the door through which Conny had just been ejected. Some of those watching concluded that he meant to go after Conny and bring him back.

Bilitza left the town hall, went down to the lake, and sat there for a while on a bench. Later he was seen on the bridge and on the causeway and at the drinking trough below the estate. Toward evening he turned up in a woodlot in Borek Forest, where people from Little Grajevo were rooting up stumps. He did not respond to any greetings, though he often stopped and stared at the torn-up root systems. He spent an especially long time gazing at several clumps of trees outside the forest. He climbed up Castle Hill and sat there on the stone wall Conny and I had built; two of the seven spruces, at whose base we had once had our private cemeteries, had been toppled by a storm.

He left Castle Hill after nightfall, but returned at dawn, in uniform, with a bag of tools on his back: saw, ax, wedges. He set to work, notching one of the giant spruces so that it would fall in the right direction, then sawing, working carefully, completely under the sway of the enormous decision he had made—you might also call it a verdict.

At any rate, no one before or after felt called upon to do what Bilitza had condemned himself to do. I have often tried to imagine him, exhausted from sawing, bent over, squinting up the rough, scarred tree trunk. I have often thought of him working there in the light of the dawn, with the lake and the huddled forest down below and the meticulous patchwork of fields in the distance. How often I have put myself in his place, given one last blow to the wedge, felt the trembling that ran through the trunk, leaped as fast as possible into the path of the falling tree, turned, and looked acceptingly toward the tree: greenness, the air whistling, the blow, then darkness.

They found him that same day; it was ascertained that he had lived a few hours after the tree knocked him down and pinned him to the ground.

I don't know, Martin, but there are forms of death for which I have to feel respect, and this is one of them. It was fitting for Bilitza, if you think of what he was and of the clamorous nonsense he dreamed up with his limited intellect. But enough of that. The newspaper obituary was written not by Conny but by our former teacher Henseleit, Bilitza's successor as chairman of the Lucknow Homeland Association.

For the time being, Conny did no more writing in our newspaper. After the funeral, which he would have attended had not Kukielka advised him to stay away, he was summoned to the office of Friedrich Maruhn. The newspaper owner served him coffee and cognac and was not sparing with murmured expressions of admiration. Then he confided to Conny some of the difficulties the newspaper was experiencing at a time when those who set the tone were calling for "texts consistent with the interests of the nation." Maruhn hinted that it was not his wish to terminate Conny's activity as a reporter, but he was powerless to do anything about the requirements laid down for him. Because he personally had come to value Conny's abilities, he suggested that Conny retain his connection with the paper. He offered him the possibility of returning to the printing plant and working there for the time being—he repeated: for the time being.

Conny accepted the offer without even taking time to think it over, as Maruhn had suggested. He was sure this was simply a temporary solution that had been worked out just for him, and when he reported his change in circumstances to us, he gave the impression that it was a welcome change. Perhaps he hoped that after an interlude in the printing plant, people would no longer ask him about Bilitza, that name he was trying to forget . . .

Pardon me? No, Martin, that was not the end of the idea of a borderland museum. By and by it was raised again by Bilitza's successor, with less fervor, to be sure, more dutifully than anything else. At least he did not turn up to inventory the weapons and tools in our collection, although he brought up the subject of the museum at every meeting of the Homeland Association.

At that time I welcomed anything that remained undecided, for our child had been born, and I, at least, felt strongly how much that event affected us and how much strength we had to summon up to deal with the unexpected alterations in our circumstances . . .

Our child: before it was born we had decided to call it Paul, Paul the little one, but when I saw him for the first time—wrinkled, chubby-legged, blue in the face from crying—I was somewhat startled, and other names came to my mind—Wolf, or Robert, or even Wolfdietrich. We generally called him Purzel, which was the Masurian name for a certain kind of yeast pastry that formed curious shapes as it rose. Purzel slept and cried, dominating us with his needs, sometimes acknowledging my caretaking and caresses with a blank look, sometimes insistently shaking his head as if to say that even at this young age he was not accepting anything on faith.

Edith was enthralled by the child. She sat for hours beside his cradle, a museum piece painted with roses and little birds. The minute I picked Paul up, she began to tremble, then to object; she was nervous if I so much as wiped the drool from his mouth. In Purzel's little old man's face she observed reactions hidden to the rest of us. She wrote down these discoveries in a pretty notebook with pink ties. This was the beginning of a long period of withdrawal for Edith. When I came into her room unexpectedly, she stopped her murmurs, tore herself away from the baby, and looked at me in consternation, as if I had broken in on a tender conspiracy apparently directed against me. She seemed completely uninterested in the news and gossip I brought home from the weaving studio. It was as if she did not hear me; often she quietly turned away and left me standing there in the middle of a sentence.

I should tell you that Sonja and I were working at that time on our largest commission, our first joint effort. It was to be a magnificent birthday rug, which Toni Lettkow had ordered in person and was going to pick up and deliver himself, a rug of unusual dimensions for the so-called Gauleiter in Königsberg. It was to be a sample of the richness of the Masurian rug-weaving art.

We had been given only general guidelines. We knew we had to work in four rotating suns, but the rest of the design was left to us. After all kinds of mysterious mullings, Sonja Turk decided on partridges and dancing girls and a stylized group of trees behind which an ear was visible. We were not particularly keen about the job, but once Sonja Turk had accepted the commission, we worked on after our usual quitting time, worked by lamplight, and some evenings it was almost midnight before I got home.

Edith seemed not to miss me. When I explained why I was getting home so late, she would look at me as if she did not know what I was talking about, then turn her attention back to the baby. Edith had no doubt that Paul recognized her and that his undirected smile was a response to her fondling. She never tired of wooing him; she would hold up a teddy bear, a little donkey, a bright-colored celluloid duck, and watch the expression in his gray-blue eyes...

No, no, Martin, we finished our first joint commission right on time and were pleased with the result. They came in a carriage from the estate and fetched the rug. They praised it to the heavens and we took it for granted that it would go straight to Königsberg to be delivered to the so-called Gauleiter on his birthday.

But a week later two horsemen came trotting across the drying meadow, thoughtlessly trampling the drying skeins of wool, two horsemen in black uniforms with bronze insignia on their chests. We came out of the weaving studio and waited for them in front of the house. They jumped the hedge, one of them slashed a piece of twine, and the rolled-up rug fell from his saddle. They did not speak. Or rather, one of them said, "Filthy Gypsies!" That was all. Then they wheeled and rode back toward the river.

We carried the rug into the house, and the more we looked at it, the better the workmanship seemed. We were thoroughly mystified by what had happened and by the angry manner in which the rug had been returned.

We never did discover exactly why the rug had been rejected. Later, to be sure, we heard from trustworthy sources that one of our symbols had involuntarily touched on a sensitive subject: it seems that one evening when he was in his cups, the so-called Gauleiter had bitten off the ear of a drinking companion . . .

In any case, we had our rug back, and we had not been paid. We sat there in silence, not even unhappy over the business, merely pensive. After a while my old teacher placed her hand on my shoulder and said, "We are blanks, Zygmunt my lad, blanks but for our connections with things, be it a star or a tree of life or a little partridge, and that's something you can't learn too young. So take this here rug home for your Purzel. Let the little rascal grow up with it. See what he can pick out as he gets older. Let him learn to see differences and be in touch with his surroundings."

Sonja Turk helped me roll up the rug again, and I borrowed a handcart and took it home, the biggest present Paulie ever received. It was so large that we had to hang it in the workshop, where it took up almost an entire wall.

You may not believe this, but when Edith carried him slowly past his rug for the first time, he crowed with pleasure at the sight of the partridges, grew anxious when he saw the three white dancers stepping solemnly across a green plane. Each time I took him in my arms and moved him past the woven pictures as if they were a film, he responded in the same way. He crowed and reached out for the partridges and wished to put his arms around their necks. At the sight of the dancers, he hid his face and breathed heavily as though there were a weight on his chest. Once when I stopped in front of the partridges and held Paul close to them, he tried to seize their heads and put them in his mouth. He whimpered with frustration, and suddenly screamed and went blue in the face. Edith begged me to keep him away from the rug for the time being.

As I said, Edith kept track of his development, and long before I noticed any traits of his, she perceived his gentleness, his excellent memory, but also the delicacy of his feelings. These qualities turned out to be lasting ones. He early proclaimed his right to have his own experiences, that is, he made clear that he did not like to be shielded from experiences that lay in his path, even dangerous ones.

What interested him most? Other children. He would patiently ride on my shoulders wherever I chose to go, but the moment he spotted another child, he came out of his reverie, pounded my chest with his heels, leaned over perilously, demanding to be set down. Once on the ground, he headed straight for the other child and grabbed for its face. Often he was not only shoved away but knocked down. Yet even if he fell on cobblestones, he never cried, just looked around in bewilderment.

At the large sandbox in the playground he let himself be pushed around so meekly that the other children could hardly believe it when one day he discovered the pleasures of pushing down others. Paul, all tenderness and curiosity: he learned the rules of the game but did not follow them for himself. He insisted—or so it seemed to me—on his own approach to life.

In our museum he favored the very objects I would have imagined: not the crossbow, lance, or double-edged sword, but the humming pot, the devil's fiddle, and the contents of the Sokolken box. When Eugen Lavrenz set the spinning wheel in motion, Paulie shut his eyes; he claimed to hear voices and a hummed tune. He liked our animal room, and would groom the stuffed specimens, brushing their fur, polishing their teeth and their glass eyes. He gave names to the dancers and the partridges on his rug, strange names he could not possibly have heard from us: Olk or Gigga or Wanna.

Edith still tried to maintain a secret pact with the child. She wanted to know everything that passed through his mind and would question him so hungrily that I found myself annoyed and embarrassed. Paul seemed to comply, but deep inside he was resisting. Just imagine: to keep him from wandering down to the riverbank, Edith fastened a long rope to a tree and tied the other end to the leather harness he wore at that time. So Purzel was staked out like a goat, and he never left the circle determined by the length of the rope. Once I noticed he was not trailing the rope behind him, and ran over to check. The little chap showed me the hairpin he had used to pick open the knot. He was proud of his feat, but he did not stray from the circle Edith had defined for him, even when he was free.

On long summer evenings we two would go down to the river and sit side by side on the grassy bank and watch the little whirl-pools forming and dissolving under the weeping willows. He had an eye for everything in the world of nature, and he trembled with the excitement of it all. I found it wonderful to sit there with him until the wind died down in the rushes and it was time to take him home to bed.

Around this time we began to worry about Edith. More and more she stayed in her room or slunk about the house with an overwrought air. She became upset so easily that we hardly dared speak to her. Any requests we made she carried out with a kind of harried, hectic subservience. Toward me in particular she displayed a curiously anxious manner. Something had hurt her, worried her, but whenever I tried to query her about it, she became evasive or listened to what I had to say without offering any answer. She treated Paulie with distracted, sometimes sorrowful tenderness. She would stand for a long time behind a hedge or at her window, watching him playing. In her soft white dress she looked like a bird about to take flight. She continued to keep a diary, noting down everything to do with Paulie. She recorded his growth and his behavior, and time and again would describe incidents illustrating his vulnerability and the signs of insight which set him apart from others his age. Edith amazed me later by the range of her observations, but she also proved that observations by themselves do little good . . .

Pardon me? Yes, dear boy, that seems to be the case: our observations by themselves do not add up to the truth. But enough about that. The thought strikes me that the fire also destroyed all the remaining pictures of Paulie. They were dim snapshots which his half-sister Henrike had had enlarged and displayed on a shelf dedicated to his memory. Yes, to the last, Henrike made sure that we remembered him. She never forgot Paulie's birthday, when she would arrange tiny bouquets in the two eggcups which flanked the photographs. By the way, all the photos showed Paulie holding a watering can, for his favorite activity was planting and transplanting. Every buttercup around our place had been transplanted by him about a dozen times . . .

Yes, Martin, that's right, I had something special in mind for your visit—ah, now it comes back to me: I was going to tell you about the attempt to wipe out Little Grajevo, that colony of cabins established at a time when no one dreamed of holding a competition for the "most beautiful town of the eastern provinces."

Henseleit, Bilitza's successor as chairman of the Homeland Association, was involved, but no more involved than others of his ilk, who conceived the plan and passed it along to certain characters who habitually took ideas and turned them into orders and action. In any case, it was during a rainy harvest season that Heini Hauser, on his way home from the estate, found a strange man face down in a puddle not far from Heini's cottage. The man was wearing striped overalls that were soaked through, and Heini thought he had only fallen and would get up any moment and continue his flight, straight toward the Hauser cottage. But he lay there without moving and did not respond when spoken to. Heini Hauser did what anyone in Little Grajevo would have done in such a case; he turned away and hastened into his house, closing the door tightly behind him. Soon afterward he and some of his family could be seen at the small window, and but for the dusk, an observer would have realized that faces were peering out from all the windows in the settlement.

But then in the darkness something happened that the people at the other windows found incomprehensible: Heini Hauser left his house, picked up the stranger, and dragged him over the soggy ground to the cottage, where he and the others managed to lay him on a cot. They took off his jacket and found two bullet holes in his back. He was dead. Standing on either side of the cot, Heini Hauser and his mother argued with one another. He was prepared to carry the man back to where he had found him, since there was nothing to be done. But the woman would not allow it. She was already washing off the man's face with a damp cloth. And once she had cleaned the man up, she crouched by the cot and stared at him penetratingly, broodingly, as though she could discover the reason for his death if she only thought hard

enough; as Heini Hauser told us later, she spent the better part of
the night like this, and at daybreak she was sitting there again and
barely looked up when Conny arrived.

Heini Hauser had sent for him after finding an initial marked
on the strap of the overalls with a laundry pen. When Conny
entered, he immediately confirmed Heini Hauser's suspicion: it
was Master Weinknecht.

Conny crossed his former master's hands over his breast and
covered him with a rag rug. He advised the Hausers against
placing lighted candles around the cot. Conny examined the spot
where Master Weinknecht had been lying, then with bowed head
climbed the slope to the Borek, and returned, systematically
searching for clues, but nothing was to be seen. The rain had
washed away all traces, this unremitting rain which turned the
paths to mud, soaked through clothing, and threatened to ruin
the harvest. Back in the cottage he and the Hausers discussed
what steps to take. He suggested that Heini go to the estate as
usual and notify the police from there.

And now you must imagine two police vans approaching in the
pouring rain from Borek Forest, preceded by an unobtrusive
automobile. The sky is so lowering, the air so heavy that the
wheels lumbering through the mud sound muffled, and if you
close your eyes, you can hardly tell from which direction they
are coming. If you saw the convoy, you realized at once that it
was not there for an ordinary investigation. The massive vehicles
halted above the settlement, rain-darkened canvas flaps were
thrown open, and armed men in gleaming rain gear jumped
down. The contingent spread out to form a chain, a ring, and any
onlooker would have seen that this was a carefully planned operation. Meanwhile, the passenger car bucked on down the soggy
slope and stopped not far from the communal pump.

Four men got out, and anyone in Little Grajevo bold enough
to still look out the window recognized that one of them was
Heini Hauser, Heini with his damp hair plastered to his forehead.
The others, all in plainclothes, were wearing hats with turned-
down brims. They had Heini take them into his cottage and
identify the other people there, including Conny, who was known
to at least one of the secret police agents. Still wearing their hats,
they bent over the man on the cot, examined the bullet wounds.

Now and then they exchanged glances, had Heini Hauser describe the precise circumstances once more. One of the men,
whom the others looked at more often, ordered Heini Hauser to
return the body to its original location "and make it snappy."
Conny, who had identified himself as a friend of the family,
helped move the corpse, while Heini's mother sobbed. They
dragged Master Weinknecht out to the path and Heini had to
arrange him just as he had been, looking like a fallen runner.
Heini had to walk away and on command approach, stopping at
the point where he had discovered the body. The police took
notes, paced off distances, photographed the scene, and specu-
lated on the direction from which the shots had come. Their
search, like Conny's, turned up no clues. The chief went over the
timing once again and mentioned the need to call in the medical
examiner.

Don't think for a moment that the investigation was over; the
police combed the cabins and asked in each place whether anyone
had heard a shot. When the people said no, they were ordered to
go out and look carefully at the face of the man lying on the
ground. They did not know him, they had heard no shots. The
policemen would not let the question rest there. They kept the
people outside in the rain and asked them again whether they had
ever seen the dead man and Heini Hauser together, and if no,
whether they had seen Heini Hauser bring the man into his
house. No one could remember that, either. They knew nothing,
they were blind and deaf. The top man of the three showed
neither surprise nor impatience; apparently he was familiar with
their chronic know-nothing attitude. And then he turned and
spoke to the circle of inscrutable villagers: solving this crime
called for careful, relentless effort; all inhabitants were to ready
themselves for immediate evacuation. They would be permitted
only hand luggage, and the trucks would be leaving in fifteen
minutes.

I've spoken before about the sense of permanence in Little
Grajevo. The people there expected that any moment their time
would be up. And if the top man was surprised that his order was
received without protest or question, he was even more so by the
way most of the villagers hastened back to their cabins and returned well ahead of the deadline, holding their children by the

hand and shouldering boxes and crates. They looked back at their pointed chimney pots, from which thick white smoke streamed; the stove fires had been hastily doused. No one locked up. They walked slowly toward the pump, seemingly intent on all arriving at the same time. Conny was among them.

Conny was carrying the carton belonging to Heini Hauser's mother, which also contained possessions of Anna's. At first he went unnoticed, waiting silently with the crowd. The policemen made a quick check of the cabins, then gave the signal for departure and accompanied the villagers up the slope to where the troops were waiting. The villagers scrambled up into the trucks one after the other, as though they had been practicing for years, while Conny hoisted up the luggage. Just as he, too, prepared to climb in, the top policeman intervened. Conny had no business here, he said. Conny replied that he regarded the entire action as a mistake and wanted to be present when the mistake was officially acknowledged. The policeman called him aside. "You are wading in too deep for your own good," he told him. "You could regret this for a long time."

What is it? No, no, Martin, I just need a drop of tea. Forgive me, but these stories get me all stirred up. As if one had to relive all this, or as if one woke up and discovered that nothing had been solved in the meantime. Or one could say the dream goes on and on.

But I wanted to tell you the rest. Conny took the hint and was on his way back to the Hausers' cabin when he heard galloping hoofs and saw Toni Lettkow flashing through the thin stand of pines on his fancy horse. He cantered right up to the car, dismounted, and casually shook the commanding officer's hand. The estate owner was clearly angry, and presumably had a right to hear what this was all about. Conny observed the two men talking back and forth, then starting down the path together. Inside the Hausers' cottage, Conny found the body of Master Weinknecht on the cot again, uncovered, where it had been deposited by the police. Hearing voices coming nearer, Conny slipped behind a curtain which hid the shelves of food supplies, just before the police agent and Toni Lettkow entered the cabin. They stood a long time before the corpse. It was so still that Conny could hear the ticking of the pocket watch one of the men carried.

Toni Lettkow broke the silence first, speaking tonelessly, more to himself than to the other man. He remarked that the dead man was in "concentration camp getup," whereupon the policeman threw in that this was an inmate from the Liekuk Camp, a man by the name of Weinknecht. The man came from Lucknow and had been interned for subversive activities. Toni Lettkow appeared to find this information sufficient. The swishing of his rain cape indicated that he was going to the door, but as he reached it, he said a few more words to the police agent. Of course, the latter was only carrying out his instructions, but as a landowner, he felt obliged to object that the operation in Little Grajevo threatened the harvest and would have a serious effect on the labor supply. In view of this, he would be lodging an immediate complaint with Reschat, the Statthalter of Lucknow . . .

What right had they? You're asking who authorized them to cart away a whole settlement? Quite simple: they had the power, and since they were always convinced their cause was just, they never suffered from pangs of conscience. They elevated ruthlessness to the status of law, so there was no need for authorization . . .

In any case, Toni Lettkow had not overestimated his influence. By early evening the people of Little Grajevo were allowed to return. They were sent home without explanation or apology. The trucks which had taken them away carted them back to the same spot. It had stopped raining, the sky was swept clean, a beautiful harvest sky which they noted as they walked down the path to their homes. If you asked them about the incident, they merely shrugged, as if they could not think of anything to say.

No, they had seen nothing, experienced nothing, and later, when Conny found proof that Master Weinknecht had been shot right outside the Liekuk Camp, thirty kilometers away, even this news elicited only another shrug from the people of Little Grajevo.

But Conny could not get over the facts his investigations turned up; he could not get over the death of his former master. Now Conny had a clearly defined goal; it was no longer a question of judging from case to case, for now there could be only one judgment, and the time had come for action.

I remember how he took us into our confidence. He was waiting for me in the weaving studio while I was helping Sonja Turk to bed. Something had happened to her sense of balance, and she was prone to falls. But Sonja insisted on hearing what it was all about. So I brought Conny to her bedroom, with its stuffed nocturnal birds. It had been some time since Conny had visited her, and her condition plainly shocked him. Her hair had grown thin and ashen, her skin had a yellowish tinge, one corner of her mouth was askew, and some of her fingers looked twisted and swollen, as though deformed by gout. She saw how shocked Conny was, and smiled sourly, swallowed a few times, and finally said, "When a person's down on his stumps, well, that's all there is to it. No reason to stare, and no reason to blubber, either, because it's too late for blubbering." She patted Conny's hand and nodded at her own words, apparently to spare him the trouble of expressing hopes for her recovery.

We seated ourselves where she could see both of us without turning her head, which seemed too heavy for the fragile neck. "If I had it to do over again," Sonja Turk said, "I'd start a school that'd teach folks to get along with each other without all this fussing and fuming." She sent me after the homemade berry wine which she always offered me after I had washed her and put her to bed, and urged us to drink "to nothing." She looked challengingly at Conny as he sat there with lowered eyes, twisting his glass in his hands. As always when she focused her entire attention on one person, she trembled slightly, as if radiating mysterious energies, while the person who was the target often felt—I speak from personal experience—like an actor on the darkened stage when the spotlight seeks him out. "A fellow like you," she said to Conny, "might need more than one hiding place. When the time comes, count on us."

Conny had come to recruit me. He was bringing greetings from his friends, who in turn had been friends of Master Weinknecht's. They had approached him on the day of the funeral, had met with him again at a small abandoned brickworks, six or seven men who had made him privy to their aims. These aims were, as I mentioned, clearly and carefully defined. First and foremost, they would help each other and people of like persuasion who were in danger. For the time being, their main concern was to survive these ghostly times which the riders to the East were arrogantly proclaiming would last a thousand years. Conny and his friends foresaw an age of terror, from which no one would be exempt. They predicted war and cataclysmic changes. They felt it was essential to give warning . . .

You ask whether I joined them. No, Martin, I did not—and I completely understand your astonishment—I did not give Conny the answer he has hoping for, less out of caution for my own safety than out of the sense that my assignment was to bring our museum safely through the difficult times ahead, our local history museum with its irreplaceable relics, many of which did not speak the official language but rather exerted what you might call the silent opposition of inanimate objects. To do this, I felt I had to remain independent. I must not give them any pretext for dissolving the collection or commandeering it for their own purposes. I'm sure I already mentioned that it had come to be the most significant collection in the entire southeast. And think what you will: not until I had to weigh the choices did I fully realize what had been entrusted to me and how much depended on me.

Conny had expected me to hesitate, and even admitted he could understand my temporary refusal, as Sonja Turk, in the role of attentive referee, understood it. "Neutrality," she said, "that's in a person's right, only he's got to ask himself how long he can afford to stay neutral." Conny was willing to wait for me to come round. In the meantime, he had some serious advice for me. "Look out for the counterfeiters, Zygmunt," he said, "the forgers of history. They will try to prove that history must be regarded from a single angle, as the saga of heroes or the chronicle of ethnic superiority. You have all the material counterproofs, with whose help you can demonstrate that history includes everything, even the insignificant, even weird old junk."

I never took up that question, for at that moment a tremendous uproar broke out in the dye room. Buckets tipped over and rolled across the floor; a door slammed shut, glass shattered. Sonja started, and pulled herself up to a sitting position. Conny and I rushed out together, parted ways in the hall. I sprinted out into the garden, while Conny ran to the dye room and threw open the door with a shout. I grinned at him from outside through the broken window. He gestured to me, and we moved on to the next room, and there we cornered the intruder.

A boy was cowering by the windowsill, a gangly fellow of at most fifteen with curly black hair. He had on a ragged shirt and pants, and homemade sandals. He was bleeding from the wrist. Don't think for a moment that he showed fear or remorse; his expression conveyed only chagrin at having been caught. You should have seen the surly shrug with which he stood up!

Several sheets of paper were thrust into his shirt, and a number of colored pencils stuck in his pocket. We propelled him into Sonja's bedroom. Even now he kept his bold front, refused to tell us anything. He remained silent in a friendly but determined way, even when the old weaver herself questioned him. Sonja Turk beckoned him to come closer, grabbed his hand, examined the wrist where broken glass had scratched the skin, had me bring the first-aid kit, and bandaged the cut.

We had to deal with the situation somehow. Conny pinned his arms while I emptied his pockets and plucked out the papers he had stored inside his shirt. As I lifted the shirt, I saw a maze of welts and bruises.

Sonja Turk went through the oddments—shell cases, prunes, a few of those little cards from cigarette packs, as well as tiny snippets of dyed wool. She collected all this in a dip in the feather bed, reached for the sheets of paper, and scanned them quickly. "This'll open your eyes, it will," she said, passing the pages to us. We recognized sections from Sonja Turk's rugs, sketched in and colored. It added up to a catalogue of all the ornaments and symbols used in the rugs, while some of the pages were scrawled with sentences from the great manual of rugmaking.

It was not reassuring to learn that the boy had been in the house several times and in the weaving studio. Apparently he had stolen in there, both during the day and at night, for the sole purpose of copying all this material, whether or not he understood it. So much he confessed to, watching us keenly, trying to interpret our words and glances. His fear seemed to be that we might confiscate his booty.

I still remember the look of puzzled gratitude he gave Sonja Turk when the old weaver gestured to him to gather up his belongings. He reached out half incredulously for the papers and, to make us some return, told us his name: Marian Jeromin.

Yes, Martin, it was under these rather unusual circumstances that I made the acquaintance of my future and favorite pupil.

We now heard, among other things, that Marian came from Rankow, not from the estate with the orchards, but from a run-down, forlorn farm, whose owner had taken him in as a sort of foster child. His own family had died in a body from mushroom poisoning: there were some dangerous varieties among our famed Masurian mushrooms.

The farmer and his wife were childless and took little interest in the toddler. But the farmer's one-eyed sister who lived with them had charge of him and set him to various chores around the farm. This woman owned a hand loom on which she wove runners and little wall hangings which she brought to Lucknow to sell for a pittance or barter for food.

These people never had visitors or received any mail. There was not even a copy of the *Masurian Almanac* in the bleak farmhouse. The only pleasure of the child's day came in the evening, when he crouched on the floor watching the one-eyed woman at her weaving. She wove the same rudimentary patterns over and over, but he still found it wonderful to see how they grew under the flying shuttle. By the time the farmer reluctantly registered the boy for school, he could already use the loom. Not that he received any encouragement for this skill. The farmer even forbade him to waste his time on such useless nonsense. Marian had to practice weaving in secret, and the farmer punished him whenever he caught him. Altogether, there were many things he was punished for. He had learned about Sonja Turk in school, in his class on local history. The teacher had mentioned her as an important person who was responsible for the third great flowering of Masurian weaving.

Shortly before the one-eyed sister died, she bequeathed the hand loom to the boy. She had also threatened a great misfortune for anyone who tried to destroy the loom. The farmer took his sister's words seriously enough to leave the loom alone, but the boy was still prohibited from using it. Marian had long practice in being furtive. So he had sought out our weaving studio, entered the place, and never once filched anything.

When he swore to Sonja Turk that he had never stolen, he

placed his right hand over his heart; with the same gesture, he told us that his one wish was to become a rugmaker. Before we sent him on his way, I rubbed soothing ointment on his back. We had told him he was welcome to visit whenever he wished. He had all his boldness back by the time he said goodbye. We watched him begin to run when he reached the drying meadow; he leaped into the air for joy. That is how we found our prodigy . . .

No, no, Martin, I told you before that I do not mean that ironically. Sonja Turk called him that, too, though she would add that a prodigy was not enough in the long run. The boy did not begin his apprenticeship right away. It was not until later that I took him on, when Sonja Turk was confined to a chair, half-paralyzed, devoting all her energies to finishing the book and drawing up a catalogue of all the rugs she had made since her childhood . . .

Pardon me? Well, well, so you visited him again, you and Henrike. Yes, I know, out there in Pudby, in the former village school of Pudby, where Master Weaver Jeromin is now training pupils of his own. Did I mention that we differed completely in our concept of rugmaking? Yes, Marian sets store on originality, while I believe in devotion to the rules of the craft. Ask him about the art of weaving and you'll see what I mean: he'll answer with phrases like "the free play of color values as means of expression" or "vibrating modulations" or the "bold shifts in rhythm that underline the refractions of light." He is a magnificent rugmaker, no doubt about it, but for his own sake I discount him when he starts going on about "effulgence" and "contrapuntal surfaces" and the like. But enough of that. I'd rather hear something about Henrike, what you and she are up to . . . Really? You're saving for a trip to Masuria? Well, I should warn you not to expect to find the things I've been telling you about. You'll find strangers there, vaguely familiar strangers. That's probably why I never went back; I did not want the images in my mind to begin to waver. But even these images, which I carried off with me as invisible baggage, are nothing one can always be sure of. They emerge from the shadows for moments, then vanish again, a bit like those fields of plankton in the Sargasso Sea that you once mentioned.

Which brings to mind a window covered with snow on the outside, steamed up on the inside, which a hand is wiping clear with a circling motion, ever faster and more furiously, until a face gradually takes shape out there, with huge flakes of snow blowing behind it. The face behind the glass acquires the features of my grandfather, and as the image gains in clarity, I realize that it is New Year's Eve, that New Year's Eve on which we witnessed a defeat with far-reaching consequences . . .

No, no, Alfons Rogalla was not still putting up at the Queen Luise . . . The chief reason was that he could not adjust to the bills, quarreled daily with the waiters, and complained daily to the management; when he began accosting diners in the restaurant, recommending that they examine their bills carefully, he was asked to move out. He rented a basement apartment near the old cavalry barracks, and laid in boxes of canned goods, soap, candles, and noodles bought on sale. But that New Year's Eve, when we might have expected anyone but him to drop by, we felt nothing but happy anticipation so long as the unknown visitor was out there clearing the snow from the window. Paulie even climbed up on a stool and began to wipe the window from the inside, trying to synchronize his motions to the circling hand outside. We were sitting around the table, and on the oilcloth lay odd little clumps of lead, which we had melted and tossed into cold water, then interpreted in the traditional New Year's Eve fortune-telling. Who knows whether my mother or Eugen Lavrenz would ever have agreed to let my grandfather in; they stared at the emerging face first with dismay, then calmly and contemptuously, without responding to his pleading expression.

It was Edith who could not resist his knocking and whining, and sent me to the door, but even she shrunk snail-like into herself when he came stamping in without a greeting, clutching something to him which looked like a pillow and turned out to be just that. He looked right past us, shaking no one's hand, his gaze fixed on Eugen Lavrenz. In the light we could see that his pinched face was dripping with sweat. He groped for the back of a chair and sat down with a thump, as if the weight of his wet coat were dragging him down. He was shivering with fever, breathing hard through opened mouth, and he leaned back as though he had a vampire sitting on his chest.

When Edith poured him a glass of mulled wine, my mother stared at her reproachfully. Alfons Rogalla reached for the glass, but his hand trembled so that some of the wine spilled, and he had to set it down again. The only way he could drink was by leaning far over the table and holding the glass with both hands. One could not expect him to tell us why he was there, but we thought we knew when he slid off the chair and went down on his knees in front of Eugen Lavrenz. His whole body shuddered. With the exception of Paulie, we all felt as if we were in the middle of a terrible dream; my limbs went stiff, and I could not have found the strength to leave the room or even to turn away.

My grandfather put his arms around Eugen Lavrenz's knees and looked up at him for a long time. He whispered something we could not make out but could deduce. He was asking forgiveness. He admitted that he had testified falsely, and begged Eugen Lavrenz's pardon for all the lost years and for whatever injury he had done him, knowingly and unwittingly. For the very first time I saw fear and sorrow in his eyes, and his head began to sway slightly as he waited for an answer.

Eugen Lavrenz said nothing, just sat there and looked at him, and his face expressed neither sadness nor disgust nor satisfaction; it seemed as though he was drained of emotion. My grandfather dragged himself to his feet, filled with disbelief that forgiveness could be withheld. He muttered angrily that a person who came ready to confess and settle accounts had a right to be forgiven.

That was the old Alfons Rogalla, demanding his rights and thinking himself in the right. He waited with growing impatience for the word or the gesture that would absolve him. Yet to those who knew him, it was clear that the sorrow and fear remained; his chapped lips twitched and his sunken eyes were filled with a restless gleam. Once, he looked in our direction as though asking for assistance, begging us to add a word of our own to his plea. He repeated his request. He took Eugen's hands. He leaned his head to one side and showed humility, a sort of absentminded humility, which he then threw aside with a strange, whining sound.

All in vain; he could not get Eugen Lavrenz to speak, and after a while he began to smile, cunningly, shaking his head at himself, and with a smile he reached for the pillow, and fumbling in his

pockets, he accused himself of forgetting something very important. He pulled out a jackknife and slit open the pillow. "Of
course," he murmured, "of course, how could I forget: the very
least I could give you after all I did." He put the knife down on
the floor and plunged both hands into the pillow, fumbling for
something. With a flourish he pulled out a handful of limp banknotes, which he tremulously held up for Eugen Lavrenz. "Look,"
he said, "see what I brought you: a little compensation, nowhere
near what you deserve, but still enough to show my good will.
Take it, take it and say you forgive me."

Even now, Martin, Eugen Lavrenz did not stir. He seemed to
look right through the man and his banknotes, indifferently, like
a statue. My grandfather lowered his hands in confusion, but he
did not give up; several times and always in the same words
he tried to force the money on Eugen Lavrenz. He begged, he
tempted, he wooed, he tried guarded threats. Again he turned to
us and demanded our help: "Come on, make him see reason." We
sat there looking at him, keeping perfectly still as he picked up
the banknotes and flung them into the air. His hatred burst into
flame. You should have seen how he gesticulated, and hurled all
kinds of names at Eugen Lavrenz.

He accused him of heartlessness and of profiteering. He apparently assumed that Eugen Lavrenz was holding out for more
money before he would grant forgiveness.

Suddenly he fell to stammering, gasping for air and making
terrible faces. He pointed furiously at the banknotes scattered on
the floor and shouted something like an ultimatum. Yet even in
his confusion he seemed to realize that, ultimatum or not, a decision had already been made. All at once he bent down, picked up
some of the bills, and twisted them into a spill, which he ignited
on the oil lamp we had used for melting the lead. The banknotes
flared up, illuminating the crazed satisfaction in the old man's
eyes, his raging triumph. He flourished the burning banknotes in
the face of Eugen Lavrenz. "He's gone mad," my mother whispered, "now he's gone mad."

If Eugen Lavrenz had moved to put a stop to these antics,
perhaps we would have been able to stir from our chairs. But the
teller of the ninety-two lake stories stayed true to his policy of
silence, even when Alfons Rogalla waved the burning spill before

his eyes. That, in turn, forced us not to intervene. No one so much as tried to put his foot on one of the banknotes, nor did we protest when Rogalla made two more spills of them.

Then he stumbled and fell down, but that was for effect, for he promptly sat up and began collecting the remaining bills and stuffing them into the pillow, even the charred ones. He sat there groaning for a while, clutching the pillow to his chest as he gathered strength to stand up . . .

Yes, Martin, you're right, none of us expected that the scene would be over that quickly. Without another word, without taking time to button his coat, he rushed off into the blizzard.

What happened next we heard from those who witnessed it. After leaving us, Alfons Rogalla headed into town and made for the Hotel Queen Luise. He was singing as he went. No one stopped him as he shambled through the crowded ballroom with snow in his hair and pushed his way up to the balcony, where he roared out something that interrupted the New Year's Eve ball. Before he opened his pillow and, laughing wildly, let feathers, money, and ashes rain down on the crowd, my grandfather announced that a new era had arrived: the age of worthless money. Well, the waiters cornered him, and two Lucknow doctors at the ball with their wives went quickly to his side. They had him committed to our insane asylum, whose grounds bordered on the cavalry barracks. Several times I saw him there, clinging to the fence and staring with mindless persistence at the horses at their training.

That's enough for today, dear boy; it's almost five-thirty, and it's not impossible that another visitor may be here in a few minutes, a visitor for whom I must save all my strength; I had almost forgotten. No need to rush, Martin, there's time enough . . .

No, you did not stay too long. You can see I'm feeling better, and this kind of rainy day agrees with me . . . Your umbrella, don't forget it. Have I already told you that my heart feels lighter when I have given you a lump of the past to take with you?

Yes? Except, of course, this sense of relief can't be depended on. It doesn't last, no.

# 10

COME on in, Martin, have a seat. Today's an anniversary, it's
your tenth visit, and to celebrate I have some home-baked pastry,
Carola's cream puffs, which taste better, and cost less, than any
baker's. Yes, my wife was here again; she was bringing me the
mail—leaflets and forms from various insurance companies,
which prove once more how reasonable the world appears once
you subordinate everything to a purpose. Everything seems simple if all you care about is preventing fires . . .

Come, try a cream puff.

A fire can start in so many ways, and how many flammable
materials there are! Actually every house should have a sprinkler
system, and every citizen should be trained as a firefighter. These
insurance company leaflets make me realize that.

But enough of that, dear boy. I have to thank you for a sacrifice you have made for the time being, I assume for my sake. No
need to look astonished—I have my sources. So you have withdrawn your application for that marine research project. I even
know where the ship is going—to the West African coast, to
have a look at some of the rarer fishes living in the depths. What
will they think of next? . . .

It's not you I'm smiling at. I was remembering how the riders
to the East tried to shape our times to their ideas, to revise history by changing all the names. From one day to the next a new
craze appeared: anyone who thought his name had too many
consonants could have himself renamed, and that went for places
and rivers, too, even objects. The new names were meant to
conceal uncertain or undesirable origins, and the familiar tongue
twisters which had served us well so long were withdrawn from
official use and replaced with fine-sounding German names.

Eugen Lavrenz ran smack into the new dispensation on what turned out to be almost his shortest journey. The urge had come over him to look to all the tiled stoves in the region, which he had neglected far too long, he said. He set out with his knapsack and spade as usual; it was the beginning of June, and he planned to be away until the potato vines smoldered in the fields. But after a week he was home again, in bad humor, and resolved to undertake no more such expeditions. "Now they've gone and done it, they've turned Masuria into a maze," he said, and he told the story of his journey. It joined the ninety-two others in his repertory, but this one he told most often, because it was the newest.

In any case, the stove builder Eugen Lavrenz was striding along the road through the birch forest to Panistrugga, a route his legs knew by heart, when he noticed that the old signs pointing to Marzinowen and Maleczewen had been replaced. The intersections were marked with signs pointing to villages called Martinshöhe and Maleten. Taking this for a mistake or some idiocy, he kept going in the direction of Panistrugga, and intended from there to head toward Skrzypken and Krzysewen as he always had. The young ferryman whom Eugen Lavrenz asked to row him across the Czerwaune responded strangely. "The old Czerwaune has dried up," he told him captiously, "so I can't row anyone across it anymore. What you see here is the Rotbach, which will never dry up, and if that's the river you mean, come along."

So Eugen crossed the river, and in fact had the impression that the banks of the old Czerwaune had actually changed: he could not locate the bare brown spots that had always reminded him of worn places on a fur coat. When he got to Thurow's Tavern in Panistrugga, he noticed that the sign giving the name of the town had been painted over; it told him he was in Herrenbach. Eugen Lavrenz felt so addled that he stopped in at the tavern for a glass of Nikolaschka. Sitting at a table in the corner was the constable, Jwaschkowski. They drank to each other's health, and the stove builder asked whether a new disease had broken out in the area, the renaming disease, whereupon the constable asked Lavrenz not to call him Jwaschkowski anymore; his name was Hausbruch, Waldemar Hausbruch.

And so it went. Eugen Lavrenz finally reached Krzysewen,

which now called itself Kreuzborn, and wanted to put up at the inn. When asked his name, he offered several choices, including Lanonowoski. They did not seem to appreciate his joke, and liked it no better when he admitted that he could no longer remember what his name was. Regulations being what they were, he had to spend the first few nights out in the open.

In the village of Lavrenzicken, Eugen Lavrenz finally remembered his name; he at once purchased a ticket and took the train back to Lucknow. He claimed to have drawn the curtains and held his ears whenever the train passed through a station, so he would not hear the names of the villages called out, for more than anything else he wanted to preserve his memories of Masuria as it had been, the Masuria he knew and felt at home in. "What good does it do if everything sounds nice and German and the names are just pasted on? Przepiorken will always be Przepiorken, no matter how often they tell you it's called Wachteldorf."

What's that you said? . . .

Yes, Martin, I agree completely; whoever wants to establish a new era is forced to do this. The names have to be changed, the signs, the flags, and whoever wants to shape the future, as the riders to the East wanted to, must make sure that all the preserved relics of the past support his cause. He's driven to sorting and selecting and purging, making much of those historic remains that are useful, destroying those that are not. We ourselves were not spared the process: after the renaming came the mopping-up operation.

No, first we received instructions by mail from Königsberg, a registered letter from the office of Professor Melzer-Tapiau, ordering us to recatalogue the inventory of our museum. Each item was to be accompanied by a precise description, as well as details of the time, place, and circumstances of the find. In the course of so doing, we were to "eliminate" any items that were of Slavic origin or whose origins could not be precisely determined. Where doubt existed, we were advised to "withdraw" the object.

Edith wanted to help me with the assignment. We brought out our old homemade catalogues and began going through our collection, trying to meet the new requirements. "What do you think?" I asked her. "Here we have these white gloves with Masurian embroidery; they were most likely worn in the Vistula region, not around here. Do they pass?" She prepared to write, but her little shrug did not escape me, and I quickly revised my note: "Let's say the gloves are from Mrossen, now called Schönhorst; they can stay."

As we moved along the shelves, my eyes fell on a group of carved and painted figures: a group of women carrying water were watching a troop of horsemen ride away, one of whom had a red and white pennant waving from his lance. Should I banish the entire group or could we merely file off the little pennant in the Polish national colors? I asked Edith. Her pencil was already poised to jot down what I said, but behind her feigned neutrality and obedience I saw that Edith was shocked at what I was doing. Occasionally I had the impression that she deliberately refused to take part in this farce; she rejoiced at my uncertainty, my embarrassment, or at least she took a perverse pleasure in seeing me forced to resolve these issues. I found myself thinking of Uncle Adam.

We went on to the bright-painted peasant chair whose crudely carved spoolings and trapeze-shaped backrest left no doubt that it came from south of the border; it had been made by a man for his own use; presumably he had brought the chair along when he came to take a job in our region, on the land, in the forests.

I ran my hand over the chair, picturing its owner. I suddenly realized that no one who had lived in this region could carry out what we had been instructed to do. No such judgments could be made without insulting those who had survived in this region, in its sandy fields, bordered by bubbling swamps, fields over which they had fought, which they took from one another and defended, and beneath whose surface they finally disappeared. How astonished Edith was when I asked for the list we had been compiling, folded it, and deliberately ripped it to shreds. How relieved and almost grateful she looked when I simply took her by the hand and led her out of the museum, without saying anything more on the question.

I hope you understand what I mean, Martin. The past belongs to all of us. It cannot be divided up or bent into shape. Things grow together, become part of each other, and to try to separate them and decide that one is pure, one impure, is to do violence to the truth.

We never sent the new lists and never responded to the instructions from the distant capital. As time went on, we began to think that Melzer-Tapiau's office had forgotten the whole business, but apparently these people never forgot the most trivial matter. For one Sunday a crooked, stooped little man with a briefcase turned up. He flashed his official badge at us and, rummaging in his briefcase, pulled out a folder, and from the folder a carbon of the instructions from Königsberg. He wanted to know whether the letter had been received, whether we had acted according to the instructions. Sizing us up with his rheumy eyes, he asked whether the lists were ready. He appeared neither disappointed nor angered when our silence told him we had received the letter but had disregarded it. He assumed that we had been expecting him, stuck the folder under his arm, and wanted to be shown through the museum.

You should have seen his reaction to Paulie. The boy was playing in the room devoted to Masurian animals. He was combing the stuffed polecat, the badger, and the fish otter, talking to them, and feeding them bits of bread. The man went through the room with not so much as a wink or a friendly word, as if the child were just one more display item and he was showing us how to make neutral decisions. To this day I wonder how I managed to keep my composure as he went about his job of sorting out the non-Aryan elements from the collection. He looked as though he were determining the sex of baby chicks. He would grab an object, look at it from all sides and angles, and whatever he found objectionable he marked with a numbered sticker and noted down on his list . . .

No, my dear boy, unfortunately that's true. I went along like a subordinate, as if I had no say here. "This decorated butter churn —we know this sort of ornamentation from the Vistula region— we can do without this; and this flax scutcher is clearly Polish in origin." So it went. He had a keen eye, no doubt about that. He stopped in front of a corner cupboard and exclaimed, "Well, how did you get here all the way from Kashubia?" and in a collection of mangle boards he went straight to the one Uncle Adam had bought from Gypsies.

I did not really put up a fight until we got to the rug room. After a coughing fit that brought tears to his eyes, the visitor fell to studying the *kuddräs* and *kotzes* in this collection, which I had enlarged so much, with Sonja Turk's help, that the *Lucknow News* had hailed it as the most comprehensive collection of Masurian weaving ever assembled. It soon became clear that he was interested in the symbols and motifs rather than in the artistic merits of the rugs. Something like a castle was above suspicion: what could it symbolize but steadfastness and strength? The leaping white hind, the emblem of hope and illusion, is considered a sacred animal in Masurian folk belief, and the official approved of it, as he approved of the divine steed, Wotan's horse, which was read as a symbol of reined-in power. The swan clearly represented purity, the stork fertility. Neither caused any objections. He accepted hens, geese, cows, and trees of life, but mythical animals, or combinations of animal and human traits, heart motifs, and especially Biblical scenes were suspect.

He waved me over and remarked that some of the items did not deserve to be exhibited in this setting, items that were alien to the Aryan spirit. These he had marked with yellow stickers. He was about to move on to the next room when I blocked his path.

"Yes? Was there something you wanted to say?" I had not planned to say as much as I did. I had only been planning to say that each rug here had its place in the historical development of Masurian rugmaking. I wasn't going to gut the collection. Then I went over to the condemned rugs and ripped off the stickers.

He turned back to the rugs as if to concede he might have been somewhat hasty. As he appreciatively ran his hand over the textures, he asked if I was aware that I could be compelled, yes, compelled to remove all "non-Aryan elements," by the authority of the Law for the Protection of the Germanic Cultural Heritage.

I declared that our museum was a private affair, founded by Uncle Adam and continued and expanded by me. He countered impassively that our museum received regular subsidies and that the public was routinely admitted. "Where such is the case," he said, "the governmental agency in charge of these matters must exercise its obligation of supervision."

At first I merely shook my head in denial. Then I demanded on what basis he was acting. He quoted the relevant decree. Still unconvinced, I asked at what moment the public could assert rights over objects which an individual had acquired and collected on his own and purely for his own edification. He rapped out a ready-made answer. "The collective judgment determines the moment at which an object acquires value for the entire people." Something inside me seemed to explode. I grabbed a knife and raised it against a rug. He watched me with a curious legalistic calm, only warning me that while I could consider the rug my property in a material sense, in the spiritual sense it belonged to the German people.

Don't ask me what I hoped to prove when I stabbed at a runner with the knife and tried to draw the blade down through the tight weave, or when I hurled two early hand looms to the floor. I was in such a frenzy that I did not even notice where the official had taken refuge. It was Edith who put an end to my rampage. She rushed over to me, wrenched the knife from my hand, and led me over to a bench.

Standing behind me with her hands on my shoulders, she asked the official to leave. She put it simply enough, and added firmly, "It's for us to decide if and when anything is changed here."

He left, with a hint of a bow. Edith stayed where she was, pressing harder on my shoulders and surveying the damage. I tried to explain what had come over me, but she said, "Shush, Zygmunt, I understand, shush." I repeated what the visitor had said. "They won't do it," Edith murmured, "they can't." For the first time I considered dissolving or even destroying the museum rather than letting it come under outside control. As though Edith sensed what I had in mind, she said, "If need be, there's always a third possibility."

I discovered later what the third possibility was. That same Sunday the official reappeared, this time accompanied by Henseleit in uniform. We ourselves were busy burying a drowned piglet washed up by the river. Paulie insisted on a proper funeral, so we left the visitors to their own devices. We found them going through the museum, Henseleit drawing up a list at the other man's bidding. Edith and I followed them. Edith stayed by me, although Paulie was calling for her outside. She linked her arm in mine and registered the man's decisions with inscrutable calm. At times she even seemed to be smiling. We trailed the two everywhere and, when they had finished, strolled behind them to the front hall. We were informed that copies would be made of the list and that we would receive ours promptly, with instructions that we carry out the purge of the inventory, likewise promptly.

At this point Edith spoke up. They could spare themselves the trouble, she said. There was no need to send a list, even to duplicate it. With utmost poise she walked across the hall and gathered up the three hand-lettered signs: one with the museum's hours, one with the entry prices for adults, children, and school classes, and finally the inevitable sign with which we expressed regret that we could not be responsible for lost or stolen property. She held them out for the two men to see, then snapped them over her knee. Once she had reduced the signs to the size of beer coasters, she handed the remains to Henseleit: "Here, you can consider this an application, our application for permission to close the museum to the public. I assume we need not wait for official notification."

You should have seen the dismay that overcame not only the visitors but me as well. For although I had considered the possibility of closing the museum, this denouement had arrived so suddenly and so naturally that it was as if we had arranged it long ago. "From today on," Edith continued, "we will consider the museum a purely private collection. That is what it originally was, and I can't imagine that anyone would object to that."

The two withdrew to a corner and there admitted their embarrassment to one another, their frustration at this sudden loss of authority. In parting, Henseleit could think of nothing more threatening to say than, "From now on, don't expect any more subsidies."

Yes, Martin, but I wouldn't call it an actual protest; at least we did not intend it as such. We had simply refused to go along with their plans for reordering our museum and giving it an ideological bias, the bias characteristic of their own peculiar version of history . . .

So we closed the museum to the public, nailing up a sign that was supposed to deter would-be visitors. "Was supposed to," I say, for we soon discovered that the sign was not entirely effective. Many people rang our bell and wondered if it was really true that the museum was closed, and why. Our standard answer, which even little Paulie learned to give, was "Personal reasons," and strictly speaking that was true . . .

No, on the contrary. To be sure, we did enjoy the quiet at first, and did not regret being spared the rowdy classes of schoolchildren. But after a while we had to admit that we did miss the visitors. It became clear that all these objects, witnesses to the past, derived their value only from being seen by people who learned something about themselves from them. Now the relics were alone again, carefully cleaned, labeled, and displayed, yet hidden, as if they had died a second, representative death. But we had to resign ourselves to this state of affairs. At least we had found peace in these difficult times. I must confess that I cherished this peace, unlike Conny, who would not lie low, who insisted on interfering in everything, for good or for ill. But, as he always said, what mattered to him was keeping the spirit of opposition alive.

That was Conny Karrasch—yet for him, too, there came a day when he felt utterly defeated and was almost ready to give up. He had become involved in something without considering the consequences, and this is the story as he told it:

It was the second Sunday in September, and Conny had gone out on Taroven Hill on his motorcycle. The wooded slope, which dominated the road like a natural fortress, had been the scene of a battle during the last war, and this heroic episode was replayed there every year at this time. Soldiers from the Lucknow garrison portrayed the Russians, in historic uniforms of the St. Petersburg Artillery, as well as the local militia.

This occasion was an important one in Lucknow. The Masovia Brewery produced a special strong beer called Taroven Brew. Bakeries displayed cakes in the form of the famous hill. The Hotel Queen Luise was decorated with flags and streamers for the great Taroven Ball, attended by at least eight hundred. Out in the village of Taroven—but to call it a village was saying too much; it was just a sprinkling of humble farmhouses—beer tents had been planted. The traditional Taroven lentil soup was bubbling in field kitchens. Souvenir booths had materialized, along with a first-aid station, a van with a public-address system, portable toilets, and a reviewing stand of fragrant new lumber.

It was quite a struggle to get through the crowd, which was packed like sardines. Still Conny managed to hear the announcements over the loudspeaker. Once again they had managed to find a veteran of the battle. In Grabnick they had ferreted out a man who presumably was the last living veteran, Bruno Baltuschat, decorated with the Iron Cross, Second Class. "Our hero, Bruno Baltuschat," the loudspeaker blared. Conny picked him out at once on the reviewing stand: there he sat, flanked by the commanding officers of the garrison, wearing a stiff new uniform, looking scared, with a blotched face and blinking little pig eyes. He had a wooden folding chair all to himself, while the others, the officers, the Lucknow town officials, the leaders in brown and black uniforms, were consigned to a bench.

The uneasiness Conny noted in Bruno Baltuschat seemed to increase with the arrival of further guests of honor—a general showed up, also representatives from the churches, the school principals, and the mayors of neighboring towns. He ignored all the cigars which well-meaning dignitaries offered him from their leather cases. Then orderlies in white jackets passed around the Taroven Brew, and the guests of honor drank to each other, clicking their heels as they raised their mugs, then grunted contentedly and wiped the foam from their lips with the backs of their hands. They cheered as the loudspeaker announced that the troops had taken up their positions and were ready to start. Field glasses were focused on the sparse stand of trees atop the hill, a single trumpet note rang out, another trumpet answered feebly from the rear, and before the sound had died away, the first shrapnel burst into the blue and white sky. I had witnessed this scene often enough myself.

Conny could not take his eyes off Bruno Baltuschat, whose nervous state was not caused by the battle, which raged out of sight at first, though noisily enough. All his attention was directed toward the spectators, whose faces he examined through the field glasses someone had lent him. The hill was stormed by the St. Petersburgers, from the rear, and true to the actual course of the historical battle, they forced our militia to withdraw: first one by one, then in groups, the soldiers in gray retreated from the copse and in disciplined fashion fled down the slope on our side to a sandy tract dotted with bushes. Already mud-colored uniforms appeared on the crest of the hill, and a trumpet signal announced victory, temporary victory. The gunfire died away. All the field glasses were pointed toward the edge of the copse, all except the veteran's borrowed pair; Conny saw Baltuschat trying to take cover behind the officers on the platform. It was apparent to Conny that the veteran had cringed at the sight of a swarthy man in a broad cape who with unconcealed interest was letting his eyes rest on each of the guests of honor in turn.

Now tremulous signals hissed up into the September sky, flares which seemed to come from the depths of the earth, since no motion could be seen at the foot of the hill. But shortly thereafter the trenches, the mounds of earth, and the bushes began to stir, tufts of grass to move, leafy branches to edge toward the hill. The whole landscape came to life, apparently about to reconstitute itself, and from the crest of the hill came the crash of explosions; mushroom clouds floated into the sky, and when the wild rattle of artillery fire broke out on the edge of the copse, a trumpet signal resounded: "Potato soup, potato soup"—the call to attack.

The general turned affably to the veteran, pointing to the militiamen who amid the hail of fire gathered their forces to storm the hill. He called his attention to the heavy, camouflaged machine guns which were laying down covering fire for the attacking troops. Baltuschat nodded obediently and hastily added a comment of his own, while his eyes once more sought out the swarthy man in the cape. The general smiled sympathetically; perhaps he was a fatherly sort who could imagine how a veteran must feel when given a chance to relive forgotten moments of fear or valor. In any case, he went on expounding the phases of the battle to Baltuschat.

The men in field gray were a good halfway up the hill when the general had an idea: he expressed the wish to hear where the veteran had been during the battle; he wanted the man to show his particular foxhole, to tell what camouflage material he had used, to retrace the path he had taken in storming the hill. For the first time at a Taroven commemoration the spectators saw a general hook his arm through a veteran's and leave the reviewing stand while the storming of the hill was still in progress. The general's entourage had to go, too, of course, and Conny unobtrusively tagged along.

So now they searched for the spot where Bruno Baltuschat might have crouched; there were measurements to be taken, memories to reexamine, and the general seemed not to mind that the man had trouble remembering. "Perhaps in this hollow?" "Yessir, might have been here, sir, but maybe not, sir." "How about that ridge there?" "Yessir, don't remember a ridge, sir." The general accepted this forgetfulness with understanding and even seemed pleased by it: heroes could not be bothered with topographical details. They followed the troops up the hill. The blanks fired by the rifles formed a chain of tiny lightning flashes; here and there one of the attackers fell and rolled convincingly down the hillside for some distance, but a friendly kick from the general brought him to his feet with a salute.

Up there in the copse hand grenades were exploding and the artillery fire intensified. In honor of the victors of yore, victory was being reenacted, heralded by a chorus of hurrahs, and the general asked the veteran to recall where he himself had fought his way into the underbrush. "Yessir, could be over there by the hazel bushes, sir, but mebbe it was over there by the pines, sir."

The militiamen occupied the wooded hillcrest, the mud-colored uniforms fled. All was well, all was glorious, and when the long elegiac trumpet call sounded, the victors removed their helmets and bowed their heads in prayer. Conny, too, bowed his head, but out of the corner of his eye he watched as the man in the cape swept noiselessly toward the tree against which Bruno Baltuschat was leaning. Something was whispered to which the veteran replied with a humble appeal for patience; more Conny did not hear, for now the general turned to Bruno Baltuschat again and dragged him off to a briefing in a clearing.

Meanwhile, Conny followed the swarthy man, whose name was Simoneit; he came from Gorlau, a village near Taroven. Conny caught up with him and asked him what he thought of this year's show. From the dogged way the man kept his opinion to himself, Conny sensed his scorn and contempt for the entire occasion. Conny invited him to join him in the beer tent, where he plied him with Taroven Brew. When he brought up the subject of Bruno Baltuschat, Simoneit merely looked at him contemptuously and pityingly, as if Conny had mentioned the name of a man who had just thrown away a future that would have been wretched in any case. No more prodding was necessary. Simoneit was ready to tell his tale.

He, Simoneit, was a veteran of the storming of Taroven Hill, but he had been repeatedly passed over for the honor of sitting on the reviewing stand because of a jail record—short sentences only, for poaching. Nothing helped his cause, neither his Iron Cross, First Class, nor the fact that the Taroven Committee, who arranged the commemoration, found it increasingly difficult to come up with a veteran who could still walk to the platform. He had imagined that he would at last have his chance, when one day he learned that a certain Bruno Baltuschat had been dredged up and was to occupy the special folding chair on the stand.

He went to visit Baltuschat in Grabnick and suggested that he decline the honor in favor of him, Simoneit. That was not all; he implied that he had more right to sit on the reviewing stand than Baltuschat. It was not Baltuschat who was obstinate but his wife and two daughters, and they stuck to their guns even when Simoneit referred to an episode whose very mention made Baltuschat pant for breath. The upshot was that Simoneit was ready to expose Bruno Baltuschat and let the public know the actual role the latter had played at the storming of Taroven Hill.

Conny heard how the detachment to which Simoneit and Baltuschat had belonged decided shortly before dawn to retreat from the hillcrest in the face of the St. Petersburgers' assault. They were under heavy fire. They had their gear to drag along. Each had to look out for himself. There was no time to notice who or what was left behind. In any case, at a roll call after a hasty retreat they had to list Militiaman Baltuschat among the missing. Then they regrouped at the foot of the hill; they agreed on signals and took up their positions. Every Lucknow schoolchild knew when and in what kind of weather they stormed the hill, how much munition was used, how long the battle went on, and how many light wounds, serious wounds, and casualties there were on both sides.

Simoneit reached the edge of the copse without injury only because, by his own account, he would run forward a few steps and then take cover behind the body of a fallen comrade. He claimed to be the first to have made it into the sheltering underbrush, for he knew the hill well from having set out his nets and traps here ever since he was a lad. He was working his way toward an old hiding place, when he came across a militiaman lying face down, with one foot and one arm caught in a pair of traps.

The militiaman did not move when Simoneit poked him with his rifle barrel. Not until he knelt down and spoke to him did the man jerk at the traps and toss his head to the side; it was Bruno Baltuschat. Simoneit freed him from the traps, which had kept him immobilized throughout the entire retreat and the attack. He bandaged the wounds on his arm. And Baltuschat did not refrain from stepping out there on the height and firing after the fleeing St. Petersburgers so steadily that he could not be ignored when decorations were handed out . . .

Yes, one might title the story "The Hero in the Spring Trap." You know Conny well enough by now to guess that he would not want to keep a story like that to himself. After Simoneit had assured him that he could do what he liked with Baltuschat's misfortunes, Conny jumped onto his motorcycle and sped back to Lucknow and the newsroom.

There was only a skeleton staff on hand; perhaps Conny would have hesitated to sit right down at the venerable Remington if Kukielka had been there, but the politest editor in Masuria had to spare his heart these days; it had been giving him trouble since the threatening letters started coming in—letters he had no desire to include in his collection. The new editor, Kudzus, a younger man, was always trying to curry favor with the established reporters, so he made no objection when Conny proposed to do a human-interest sketch in connection with the Taroven Commemoration—under a pseudonym. It would be printed along with the feature article. And so Conny wrote up the story of a soldier who had been caught in a poacher's traps and had thus survived the battle, the story of the veteran Baltuschat, whose accident had put him in the position of being decorated for an honor he had not earned.

Kudzus, who abhorred buttermilk but was partial to gin, read the text, saw nothing wrong with it, approved the manuscript for printing, and was so pleased that he said he hoped Conny would regularly contribute such items, under an assumed name for the time being. He offered Conny a shot of gin, and they sat and drank together. Kudzus asked questions more or less at random to help him form a picture of Conny's circumstances, and appeared to want to know him better. Then the floor began to vibrate as the presses started to roll, and Kudzus invited Conny to accompany him to the so-called House of Comradeship. He seemed so affable that he could not be refused.

They set out on Conny's motorcycle. The house, a spacious villa on the lakeshore promenade, had belonged to Dr. Fantl, who for more than forty years had attended to the Lucknowers' teeth, in reward for which he had been allowed to emigrate to join his daughter in London, minus his personal property, of course. All the windows were lit up, some of them open, and from them wafted phonograph music and the click of billiard balls. The heavy door was locked. Kudzus pressed three times on the bell, whereupon a peephole opened. A pair of blue eyes looked them over before a key turned in the lock, and a bull-necked giant let them enter. They signed their names in a guestbook in the hall, which was decorated with framed portraits of the Führer. The high French doors were open. Kudzus showed Conny the meeting hall, the billiard room, the reading room, and finally the paneled schoolroom. Here Conny suddenly went weak in the knees and felt such a pounding in his head that he had to excuse himself and sit down on one of the desks. The walls were hung with posters and diagrams on which various skull and facial forms were portrayed; without exception they were repulsive faces with receding or bulging foreheads, with outsized ears and exaggerated noses. Conny gagged; his only thought was to get out of this so-called House of Comradeship, but Kudzus apparently laid great store by his company. He insisted on leading his guest to the bar. Here, in what had once been the dental office, a counter had been set up and stocky peasant chairs and tables brought in. Kudzus's comrades were drinking Taroven Brew from pewter mugs. Most of them were in uniform. The few civilians wore on their lapels the emblem which united them, to which they had sworn undying loyalty, and they were all gathered around Toni Lettkow, who was apparently amusing them with anecdotes about his cavalry brigade.

Conny described to us how Kudzus froze in front of Toni Lettkow, snapped his arm up in the salute, and remained rigid until a casual nod released him. Then they went over to the bar, where the bull-necked fellow presided in a heavy leather apron. One wall was covered with weapons captured in various historic battles—French daggers, Russian bayonets, two English airplane propellers, all the weapons arranged to form crosses. Another wall was decorated with old general staff maps seized in various wars. Through the blue haze of smoke Conny spied familiar faces, Struppek and Henseleit, for instance, but also the owner of the Hotel Queen Luise and two Lucknow judges. People toasted him. He raised his pewter mug and drank, watching over the rim two men who bent their heads together and whispered, glancing toward him now and then.

Kudzus confessed that he had been meaning to bring Conny here for some time. He steered Conny over to a table with baskets of rolls and hard sausage. The group around Toni Lettkow abruptly burst into song, rose from their seats, stood at attention, and raised their mugs to the estate owner.

Kudzus talked about the newspaper, their *Lucknow News*. He had frank words to say about the paper's backward, conservative policy. "Maruhn and his ilk," he said, "have never moved beyond the spirit of Tannenberg." His criticism was anything but veiled. The main point was that the paper should fall into line with the new movement. He and his comrades, of course, possessed the means to neutralize Maruhn's influence, but in this case they chose to handle matters differently. He talked and talked, without attempting to discover where Conny stood. To the last Conny was not sure whether Kudzus hoped to find an ally in him, or was only showing his cards in order to make Conny expose his own.

Conny's mug was empty and he shook his head when Kudzus suggested another beer. He searched for an excuse to leave. Kudzus broke off a piece of bread and shared it with him and offered him a slice of sausage on the tip of a knife.

Suddenly the bull-necked fellow stepped up to their table, a half-dozen beer mugs in his huge hands. He bent over Conny and hissed, "Stand up, make it snappy." He put the mugs down on the counter, gestured Conny over to him, and pointed to the exit. Conny did not even have time to say goodbye. From the door he looked back at Kudzus, who was standing there dumbfounded; his surprise was genuine. Without a word of explanation Bullneck opened the door, and assumed the posture of a traffic policeman, one arm pointing forcefully to the outside.

Conny went straight to his motorcycle, jumped on, and roared off at top speed. On his way back, he stopped by the Hotel Queen Luise and watched the guests arrive for the Taroven Ball, among them Friedrich Maruhn with his ailing wife, who was dressed in her usual black. Conny managed to wave to him.

Then he rode home, packed his knapsack, and left that same evening for Rumeyken on Lake Glocken. He made himself a bed in the reeds, built a fire, roasted potatoes, and lay there watching the moonlight glancing off the lake. He listened to the calls of the nocturnal birds and the rustling in the reeds. The place had become a familiar refuge, where he often spent his weekend. He would sleep in the open, bathe in the lake the next morning, fix breakfast over the open fire, and lie in the sun for hours, reading. Monday morning he always returned to Lucknow just as the sky was growing light over the lake. On the way home he would stop at a country bakery and buy rolls fresh from the oven.

In any case, Rumeyken was where he made for that eventful Taroven Day, and in his hideout he decided to speak to Friedrich Maruhn, though not in the hectic atmosphere of the office but at the publisher's home, an old villa overgrown with grapevines, with terraced grounds descending to the lake. But the moment he entered the printing plant an apprentice told him that the boss had been asking for him and he had better get right up there.

Conny went upstairs to the second-floor wing, where the corridors had cocomat runners. This time Maruhn's old secretary did not have her usual encouraging wink for Conny; she did not invite Conny to sit down. Friedrich Maruhn asked him in. This time there was no coffee, no cognac, just a gesture asking him to take a seat in one of the leather armchairs. Maruhn's eyes: as Conny put it, you could read in Maruhn's eyes all the principles for which the man stood, and Conny added, "Say what you will against a liberal conservative—you can count on him to be consistent." The publisher was sorting through the supply of cigars meant for visitors. He had emptied the contents of the box on his desk and was carefully inspecting each cigar, occasionally slipping one into his case for his personal use. He spoke his first sentences softly in the direction of his desk top; Conny caught only snatches. Apparently there had been a storm of indignation, scores of letters canceling subscriptions, threats and invective; the glory of a Masurian day of commemoration had been tarnished. Maruhn stood up and walked over to a map on which the twenty-nine military cemeteries of Lucknow District, including that of Taroven, were marked with heavy black crosses. "There was no need," he said quietly, "for revealing embarrassing details about the battle of Taroven. There was no need." He remained standing in front of the map; two of the crosses marked the cemeteries at Bobern and Borschymmen, where his brothers lay buried. The old man paced to the window and from there to the bookcase, and as he passed Conny, he briefly placed a hand on the young man's shoulder. His voice held no hint of reproach as he said, "Look sharp, speak out, serve the truth: all that is well and good. But to further the truth that matters for all of us, we must be willing to forgo some of the minor truths. A person who cares about the truth must despise the perverse satisfaction one can derive from cheap revelations. The shadow of Taroven will darken the graves of all our war dead from now on."

And then he went to the door and opened it and stood with lowered eyes until Conny had gone through. The secretary was waiting with a batch of papers in her hand, his papers. She said, "You must excuse the boss; he's just been called to Town Hall." Conny took his papers and looked into the woman's eyes. The lids were slightly swollen. In the anteroom there was the look of things being tidied and packed up.

He emptied out his locker in the printing plant and could think of nothing more to do but to come out to our house, where he told us the whole story. But Conny could never bear to leave things undecided. So after eating with us he took his working papers and was off again, without mentioning where he was going. He went to see Grigo, head of the oldest printshop in Lucknow, and in less than an hour he had persuaded the taciturn boss and his son to take him on. Back home he told us his plans for expanding the little family business. "We'll print cards of congratulations," Conny said, "because most people have trouble thinking what to say on happy occasions." He also visualized a wall calendar with a page for every day and a motto on every page, likewise calling cards and the first Lucknow directory. "The Grigos will be amazed at what their presses can do," Conny remarked, and went on home to Frau Weinknecht, who was still his landlady.

It was about a year later, toward the end of July, that Conny and I were taken prisoner, on a hot, newly mowed field between Borek Forest and Lake Lucknow. That was another custom in our part of the world, the taking of prisoners to mark the end of the grain harvest. We had just left Little Grajevo on Conny's motorcycle and had had to stop because a nail had punctured the rear tire. We were pushing the heavy motorcycle in the blazing sun, and the heat, the dust from the fields of stubble, and the gasoline fumes combined to make us rather groggy.

As we passed the field, we suddenly heard the scythe concert. It came from a hollow near the wild pear trees; the mowers were beating their grindstones against their scythe blades in a wild and merry rhythm as a sign that they had finished the last field. And as the concert faded away, people came running from all directions. They encircled us, blocking our way, twenty or thirty men and women, some with rakes and scythes, some with newly braided ropes of wheat straw, with which they "bound" us, as tradition required.

They threw the ropes around our necks, tied our arms together. Custom called for us to submit without a struggle, even when they searched our pockets, counted our money, and took enough to cover a round of herb brandy for the whole company.

They heaved the motorcycle onto a farm cart that came lumbering up from the hollow. It was loaded with just a few sheaves of wheat, on top of which lay the harvest wreath, embellished with silk bows and sunflowers, as well as the Oole, a bundle of straw cleverly formed into the figure of a woman. Crowned by a sunbonnet, she rode triumphantly in the harvest wagon. They hitched us to the wagon, so that we had to walk beside the creaking wheel, and in the spirit of the thing we stumbled along with hanging heads and dragging feet, as real prisoners might do.

The mowers and the girls who had been binding the sheaves and had taken us captive spoke roughly to us, cuffed us playfully. A few of the girls kissed us, to prove how much we were at the mercy of their whims. In this jolly procession we rolled along to the estate, for it was the estate field hands who had taken us prisoner. On the edge of the farmyard, in front of the great wine-colored barn door, stood Toni Lettkow, wearing his usual riding boots and a light-colored windbreaker.

As the wagon pulled into the yard, the dogs began barking. The smithy pounded out a resounding welcome, doors and shutters flew open, the milkers dashed out in their clean red-and-white-checked shirts, and out came the maids and carters and stableboys. They all crowded around the wagon as it creaked down the lane formed by pails and milk cans and halted about forty feet from Toni Lettkow.

Two mowers hooked the handle of a pitchfork through the harvest wreath and solemnly bore it to Toni Lettkow. They held it out so that he could easily reach out and touch it, then set it down, doffed their caps, and stood there as if overwhelmed by the applause of the crowd. Toni Lettkow thanked them with a traditional phrase. The head sheaf binder now swooped up the straw harvest bride, patted her into shape, straightened her sunbonnet, and carried her to Toni Lettkow, who received her timidly but respectfully. And finally we, the captives, were presented to him, and he had no choice but to free us from our plaited bonds and invite us to the harvest festival.

In a second traditional phrase supplemented with some words of his own, Toni Lettkow thanked all the hands for their labor. Rather than singling anyone out, he stressed the benefits of working together and called for continued collective efforts. Even as he spoke, there was a perceptible stirring among the listeners. People were shifting positions, little groups were forming as close as possible to the lineup of pails and milk cans: the farmhands were getting ready for the water fight. The rules were as follows: all those returning from the fields belonged to one side, while those whose work kept them around the farmyard formed the other. As if they had old accounts to settle, they went at it, dipping and spraying and splattering, even pouring whole buckets over one another—you can imagine the uproar, a joyous uproar. Shirts and light summer dresses darkened and clung to bodies. Soon the yard was full of puddles, and a fine mist rose as high as the heads of the sunflowers, which reached up to the roof of the manse. We received our share, too, as did Toni Lettkow, over whose back someone emptied an entire bucket; he took it with composure.

Suddenly Conny pointed out Heini Hauser to me. He was sneaking toward the steps of the manse, carrying a basin of water. There stood Toni Lettkow's wife, dressed as always in pale blue, the usual white gloves in her hand. She had turned up at the estate one day with piles of luggage, from Königsberg, people said, a haughty woman who did not even try to win over the servants and farmhands, but who also, it should be said, did not care to test how far her authority reached. It was reported she did a great deal of reading, and often stayed indoors for days on end. Toni Lettkow himself regularly brought back packages of books for her from Lucknow. The hands called her "the lady in blue."

So there she stood on the steps, presumably attracted by the noise of the water battle, or perhaps annoyed by it. She gazed expressionlessly at her husband, who was wringing out his wet windbreaker. She was a bony, long-limbed woman, said to come from one of the oldest families of the Samland. Her name was Malvine, if you can believe that, yes, Malvine. She did not notice Heini Hauser creeping up on her with his basin, and even if she had, it would never have entered her mind that his approach had anything to do with her. He reached the steps unseen, crouched down, looked over toward us, and in response to our encouraging gestures dipped his hand into the water and flicked a few drops at the woman.

She seemed not to feel them, and in the knowledge that custom was on his side this day, he suddenly straightened up and sprayed and sprinkled her all over her light-blue dress. If she had been anyone else, Heini Hauser would simply have emptied the contents of the basin over her, but with Toni Lettkow's wife he dared not, out of respect or nervousness, or simply because she had never said a word to him in all the times he had crossed her path. When the woman turned toward him, Heini Hauser smiled awkwardly and shrugged as if to say, "No harm meant." The woman looked neither outraged nor amused. She simply leaned forward slightly and snapped her long, white glove in the man's face with a flick of the wrist, and only then did she look down at the dark spots of water on her dress, while Heini Hauser stared up at her in disbelief, as if he expected an explanation or an apology. We watched as he walked away with an expression of profound hurt. He stopped and hurled the empty basin into the garden like a discus. Then the attack on the barn began, sweeping everyone through the open doors to the laden tables.

Still dripping with water, the farmhands hurled themselves upon the food, and the feasting commenced. Toni Lettkow sat next to the head sheaf binder in the shadow of the gate, looking so relaxed and exhausted that he might have been taken for one of them. The maids kept refilling the bowls and baskets with our Masurian specialties, and we stuffed ourselves until it seemed a good idea to help along our digestions with herb brandy and home brew. Sitting on the ground, we drank to each other, and especially to Toni Lettkow, who went around clinking glasses with everyone, including us, the harvest captives, and the people of Little Grajevo.

Finally the hired musicians arrived, three dark-haired men with ferocious mustaches who played fiddle, flute, and double bass. They approached with practiced dignity, acknowledging our stormy applause with only the slightest of nods. We formed a large circle around them, and the head sheaf binder held the harvest bride on his lap; according to ancient custom, she was to be danced to pieces, yes.

The music began. Toni Lettkow stepped into the center of the circle, bowed before the head sheaf binder, who with a laugh threw the harvest bride to him. He caught the effigy, pressed her to him, and devotedly snuggled his head against her straw cheek. Then he danced, full of expression and undeterred by the limp straw legs that dangled between his own and grew looser with the whirling and stamping.

Out of breath, he tossed the bride to the head mower, who almost wrenched out one of her arms as he caught her just in the nick of time. And the first mower, too, went through his dance, a daring dance, by the way, a sort of tango, which called for his clapping one hand on the harvest bride's shredding straw bottom. The dancers changed off faster and faster, and the harvest bride lost more and more of her substance as she switched partners. Finally, all that was left of her was a limp bundle of straw, which Conny threw high over his head; then he stopped dead to let the last blades rain down on him. The rest of us crowded in and celebrated the end of the harvest bride with a round dance.

No, no, the celebration was not over yet. Having done our duty by the old customs, we let the musicians head for the food, and while they were putting it away as though they had to strengthen themselves for the winter ahead, out came casks of beer and bottles of herb brandy and liqueur. We settled back on sheaves of straw. As dusk fell, a girl from Little Grajevo, urged on by her girl friends, began to sing. Her song said that happiness would never come if one asked too much from life, demanded too much. After her, a mower sang, a song in which rock and iron argued over which could strike the most brilliant sparks. To our surprise, Toni Lettkow also sang, an old harvest song.

Couples were sitting shoulder to shoulder or hand in hand, and no one was in a great hurry to light the lanterns. On that warm summer evening, most of us were tired and relaxed and at one with ourselves. You could feel the sense of harmony in the air, see it in the faces, at least so long as we were sitting on the straw, singing, or merely listening to the ponderous movements of the animals in the enclosures.

Then the musicians struck up the harvest dance, which by custom lasted until daybreak, and would do so again this year. I slipped away alone. As I walked toward Lucknow, the music followed me, and I was filled with an unfamiliar sensation, the sensation of being carried along by the stamina and good cheer of the others. I had everything I wanted.

In the corridors of Masuria's most beautiful prison the night lights were on; the cells were dark. In the moonlight the glass shards atop the whitewashed walls glittered. From the boathouse a group of tipsy rowers approached; they encircled me, trapped me, danced around me, threatened me, all in fun; by way of amends, their spokesman offered me a huge paper cornflower.

Alone through the park along the lake—no, not alone; I felt as if I were walking behind and next to myself, I accompanied the man with the paper flower all the way to the wooden bridge across the Lucknow River . . .

How so, is it that time again? . . .

Too bad; no, of course there's no help for it. If you have to go, you must leave. But just let me tell you this one more thing: how the illusion of permanence can be destroyed from one moment to the next, how quickly we can be thrown out of an equilibrium that we thought we could count on for a good, long time . . .

No, not by anything particularly extraordinary. Conny stuck it out until morning at the estate, and after breakfast in the farmyard, the smith helped him repair his inner tube and changed his spark plugs. Before he roared down to the causeway, he apparently took one last spin around the farmyard, a spin calculated to jolt even the deepest sleeper from his dreams in the haymow.

Conny did not know that the Lucknow Engineering Corps was planning to lay a pontoon bridge across the river on this particular day. He rattled along the lakeshore as was his wont, honked at the three or four places where visibility was poor, trusting that anything on the road would get out of his way; that had always been the case. He had not expected to meet a heavy tractor hauling a still heavier pontoon, just turning onto the lakeshore road from Kaiser Wilhelmstrasse, a mass of battlefield gray blocking the entire passage to the river. Conny steered toward a hedge of arborvitae, crashed through it, was thrown off his motorcycle, and landed on a heap of rolled-up fencing, which had been stored there pending the repair of the fences along the shore . . .

That's true, but they kept him in the hospital for weeks, for weeks . . .

I know, dear boy, and I really mustn't keep you . . . for weeks, in which he had to learn many things from scratch . . .

Thank you, the same to you . . . So, till tomorrow.

# II

No letter, no message: a little boy delivered these flowers for me, leaving them in the lobby—that's all I know—and by now I have reached the point where I especially value such anonymous gestures. Nice to think that this bouquet might come from this person or that. I hope you don't have the solution to this mystery, Martin . . .

No? That's reassuring.

Well, to continue my story: one day we were marching along in single file—Eugen Lavrenz first, then Paulie, with me bringing up the rear. Each of us had a rucksack, and each rucksack held a packet of sandwiches my mother had made up the night before and wrapped in waxed paper. We were headed for the border, staying away from roads and highways and sticking to footpaths. Our destination was Kartossen, an insignificant village with a humble little railroad station.

If Eugen Lavrenz had had his way, we would have broken off our journey shortly after we set out, before dawn; he was completely disconcerted by this landscape in which, as he expressed it, "nothing is the way it should be." Vexedly he pointed out clumps of bushes which had sprung up overnight along a railway embankment or a bridge. He called our attention to a field which had mysteriously sprouted hundreds of kaddik bushes, or warned us to take care as we passed a copse whose trees did not grow straight up, as was normal, but leaned against each other diagonally. A familiar dip in the ground was covered with a net, out of which poked three tree trunks without crowns. We stumbled upon a collection of massive, motionless crates, all the same size, all covered with leafy birch branches. As I said, Eugen Lavrenz was enough disturbed by these oddities to want to turn around, but Paulie and I were determined to press on toward Kartossen.

It was no accident that each of us was carrying a rucksack. Several times each fall we made this trip to Kartossen because, insignificant though the station might be, it was the border-crossing point for the world-famous Polish geese. A superannuated locomotive dragged entire trains of these clever and nutritious birds to the border for export. We called these the goose trains. There was a honking and hissing from the cars, and when the customs officials slid back the doors, they stood in a blizzard of feathers.

The goose trains were always whisked through customs; the freight attendant made sure that everyone responsible for checking bills of lading had a chance to verify the quality of the shipment back home with his family. We ourselves would walk out into the no-man's-land between the borders and wait at the spot where the train had to stop for the switches to be changed. The freight attendant, who was always short of change and tobacco, acted gruff when we asked him about damaged birds. However, the moment we held out our palms to indicate that we would remunerate his pains, he simply reached in, grabbed a goose with a broken wing, entered it on his loss allowance, and stuffed it into one of our rucksacks. If all the geese around him happened to be in prime condition, he demonstrated how two quick motions could transform a healthy goose that met all the export regulations into a sad creature with drooping wings worth at most a small token of recognition.

It was these damaged but still wonderfully tasty geese that lured us to Kartossen on that September 1, a day on which the changes in the landscape posed a few disturbing puzzles, but the sunrise taking shape across the border promised a fair day almost free of wind.

When we arrived, the border station was deserted, the customs booth still closed. We waited around, but no one turned up. The broad window through which an equally broad woman usually served piping hot coffee remained shuttered. No van brought the customs officers, and in the wood huts that made up the village, people were apparently going without breakfast, for not a single column of smoke rose above the mossy roofs. Had all of Kartossen left for vacation? Had the border crossing perhaps been moved to another location? I strolled around the official buildings and was glad to see that all the prohibitions and customs regulations were still posted and the signs pointing to the spittoons had not been taken down.

But still no one appeared on our side as the goose train crept into sight to the south, and that mystified me. The train jerked along through the meadows, and tooted a few times to announce itself, but apparently it was expected only on the Polish side of the border. There a dapper stationmaster had stepped out in front of his little station building and straightened his uniform to greet the approaching train. We three advanced into the no-man's-land and sat down expectantly on the slope of the embankment. The polished brass fittings on the locomotive gleamed, and smoke floated above its stack, as if in a picture by Paulie.

Suddenly—just as the stationmaster was greeting the arriving train—the whole embankment shook, the ground trembled, and tumult swept through the drooping branches of the birches. There was a rumbling and a roaring, and we threw ourselves to the ground and peeped over the rails toward the horizon, beyond which the events of which we were feeling the reverberations must be taking place. Suddenly the sky was illuminated from below, and flashes of light and flame competed with the sunrise as a backdrop to flawless formations of aircraft heading south.

Over by the Polish stationhouse the stationmaster, the engineer, the stoker, and the freight attendant were standing, listening to the commotion beyond the horizon and also watching the airplanes, which they were trying to count. They huddled together to take counsel. The stationmaster called across to the German side, blew his whistle as a signal. When he could rouse no one, they conferred again, and apparently decided to observe the customs regulations and send the goose train on, out of their realm of responsibility, as they had always done.

So the crew scrambled onto the ancient locomotive, with the shipping documents between their teeth. They signaled their departure to the stationmaster, got up steam, and rolled and jerked into the no-man's-land in order to deliver their honking freight to its proper destination. We held ourselves in readiness, groping for coins and checking to make sure we had the tobacco.

At that moment two airplanes appeared above a wooded hill,

dipped into a hollow, soared up again, and held course toward us, two two-engine planes with shark faces painted on: slightly squinting shark eyes and shark's teeth ready to snap shut. I could make them out clearly and could also see the silhouettes of the pilots and soon afterward the emblem on the wings. I had to hold down Paulie, who wanted to leap up at the sight of the planes; I had to slap him hard to keep him from waving his arms to greet the planes . . .

Yes, that's just how it was, Martin; there was a flash from the planes, and the trail of the tracers arched down to the embankment, leaped over the ground, sending earth and stones shooting into the air, and headed for the slowly advancing train. It was hardly possible to take in with one's eyes all that was happening. With their cannon and 50-caliber machine guns they sewed a heavy seam around the russet railway cars; there was a cracking of wooden sides, the twittering of shells, the humming of iron, the bursting of brake housings, and from a shattered conduction pipe on the locomotive trapped steam issued with a mighty hiss.

The train derailed, but only after the second pass by the aircraft, and chiefly because no one was there to change the switches in the no-man's-land. When the stoker leaped down and tried to take care of the matter himself, his locomotive already had its right wheels in the air and was listing like a ship whose cargo had slipped. It tipped toward where we were posted, and dragged the first two cars with it as it lurched over, with the result that the following cars jumped the rails and collapsed into one another like the bellows of an accordion. Wheels spun helplessly in the air, steam and smoke shrouded the locomotive. Here and there something cracked. An iron chain rattled against a step. And from beside me came Eugen Lavrenz's voice—I will never forget it—"Seems to me, Zygmunt, we're at war again."

More he could not say, for at that moment we heard a rusty trumpet blast, and a huge gander hurled himself from a splintered boxcar. He almost turned a somersault as he landed, and once on the ground he drew his head back and uttered that rusty call again, whereupon from all the gaps and hatches crowded and shoved the fattened geese. They plumped to the ground, honking crazily, and went flapping after the gander, who had apparently given the signal to head for the murky peat ponds.

What a tumult. The cries and the wild flapping of this panicky white armada; Paulie clung to me in alarm. You can picture the scene: one goose had a wing dragging, another hobbled on one leg, a third had had its hindquarters shot off, a fourth staggered past with blood-spattered breast. White and red, innocence and blood. Many a bird lay where it fell, neck outstretched, wings twitching convulsively. They lay there in the shadow of the embankment like little heaps of snow which the sun had not reached. On the peat ponds a festival of joy was being celebrated by the survivors; they beat noisily on the brackish water, made exaggerated attempts at diving, paddled around in narrow circles, and splashed with their wings, honking at each other incessantly.

Eugen Lavrenz told Paulie to remain lying in the shelter of the embankment. I was to accompany Eugen and give him a leg up into one of the cars, which had had its side shot away. First a sigh, then an exclamation; he asked me to hand him my rucksack. I bent to look at the inside and for a moment felt as if I were looking into the smashed display window of a poultry shop; to be sure, the birds were lying there with gracefully bent necks and handsomely spread wings, but part of the damply gleaming innards, so essential for black pudding, appeared to have spurted all over the car. "Goose giblets—here's as much goose giblets as a body could want," Eugen Lavrenz commented, and when he had stowed away two slightly bleeding, still warm bodies in our rucksacks, he fetched out a few sheets of waxed paper and with the help of a jar lid he happened to have on him began to scoop up stomachs and livers. He also collected a few webbed feet and shiny strings of intestine and skillfully wrapped it all in the waxed paper.

Paulie called out a warning, and Eugen Lavrenz jumped down to where I was standing. We shouldered our booty and ran. As we looked over our shoulders, we spied the desperate stationmaster running along the goose train, calling out names. Suddenly he fell to his knees at the spot where the legs of the crushed stoker showed from under the capsized locomotive. We ran past the buildings on the German side—they were still empty. The humming in the air and the pounding and roaring followed us all the way to the birch forest and had still not let up when we reached the swampy Wossock woods.

There we met a shepherd out looking for a ewe that had strayed from the flock. He was an old man in a black, buttoned-up coat. We had never seen him before, but that did not keep him from rushing up to Eugen Lavrenz, seizing him by the shoulders, and in an access of fraternization embracing him: "We're at war, friend," he exclaimed. "Poland will soon be done for." Hopping on ahead of us, he led us past water holes and recumbent but living trees to a hill from which we had a view of the great border highway, whose building Conny had once celebrated in an article. There they were, marching to the south.

Yes, Martin: how alike the two scenes were! Once more I stood and watched an army heading for the "field of honor," to be sure in the opposite direction this time, and well equipped with the latest military hardware, but carried along by the same old obedience and the same old blind courage, or if not that, at least by a sense of duty which gave the men's faces that look of unshakable equanimity.

We headed back to Lucknow, through fields and meadows, keeping parallel to the border highway. This time no church bells were ringing. There was no cellophane crackle in the air, and the bridges were secured not with rusty plows and harrows but with two 3.7-caliber antitank guns. Paulie stayed behind with the soldiers manning the guns, while we continued into town. The army was marching down the main street, and the people of Lucknow were clapping and waving and tossing cigarettes and candy to the soldiers. The flower shops were open for people to help themselves; anyone could take an armful of carnations or asters and decorate the soldiers, sticking flowers into the barrels of their guns. Bakers hauled out baskets of rolls and buns and handed them up to the men on the gun carriages or tanks. Butchers' apprentices hacked off sausages from their coils and tossed them onto the personnel carriers. Incredible what Lucknow's tradesmen were willing to do to give our army a good start.

Eugen Lavrenz pulled me out of the enthusiastic crowd lining the street, and we hurried toward our house at the bend in the river. Airplane formations were still passing overhead, and we could still feel the shudder of distant explosions. On the bench in front of the house sat Edith, her coat on her lap and the big suitcase beside her. She jumped up and came to meet us, wanting only to know when we were leaving. "Leaving?" I asked. She replied, as if we were still in ignorance, "We're at war, Zygmunt." Suddenly she realized that Paulie was not with us. She demanded to know where we had left him and, without a further word, rushed off angrily to find him.

We had no chance to show her our booty. We took our rucksacks into the kitchen, where my mother was comfortably ensconced amid bowls and basins, the image of placid expectation. No sooner had I unstrapped the rucksack than her hand was already inside, feeling around. She triumphantly pulled a goose out by the neck and went to work, plucking the birds. What gave her more pleasure than the geese themselves were the giblets. "There's hardly any cleaning to do," she remarked admiringly. "The war did as good a job as we could have. We can really celebrate this fall." We left her to do what she had often enough described as her favorite job; we could tell it still was by the way she sang as she worked . . .

Departure? You are asking whether it would have been possible for us to leave Lucknow, so close to the border? I believe so; but what Edith had in mind—"go somewhere where there's no war"—or what Conny suggested that same day, would probably not have been all that easy.

But of course . . .

Conny came over right after work, avoiding the town by cutting through the gardens along the lakeshore. Under his arm he was carrying a flat package wrapped in brown paper, and from the way he walked it was clear he was hoping not to run into an acquaintance. He handed me the packet with the explanation, "That's for your museum—signs of the times."

They were signs, literally, a collection of posters the Grigos' printshop had just run off. They preached the need for conserving essential energy. They recommended being careful about strangers, since the enemy was listening everywhere. They proclaimed the necessity of the blackout, the importance of collecting scrap metal, the certainty of victory. One poster, which showed a farmer and a soldier clasping hands across a landscape of lakes and forests, claimed that the homeland and the front were united in pursuit of the same great goal. Conny avoided looking at the posters himself; he eyed me to see what my reaction would be, and when I did not respond soon enough for his taste, he fished out of his wallet a batch of freshly printed rationing stamps and placed them on top of the pile of posters.

I still recall how slow I was to catch his meaning when he said, "There's still time to go to Haparanda." "Haparanda?" I asked. "How come?" And he replied with feigned, but not completely feigned, disappointment, "I thought, Zygmunt, that you and Edith and I had a rendezvous in Haparanda. We had it all planned, long ago. This would be the moment to set out."

I had no doubt Conny was serious about his proposal. He did not want to act in haste; he merely asked me to think over the old plan and discuss it with Edith. I promised to do so, although I already knew I would not leave. Too much kept me in Lucknow —my people, my work, the museum—yes, the museum, which meant more and more to us, the more stridently the homeland was declared a so-called community of destiny.

At the time I found it out of the question to give up the collection, or even to entrust it temporarily to others. My relationship to the objects, the "unimpeachable witnesses," as Uncle Adam had called them, had changed imperceptibly. Now whenever I was alone with them, they seemed to promise me something: that one day all the nonsense and bombast of the present would be refuted. The museum thus came to offer consolation. Obsessed as only a collector can be, I began creating a special room that would show every possible aspect of the "homeland at war." I decided to save everything, even the most insignificant-seeming items, and to arrange the ensemble in such a way as to show the marks left by the war, the demands it made on us, the expectations and illusions it awakened, and the sorrow and want it had brought down upon us. My first accessions were the posters and freshly minted rationing stamps Conny had brought . . .

You wonder when our turn came? Well, you know how well the war went at first. Every day formations of war planes passed overhead on their way south. They attacked Mlawa, Lomza, and Modlin, and some showed what they could do over Warsaw, after the city had been designated a fortress in order to legitimize bombing it. In any case, the ring had just closed around Bzura when Conny and I received our call-up notices. We received them the same day and went together to our former elementary school. The review panel which had set up quarters in our old classroom consisted of a major, an army doctor, a stenographer, a messenger, and probably a few witnesses . . .

Conny had brought along a large brown envelope, which he did not put down even when he was being weighed and measured. He said not a word about its contents, not even to me, though I was favored with a wink and a soft whistle, which seemed to say, "Just wait, Zygmunt, you'll soon see what this's good for." Simon Gayko was leaving as we entered; the bow-legged Bosnian had been examined just before us, and he was only partly satisfied. They had not found the dedicated builder of model ships fit for a naval command, but only for the coastal artillery. So we came next, and we had barely been ushered before the panel when Conny handed his envelope to the doctor with a hint of a bow. The doctor nodded calmly and drew out two X rays, which he held up to the light for a long moment. As he read the accompanying statement, he nodded in confirmation. There was a brief exchange between the doctor and the major; then they gestured to Conny, and he was dismissed, "deferred until further notice" was the official expression, because of a spinal infirmity—the result of his motorcycle accident.

The major could not believe that I did not care where they put me. Determined to find me a place that suited my special abilities, or rather where I would shine, he discussed the requirements and duties associated with each of the units. Things were going so well at that point that he could take time for such a lengthy process. He initiated me into the possibilities open to the artillery, explained the wide range of functions performed by the Engineering Corps, and revealed why, in the final analysis, everything depended on the infantry—yet I could not make up my mind. I raised no objections when he assigned me to a supply battalion. My basic training took place in the varied and lovely landscape of Lötzen, so close to Lucknow that after two months I was already permitted a weekend furlough at home, in uniform. And thus began my short engagement with the theater of war . . .

That's probably the nurse with the tray; help her, Martin; I'm sure she's brought a cup for you, too . . .

There, you see . . .

Yes, Nurse, Herr Witt is here again, my companion in the

jungle of the past, if you don't mind my calling you that, Martin . . .

Thank you, Nurse, I'll take care of that myself. Little by little I'm able to relieve you of all those chores. Soon I'll be handing you my personal declaration of independence, in woven form . . .

No, don't ask me anything, I'm not telling . . .

I'll do it, I promise you; I'll ring before suppertime. Thank you, Nurse . . .

But where were we? Right, we were talking about my guest performance in the war. We were responsible for supplying the thinly spread occupation troops around the great bend in the Narev, to the northwest of Bialystok. We brought our loaded vehicles to Bialystok on freight cars. There we rolled off the flatbed cars and rumbled away in a motorized column that shrank with increasing distance, across flat, boggy countryside that stretched endlessly in all directions. We stopped at garrison and staff headquarters and at isolated outposts, where we were always warmly received and urged to stay by soldiers eager to catch the latest news. On our journeys we were accompanied by a half-track, which, however, stayed behind when the heavy snows came and was replaced by a snowplow with a three-man escort equipped with a 30-caliber machine gun. Many of the local inhabitants also welcomed us. They were small farmers, craftsmen, tradesmen. They already knew the route our column took, knew where separate trucks left the convoy and rolled on alone over the land forever dimmed by falling snow. We never asked ourselves how they had managed to hang on to all the gold zlotys through the years, how they had hidden the silver from generations of pillagers and the hams and geese from requisition commandos. Out there in the clearings or on the frozen bogs we took what they offered us, and in return we gave them gasoline and medicine, coffee and tobacco. After a while we knew our business partners by name, brought them special orders or arranged special deals, and if anything still surprised us, it was that they knew just when we would be coming through and the precise route. They always waited for us far from the villages and outlying farms.

Then, in one of those fierce snowstorms that swept over the countryside from the northeast, a loaded truck disappeared, along with the three soldiers escorting it. A major search was launched. There was evidence that it had passed Bialystok, and its route could be traced through several fortified dams in the swamps of the Narev River. But the scent was lost in the miserable little village of Kobrikovo or thereabouts—even the sign with the village's name was drifted over with snow.

A special investigation squad was sent from Bialystok to this village, inhabited almost exclusively by river fishermen and peat cutters. The investigators reconstructed the truck's last journey, interrogated the villagers, then ordered the village elder to pick three men—for the gallows. The village elder refused, whereupon the investigation squad seized three inhabitants at random and hanged them in the middle of a snowstorm, with orders that they be left on the gallows for three days. We drove past the gallows and stopped briefly. I saw them hanging there, swinging in the icy wind, and I still recall their boots, which had split and been patched several times and had no heels left to speak of. From this day on, no one was waiting for us at any of the swapping points.

Yes, Martin, and it was here near Kobrikovo that our tires jumped the frozen ruts, the truck skidded backward with its heavy load, and no matter how often we tried, we could not get back onto the road. I had to fetch help, had to summon some men from the cottages. Some of them actually said goodbye to their families before they came out in those shapeless jackets of theirs, which made them look like great bundles of cloth. At the last cottage a tall, lean, old man opened the door. His bearing combined dignity and casualness, and he appeared neither surprised nor startled to see the foreign uniform.

"Yes, soldier?" he asked. Behind him I saw the low-ceilinged warm room, where close to a snow-covered window, opposite a glowing tiled stove, stood a loom. This was how I found Michal Mamino, the most respected rug master in the Bialystok, Suwalki, and Lomza region, the legendary weaver whom even Sonja Turk referred to as a supreme authority, although he was no older than she, as I could see. Of course, I did not yet know it was he.

I was standing at the loom. The master was working on a pictorial rug, "Jesus in the Storm." The sea was green and black, the apostles wore earth-colored robes, and Christ, who was sleeping, wore white. What a challenge: the mighty waves with their glowing crests, the tiny ship without oars or sail or rudder; and while the disciples huddled together and tried to measure the danger of the waves, Christ slept at their feet. "What is it you want, soldier?" the old man asked evenly. Instead of answering that, I asked him if I might come back some time. He demurred and let me know he made no sales and took on no commissions. Only after I had told him my profession did he give me leave, but even then seemed not exactly overjoyed.

In any case, I did come back, and knocked on the window, as he had instructed me. He let me in through a wooden outbuilding which housed a dovecote. He made a pot of linden tea and offered me a sort of brown cookie, hard as rock, which he dipped in the tea to soften it. He smiled only once, and that was when I asked him if he had ever met Michal Mamino. I said, "The great Michal Mamino, whom even my teacher, Sonja Turk, regarded as an authority." With a smile he took a little box from a corner cupboard, drew out a bundle of letters, and finally handed me an old newspaper clipping. It was a photograph showing Sonja Turk and Michal Mamino, the two winners of the first prize at the rug exhibition in Kaunas.

He wanted to hear about our work, but even more he wanted to hear about Sonja's illness and her apparent acceptance of what the illness brought with it. He said not a word about the war, although he continued to call me "soldier," even after he had learned my name. Now and then I had the impression that he tolerated my visit only to fulfill a self-imposed obligation. Before I left, he wrote a letter to Sonja Turk. The pen sped over the paper without a moment's pause, as if the connection between the two weavers had never broken off. "Perhaps she will write back," he said, and watched intently as I placed the letter in my wallet.

I did not have to wait until my next furlough to deliver the letter. Not long afterward we stopped in Lucknow to drop our empty containers at the large supply depot which at a later date was literally to dissolve into a cloud of dust and smoke from the explosion of hundreds of bazookas stored there. Loaded down with canned meat, coffee, and sugar, I made my way home, where I dropped off the family's share. Then I took the rest over the bridge to the house by the drinking trough. Nowadays

Sonja's house had a neglected look. Sonja surprised me: for all her pleasure at receiving Michal Mamino's letter, she seemed to take it almost for granted. Her expression of sly satisfaction suggested that some matter had just been resolved, a matter she had never forgotten . . .

No, Martin, you'll never guess, and I myself found out only from the letter she dictated to me. Her joints were so swollen that she could no longer hold a pen.

It had to do with a long-ago argument between these two great weavers, an argument that at first may sound rather pointless, but which for the two of them—and that means also for us—touched on issues of fundamental importance. Sonja Turk had asserted that a truly original piece of weaving could never be repeated. Michal Mamino had argued that repetition was possible if one followed precisely the procedure by which the original had been woven. Thereupon Sonja Turk had publicly challenged her colleague to show that it could be done, and he had accepted the challenge, while refusing the wager Sonja Turk had made: fifty gold zlotys.

All that took place when they were both young, and although nothing came of the matter at the time, Michal Mamino remained secretly determined to prove his point. After a lifetime of vain attempts, he had to admit that Sonja Turk had been right. And this is what he had told her in his letter: that in spite of many tries, he had never succeeded in perfectly reproducing a rug . . .

His work? You want to know whether I got to see his weaving? Just a few pieces, Martin, although I never failed to stop by when we came through Kobrikovo; he showed me those only because I asked so persistently. You see, he was not so very cordial; I never felt that my visits meant anything to him. He merely seemed to put himself at my disposal for a short while. While I was there, he never touched the presents I brought him —including a jar of brandied fruit from Sonja Turk. I would put the presents down on a table, and they remained there unopened until I left. He never thanked me for them.

But there was one large rug which I did see, a rug meant to be most effective at a distance. It used strong masses of color— cadmium green and cadmium yellow. He called it "Doves and Fishes." I saw it before two taciturn men came to fetch it, or pretended they had to fetch it. On the rug the doves and the fishes had changed places; schools of spindle-shaped fish shot through a clear blue sky, while orderly ranks of doves flapped their way through the glimmering depths. The piece had a strange, impressive beauty. By the way, the fish and the doves were moving in opposite directions, but both were about to plunge into a golden gleam of light, behind which brooded a dark, netlike pattern. Later Sonja Turk and I tried in vain to find a clear interpretation for the symbols.

I asked the men where they were taking the rug. They looked at me uncomprehendingly, and after a bit Michal Mamino answered for them: "To the church," he said. "I have given the rug to our church."

For Sonja Turk's sake I continued the visits, for since I had told her about Michal Mamino, she plagued me with questions about him and his circumstances. In a fit of self-delusion she even considered arranging a reunion. And precisely because I continued my visits I observed the regulations our batallion had established for us: I never left the truck without arming myself, and making sure that at least one of us stayed behind to guard the vehicle. For on the new maps we had recently received, several so-called unsafe areas were marked, and the red hatching extended as far as Kobrikovo . . .

The forest just before Kobrikovo was not yet hatched on the map. One late afternoon, we were lumbering along, two heavily laden trucks from our column, the stronger one going ahead with a plow, we at some distance behind for safety. The route was familiar, and we drove, not expecting trouble, moving steadily through this region of cold and silence, not very fast, but at an even pace. We knew that our comrades at the strong points and batallion headquarters were counting on us. This is where we were ambushed.

It was not yet dark, but both trucks already had their headlights on. The road began to climb, and the moment the front truck stopped, I could see the two giant tree trunks, which were not lying straight across the road—this would surely have aroused our suspicion—but at an angle, as if they had slid off a logging truck. The men from the first truck got out, kicked the trunks, and debated what should be done. They apparently did not trust the snowplow to move the obstacle, and there was no way to drive around, for the ancient pines clustered right up to the edge of the road, trees with trunks so thick a man could not encircle them with his arms. "They'll have to get the winch," our driver said. "Hitch up each of the logs separately, back up, and pull them to the side." He climbed out of the truck and went up ahead, gesticulating to explain his plan, and they seemed to have reached agreement when suddenly a curiously echo-less hoarse rattle broke the stillness.

Three of our men collapsed and fell. The driver raised his head once more, doubled up, looked as though he wanted to pull himself up by one of the tree trunks, and was hurled down by a new burst of fire. Suddenly everything went still, but it was no longer the neutral stillness that had reigned on all our previous trips through this forest; it was a tense stillness produced by fright and astonishment and sudden death. I wondered what had happened to Treuburger, who was in the first truck—our column leader, a thickset, hot-tempered man rumored to have been an officer who was demoted. He was a loner who seemed disgusted by everything, even his own authority.

I don't know how he managed to leave his vehicle unseen, to crawl under it and get to me in the second truck. He tossed me his submachine gun, started up the engine, and ordered me to rake the forest through the open window. "Just keep up a steady fire," he said, as he turned off the headlights, shifted into reverse, and started to move. When the horn began to blare without a stop, I at first thought this was part of his escape strategy, but suddenly the rear of the truck rammed past a number of trees, the canvas ripped, the truck swayed, left the route, crashed past trees, and stopped dead because it was jammed and could go no farther. Treuburger was lying with his face on the wheel, his forehead pressing against the horn. I laid him out on the seat and turned off the engine. They had shot him in the forehead.

Don't ask what I was hoping for or what thoughts crossed my mind as I opened the door and slid out into the snow, uncertain whether they had already spotted me. There was not a sound— no whispers, no crackling in the bushes. I raised my head to listen, and then I saw, high up in a still pine, a brief white flash and felt a shock run through my hand as the bullet bit into the door of the truck. A short burst of fire from my submachine gun, not aimed or planned, but more a reflex action, and then, as if in slow motion, a body began to fall from branch to branch of the pine tree, followed by clouds of snow. The branches slowed his fall, and then he landed on the hood, and I recognized the dead man's face: he was one of the two men who had come for the rug that time.

Presumably the rest of them were also perched in the trees, subdued now behind their camouflage of branches, and not about to betray themselves by firing, as their comrade had done. They had accomplished most of what they wanted, and I had forced them to acknowledge the superiority of an automatic weapon. But they probably had other reasons for letting me go, stumbling along up to my knees in snow. I had not lost my sense of direction and knew that the forest thinned out toward the meadows along the Narev, beyond which lay Kobrikovo . . .

No, Martin, our side had no military presence in Kobrikovo, but Michal Mamino was there, and the priest had a telephone. So I went on through the forest and over the snow-packed meadows, reaching the wooden bridge, whose supports were being rammed by ice floes. Around midnight not a single light could be seen in the village, but when I knocked at Michal Mamino's cottage, he was fully dressed and impassively let me in. He did not ask me to sit down, although he could see I was exhausted. Standing there, he waited for me to explain this late visit. I apologized and asked him to come with me to the priest's house to act as interpreter. He refused, with a fleeting expression of regret, and standing there, composed and distant, looked at me in such a way as to remind me that I had brought my weapon along. Suddenly he left the room, and almost immediately several men entered, tired, unshaven men in black fur caps who carried hunting rifles. They disarmed me, tied my hands together, and took me out into the night, not as if I were their prisoner, but as if I were a fellow conspirator. The men whispered to one another, quickly reached an agreement, and led me along the iced-up banks of the Narev to a low but roomy shed where the fishermen of Kobrikovo stored their gear for the winter. I was allowed to sit down. One of them rolled me a cigarette, and we sat there in silence and smoked and listened to the sounds of firing in the distance. And in that shed

the war came to an end for me, or at least the role that had been
reserved for me in the war.

The men were thrown into confusion when the stillness of
early morning was smashed by the rumbling, squeaking, rattling
of moving tanks, a sound they had probably never heard before.
Two tanks came crunching over the frozen meadows, behind
them several armed personnel carriers, a display of might that
seemed so out of proportion to my captors' equipment that they
may well have believed it was all a mistake. But then the first
grenades slammed into the chunks of ice heaped along the banks.
I could not keep the men from taking up positions behind the
hatches and the partly opened door and returning fire with their
hunting rifles; I lay down in a little fisherman's boat, closed my
eyes, and waited. A flash and a burning pain: I perceived them
simultaneously during that instant when a ball of incredible
brightness burst in, accompanied by deep, hard thumps.

I learned the rest in Bialystok, in a little military hospital where
they removed no less than seven splinters from my body. Seven,
and that was two too few. Because of the two splinters left in me,
I was transferred to Lucknow, and it was from Edith, not the
doctors, that I heard why they kept putting off the operation:
the two minuscule splinters were embedded close to the heart and
could be reached only at considerable risk. Since they did not
threaten the heart directly, the doctors preferred to leave them
inside me for the time being, at least so long as they showed no
inclination to wander. What caused trouble at first was the pressure, a sharp pressure which was less painful when I was walking
than sitting down, that's right.

In any case, when there seemed hardly any doubt that the
splinters would become encapsulated, they released me, and all
my people came to fetch me, including Conny. At home Sonja
Turk was waiting, brought over in her wheelchair by Marian
Jeromin. And there was black pudding, and the radio had a special bulletin: some eighty metric tons of enemy shipping had
been sunk in the Atlantic. "Just like we'd ordered it," my mother
commented. "Serves them right for tangling with us."

No, never again. There was no more word of Michal Mamino.
The letter I wrote for Sonja Turk was returned as undeliverable.
A fellow soldier from my unit whom I delegated to search for

the weaver could bring me no news. The inhabitants of Kobri-kovo purported not to remember any man by that name. No, Michal Mamino never did turn up . . .

What would you like to know? Ah yes, while greetings and photographs arrived from Simon Gayko from Danish, Nor-wegian, and soon afterward French coastal installations where he was stationed, I quietly opened our museum to the public. We posted no signs, set no visiting hours, collected no entrance fees. We did nothing that could have attracted the attention of offi-cialdom and were content that certain people found their way to us, to ponder our exhibit of futility and interminable loss.

Do you want to know what Conny said one day, after he had seen several pupils from Paulie's class leaving the museum? He shook his head and said, "Conquering the world with the home-land in your heart: when will you see that the homeland is noth-ing but the sanctuary of arrogance and narrow-minded self-congratulation: an alibi?" And would we mind turning off the radio; the request concert they were broadcasting was making him sick.

This occurred at a time when all of Lucknow was up in arms over Conny, when the guests in a restaurant would get up and leave in a body, rather than be under the same roof with him. Wounded veterans would come up to him and spit on the ground, uniformed members of the youth organizations crowded him off the sidewalk. One evening, on the way home, he was beaten up. But it also happened that a retired schoolteacher dis-creetly tipped his hat to him. Letters came, most of them anony-mous, congratulating him and urging him to keep up the fight for justice.

The whole business had begun out in Borek Forest one day, by the tumbling brook behind Frenchman's Hill which disappeared underground near Little Grajevo and found its way to Lake Lucknow. A soldier was kneeling by the brook. Conny stood on the wooded slope and watched the soldier bend his face far over one of its pools, as if he were trying to see his reflection. Then he washed his face and hands hastily, dried them with his handker-chief, jumped up, and began to brush off his uniform, paying special attention to his knees, but also to his jacket, which he wore unbuttoned. He rubbed and brushed, dampened the cloth and scrubbed frantically, pausing time and again to listen and make sure he was unobserved. He buried the handkerchief in the soft earth of the bank, grabbed a handful of leaves to clean off his boots, then went down on all fours and leaned out perilously over the water to check his reflection again.

Then Conny's shadow fell over him, or he noticed the wavy reflection of someone standing behind him; in any case, he leaped up. Conny saw that the soldier was not especially young, a man with a broad, open face over whose left cheek two thin, flaming scratches ran, almost down to his neck. The soldier stared at him, panting and startled.

Conny did not even have a word with him, for the soldier turned and ran, leaping through the blueberry bushes and over anthills toward the main wood road. After digging up the handkerchief, Conny came to our house. That was all, but it was the beginning of a very hard time for Conny.

Less than five days later we read in the *Lucknow News* that children picking blueberries in the Borek Forest had found the body of a woman, covered with branches. The police identified the body as that of Anna Hauser from Little Grajevo, and that was not all; they had taken into custody a certain Henryk Gutkelch, a man Anna Hauser had lived with for several years and whom she had left shortly before the murder. The paper reported that the man refused to confess to the crime.

Conny rode out to Little Grajevo and sat up talking most of the night with Heini Hauser. He asked about Anna's relationship with Henryk Gutkelch and put together a picture of the man. The next morning he went to the police and not only testified about his encounter with the soldier in the woods but also handed over the handkerchief—for which he, of course, demanded a receipt. There matters remained for the time being.

We assumed that a search was underway in all the Lucknow barracks, a reluctant search involving roll calls and alibi checks. We gathered that the police were not very welcome in military barracks, and concluded that the investigation would go slowly. All Conny could discover was that the handkerchief had been analyzed and traces of blood found belonging to two different blood groups. Then nothing more was heard; it seemed as if the whole inquiry had run aground on the inexorable requirements of war.

But suddenly the war itself gave events a turn that did not solve the case but provided some unexpected information that brought the matter out of the realm of uncertainty: Conny ran across the name of the soldier. He pulled a newspaper out of his pocket and pointed to the picture on the front page. There was a sturdy soldier trying in vain to suppress a smile while his commander in chief hung a very high decoration around his neck. The soldier was called Lothar Sentek. "That's him," Conny said, "there can't be any mistake."

So it was Lothar Sentek from Hindenburgstrasse, the first Lucknow man to receive the *Ritterkreuz*, a hero whose flame thrower had made short work of bunkers, forts, and fortifications from Modlin to the Maginot Line.

We read the article about Lothar Sentek and noted that the city fathers meant to give him a hero's welcome on his next home leave. "Will you really go ahead with it?" Edith asked her brother. Conny looked out the window and said reflectively, "I have no choice."

Yes, Martin, you're right, and after a moment Conny, too, realized what he was up against. But he was never one to play it safe. "One way or the other—if we don't get them, they'll get us," he decided. So off he went to the office of the Lucknow detective division, and asked to see the chief of detectives, Joseph von Intelmann, who had taken over the case of Hauser, Anna, and brought it to the point at which everything was blocked by the obstacles the war threw in its path. The neat little man with snow-white hair rose behind his desk as Conny was shown in. Conny presented him with the newspaper, folded so that Sentek's picture and the article on him were prominent.

"Here," Conny said, "here's who it was." And Intelmann read, then looked up irritably, as if Conny had made a mistake. But Conny only nodded and insisted, "That's the one—there's no doubt about the face." Joseph von Intelmann stood up. He was nettled, not so much because he distrusted Conny as because Conny seemed to be asking him to embark on a course that violated the spirit of the times. "Do you know what you are saying!" he exclaimed. "Have you any idea where your testimony could lead! Our country is at war, in case you've forgotten!"

"How about Henryk Gutkelch?" Conny asked. "He's still in custody, isn't he?" "He will be released—conditionally," von Intelmann replied, and he began pacing the room, shaking his head as if to rid it of absurd notions. Perhaps Conny's certainty provoked him; in any case, his voice took on an accusatory tone as he pointed out the impossibility of what Conny was asking of him. First there was the question of finding the man, who could be anywhere between the North Cape and Athens. But, of course, the military mail system would help, provided there were adequate grounds. Well, supposing they did track him down with his unit, in Norway, Rumania, or Yugoslavia—would a military court accept a subpoena from Lucknow? What if he were in the midst of a siege, with much depending on that flame thrower of his? How would this highly decorated soldier's superior officers react when they received a subpoena from an obscure little town in Masuria? Finally, what conclusions would his fellow soldiers draw when one of their own, who daily earned their trust and admiration, was stigmatized in this way?

Intelmann even hinted that the first problem would arise in Lucknow itself, among the town dignitaries. After this tirade he waved wearily, as if to say, "Enough," and looked straight at Conny with an expression of sorrow and dismay. "So"—he asked —"have I made the situation clear?" Conny shot back a question: "What do you intend to do?" whereupon the little white-haired chief of detectives answered with a shrug, "What do you think? First we'll file suit with the appropriate court-martial for permission to interrogate."

More time passed in which the case seemed at a standstill, and we had to assume that the petition from Lucknow had been sidetracked on a distant front in staff headquarters, or perhaps lost or destroyed in the confusion of battle. Conny even began to wonder whether Intelmann had only pretended to be pursuing the matter and had actually long since laid it to rest.

But shortly after this Conny became ashamed of his suspicion. He chanced to meet Intelmann at the local movie house where they sat together watching the film *La Habanera*. During the moments when the beloved star Zarah Leander was not singing, the detective informed Conny of the status of the investigation. He had traced Lothar Sentek to Sicily, from there to Crete, and from there to Montenegro, where the trail abruptly ended; part of his unit had disappeared while fighting the partisans and was classified as missing. But Intelmann had not given up, and with the cooperation of a few officers he had known in the previous war, he picked up a new trail which led to a military hospital in Innsbruck, from there to Breslau and Königsberg, and then to Lötzen . . .

Yes, Martin, in the immediate vicinity of Lucknow, in the charming landscape where I had done my basic training, Lothar Sentek was acting as instructor for the Corps of Engineers. Joseph von Intelmann decided to go there himself and take the measure of this man, whom the fortunes of war had carried to such distant places. He was allowed to speak with him in the mess hall, and they had barely sat down and ordered coffee when the soldier admitted that he had been on Frenchman's Hill in the Borek that day. He did not deny having met a woman there—he knew only her first name, Anna—or that in a specific context they had had an argument, actually a playful one, not a serious, violent one, and certainly not the kind that could have led to such a terrible outcome. He spoke with horror and regret of what had happened, and offered to appear as a witness at any court trial, should he be needed.

Joseph von Intelmann had to admit that the soldier gave an impression of integrity and openness which spoke in his favor. Nevertheless, he did not consider Lothar Sentek innocent.

Somehow all of this came to the ears of Kudzus of the *Lucknow News*—probably he was informed by certain people for certain reasons—who brought it to public attention. At any rate, the paper broke the story that our town's most outstanding soldier was under suspicion of murder. The article reviewed all of Lothar Sentek's heroic deeds and contrasted this sterling career with the insignificant life of the woman from Little Grajevo, which he was supposed to have on his conscience. While nothing specific was said, imputations were made concerning Anna's

morality. The name of the person who had implicated Lothar
Sentek was not given, but before the day was out, all Lucknow
knew.

Conny was neither surprised nor upset to find himself surrounded by hatred on all sides; he could even summon up some
understanding for the general feeling. By now Conny completely
accepted his role as the most hated man in Lucknow. What kept
him going and gave him strength to bear hatred, loneliness, and
insomnia was his conviction that even in wartime justice had to
be done.

Yes, that's how it is, Martin—it's just a word, and yet so much
more than a word: a symbol, an invincible atoll . . . And that is
why Conny took the burden upon himself, and when Toni
Lettkow confronted him by Lake Tartar and without dismount-
ing from his horse said only, "I do not wish to see you on my
land," Conny accepted the ban and conscientiously avoided setting foot on any part of the estate holdings. But Grigo stuck by
him; the owner of the oldest printshop in Lucknow, whose son
was busy over Coventry, London, and Birmingham, whistled
through his teeth and shook his head when he heard what Conny
was up to, but backed him up. Grigo reportedly commented,
"Even in wartime there's got to be something besides just war."

And then an indictment was handed down, and while Rommel
captured Agedabia and advanced toward Bardia, the Lothar Sentek trial got underway in Lucknow. Spectators came from Allen-
stein, Elbing, and even from Königsberg, and everyone agreed
that what aroused this extraordinary interest was not so much the
expected outcome of the trial as the fact that such a trial could be
held at all.

When the trial began, the crowd was so great that the courtroom had to be closed. Edith and I did not manage to get in,
because people in uniform received preferential treatment. Most
of them were members of the Lucknow Corps of Engineers,
Lothar Sentek's old outfit. So we missed Conny's appearance,
the muttering that arose as he stepped to the witness stand, and
the manifestations of disapproval and anger that grew so noisy
that the judge threatened to clear the courtroom if the disorder
continued. Conny himself told us that he had been bracing him-

self for this, and worse; what unnerved him was the presence of a silent old couple, the defendant's parents, who sat there motionless in their Sunday best and stared at him without hostility, just incredulously.

Yes, dear boy, and then Conny gave his testimony, calmly and quietly, and the cross examination proved unable to shake his story. We heard later that he had prefaced it by saying that he was not out to prove anything, just to state what he had seen. This might have sounded like an apology if he had not added firmly that he recognized only one obligation, and that was the obligation to serve the truth.

The presentations by the prosecution and the defense took the form they had to take, the only form they could take in those days. Under the glassy stare of the man from Braunau with the stiff little mustache who claimed to be on intimate terms with Providence, both state's attorney and defense counsel went on at length about the requirements of the historic moment. They spoke of the "fateful struggle," of the "heroic battle," and of the "homeland's solemn vow." Conny commented later that they might as well have read aloud newspaper editorials. But he had to concede that beneath all the bombast and legal sophistry a real confrontation was taking place. Here two entirely different concepts of justice clashed head-on. It went over the heads of the spectators but was not lost on Conny. When the court withdrew to consider, Conny had no doubt about the verdict: acquittal.

But it was acquittal not on the basis of proven innocence but rather on the basis of insufficient evidence. This did not keep many of the spectators from greeting the verdict with tumultuous applause, and Sentek's comrades were moved to bear the hero out of the courthouse on their shoulders. At the bottom of the steps the picture was taken that appeared the next day in the *Lucknow News* with the caption *Victor Remains Victorious*.

We were waiting outside the courtroom doors for Conny. We took him between us and tried to protect him as we shoved our way toward the besieged entrance. Suddenly we found ourselves facing Joseph von Intelmann; to this day I do not know whether he overlooked Conny's outstretched hand on purpose. He lowered his eyes—that was his entire greeting. He seemed at once shaken and relieved. But his eyes had an inconsolable expression.

"Never again": that is what he is supposed to have murmured as Conny brushed past him. "I tell you: never again." We ourselves did not hear it.

After the trial we persuaded Conny to spend a few days at our house. He came with a battered suitcase held together with rope and a bottomless duffel bag. "You know, Zygmunt," he remarked, "you should have only as many possessions as you can carry yourself." We saw little of him during his stay. He took his meals with us in silence, then withdrew to his room to read or make notes or study the daily bulletins from the field, bent over a map of Europe. He analyzed and interpreted them in his own way . . .

No, Martin, not very much, although the *Lucknow News* began to carry the first reports of casualties. For, as I said, at the beginning the war went well, and the folks at home reaped the benefits: reindeer steaks from Norway, fancy soaps from Paris, currants and retsina from Greece, extract of roses from Bulgaria, and from neighboring Poland we still received, in spite of merciless import duties, mushrooms and geese, as we had from time immemorial. Although at first we escaped the direct effects of war, our fellow Germans to the west and northwest were not so fortunate; this we concluded from the fact that, before we realized it, Lucknow was flooded with strangers. All of a sudden one heard Cologne dialect and the refined accents of Hamburg and the even more refined ones of Bremen. Those who came were for the most part older or elderly folk, some of whom could afford to take rooms at the Hotel Queen Luise. The town's few pensions soon filled up, and the banks announced that they had no more safe-deposit boxes available for the storage of valuables. A peaceful army of occupation had arrived; they spent their time wandering through the lakeside park, crowding into the cafés at teatime, or monopolizing the public benches, where they sat reading letters.

Yes, I remember that shortly afterward the first trainloads of schoolchildren arrived, entire classes with their teachers. The faces of these city children looked pale from nights spent in air-raid shelters, their expressions knowing and cynical beyond their years.

We, too, had a long-term visitor, Rosita Riesmöller from

Bremen, whose father served as chief engineer on a submarine. There had been a brief exchange of letters before her arrival. Paulie and I went with the sled to fetch her at the station. The coat she had on was much too short for her. Her long legs in gray knitted tights resembled a foal's. With a self-assured air that took Paulie aback she said, "Well, here we are," and asked us to be careful about her suitcase: "There're some presents in it." She was taller than Paulie, and older. Even before we left the station she remarked in her prim little way, "So it's true: you have no ruins here," and when Paulie asked what she meant, she replied in a schoolmarmish tone, "Ruins are the result of the aerial attacks. Sometimes you see just one house in ruins, sometimes a whole street. We've only been bombed out once."

That was the first time I had heard the phrase.

At lunchtime Rosita distributed her presents with touching seriousness: sugar tongs for Edith, a napkin ring for my mother, for Paulie a nutcracker, and for me a cigar trimmer; Eugen Lavrenz, for whose presence she had not been prepared, received a bar of soap. She watched us, not only as we unwrapped our presents, but in whatever we did and said, as if she wanted to have certain expectations confirmed. The nature of these expectations we discovered one evening when she asked with disarming frankness whether all Masurians were really modest, superstitious, and sly; she had learned that in school, in a special geography unit designed to prepare her for the distant province and its inhabitants. Eugen Lavrenz promptly said yes, that was the way we were, and he solemnly enumerated other attributes of the Masurians: "You'll soon find out that we are tough, tough and canny, and probably heathen, too, but only in secret; humble, certainly; honest, especially in dealings among ourselves; reliable, especially when things are going well; given to brooding, et cetera; and besides, we bite the heads off live crows—isn't that true, Zygmunt?" I corroborated every word. It so amused us to hear how they viewed us in distant Bremen that we begged Rosita to tell us more. We clapped with delight when she offered to fetch her geography notebook and read aloud the official wisdom about Masuria. She trotted the information out as if reading a recipe: we were backward, often lived in one room with our domestic animals, especially chickens, piglets, and calves; we still used the wooden plow, and many of us still ate from wooden plates. That in the eighteenth century we had been the poorhouse of Germany was true, but she had also been told that we worshipped trees, especially linden trees and oaks, and that drunks were often found lying in the furrows of our potato fields, since we were hopelessly addicted to alcohol.

What else? Oh, yes, we had to submit to being characterized as steadfast—"As soldiers they are steadfast"—and the physical description called for our having round heads and stocky builds. As far as our clothing was concerned, in Bremen they thought we went around all muffled up in gray. At the same time, the muffling up did not prevent us from being "born dancers"; at every occasion old and young could be seen spinning around in our favorite dance, the mazurka. And finally we learned what our countryside was ideally suited for: paddleboat expeditions, which could be undertaken alone or in pairs, on our endless, untouched lakes, which, for greater convenience, were linked by rivers and canals.

We did not contest or correct any of these stereotypes; we accepted them all, not so much out of politeness as out of the desire to have her examine the assumptions for herself in the course of her stay with us.

Before long I found her alone in the museum, squatting on the floor to sketch our musical instruments, the devil's fiddle and the humming pot; she planned to draw the entire collection and send the pictures home. "What for?" I asked, and Rosita replied with winning candor, "So they'll envy me." Not long afterward she asked one morning at breakfast, "Could I please have a little drop of milk and another little roll?" She had adopted our habit of using the diminutive, or rather, it had taken possession of her, this diminutive which formed such a characteristic feature of our dialect . . .

Pardon me? Yes, precisely: Henrike uses it all the time, probably more often and more consciously than we ourselves used it . . . I hope Henrike is straightening out. I hope she realizes that I had no choice . . .

But enough of that, I don't want to get ahead of myself . . .

Yes, I know it's time for you to leave again; I can tell by how worn-out I feel . . . All right, Martin, that's good news that

I'll see you again tomorrow . . . I still haven't given up the idea of having you all here someday—you and Carola and Simon Gayko and even Marian Jeromin. Then the whole extended family can sit in judgment, or we can add up our losses together . . . All right, till tomorrow then . . .

# 12

COME in, come in, son; I've been dying to see someone so I
might tell him that this is the best day I've had since I got here. I
simply have to pass on the good news from my doctor: the skin
grafts have taken, Martin, they've made peace with their new
surroundings . . . You understand what I mean, don't you? And
now grab a chair and find yourself a peach; this whole fruit
basket was delivered anonymously, like those flowers a while
back. I must say, that's a real gift when the giver doesn't let you
even say thank you . . .

Pardon me? Really? You think it was Henrike? . . . That's
strange: yesterday after you had left, I fell asleep, napping as one
learns to nap in the hospital so one won't be disturbed by the
constant coming and going of the nurses. I woke up because
someone was standing by my bed and looking at me. I could feel
it through my sleep, but when I opened my eyes it was already
too late; I saw only an arm, and the door closing gently. And
this fruit basket stood on the bedside table . . .

So you're pretty sure you saw her at the bus stop; maybe she
even saw you and waited for you to leave before she dared to
come up. We'll see. Let's leave it uncertain for now. We don't
have to solve every mystery right off; I've long since grown
accustomed to living with uncertainties, to letting them linger on
as continuing but unsolvable tasks.

The uncertainties began to pile up as the war wore on and, so
far as we could tell from our Lucknow vantage point, was no
longer going so well. I still remember the mild shock when the
outcome of the war first came into doubt, a shock which all of us
in the house on the bend in the river felt, even though the battle

reports continued reassuring. The period of certainty ended when Albin Jakubzik, whom we at school had always called the beanpole because of his gangling height, came home on leave from the eastern front parading an unfamiliar red decoration, the so-called Frozen Meat decoration, the receipt of which he explained to anyone who would listen.

It sounded utterly incredible: the army was freezing. This army, so accustomed to victory, which had battled its way successfully to the outskirts of Moscow, was shivering and trembling, its teeth chattering. Not far from the hearths of Moscow, which would have made the winter bearable, this army found itself ambushed by a frost that transformed the conquered territory into a desert of ice across which men, horses, and vehicles skidded helplessly in temperatures as low as 60 degrees below zero. Lined gloves would have prevented chilblains, but they had no lined gloves. Lined boots or felt inserts would have averted freezing and amputations, but they had neither. The army was equipped for summer battles and summer victories, and no one had given any thought to fur caps or earmuffs, wristlets, lined coats, or woolen underwear . . .

Yes, Martin, as you say, the great Napoleonic army had also dreamed of summer victories until the cold struck and put an end to all its arrogance. We in Masuria had always paid proper respect to the merciless lash of winter and knew how to make preparations . . .

The thought of an army freezing to death shook our confidence; we knew too much about the power of this kind of winter. Our own experience helped us interpret the images Albin Jakubzik conjured up in his accounts: men hobbling along in the cutting wind; wounded soldiers frozen stiff on their stretchers; balking equipment to which the soldiers' skin stuck; horses' legs sticking up out of the snowdrifts along the route of the retreat. My mother was beside herself when she learned of the fate of the army; she wept soundlessly and snuffled, and suddenly in her sympathy she had an idea: "The one thing that will help is knitting; if someone gave an order that everybody back home had to knit till their needles shot sparks, sooner or later they'd be warm and cozy out there in their war."

Such an order would probably have come too late, but an

appeal for contributions went out to the people of Lucknow, an appeal to collect warm winter clothing for the stranded army. Posters to that effect appeared on trees and walls everywhere, the newspaper was full of it, and you should have seen how the people of Lucknow sprang into action.

The morning the collection point opened in the gym of my old school, people stood lined up in a double row, jabbering away and peering at what everyone else had brought. You would not have thought it possible that so much could be fetched out of trunks and closets, boxes and dim storage spaces: not only lined trousers, fur-lined boots and windproof coats, but also ancient fur caps, gaudy crocheted earmuffs, moleskin muffs, and pelts and skins from all of Masuria's fauna: foxtails sewn together, rabbit and otter pelts, warm dickeys from polecat skins, detachable coat linings from colts, body warmers of cat and badger fur, and finally double-knit face masks, mufflers, and wrist warmers. What had helped generations of Lucknowers get through the Masurian winter was now supposed to see the afflicted army through its Russian ordeal.

Among the volunteers who received the contributions, checked them over, and sorted them was Eugen Lavrenz. He wanted to "help out" between two trips; he spent a good deal of time on the road now, because too many stoves smoked and drew poorly, having been converted from coal and charcoal to peat as the situation demanded. Eugen Lavrenz had been installed as a sort of ultimate authority; he had the last word on which contributions could be accepted and which were simply not "fit for the front," even with the best will in the world.

You probably cannot imagine how offended people felt if their contributions were rejected. They became positively threatening if he turned away a pair of terribly worn goat-hair innersoles or a moth-eaten rabbit jacket. It was quite an experience. Another experience was the special appearance of the "lady in blue," the wife of Toni Lettkow, who, by the way, was stalled outside Leningrad with his regiment, destined to witness all four seasons there twice around. The lady from the estate came straight into the gym, disregarding the long line of people waiting their turn. She turned to Eugen Lavrenz to ask whether this was the collection point and ordered him to come outside to the sleigh, which stood there loaded down with furs and blankets and lined clothes. He had to carry in this fantastic contribution, at the sight of which the bystanders nudged each other and began to mutter, not because they wondered how anyone could part with such precious possessions, but because it seemed inconceivable that any one household could own so much—and presumably there was more where this came from. After the woman had indifferently accepted the voucher for her contributions, she ordered Eugen Lavrenz to help her out of her fur coat, and as he paused indecisively, she pointed to a heap onto which he was to throw the coat. "That's where it belongs, I should think," she said, and then she left. Who would have dreamed that this incident marked the beginning of Eugen Lavrenz's downfall, a downfall born of thoughtlessness and misplaced trust, a downfall he could neither interpret nor understand, since no one could persuade him that he was at fault.

The collection point remained open for seven days, and by the last day clothing had to be put in the equipment room. There was enough to outfit an entire combat-strength regiment against the most brutal winter. Then two trucks arrived and began to shuttle back and forth between the gym and the freight yard with the sorted and bundled clothing. A train had been brought in, its cars painted with the slogan THE HOMELAND THANKS THE FRONT. Car after car was loaded to the roof, and they continued loading by moonlight until not an inch remained in all the cars. The locomotive had already been coupled on when the Rhenish sergeant-major in charge realized that no room remained for the escort squad. He ordered part of the last car cleared of freight so that three men could get in. Not too many items had to be left behind; the sergeant-major caught them himself as they were tossed out, and in a burst of generosity threw them to the French prisoners of war who had been diverted from their work on the tracks to help load the cars. "There, good against the German winter," he said.

He had no trouble at all disposing of the remaining clothing; everyone in his vicinity got something as the items came flying and had to be caught. Eugen Lavrenz found himself in possession of a three-quarter-length jacket, gray leather warmly lined with badger fur. And then the escort squad checked to make sure they would have enough space, stowed away their weapons and other gear, and laid out candles and flashlights for the trip to the deserts of ice. The sergeant-major signaled the engineer with his flashlight, and the train pulled out.

Thus it began, and all would have been well if Eugen Lavrenz the very next day had not set out on another stove-fixing expedition to Nussberg or Schönhorst wearing his warm new acquisition. He headed across the causeway toward the estate, then followed the lakeshore, past the spot where nothing remained of the tiny house where he had once lived. By the monument to a drowned officer he climbed toward the woods and continued on along the well-traveled highway, which had been smoothed by the steel runners of many sleighs. Before long he heard the jingle of sleigh bells behind him, and Eugen Lavrenz stepped into the track, sure that the light sleigh, which carried only two passengers, would stop and give him a ride. But the sleigh came closer and closer without showing signs of slowing down, and Eugen Lavrenz had to leap to the side to avoid being run over.

He had recognized the faces, a grumpy driver and the "lady in blue," but in the moment of recognition he had to think of his own safety, so he failed to notice the look of sudden consternation that crossed the woman's face. He did not hear her brusquely order the driver to stop; he only saw the sleigh unexpectedly skid to a halt, and had to assume that they had decided after all to give him a lift. He was wrong. They waited for him to catch up with the sleigh, and as he prepared to scramble in, the woman stopped him with a cold stare. She reached out and touched the jacket and said, "From the collection point, right? You were at the collection point, weren't you?" to which Eugen Lavrenz replied innocently, "Yes, all seven days." This answer satisfied the woman. She looked up and stared out into the glittering, snow-covered countryside, and the driver set the sleigh in motion.

Things took their course, Martin; the skids had been laid, even though the person most affected had no idea what was pending. In any case, it seemed surprising but not disturbing when one evening two men in long, fur-lined leather coats turned up and wanted to speak with Eugen Lavrenz. Their manner had nothing urgent or dramatic about it; they acted as though they simply wanted him to corroborate something, and we willingly told them where he had been bound and when we expected him back. The men seemed pleased with the information, and we did not see them again. But neither did we see Eugen Lavrenz; he simply did not return from Nussberg or Schönhorst. After waiting what seemed a reasonable time, we went to the police and reported him missing. Since we heard nothing, we stopped by the police station from time to time, reminded them and badgered them, to which the police always replied with the same shrug. Finally, we ascertained his whereabouts: he was in the custody of the security police. More they could not tell us at the station, for this special police had its own powers and was not obliged to give out information or respect the usual regulations. The Lucknow police frankly admitted their own impotence . . .

I'm getting to it, son, just be patient. Conny suggested that we ask Albin Jakubzik to help us. He was still home, not yet recovered from the effects of serious frostbite. Albin Jakubzik put on his parade uniform, attached his brand-new decoration to his buttonhole, and betook himself to the inconspicuous office of the security police, where he, according to his own account, received only curt attention and was not even invited to sit, despite his cane. And presumably they would have sent him packing without any explanation had he not run into Masuch in the corridor, puny Masuch from our class, now head of this office, or at least deputy to the head. What Jakubzik found out, he owed not to his uniform, not to his injuries, and not to the Frozen Meat medal, but only to his former classmate, who greeted him warmly and steered him into the director's office, where he promptly offered him a chair, a monster of a chair that had obviously once served other masters in another setting. Masuch sent for real coffee and offered an assortment of European cigarettes, as well as a silver canister full of candies. He settled back and said, "So, what's been going on with you? . . ."

That was how we learned what had happened to Eugen Lavrenz. When Toni Lettkow's wife saw the man standing in the path of her sleigh, her first thought was that this was her own husband, wearing the three-quarter-length jacket she had given him for winter hunting. When she passed him and recognized the face, she instantly put two and two together and concluded that the man from the collection depot had appropriated the garment. Her indignation was such that she notified the police that very day. Eugen Lavrenz admitted immediately that the coat had come from the collection center, but he denied having picked it out for himself. He repeatedly explained how he had come by the coat; he either forgot to or deliberately did not mention that the French prisoners of war had likewise been provided with winter clothing. The number of the train, the day of its departure, and the exact time could all be determined, but Eugen Lavrenz's story could not be checked with the escort squad, for in the forest of Orsacha the train had passed over a mine and derailed. The engineer and the stoker died in the derailment, and the escort soldiers perished in a hail of partisan bullets.

Since nothing turned up in Eugen Lavrenz's defense, they classified him as a "saboteur" and transferred him to the Liekuk concentration camp, which no one came out of alive, as one of its commandants later testified. He could receive neither mail nor visits, and after trying in vain to get in touch with him, we had to accept the idea that Eugen Lavrenz was as good as dead.

Yes, that was how things went that winter when the cold humbled an arrogant army and revealed it to be utterly vulnerable and helpless. Misfortune sharpened our wits, and we no longer believed the official rhetoric about a glorious victory. We felt shaken and bitter at how badly we had been misled.

Marian Jeromin, our prodigy, was called up; in contrast to me, he knew exactly which unit suited him. The first photo he sent us showed him being trained as a medic, standing next to a stretcher. The next reached us from a military hospital on the Dwina: Marian between two wounded soldiers he had bandaged himself, and in the background the sluggish river.

We expected Conny to be called up any day, but it appeared that Grigo's printshop was considered "vital for the war effort." We gauged the effectiveness of the sample posters he managed to bring us from every new batch: appeals, slogans, warnings, threatening announcements in two languages for the occupied territories, colorful promises, regulations, and so on. He also brought passes of various sorts, licenses and authorizations for just about everything. Grigo's son had been shot down over London and wrote from a prisoner-of-war camp in Texas that

when a shortage of powdered chalk for marking the lines on a
football field had occurred, helpful private citizens had contributed confectioner's sugar to do the job. If Conny had not
been there, Grigo would have had to close the shop . . .

But what did I want to tell you? Oh, yes, after they drafted
Marian Jeromin, I had to persuade Sonja Turk that she could not
remain alone in her house. It was not easy for her to part with
everything that had constituted her life, not only the material
objects, but also the projects and dreams that had never been
carried out. I wheeled her through the rooms so she could decide
what should be packed and brought to our house. Sonja and I
looked over the indispensables, such as clothing, bedding, and
dishes. We stowed documents and correspondence in a trunk,
along with some of the things Sonja had inherited from Bianca,
and I thought it natural that Sonja wanted to take along a stuffed
owl. On top of the heap she had me place the book, the manual of
Masurian weaving lore. Then she nodded at the looms and said,
"Off we go, Zygmunt dear, to the last waiting room." . . .

Ah, you want to know whether we abandoned the looms. No,
Martin; but from that day on I worked alone in Sonja Turk's
house . . .

And so the great teacher moved in with us, to the delight of
the children, who could not get enough of the glass balls and
mirrors and tablets with colored symbols in Sonja's room. Sonja
willingly explained the wondrous powers of the objects to the
children, and told them stories, gave them puzzles to solve, assigned them things to draw, and generally kept them busy and
interested. When they got home from school, they could hardly
wait to seek her out in the first-floor room that we had put at her
disposal.

Edith did not oppose the move, but Sonja Turk had always
affected her with a sort of paralyzing timidity, a painful shyness,
so that Sonja's coming to live with us seemed to pose a task she
felt unequal to. It was around this time that Edith threw us into
confusion by announcing she had taken a job. She had already
received a special permit allowing her unrestricted access to the
railroad yards, and she showed us her armband. Edith had volunteered for the railway rescue mission. She never told me why she
had done it, and from the way she had gone about making all the

arrangements on her own, we realized that any attempt to dissuade her would be pointless.

She worked in the evening. At the beginning she still said goodbye before leaving the house. Later she just slipped out and made her way to the roomy wooden shed, which in winter was always overheated; besides a furnace there was a field kitchen providing warmth. On long oilcloth-covered tables loaves of bread were sliced, loops of sausages and blocks of margarine were cut into servings, tubs of jam were spooned into little cardboard containers, and gallons of malt coffee were brewed over the fire. All this was intended for the soldiers returning from the front on furlough or being shipped back to the front. In those days many trains passed through Lucknow, not only furlough trains but also hospital trains, prisoner transports, and trains carrying reinforcements to the front. And, as Edith discovered, in the middle of the night sealed freight trains stopped on unlit sidings and voices called for help in all the languages of Europe.

I sometimes watched Edith from a distance as she ran beside the trains pulling in. She carried an enameled container of steaming coffee, and soldiers were crowded at the open windows of the train, waving, beckoning, holding out their tin cups and mess kits. Other women hurried from window to window with baskets full of bread and packets of sausage and margarine. I marveled at the calm, businesslike air with which Edith attended to her work; she did not react to the jokes or flirtatious remarks and steered clear of all conversation. She matter-of-factly accepted letters to mail at the nearest mailbox, and she waved back mechanically as the soldiers waved to her from the departing train.

She usually got home around midnight. In the beginning she felt the urge to sit by my bed and tell me about the evening's encounters and experiences. For at the station she heard what could be found in none of the newspapers: firsthand accounts of the war. The witnesses, the participants, the victims spoke to her, suppressing nothing, revealing their feelings and their moods, apparently emboldened by the setting, which reduced the risk of telling the truth and encouraged confidences. Edith made no particular attempt to collect information; she heard unintentionally about successful retreats and the casual abandoning of entire armies; she heard about the burning cities in the West, about the creation of a battalion of deaf soldiers, about the shortages on the home front. In most of the faces that appeared in the windows above her she recognized fear and exhaustion.

She also told me she had not been able to withstand the timid voices calling to her from the sealed boxcars. When the transports were not accompanied by guards who patrolled the cars during the station stop, she had taken the leftover ration packets and pushed bread, sausage, and margarine through the cracks in the cars. "Sometimes you get the impression that all the sorrow in the world passes through the Lucknow station," she said. She carefully kept the items which the prisoners shoved back through the cracks as a way of showing gratitude: a page from a Hungarian calendar, a flat piece of Russian carving, a saint's picture with an Italian inscription, often just a scrap of paper with a scribbled address: Amsterdam, Namur. I suspected she kept them so that one day they would testify to the reality of a part of her life which often seemed like a dream.

But then one day she stopped talking about her experiences. She came in without a word, undressed in the dark, without trying to see whether I was still awake. When I asked her about work, she played down the night's incidents as if they had been nothing special, just the usual.

She became filled with anxiety, at first only in fits, but so noticeably that even Sonja Turk asked me about it. Had something happened to Edith or was she expecting? I would never have dreamed that I myself might be the source of her anxiety, at least the original anxiety; she was tormented by the thought that I might send her away. She even assured me that I had a perfect right to send her away, since she was not the person I took her for.

You should have heard her self-recriminations. She dredged up insignificant mistakes she had made and built them up into capital crimes. She went so far as to describe herself as unworthy, unworthy of living with us. She would sit for hours, brooding and depressed, and nothing I said could help her.

Suddenly, as if this anxiety had run its course, she startled us with another fear. Quite by chance I discovered that when she returned from work she regularly stopped off in the pantry before coming up to bed. I searched the pantry and found a cubbyhole where she had accumulated an extraordinary store of supplies, leftovers she had brought home from work. She had given no thought to whether the foods were perishable or not. Heaped up at random were bread, sausages, tubs of marmalade, bags of tropical fruit, choco-cola, bags of noodles, and split peas. I stopped her one evening after she had stowed away a large hunk of cheese, and spoke soothingly to her, until she admitted that she was afraid of starving, or rather, afraid that we would let her starve. So she had better lay in supplies. Yet at the same time she often sat at the table exhausted and preoccupied, unable to eat any of what was placed before her. She probably agreed to my clearing out the cache only because she was too worn-out to object.

There was nothing we could do but accept these changes in Edith, and that meant also being prepared for the unexpected. For a time she struck us as less frightened and depressed, especially after she started taking aromatic baths, with herbs prescribed by Sonja Turk. But by and by a new fear seized her, leading her to actions that in turn introduced a previously unknown element of suspicion into the house.

The children were the first to notice items missing from our collection. They led me from display to display, and stood silently by to see whether I would discover what they had already discovered. When I did not name the missing items fast enough, they pointed sternly at the little cards, or traced the object in the air with their hands. The losses grew more painful each time they led me through the rooms. I tried to recall the most recent visitors to the museum, especially those who had come more than once. Brooding over the evidence, I found myself thoroughly perplexed when I realized how many grounds for suspicion one could find without even trying. You must know the experience: goaded by suspicion, undermined by mistrust, one ends up suspecting almost everyone, and in fact, my suspicions attached themselves to all the visitors . . .

The police? Certainly, we intended to report it to the police, but that was to be a last resort, in case our plan of extreme watchfulness should fail . . .

Yes, Martin, there followed agonizing waiting and watching. Often I had to apologize to the museum visitors and invent some white lie to explain why I was dogging them. Often, when my behavior seemed too strange, I worried that visitors would be frightened away. No matter how I tried, I could find no sign of the thief, and I had almost given up when, on a warm night shortly after a thunderstorm, I happened to look out the window into the garden. I saw a figure down by the river, digging in the bank among the willows, digging hastily, then bending down for a moment before beginning to shovel back the earth, which was wet and made a slapping noise.

It was Edith. I lay down and pretended to be asleep when she came in. The next day, after she had left for work—she no longer went regularly and often found the oddest excuses for staying home—I slipped down to the willows by the river and carefully examined the riverbank. There were a number of barely discernible humps which had been flattened down, some of them even masked with pieces of sod. Even before I dug out these humble little graves, I knew I had found the cemetery Edith had established for the vanished relics, those same objects Uncle Adam had once painstakingly dug out of the earth or out of oblivion, in order that they might be witness to the life of bygone times. Now they had almost been lost a second time, and with them their message for the living.

I dug the things out, took them to the workshop, and spent several days cleaning them. I lined them up on the floor and called Edith to come and see. She displayed no guilt, no remorse, no agitation; all she would say was that we should bury the things we valued while we still had time and that the safest hiding place was still in the ground. With that she left me there. The next morning she did not get up. She softly explained that she could not dress herself or face any of the demands of the day. She wanted only to be quiet, not to move. Yet it turned out that even under these conditions, anxiety gripped her, a "fear from the depths of the heart," as she put it. This fear expressed itself in a special way: through plucking. We knew at once how things stood with Edith when she began to pluck at the bedspread, at her fingers, at her hair. It was a mechanical, sometimes rhythmic movement originating inside her. Even when I stopped her by holding her hands between my own, I could feel a slight jerking that continued in her body.

It was about this time that I began to notice the poster. It appeared on the breastwork of the bridge, at about knee level, on the bridge pilings at eye level, on the wall of the railroad station, on the church, on the whitewashed walls of the prison, even on trees in Borek Forest: simply a black poster with a white question mark in the middle. It was the sort of thing you looked right past and then turned around to stare at, puzzled, as though you would not have thought a simple question mark could exert such fascination. When I scrambled down the bank to look at one of the posters on the bridge piling from close up, I grew nervous, as if simply by looking at it I were taking part in a conspiracy. And I cautiously looked around to see if anyone was watching me.

At first the town authorities did not attempt to discover the person or persons responsible for the posters; they concentrated their efforts on removing them as soon as they appeared . . .

Conny's reaction to the posters? All he said was that he found the curved part of the question mark too well nourished; it should have been leaner, more sickle-shaped. That was all we could get out of him . . .

No, no, dear boy, go ahead and ask. Work, you said? You wonder whether work was even possible during that time . . .

No, Martin, I don't consider that an irrelevant question, not at all. To understand a person in any significant way, I want to know what work he does, or at least what relationship he has to work. Overspiritualized types don't interest me much . . .

Now listen and be amazed: about the time our hoarded supplies of wool and dyes began to run out, after Minsk had fallen and Rokossovski's divisions had already reached Warsaw, we received probably the largest, most lucrative commission ever given to a Masurian rug weaver, a commission practically Oriental in scope, when one considers the assurances, privileges, compensation, and special authorizations that went along with it. Sonja Turk, who urged me for a number of reasons to accept the commission, apparently foresaw its fate from the very beginning, for she always called our last weaving job the "unfinished monster," and monster, as you know, suggests not only size but also something fearsome.

But here's how it came about. Conny continued to analyze the military communiqués, bending over his map of Europe. He had just extended the broad arrows coming from the east as far as the Vistula and Memel Rivers and had used blue hatching to mark the two basins around Vitebsk and Bobruisk—our last letter from Marian Jeromin had come from Vitebsk—when we received an unexpected visit. An open jeep pulled up in front of the house, and out jumped a young officer, of very high rank for his age. He wore the aiguillettes of an adjutant and the silver medal of those wounded in action. He greeted me in a friendly manner and asked if this was the residence of Sonja Turk. I led him into the house and took him to the old master weaver, who was just attempting to spoon up her gruel, assisted by Paulie. The officer introduced himself—we gathered that he belonged to some highly placed staff or even to supreme headquarters—and waited until Sonja Turk had offered him a seat. He took no offense at her asking me to stay in the room.

He had come not on his own behalf but on that of his staff. Before explaining his business, he wanted to make certain that he had indeed found the noted weaving master Turk. Then he described what was wanted: a rug, a large hunting rug meant to cover an entire wall in a rustic castle that served as a hunting lodge. He would give us the exact measurements later.

The hanging was to be a gift from the staff to its commander in chief, who also bore the title of Reichsjägermeister, Reich master of the hunt, and would soon be celebrating an anniversary, the anniversary of his accession, so to speak.

His reason for seeking out Sonja Turk was simple enough: during the most recent organized hunt on the Rominten Heath the Reichsjägermeister had been remarkably taken with a little wall hanging he saw in the house of a high-ranking forester. It came from the Lucknow weaving studio. Artistically we would have complete freedom, so long as we portrayed, or "worked in," every type of wild animal that could be hunted; the design should evoke "the joy of the hunt," or at least joyful memory of the hunt.

Sonja Turk let him have his say, then silently held out her hands to the young officer, those hands with their knotted joints, swollen by calcium deposits. "They've served their time," she said, "they can hardly hold so much as a spoon anymore. You

can't expect anything more from these hands, not even a rag
rug." The officer looked disbelievingly at her hands, which were
bent and distorted, with the skin in some spots of a curious shiny
smoothness, but clearly what troubled him was not so much the
condition of her hands as having to give up the plan that had been
so carefully and hopefully hatched in his staff. "Does that mean,"
he asked, "that you cannot accept the commission under any
conditions?"

"No," Sonja Turk said—and now I had my turn at being surprised—"we accept the commission, yes. We will work out the
design together; the execution will be up to Master Rogalla."

I found myself remembering an earlier commission that had
gone bad, remembering the manner in which they had thrown
our work back in our faces, and I said, "Can't be done, we've
exhausted our supply of materials." The officer assured me at
once: "We will provide you with all the materials you need and
more." Turning to Sonja Turk, I went on with my arguments for
saying no: "Even if I wanted to, I could not do it without our
helper; a piece of this size can't be done single-handed." "We'll
see to it that you have him," the officer said. "But our helper,
Marian Jeromin, is in Russia," I told him, "presumably in the
Vitebsk Basin." "In that case all I need is his military address,
name, and rank. We'll place the fastest available transportation at
his disposal."

We went back and forth, and he swept all my objections aside,
in the process giving us a glimpse of how far his powers extended. All he needed was my acquiescence, which I finally gave,
with a shrug, since Sonja Turk had ignored all my unspoken
appeals for help and had long since made up her mind. The
officer thanked us, took a few notes, and promised we would
soon have written confirmation and another visit from him. Before departing he swore us to utmost secrecy. As he clambered
into the jeep, stretched, and slapped his thighs, he looked like a
man who had reason to be pleased with himself.

"This is an impossible commission for us," I told Sonja Turk
after he had roared off, and she replied, with a resignation I had
never seen in her before, "You know, in these times people have
no choice. Where you're offered protection, you've got to take

it. And this commission brings us protection. I've an awful feeling we're going to need it. And as far as the hunting rug goes, as I see it, it'll be our unfinished monster."

A few days later an orderly arrived with the written confirmation and a batch of authorizations and papers stating that the holder was engaged in a special project for the Reichsjägermeister. An advance, which to my astonishment my teacher had requested, arrived promptly to replenish our depleted bank account. And then who should turn up, still green in the face from a bumpy flight in a transport plane, but Marian Jeromin, ordered to report for special duty, as his marching orders put it. He had no idea what it all meant until we told him about the project.

The three of us made our calculations, decided on the stages of the job, and set up a provisional schedule. Sonja Turk by no means confined herself to listening; she took part in all the discussions, responding vigorously to our suggestions and offering advice.

Then, armed with our papers and authorizations, Marian and I took our handcart and trundled over to the depot, where we again received evidence of the power of those who had commissioned us. The sentry, accustomed to open the barrier for entire columns of trucks, smiled condescendingly when he saw us approaching with our cart, but once he had pored over our documents, he turned businesslike, almost obsequious, and telephoned to the central office, which sent down a soldier in overalls to look after us.

What a labyrinth of fabulous goods! It was an underground treasure house, full of everything from weapons and foodstuffs to medical equipment and fabric. A system of railway tracks led like rays into dimly lit tunnels; trains and trucks were constantly pulling up to the loading ramps or heading off for distant storage areas. The staff corporal in charge of filling our order checked the inventory list, with its more than eight hundred items, and found without difficulty raw wool, linen, all kinds of thread in every gauge, and the whole spectrum of dyes. We ourselves waited in the main office, where we listened to the orders coming in, astounded at the range of wishes that could be fulfilled from the seemingly endless stores of the depot. Our number was called and we went to the loading dock to receive our order; as we fastened down our load, Marian Jeromin looked up at me and said, "This is really happening, isn't it? Or is it all a dream?"

Yes, not too long afterward these catacombs of plenty blew sky-high because seventeen thousand or seventy thousand bazookas exploded, setting off a chain reaction of explosions. The earth shook, a column of ash and dirt and shredded brush rose into the air, and in Lucknow all the windows shattered.

But for the time being the catacombs remained at our disposal. We carted the materials to the workshop, and as the Middle Army successfully withdrew to the Narev, we went to work on the sketches for the great hunt rug. Marian and I did not know or even suspect that this would be our last work woven on a Lucknow loom, though Sonja Turk probably realized it, for, as I said, she always referred to the project as our "unfinished monster." Her first question was, "What story do we want our unfinished monster to tell? What meaning should we give it, seeing as how we have to get all the animals in? As if one could ever capture the whole of anything."

Finally, after much trial and error, we decided to accept her idea: hunters looking over hunting weapons and seeing in their mind's eye the noble game. You get the point: in using scenes from the history of the hunt we had a pretext for including all the different sorts of game animals and showing the ritual death appropriate to each. We started stringing the loom about the time the Third White Russian Front took Kaunas and advanced on Mariampol. The officer, who visited us twice at short intervals, wanted to be sure that the weaving was underway and making progress. When we showed him the few inches we had finished, he turned speechless at the prospect that all his efforts might be for nought. "You're not going to stand us up?" he asked nervously. We assured him we had never missed a deadline. To encourage us to keep at it, he brought us cans of cocoa, real coffee, and beef. This turned out to be his last visit. We lost no sleep over his subsequent absence. In light of his high rank and the unfortunate turn the war had taken, we found it easy to imagine that he was needed elsewhere for the moment. We continued working, and whenever we needed materials, we set out with our handcart for the underground depot. In time we managed to build up an excellent supply of our own. We took our last load home just days before the great explosion . . .

I don't know, Martin, but it was rumored that the Lucknow depot was blown up by men who had parachuted over the Borek and the State Forest, jumping out of the planes that slowly circled over the town every night and were popularly referred to as "sewing machines" . . .

And then one day nothing counted, not even our special papers. A general call-up forced us to break off work on the rug. We had to find shovels, picks, and spades and report to the old Lucknow cattle market, southeast of the town. Everyone capable of shouldering a tool had to appear there, regardless of his position or profession, and the men of Lucknow closed their shops and offices, left their workplaces, put on their oldest clothes, and streamed out to the market. There names were called out from lists, and we were assigned to so-called platoons. Each platoon received a leader and his deputy, and we had to line up in a square formation. Ludwig Krimkowski, director of the Lucknow Firemen's Academy, stepped forward, flanked by several sergeants from the Corps of Engineers and a number of men in brown party uniforms. The high and mighty Reschat also appeared, the Statthalter of Lucknow, sporting his golden oak leaves. Apparently Krimkowski was to acquaint us with our assignment. The "Firefighter General," as we called him, stood there in the uniform he had designed himself—with two crossed hose nozzles as collar insignia!—and spoke of a temporary threat to Lucknow posed by an enemy that had only numerical superiority. The local leadership was determined to prevent this enemy from seizing so much as an inch of the beloved homeland.

He charged us to join the men from neighboring townships in building a trench which would halt the flood from the east and break its force. He trotted out some slogans about our strength in time of need, cited a historical example, and held out a vision: this unique trench would be the trap and final grave into which men and equipment would disappear head over heels, but especially the rumbling herds of T-34's, which he could already picture tipping and hurtling down, helpless as turtles on their backs.

Accompanied by some Engineering Corpsmen and the brown

uniforms, we tramped out to the section allotted us. We passed the spot by Maraune Brook where my father had gone up in a blaze of glory, and marched along in sight of the Rankow orchards. Parallel to the railway embankment, behind which thirty years earlier Samsonov's grim mortars had taken cover, the Engineers marked off the line of the trench. From there it cut across a sandy field and followed the edge of the orchard, some of whose trees would have to go, then climbed the hill to the wooded crest and continued toward the horizon, where men from neighboring villages were already working their way toward us with picks and shovels.

We drove our spades into the earth, this earth saturated and leavened with the sufferings of our people. We had to proceed carefully, since the walls of the trench were to slope at such an angle that the tanks would fall in of their own weight and be caught in the pit that grew narrower toward the bottom and made it impossible for them to climb the opposite wall or back out. Some of us wondered what the observers in the foreign planes flying high overhead must think of our combined efforts and this simple, interminable construction project, which grew from day to day and cut across the countryside like a dried-up canal. Still, we did not doubt that when they analyzed the aerial photographs, they would at least be impressed by the speed with which we were laying the protecting trench around Lucknow.

Yes, Martin, and there near the wooded hills, when we had almost reached the desired depth for the trench, Conny's pick struck an urn cover; it pierced it, producing a ringing sound, which made everyone nearby look up. And I was still scraping away the dirt and trying to rub the urn clean when we heard an exclamation of surprise and the same ringing sound. They came running over to show me another urn, a bronze urn which had not been damaged at all. My appeal for carefulness bore fruit; one man found a hair clasp, another a finger-length knife blade, another several ointment pots—altogether, it was an interesting cache of grave goods that we laid out on my handkerchief.

Conny grinned and murmured to me, "See, we have one winner already—ye olde museum." But it was he who took the greatest pains to rescue the remains on which we had stumbled. And during our breaks he impressed upon the others that they should dig cautiously and keep a sharp lookout for anything that seemed significant.

The men kept calling me over or bringing objects to me: rusty iron parts of agricultural implements, petrified wood that aroused their imagination, pieces of brick, shards, bones, bottle stoppers, and who knows what else, and I had to identify them, establish their value, and estimate their age. The men felt terribly disappointed when I tossed their finds away, so eager were they to be involved in something more meaningful to them than this ditch digging. If Uncle Adam could have seen this army of men coaxing treasures out of the Masurian soil, it would have been the happiest day of his life.

In the evening, when our procession toiled home, Conny carried my pick, while I carried the tarpaulin containing our day's booty. I took it straight to the workshop, where Paulie was already waiting impatiently. Together we cleaned and sorted the objects, relics from the Neolithic Age and the Bronze Age for the most part, certainly the most important finds that had ever been made in the Lucknow area. We had no time to display them properly, so we just labeled them and took them up to the attic. I thought of setting up a special room for the objects that had been found during the digging of the tank trap.

Each time we linked two separate sections of the trench we passed around a bottle, while the Engineers praised us and our trench and told us how our project would prove fatal to the enemy tanks advancing from the east and southeast.

But we were shocked one day when, just after we had drunk to the joining of another two sections, the rumbling of bursting grenades became audible. The sound was far away, but so loud that we felt as if an irresistible ball of fire were hurtling toward us. And the rumbling came from the north.

"That's to the north," Conny said tensely. "They've broken through in the north," and this observation bore not only on the danger itself but also on the value of our entire defensive enterprise. Reschat overheard Conny; Golden Oakleaf had turned up to congratulate our team and pass out cigarettes, since he, and not the military authorities, had responsibility for the construction of the trench. "A temporary breakthrough," he said, in a confident tone meant to forestall further questions. "It will be halted. Fresh units are on their way. Besides, tomorrow the Volkssturm will will be mobilized all over the country. The last great offensive by our entire population will usher in the turning point."

Such was his rhetoric, while we stood there unnerved, staring toward the north, where a great force shook the earth. Don't imagine for a moment that we stopped our work or that Reschat thought better of the whole project. He ordered us to dig on, even after a formation of low-flying Russian bombers roared over us, coming from the north. They raked our construction project with fire. We carried off the wounded and returned to our digging.

We could tell something was amiss from the change in traffic patterns on the railway embankment. There were hardly any trains going east now, while a steady stream headed west: first a few camouflage-painted special trains with their own antiaircraft guns and a forest of antennas over the communications center, then hospital trains marked with the Red Cross, and finally flatbed cars full of equipment shrouded in tarpaulins and cattle cars pulled by the locomotives that usually pulled expresses.

Reschat's men paced up and down the trench, spurring us on when we paused too long to gaze after the trains. "Come on, fellows," they urged us, "this trench must be finished." At the beginning they had tolerated the delays when the men brought me their archaeological finds, but now they reacted irritably.

Ah, yes, I still remember how we felled a row of apple trees laden with fruit, without taking the trouble to pick the apples first. We hacked off the roots and dragged out the stumps with a fierce cracking sound that reminded me of a whip. I was expecting nothing in particular when from the corner of my eye I saw Dr. Duddek, the local physician, bend down and pick up something, which he blew on and then polished with his sleeve. When he raised his head, I could tell he was looking for me.

From quite a distance he stretched his hand toward me, triumphantly, as if he had a major announcement to make. He trudged over and held out his palm, on which lay a compact object still caked with earth. He let me hold it, and I was astonished at the weight. "Iron slag," he said, as though an old hunch of his was hereby confirmed. "If I'm not terribly mistaken, they were smelting iron ore in Lucknow a thousand years ago." He took the piece back. He wanted to examine it under his microscope and have it analyzed, after which he would give it to our museum . . .

Pardon me? You wonder what such a discovery is worth? Whom such a discovery benefits?

Of course, one may ask such questions, Martin, and perhaps one must . . .

In any case, we were still standing together discussing the find when first one of Reschat's men and then Golden Oakleaf himself urged us rather roughly to go back to work. When we did not immediately pick up our tools again, Reschat demanded an explanation of why we were standing around idle, whereupon Dr. Duddek held out the lump of iron slag and said in a condescending tone, "Here. This is something for the historical-minded. Slag from ore smelting a thousand years ago, local slag."

Reschat took the lump. He obviously saw this as a challenge, both to his authority and to his intellect. Dr. Duddek followed up his advantage by remarking, "Those who have eyes to see can draw conclusions even from a lump of slag." Golden Oakleaf quivered with rage and hurled the slag down the bank into the Maraune. "We can't afford these little refinements just now," he said bitingly. "Get back to work." He would simply have stalked off if the old doctor had not hurled a word after him.

Reschat turned and walked back slowly. He demanded to have the word repeated, and Dr. Duddek said, between clenched teeth, " 'Barbarian' is what I said, and I'll say it again: barbarian!" The next morning, when they distributed the armbands to us, when they turned us into the Volkssturm by means of armbands and captured carbines, Dr. Duddek was not of our party.

Yes, Martin, the discoverer of the first ore smelting in the forests of Lucknow did not appear. He was not able to make anything of his extraordinary find, nor was he forced to join in the final effort that got underway when all was already lost and the end inevitable.

So once more the ordinary folk had to lay their necks on the block; after all they had endured and sacrificed, they were supposed to throw themselves into the breach and turn things around.

You should have seen the Lucknow Volkssturm marching out

to Castle Hill under the command of two wounded officers. Well, marching is hardly the word; I should say straggling. On the site of that old stronghold, above the terraces Uncle Adam had once carved out, we practiced assault tactics and learned how to clean and repair our weapons. While we tried to obey all the orders and instructions, I stared at the headgear, fascinated by the conductors' and mailmen's caps, the dark-green woolen caps of the woodsmen, the broad-visored chapkas, and the felt hats that characterized our civil servants. It was anything but a military sight.

Conny and I stuck together as we took cover behind tree trunks or the stone wall we had built long ago. "You remember?" —"I remember"—that was all that had to be said.

A continuous rumbling came from the north, the sound of mortar shells exploding and aerial bombardment. We had to take turns storming and defending Castle Hill or swarming up to the highway, where we jumped into already-dug foxholes and peered out at the trucks, tracked vehicles, and horse-drawn wagons rolling westward. Entire military staffs and civilian offices were on the move. The wagons plodding along amid the military vehicles were heaped high with expensive furniture, trunks, sacks, and suitcases. "It's time for us to start making our own plans," Conny whispered as we lay there in the brown grass.

That same evening, after we had taken off the armbands and turned in the carbines, we came to a decision. But it turned out that it was already too late, too late because someone else had reached a decision before us: Masuch.

We had just come out of our camouflaged positions and reported at the bottom of Castle Hill for coffee. Our former classmate was standing there between the two officers, chatting casually and smoking; from his bearing you could never have guessed what had brought him out here. Conny and I were chilled and eager for something hot, so we lined up and worked our way toward the field kitchen, which meant closer to him, who showed no interest in the men or in getting a hot drink. Then one step put him so close to Conny that their sleeves brushed, and still he gave no sign that he was there in his official capacity.

He did not say hello to Conny or even look him in the eye. He only murmured, under his breath, "You're coming along with me, but drink your coffee first." No one heard what he said but the two of us, and after we had finished our coffee, Conny winked at me, nodded jauntily, and said, "Well, defend our Castle Hill; I'll be back tomorrow to help you." With that he strolled away, accompanied by our former classmate, who was still puny. How could we have known that we would not see each other again for six years? Yes, six whole years . . .

Yes, Martin, you've guessed it. They had discovered that the posters with the question marks came from Grigo's printshop, and that Conny had designed them, printed them, and posted them all by himself. At first they had simply ignored those meaningless white symbols on a black background, but the longer they were around, the more irritating they became, especially when hand-drawn exclamation points appeared on the posters. The mysterious sign began to seem subversive, an incitement to doubt. That at least was what they told Conny at the office of the security police.

Conny explained that he intended his question marks to make people ask, "Have you done enough? Do you realize what's at stake?" That was absolutely all he had in mind. The security people weren't buying that. They showed him statements by citizens of Lucknow, all of whom read the poster as an attempt to spread uncertainty and undermine morale. Then Masuch himself wanted some words with Conny. He seemed to take an interest not only in this case but in a few other shady matters in Conny's record; apparently they knew more about Conny than we, his closest friends and relatives.

Although Masuch offered his former classmate the most comfortable visitor's chair and had tea, pastry, and Egyptian cigarettes brought in, Conny proved unable to help him when it came to tracing hidden connections. In particular, Conny had nothing to say when Masuch raised the question of the so-called Weinknecht Group, which had just been rounded up in nearby Goldap. By the time they had done talking, Masuch had decided that Conny should spend the night at the office, in a room without windows. The following morning he came in with a pleasant "Good morning" and an arrest warrant.

And now you must imagine—as I have so often imagined—the two of them marching down the street to the station, shoulder to shoulder, moving their feet in unison. Picture them passing the control barrier on the strength of Masuch's badge, and going up the steps to the railroad platform, stopping simultaneously, moving ahead simultaneously, and always trying to be as inconspicuous as possible. But had anyone been looking, he would have seen, just for a moment, the handcuffs that linked their wrists together.

Conny told me later that from the train they had seen camouflaged clusters of tanks and artillery that had taken cover in the autumnal forests, and on a military airstrip they counted a dozen planes, under camouflage nets, that remained on the ground in spite of other planes that came swooping over the horizon at low altitude. On both sides of the sandy roads soldiers with heavy packs streamed northward, past antiaircraft stations and antitank cannon which had been set up on harvested fields. Several times the train had to halt because columns of trucks and wagons were crossing the tracks. Around dusk they reached Goldap.

Once there, they had no need to practice any special concealment, because as they got out on the platform the first salvos began, with mortar shelling and flashes of fire and rumbling from the artillery on the other side of the lake. To everyone's surprise, the Russians were attacking Goldap. Before sending in their tanks, they pounded the town, and the howling of shells and the whistle of grenades filled the air. The defenders of the town were caught as much unawares as the civilian population. No one had expected it to happen this way.

Conny left it to Masuch to choose their route and establish their pace. He trotted along beside him, with no wish but to get away from the dangerous area around the station. The streets were jammed with people and vehicles with their headlights off, all in flight from the town. No one paid any attention to cries for help or shouted orders. The first houses were beginning to burn. Conny and Masuch slipped into a side street. To avoid an oncoming wagon, they scrambled over a garden fence. They were about to cross the sloping lawn when they were simply pushed off course by a bomb blast. Conny later described how the vibrations picked them up and hurled them against a tumbledown wooden gazebo. After they had both come to, they crouched for a while by the wall, groping for their caps and the briefcase. "The key—get out the key," Masuch said. Conny squeezed his hand into his captor's right side pocket, but found no key. It was not in the left pocket, either. Simultaneously the two went down on all fours and crawled over the sloping lawn, feeling for the key as they went. They retraced their path and circled the gazebo, but without success.

There was nothing to do but struggle through to headquarters. Masuch voiced this idea to Conny and waited for Conny to offer a countersuggestion. But Conny was in no mood to take the initiative.

The firing was letting up, and the streets had emptied, people having sought shelter in the cellars or made it through to the artery leading west. Burning houses illuminated what seemed like a deserted town. And then, Conny said, they heard another sound, a mighty rustling which drowned out the rattling of automatic weapons and the burst of grenades. Two soldiers hastening by on a single bicycle shouted, "Get off the street, clear out. The tanks are coming!"

Masuch pulled Conny to one side, and for the first time the handcuff bit into his wrist. They pushed open a swinging door and hurtled into the lobby of a bank. They groped their way along dark corridors and finally descended a metal staircase to the boiler room, where they hid. They huddled there in silence. Masuch shared his remaining cigarettes with his prisoner, and they slept, sitting side by side.

But then the dry barking of the tank guns came closer, and in the building above them they heard shouts and whistles . . .

Yes, Martin, Goldap was retaken, but they did not realize that until they heard the voices of their own soldiers in the lobby and corridors above them. They left their hiding place, and went through the smoldering streets, where no one paid them the slightest attention. Civilians were busy carrying their belongings into the street, where they bundled them up and prepared to set out on the trek.

The headquarters, a large private villa, turned out to be undamaged but abandoned, except for the janitor. He asked to see Masuch's identification before admitting them. He not only undid the handcuffs with a special key; he also, on Masuch's request, furnished a new pair of standard handcuffs, which he placed beside the tray on which he brought freshly made coffee.

They drank their coffee in a leisurely manner and smoked; then Masuch with an expression of regret asked for Conny's wrists and snapped the cuffs shut. Since he himself had to draw up the necessary report, he then turned Conny over to the janitor, who locked him up in one of the many rooms. There Conny stayed until the little town was again taken by the Russians, this time for good. When the door was kicked open, Conny stepped out of his corner and held up his bound hands to the soldiers storming in . . .

What's that you say? Safety? Safety in the lion's den? I don't know whether experience bears that out, Martin; I have my doubts. After all, Conny told me that the people of the so-called Weinknecht Group, whom he was supposed to confront, also wore handcuffs when their bodies with blood-encrusted holes in their necks were found in a cellar.

In any case, the rest of us back in Lucknow had to do without Conny. We were still drilling on Castle Hill. We sat on the overgrown terraces and spooned up thick soup from the field kitchen. We watched Russian planes fly overhead and were badgered and bullied by a bevy of Reschats into believing in our own superiority and facing the impending "decisive struggle" with confidence.

They exploited the idea of the homeland to the utmost. They talked about homeland divisions which would show exemplary determination. Love of homeland was to generate defensive valor. Soil of the homeland, pride of homeland, the sounds of the homeland—all these slogans were to inspire us, uplift us, fire us to action. The Reschats, and not only those in Lucknow, kept exhorting us to stay, and did everything to see that we did. Meanwhile, their own vehicles were tanked up for the flight, their special train compartments reserved, their speedboats and icebreakers had built up steam to carry them across the Baltic. From the way we were dug in around Lucknow, one might have thought the town had been declared a stronghold. Although the First White Russian Front in the west threatened to cut off all of Masuria, still there were no mass departures from the city.

The snow came early that winter. Our reliable swamps, which had once been called our greatest protection, froze solid, and the lakes, too, froze over. We received permission to cut wood in the Borek. Flocks of crows, larger and more raucous than ever before, passed overhead. The ice fishermen spoke of extraordinary catches. In Little Grajevo a quiet wedding took place: Heini Hauser married Irina Gutkelch. I was invited, but had to leave my plate untouched when the siren went off, summoning me to an air-raid drill on Castle Hill.

On those evenings when the northeaster battered the house, that same northeaster that carried distant sounds of fighting to us, on those evenings when work seemed impossible, I slipped into the museum, where I began to sort and select. Here and there I packed certain items into boxes and wicker hampers. In spite of the pressure on us to stay, to resist, and our will to comply, I could not help making preparations to save the objects entrusted to me. Don't ask me why I started with the "fauna of the homeland." I simply followed a hunch, and the first animal to find its way into the great hamper was the stuffed wolf with the blue-gray glass eyes. I put in the fox and the polecat to keep him company, placed the stuffed beaver across his neck, slipped the black stork between his paws, and, carefully filling in the gaps, stowed away snakeskins, blown eggs, skeletons, antlers. One time Edith came and stood there for a long time, staring at me blankly, then asked, "Everything? Is everything supposed to go along?" "If we have to go," I said, "we won't be able to take enough with us." Please believe me: I was not doing this so that these reminders and remains of our deeply intertwined existence might someday form the basis of a claim or an assertion of rights. Rather, I was packing these things simply because they were our heritage, part of us, of our region, of our life, of the knowledge that had been acquired about our past, so that with their help we could trace back the winding paths to our origins ...

That's enough for now, Martin; let's have what's left of the tea, and you finish your cigarette. Then I have to nap a little. The day after tomorrow—I hope you will be coming the day after tomorrow, as you said—anyway, when you come back, I will corroborate for you that the past always looks clearer, the farther away it is ...

The ashes? Just put them in the sink and rinse them away ...

Clearer, I said: yes, that became evident to me on the ship crossing the wintry Baltic. As I looked back toward the darkening horizon, I felt distinctly: There is no return, no one can ever return to what once was, even if some miracle and a good memory let us take up the broken threads again and knot them together for a short while. "Once broken, they're broken forever," as Sonja Turk said. "It doesn't do any good to start over."

# 13

I assure you, none of us ever really thought we might be evacuated or, worse still, forced to flee; we simply could not imagine giving up Lucknow. To us the town symbolized permanence and shelter, and we secretly believed that we and the town belonged together for all eternity.

But then on a frosty January morning during the last year of the war we received the order to evacuate. The city was under fire from long-range guns. Veils of dust swept over the roofs, and through the pounding of the shells one heard the wail of the sirens. Marian and I rushed to the estate, and with our special authorizations, showing that we were engaged in a project for the Reichsjägermeister, we qualified for two vehicles: a sleigh and a rack wagon. We hitched up the horses, who smelled fire and were skittish. We had to keep them reined in because the road glistened with a thin layer of ice. In two hours everyone had to gather at the estate; that was all the time we had been given for packing.

In the house on the bend in the river, no one had lifted a finger. "Is this really it? Do we really have to flee? I just hope it isn't a mistake," my mother babbled almost incoherently.

We told them what we had heard, but they still refused to believe the evacuation order. Not until Marian told them the deadline and tore past them to get to work did they begin to grasp it. The true meaning hit them as they began to look around and realized they might have to part with some of their possessions.

I rushed into the museum, determined to drag the crates and hampers I had packed—which contained only a small part of the collection—to the wagon. But then, in the midst of the objects, many of them still on their shelves, I was swept by paralyzing indecision. For a moment I considered leaving everything there, in its completeness, so that it could bear coherent witness. I felt I should not separate things that silently complemented each other. I saw no way to set priorities.

In a daze I opened a window and looked out. Downstairs they were hauling chairs, the wall clock, the checked bedding outside and depositing the stuff next to the wagon—a load which would already fill a third of the wagon. And when Marian came out with the dining-room table on his back, I turned away, stepped over to a glass case, and tipped the jewelry collection into a crate. Don't ask me how I decided to condemn the humming pot and the devil's fiddle to stay but granted the old Masurian spinning wheel a place on the wagon.

I gathered up at random whatever caught my eye: documents, coins, costumes. Historic kitchen implements found a cozy nest among rag rugs, Bronze Age weapons were thrown in with toys and the "flora of the homeland." I can't explain why, numb and sweaty as I was, I chose to take along certain objects that had come to us from over the border: a hand-carved easy chair, a Masovian fancy vest, an old saddle and bridle, and wooden agricultural implements—I picked them just as randomly as the other objects, like the Sudauese urn or the straw crown.

Curiously enough, as I was packing the objects almost in a trance, I knew exactly where each one came from and what its story was.

I did not even answer Paulie when he came in and began gathering objects he particularly cherished, asking, "How about this, can it come along?" I watched in silence as he took our collection of "soil of the homeland" and, to save space, poured it all into a bag, which he stowed away in his school satchel: limestone and gravel, quartz, mica, and clay samples which had been displayed in bottles and test tubes. It was Paulie who placed the book in my hands, Sonja Turk's manual of Masurian weaving lore, the first thing I carried down to the wagon, along with some ancient tools.

Two passing soldiers had hung their guns on the fence and were helping Marian and the women heave the heavy baggage onto the two vehicles, or rather, the soldiers were loading while the women kept running back into the house to bring out things that simply could not be left behind. Racked by dry sobs and driven by an insatiable need, my mother hauled out everything transportable, regardless of weight or value. Edith worked in silence, her lips pressed tightly together. She apparently did not hear me when I called to her, and once, when we met on the stairs, she looked at me so expressionlessly that I was horrified. Sonja Turk sat apathetically in the sleigh, a black crocheted shawl around her. She was propped up with pillows, and her wheelchair had been jammed in amid the other stuff to shield her from the wind. She seemed no longer affected by what went on around her.

How quickly the vehicles filled up, and in the trampled snow around them lay as much again, all supposed to go along. None of the containers was labeled, not even the contents of the museum that I had so carefully packed earlier. And suddenly, while across the lake the first wagons rumbled to the collecting point, there began a frenzy of trying to locate things. "Do we have the album?" "How about the hot-water bottle?" "Where, my boy, is the iron?" "The honey?" "And the big mirror—did we pack that?" And so on. No help for it: we had to start rummaging through the loads. I still remember how startled I was to come upon the Tartar Stone, that pockmarked granite ball, enclosed in wooden slats—apparently the soldiers had heaved it onto the wagon. It was too late to ditch it and repack the load. So that massive missile which had proved fatal to the leader of the Tartars in 1656 had to go along.

I can't tell you how often I gave the signal for departure; they simply could not tear themselves away from the articles left in the snow. They wanted to carry them inside or cover them with burlap bags to protect them from the bitter winds of January. Marian and I had to scramble down, lead the women away, and help them up onto the loads, where they finally made little hollows in which to sit, between table legs sticking up in the air, bedding, and rolled-up rugs. But even now the questions about this or that object did not cease ...

Ah, you wonder whether we thought about returning, whether the evacuation seemed like a temporary measure. Yes,

Martin, I have often wondered that myself. But when I reconstruct the thoughts and feelings of that moment, I have to say that I at least was filled with only one wish: to escape with what had been entrusted to me, to escape . . .

In any case, the guns were pounding away as we set out. I took the reins of the rack wagon and did not look back. As we bumped down the sloping road to the lake, the wind seized hold of us, and we turned up our collars. Along our route we passed house after house with its doors wide open, abandoned furniture and housewares out in front. As we climbed toward the bridge we overtook a procession of bundled-up women, children, and old men with canes, a contingent that had set out on foot and was now slipping and sliding up the icy slope; some of them clung to our vehicles. The wooden gate of the prison stood open, the prisoners having long since left. And the squat, whitewashed house on the lake where I had spent my childhood amid multicolored vapor clouds also stood open. The causeway leading to the estate was already crowded, the procession creeping along. Someone who caught sight of our wagon remarked, "Look at that, the museum's coming along. So we'll have everything we could need."

Finally, we drove into one of the enclosures at the estate. A hundred or even a hundred and twenty vehicles had gathered there. We all received oats and straw, and Ludwig Krimkowski, the firefighter general, introduced himself as leader of the cavalcade and pledged that he would get us safely and without a single loss to our goal: Dirschau on the Vistula.

We were still standing around in the frozen courtyard when out of the manor house came Toni Lettkow's wife, the woman in blue, in laced boots and a short woolen coat. She came toward us, nodded haughtily and distantly as she passed. When she reached her coach, she held out her arm to Heini Hauser, who was supposed to help her in. He hesitated—I saw it clearly, but when she looked at him irritably, he put his hand under her elbow as she climbed onto the coachman's box.

Heini Hauser had decided to stay. He wished me a good trip, not a safe return; then he unhurriedly walked to the middle of the courtyard and from there watched our departure. His expression showed no joy or satisfaction. He just stood there, looking unmoved and patient, a lonely figure with the long row of stalls behind him . . .

Yes, Martin, we had animals with us, but only horses and some of the cattle. So-called small animals were not allowed to be taken. We kept the animals tied to the back of the vehicles, and they trotted along willingly in the crunchy snow, including Toni Lettkow's two East Prussian grays, which were hitched to the coach of the "lady in blue." Anyone seeing us from a distance might have thought us pioneers setting out to find new land, new possibilities, new beginnings in the west. We moved along in darkness, and the cottages and farms we passed also lay in darkness. Only the snow gave light.

We did not pause as we passed Castle Hill with its ancient legends of courage and triumph. We took shelter from the wind in the forests, where the pounding of distant guns faded or was absorbed in the icy stillness. We rested under the fir trees, having put eight miles between ourselves and Lucknow. To the rear of the column, a fire was built to heat milk and warm stones, which they wanted to wrap in their clammy blankets. As if on command, various figures jumped down from the vehicles and began to heap branches and pine cones on top of a layer of straw. But before other fires leaped up, Krimkowski and his assistants came storming along with shouted warnings and smothered the flames with snow.

So without fires to keep us warm, we spent the rest of the night on top of the wagons. The frost crackled in the forest, and the cold crept into our bodies. The animals pawed the ground and tossed their heads. There was no need to post guards, since everyone remained awake. On all the vehicles people were going over the things they had brought along and the things they had left behind. Only now, in retrospect, did they realize how they valued the possessions they had accumulated over the years.

At daybreak we set out again. No one troubled to round up the animals that had broken their tethers and fled into the depths of the forest. As we jogged along the rather broad wood road, people were eating on all the wagons and sleighs. My mother cut bread and hard sausage for everyone, passed around dried apple slices, and poured us brandy diluted with tea from an enameled flask. Paulie ran alongside to deliver the breakfast to the sleigh, where only Marian was to be seen. Sonja Turk seemed to have sunk out of sight amid rolled-up rugs and bedding. The forest thinned out and we found ourselves on the snow-covered highway to Arys. Then the sun came up and the ice coating the birches began to glitter like a crystal chandelier. As we rode along, we were joined by wagons coming in from the side roads, but also by motorcycle couriers, military ambulances, and columns of soldiers who had become separated from their regiments. They all attached themselves to us, as if our procession would lead them to safety. Our column had already doubled its length. One time we passed a small, deserted railway station. Beside the snow-covered tracks stood heaps of trunks, furniture, bundles, and hampers, left there when their owners had managed to catch the last train out and had had to sacrifice their baggage. Edith drew a blanket over her face and began to cry.

From an elevation I could look out across the whole countryside, a white desert under a pale sun. I looked back over the winding highway and our bobbing procession. Coming toward it from the northeast was a motorized column, moving along briskly—tanks, open-tracked vehicles, and military trucks, possibly under orders to secure Lucknow or even to liberate it. We pulled up, and as we were still conferring, a motorcycle courier came roaring by and called out as he passed, "Everyone off the road, make it snappy!"—and seemed not to hear what we shouted to him. People hesitated, trying to estimate the risk of moving off the road into the drifts to the side. Instead, they tried pulling over close to the birches that lined the road. But that was not sufficient. Even before the motorcycle courier returned, the wagons ahead began to scatter, forced off the road by the heavy tanks that came trundling along without even slowing down. The horses bucked and sank knee deep into the drifts. At first their legs began to flounder, but then they found a foothold and began to pull steadily, straining to reach the field. One wagon after another lurched off the road. Some of them tipped over in the attempt to climb the ditch. People were pinned underneath, loads landed in the snow. Shafts, axles, and runners broke. The cracking of whips was drowned out by shouts, cries, and confused voices.

I dismounted and gestured to Marian and the others to climb down, except for Sonja Turk. Then I urged the horses on, and they waded into the drifts, their eyes white with fear. They took the opposite side of the ditch at an angle, their hoofs hammering and stamping the snow. The wagon swayed, the load shifted under the ropes, but the horses' steady pulling prevented a spill. We made it over, first the rack wagon, then the sleigh. From the hummocky field we watched the military column passing by. The tank commanders stood in their open turrets and looked straight ahead, while in personnel carriers very young soldiers huddled together. You might have thought they were trying not to see us. The column was moving toward what it thought was the front, proceeding under its dirty white camouflage paint, obedient but without conviction.

This was the beginning of the gradual dissolution of our group. At the beginning we still helped one another repair broken vehicles and gather scattered baggage, or we assigned people to undamaged vehicles. But some people insisted on staying behind with their vehicles to fix them. Those who did never rejoined us, for our route did not follow the course charted at the beginning. It depended, we soon recognized, on changing conditions— the movements and countermovements of innumerable other marchers, of retreating divisions, and also on the incalculable forward thrusts of the Russian tank divisions.

We pushed on, making headway toward the northwest, across frozen fields, sometimes over the thick ice of lakes. Where was it that the two artilleries, theirs and ours, exchanged fire across our column? We came to a halt in a little valley, heard the missiles whining overhead, and had trouble keeping the horses from bolting. We did not see either army, just heard the firing and felt the frozen ground tremble under our wheels.

Yes, now I remember, it was the valley of Wilucken. Shortly afterward we passed the forest which had given the village its name. Not only military trucks and guns had taken cover there. We encountered part of another column which must have sought shelter there and been surprised by the artillery fire. Horses lay strewn about. Smashed vehicles sprawled in the snow. Belongings were scattered under battered trees that tilted at crazy angles. I will never forget the sight of the wheel of an overturned wagon, rotating all by itself in the air. An old man was being helped by several soldiers to drag stiff corpses to the edge of a shell crater and gently push them in. Cartons, hampers, and bundles had emptied their contents all over the ground. Everywhere there was bedding, spotted, grimy bedding, and the smell of burned rubber filled the air. No one from our party dismounted to help, and those who had survived the attack seemed to expect nothing of us. They scarcely noticed us as we toiled past.

Not long after we had passed this scene, a cry of horror from my mother announced a terrible discovery. The lids on a crock and several jars of honey had loosened and the honey had trickled over our Sunday clothes. She hurled the clothes about and tried to rub off the stickiness with a rag. As she scrubbed, she could not resist licking the congealed sweetness off her fingers. For the next few hours she brooded bitterly over this misfortune.

Ah, all those losses, that long trail of ruins and lost possessions! You could trace the fortunes of the refugees by the goods they left behind along the route. How completely winter and the open air transformed them from prized possessions into pathetic junk!

But I must tell you about the evening when we were forced to change the direction of our flight.

We had turned off the highway and swayed up a bare avenue lined with linden trees, Krimkowski's wagon in the lead, to an abandoned estate. The barn and stables had been hit by grenades, but not the manor house, whose broken windows we hoped to be able to stuff with straw and burlap bags. We had barely driven up when the firefighter general called the team drivers for our usual evening conference. We walked stiffly across the terrace, stumbling over broken flower pots and loose mortar. The French doors banged in the wind, and shredded curtains flapped in the windows. The self-appointed leader of our party awaited us there. He gazed over our heads toward the gentle white slopes which descended to an oval lake. As he stood there with his coat open and the crossed hose nozzles on his collar, he seemed confident and optimistic, this leader of ours.

As he did every evening, he repeated his instructions for feeding the animals, allocating rooms, relieving the watch, and taking precautions against fires and misconduct. And as always, at the end he asked for questions.

Two or three arms went up, but he overlooked them, seeming suddenly to have other matters on his mind. He was staring so fixedly at the slopes across the way that we involuntarily turned. We instantly spotted the horseman storming down toward the lake—a single dark figure riding not only fast but also cautiously, avoiding the snowdrifts like one who was fully familiar with this countryside. Man and horse seemed inseparable as they flew along the shore of the lake. They jumped a brook, crashed into the crackling reeds, turned, and came charging up to the estate, still not slowing their pace, although the rider must have long since taken note of our vehicles. He galloped past us, slid out of his saddle by the approach to the manor house, pulled a carbine out of its case, and, without tying up the horse, made his way among our vehicles into the stables. Not until the first shot rang out did some of us run over to see what he was doing . . .

No, Martin, not that. No, there were more than a dozen wounded horses there in the stables, Arabians and East Prussian grays, which no one had been able to look to when tank grenades forced the people of the estate to flee. The horses stood and lay in their boxes with severed forelegs, with flanks split open. They waited there, not whinnying, at most panting softly into the straw. They stood there with blood gleaming on their coats, with bones laid bare, one of them sniffing at his slippery innards; this, too, quietly. All one heard was a feeble pawing of the ground.

The man stumbled from box to box in the last daylight that entered the stable from the gaps the grenades had smashed in the building. At each box he stood motionless for a moment, then raised the carbine with only his right hand and fired at close range, always right behind the ear. One horse after another collapsed. Those that were already lying in the straw tossed their heads after the impact of the bullet and raked the ground with their front hoofs before they stretched out dead. How long the bodies continued to tremble! We had no doubt that the man was the horses' owner. We saw how some of the horses raised their heads and nodded at the sight of him, as if to greet him, yes. When he reloaded, I saw that his left hand wore a suede glove. It was a wooden hand.

Then he sat down on an oat trough, lit a cigarette, and leaned his forehead against one of the rough pillars of the barn. We respected his need and did not crowd around him. And you should have seen his face when he finally got up and staggered toward us, overcome with grief and at the same time filled with a bitter satisfaction. He was a man of few words, as we discovered, this estate owner who had ridden twenty miles to put the wounded horses out of their misery and now was going to return to where his people had camped for the night. He did not stay around, showed no interest in where we had come from or where we were headed. Without even glancing at the buildings, he pushed his way past our vehicles and whistled to his horse. It trotted up obediently, and he swung himself into the saddle. Only then did he seem to become aware of us. "You can't get through anymore to the west," he said. "They've advanced as far as Elbing and have blocked the last open route." Having said that, he wheeled on his horse and rode off without another word. We stood there and watched him until he had reached the opposite slopes.

We went back into the cold manor house and debated what to do, or rather, it was clear that we had only one choice and that was to take the route that would get us across the frozen lagoon and then over the wintry Baltic. Then each of us went to his people to tell them what to expect on the journey north. No protests, no grumbling; they numbly submitted to the new plan. Ah, we were ready for anything so long as it held out the slightest prospect of escape.

We spent the night on the floor, crowded close together for warmth, fully dressed, and wrapped in our clammy blankets. There was an uninterrupted rustling, whispering, and whimpering, the babbling of an old man who was fumbling through his possessions. It did no good when here and there someone asked for quiet. Some murmured in their dreams or cried out, others ate surreptitiously under the covers or muttered constantly to themselves. Nevertheless, I did manage to catch a few winks at a time.

That was the night when Sonja Turk spoke her last words. Not that she died or had a stroke; she just stopped speaking. It all began when someone came rushing in from outside, shouting,

"It's snowing, it's a blizzard," whereupon people went to the windows, where they stood staring out dazedly. I heard the wind rising and flailing around the house. I was thinking about starting out the next morning, about roads erased by snow, about vehicles foundering in the drifts, when I felt a hand groping down my arm. I thought it was Marian's, and that he had some suggestion for tomorrow, but it was Sonja Turk, who asked softly, "Are you asleep? Are you asleep, Zygmunt?" She took my wrist and drew me closer, so close that I could feel her breath on my face and she could be certain no one heard us. First she wanted to know whether it were really snowing, and when I said it was, my old teacher sang the praises of the snow. She sang the praises of the snow before she asked me to do her one last favor.

From her place up on the sleigh she had noticed a patch of undergrowth alongside the orchard. I was to take her there, at once, and without a word, "so's no one comes traipsing after us," and there I was to set her down in the snow and leave her to herself. She wanted a rug—"you know, the one with the staring eye"—and she would lie under it, "snug as can be," and be gone, out of sight. She thought she could promise that it would all remain "just between us." She gave me a free hand with her property and averred that this would make everything easier on our journey north.

I patiently tried to talk her out of the idea, stressing how much she meant to us and that she was not a burden to anyone. I went so far as to conjure up a studio on a distant, peaceful coast where she could watch over the training of intelligent weaving pupils who would receive and carry on her wisdom. As I talked, she gradually moved farther and farther away from me; she said less and less by way of opposition, and finally she simply ignored my words and lay there in complete indifference, determined to speak no more. She would not even speak to Paulie the next morning.

Yes, that happened often: we buried our dead at dawn—but bury is perhaps too fine a word. When possible we chopped a cavity in the frozen ground with a pickax, but often we only covered them with branches or left them under a heap of snow, beside the highway, with an unspoken promise to return someday and attend to what we had no time for now. And they, too, marked our trail, the ice graves, the snow graves, the hastily patted-down mounds in which the wooden crosses did not remain standing for long.

On, on, we had to go on, obedient to compulsion and fear and the prevailing laws of motion; on, because daylight was coming and gruff orders drove us onward, because the rumbling and the flash of gunfire came creeping over the horizon, on and on, because we were now filled with a terrible vision: the last ship pulling away just as we reached the deserted pier. With brooms and shovels we freed our vehicles of snow and dug them out. We fed the horses with the supplies we found in the stables, and shoveled a path back to the highway. Whips cracked and the cavalcade jerked into motion. Our wagon began to skid and landed against a linden tree. Some of the wagon's rungs splintered on impact, and it must have been then that we lost the coin collection. Unless it was later, when we were strafed out there in the dunes and the boxes and trunks fell off the wagon. So now we were deprived of the coins, which bore witness to the many-tongued and colorful occupations of Lucknow. They showed the profiles of all the khans and kings who had stripped the town of its valuables time and again.

Several other vehicles skidded along the linden avenue. One of them crashed, breaking both its axles. We rescued the baggage and divided its occupants among the other wagons. We, too, received a new passenger, Joseph von Intelmann, the retired chief of the Lucknow detective division. He scrambled onto our wagon with a roomy valise. He introduced himself to each one of us, including Paulie. Pretty soon we learned that his valise contained documents, records of the more unusual criminal cases which he had helped solve. He wanted to rescue the documents to use for his memoirs or a book on police methods. That same day we were joined by one of Krimkowski's men, a shapeless, fluttery fellow whose own sleigh had been smashed. Somehow he still managed to foresee a happy end to our flight, and in fact to the war itself . . .

You ask how that was possible. Well, that's what we wondered, too, all of us who had been condemned to be eyewitnesses and who even when we closed our eyes had taken in enough to be immune to any kind of promises or rosy predictions. Yet those who needed us to prolong their shabby power probably could not help it; they had to interpret events in their own favor.

Przytulla, who now sat next to Intelmann on the wagon, showed us how it was done. If one of our planes chanced to appear in the low-hanging snowy sky, he saw our "mastery of the skies" restored. If one of our own tank columns forced us into the ditch, he predicted our imminent return to the homeland. If we passed grenadiers digging in behind a hill, for him it signaled the beginning of a defensive battle that would reverse the score. Even when we passed a group of trees from whose branches dangled hanged soldiers, bareheaded and twisting in the wind— even at the sight of these fellows convicted by summary martial law—he felt that things were "looking up" again, now that the leadership had decided to restore discipline by any and all means. It is terrifying, Martin, to see how things can have such diverse meanings, what diverse meanings we ourselves can have. Sometimes you have to assume that truth itself is frighteningly diverse.

It was inevitable that Intelmann and Przytulla should be at loggerheads. Every experience, every remark fueled their continuing argument. When they learned that they were riding on top of the Masurian museum, they found endless pretexts for bickering.

Intelmann simply could not see us returning home soon after the end of the war. He cited various movements of peoples in history that had resulted in totally new constellations. He questioned whether the homeland could be immutable, guaranteed for good, and he attributed only a sentimental, or at best a cultural-historical significance to the artifacts that traveled with us.

Przytulla, on the other hand, was convinced that we would soon be returning home. He spoke of the "right of homeland." This right could not be tampered with because it was an expression of an innate need. Intelmann's reference to historical movements struck him as an attempt to downgrade the idea of homeland to a matter of mere geography. He viewed the inventory of our museum as the modest but irrefutable evidence of a long-lasting claim. I let the two of them fight it out and concentrated on the road.

How often I read the same names of villages and towns on the signs we passed; I thought I recognized bridges and forests which we had seen before. One night I dreamed that the last highway signs in East Prussia had all been turned around. We could not be sure we were really making headway, since rumors and watchwords, but also unrealistic instructions sent us back and forth and in circles. At every other intersection we ran into barriers and checkpoints. The straggling soldiers who had attached themselves to our party were pulled out and organized into emergency units. But we were waved on, once we had shown our special authorizations from the Reichsjägermeister. Yes, we were given preferential treatment and allowed to pass on.

Who knows whether we would ever have made it to the Baltic lagoon if we had not attached ourselves to an ambulance unit, a column of loaded and damaged vehicles, some of them being towed by their stronger brethren. They were high-axled panel trucks burning synthetic fuel. Following them, we rattled along the potholed road into the dunes. And there, beyond the ragged scrub pines, was the lagoon.

The lagoon lay there, a gray expanse of precarious ice, pierced by dark channels in which crushed ice glittered. Buoys stood at crazy angles, frozen into the ice. A convoy of tugboats, lighters, cutters, and landing boats was sailing northward, following a rusty icebreaker which left a trail of smoke over the channel. Where we stood, we could hear the crashing sound of the boats ramming through the ice. I let my eyes trace the channel back to the stone lighthouse, to the jetty, to the little harbor of this town, whose houses clustered around the harbor basin and on both banks of a river that flowed into the lagoon. Tied up at the jetty lay the rumps of two minesweepers, rust-red, without their superstructures.

You can imagine how the sight excited us. We could not wait to reach the harbor. The sleighs left the road and went slithering down the hill, while the wagons trundled down the bumpy track toward the last loophole, the portal of hope; they had reached the harbor where their long wandering was to end.

We could not enter the town. Where the road led out of the dunes, we were halted by riflemen who forced us to turn back and informed us that we would have to wait—"might be three, four days." They assigned us a spot, a shallow dip amid the scrub pines, where we drew up our vehicles in a circle, cleared away the snow, and built fires on the frozen sand. Soon iron kettles dangled from tripods and tents began to go up.

Marian Jeromin handed me his binoculars. Scanning the coastline, I picked out other groups waiting everywhere, gathered into wagon encampments or scattered through the dunes. On the shore where tides had left marks which were now frozen solid, entire arsenals of weapons and military equipment lay heaped up, guns of all calibers, for which there were no munitions, communications vans which had nothing more to communicate, mounds of empty containers, and a pile of camouflage netting which camouflaged only itself now. I turned to look at the town, whose streets were jammed with columns of waiting vehicles. On the two larger town squares, round tents displaying the Red Cross had been set up. One of the bridges over the river had buckled under the weight of a tank. Although the transport ships had just left the harbor, the pier was already crowded with prospective passengers, all of them bandaged soldiers . . .

You want to know whether we were encircled. Yes, Martin, encircled and locked in; that became clear when Krimkowski called the team leaders together and prepared us for waiting not three, but more likely five days for our ship. He had heard that over six thousand wounded soldiers were to be taken out first, and after them the most essential war material. We went back to our wagons in silence. We dug deeper into the sand, stretched tarpaulins over the hollows, built up walls of sand to serve as windbreaks. A dead cow, already almost frozen, was chopped up; with saws and axes we dressed the meat and distributed it. On orders we extinguished our fires at dusk. The night was not dark; the sky remained dark gray, and under this cover the ships returned to the harbor, without board lights, restricted to the channel which the old icebreaker kept plowing open.

As the vessels tied up, we listened intently to the rattling of the hatches and the creaking of the loading cranes, the hum of the engines and the blasts of their horns. We kept count incessantly, mentally loading one ship after another, adding up the number of those left behind, and trying to figure our own chances for getting out in time.

For the time being only individual aircraft flew over the basin by night to drop their bombs on the harbor; we could not detect any damage the next morning. There was only an indistinct rumbling beyond the horizon, distant enough so that one stopped hearing it after a while. But when a firebomb dropped, illuminating the harbor with its cold light, our fears assumed clearer form. We began to wonder how long the small harbor would remain usable, and watched with growing dismay as more and more columns of ambulances rolled across the dunes, rattled down to the shore, and did not even attempt to drive through town to the harbor but stopped by the beach to deposit the wounded in long rows of stretchers. And new groups of civilians came straggling in from the west, where they had waited by small harbors, one after the other of which had been lost. Now they poured into the dunes, swelling the numbers and the confusion.

Then one afternoon Krimkowski came running along the line of wagons shouting, "Get yourselves ready!" So our turn had come at last. The Lucknowers crept out of their dugouts and milled about, packing, tying down the loads, harnessing up for the shortest stretch of our journey: there remained only the winding road through town to the harbor, which lay empty and gleaming in the wintry sun. A faint life appeared in the faces, which had grown stony from long waiting and fear. We nodded at one another, generously shared our last crumbs of tobacco.

We set out much too early; when we reached the harbor, the ships were not yet in sight and the pier was still crowded with people who had more right to a space than we did. Still, we managed to inch forward. Vehicles were jammed in so tightly that there was hardly a finger's breadth between them.

Yes, Martin, and then that indomitable hodgepodge armada heaved into view on the horizon, came steaming up, and glided into the harbor basin. The ships' screws whipped up the ice soup during the complicated tying-up maneuvers. Ropes were tossed to shore, gangplanks were lowered, and in no time there was a tramping and a rolling and a heaving of objects through the air; you have never seen a faster loading. We inched along, holding our documents in readiness, the special authorizations and special papers, or rather, I gave them to Marian, whose sleigh was in front of my wagon. We were determined to bring as much of our baggage on board as possible . . .

The horses? Oh, a squad of riflemen took them over when we came to the harbor and led them by back ways to the shore, to a receiving pen, a death pen.

So our party had reached the harbor, and the battered sides of the ships were almost close enough to touch, when several air-raid sirens began to wail in town. No one left the ships, no one tried to take shelter. Our goal was too close. Now the warning horns of the lighters, cutters, and landing boats went off, and we saw the soldiers who manned the antiaircraft guns rush to their platforms. Perhaps we would have run for the shelter of the jetty if just one person had made a move in that direction, but fear of losing our places in line kept us rooted to the spot.

They were coming from inland, three waves of low-flying aircraft. We did not hear the sound of their engines until they shot out over the dunes, then climbed steeply, swerved when they were out over the lagoon, and thundered back toward the shore. The blast of their shots plunged white-hot into the ice and sent frozen sand spurting into the air. They hammered over the jetty, over the ships, over the people, and over the endless piles of material. Bombs fell. The first ones enlarged the channel. The next smashed the poor lighthouse to smithereens. They found the harbor, sending up fountains of water, shattering the decks of the ships, exploding on the pier, slapping down the narrow houses with the high gables, peppering the holding pen. Smoke and clouds of sand obscured the harbor basin, and one ship went up in flames. Our horses panicked, rearing up and trying to break out, but there was no gap through which they could escape; the ve-hicles were crowded in so tightly. The ships emptied out. A terror-stricken horde flooded toward the town, dragging with it anything that stood in its way. I can still see that mast, the highest mast in the harbor, which began to tremble and list, listed until it was almost horizontal, and then dove down into the water almost gently as the cutter capsized. And then . . .

No, no, it's all right. I'll manage, it's just that old feeling of pressure, as if you were under a huge screw and it were being tightened. I'm afraid this feeling will stay with me. You needn't call the nurse, just open the window a little, that'll do . . .

There's no help for it, I have to tell you this, too . . .

I can still hear Edith calling out my name wildly; I can still see her sitting there among the bedding and the rolled-up rugs, and on her lap Paulie's motionless face and the blood trickling from his forehead. I can still see her dragging the child's sled, onto which she had loaded the boy, disappearing into the crowd without heeding my shouts and desperate waving. I simply could not prevent her from climbing down, lifting the boy from the wagon, and transferring him to a sled that had been leaning against a tree. For as soon as the airplanes had disappeared behind the dunes, a high-ranking officer waved the Lucknow contingent to the jetty where the rumps of the rusty-red minesweepers were tied up. He drove us along, he hustled us, and I could not hand over the reins fast enough. I did not jump down until Edith had already merged with the frantic crowd and was being swept back toward town. I ran after her, or rather, I staggered, stumbled, was dragged along. You mustn't fall, I thought, don't let yourself fall, but the crowd rushing through the narrow streets carried me along and would not have let me fall if I had wanted to.

On the square where the round Red Cross tents still stood, the pressure let up, the hordes thinned out. I managed to work my way to the edge and stood there for a while pressed up against a building, looking for a woman with a sled. I hurried into the tents, searched the rows of wounded soldiers and civilians. I made my way among the straw pallets to a curtain, behind which I could see the silhouettes of the doctors doing surgery. But Edith and the boy were nowhere to be found.

She may have taken the boy to the hospital, I thought, and I rushed out and asked directions. No sled at the entrance, but the steps and the trampled snow were covered with the wounded sprawled there, keeping their eyes on the brick building. They hardly noticed as I stumbled by them; they did not even move over as I came up the steps. The corridor was impassable, blocked by the more serious casualties; I waited at the entrance until a nurse appeared, but she shook her head even before I had a chance to ask her about a woman and a little boy. She pointed at the people lying there and said, "Have a look yourself."

Could I have some water, Martin, just a glass of water . . .

And see that flat box—you have to push the cover open with your thumb—could you give me half of one of those pills? Just break it down the middle, that's right. Thank you . . .

398 ‡ Siegfried Lenz

I looked and I looked, but in vain. I finally stopped asking, for I kept encountering other people who asked me whether I had seen their children, their companions, their relatives, telling me how they were dressed, mentioning a stuffed animal or a crutch. I gave up searching in the town and returned, filled with sudden new hope, to the harbor. She must be here, I thought, she must have found her way back to our contingent by now. And I told myself that she would have been given preferential treatment, processed and allowed to board one of the ships, which were once again taking on people and baggage amid all the confusion and smoke and ships' booms sticking up out of the water.

I stood in the harbor and tried to find my bearings. Our party was no longer where I had left it; all the wagons and sleighs had turned over their contents to the two unfinished minesweepers, and the vehicles had been moved from the pier to the beach. Our people were milling around on the ships, piling up their luggage; from the iron decks which still lacked their superstructures they called out to me and waved: "Hurry, hurry, we're leaving," and I saw a hawser flung to the old icebreaker from the bow of the closest minesweeper. So the sturdy old ship was going to tow us out of the harbor.

Edith and the boy had to be on board already—I could see no other possibility. You understand that I simply had to assume that, otherwise I would never have run over to the overloaded ship's rump and grabbed Marian Jeromin's outstretched hand and let myself be hauled on board. As I landed on the deck, the tow hawser had pulled taut, and as our distance from the jetty steadily increased, I started combing the ship, looking intently into every face above and below deck, softly calling out the names of Edith and Paulie. I groped my way through the entire ship, but no one answered me.

Back on deck I saw our procession gliding out of the harbor, the icebreaker in the lead, then our ship, and then the second ship's rump—all connected by steel cables. From the stern I watched the ship behind us, scrutinizing the people on deck as best I could at that distance, and I heard Marian saying, "They're over there, and some of our things are over there, too. Too many people were helping with the loading, and it was impossible to keep everything together." He pointed to a heap of luggage on which my mother sat fatalistically. He also pointed out a stack of bedding which served Sonja Turk as a windbreak. Edith and the boy were not to be seen . . .

Without a trace, Martin, they had disappeared without a trace. To be sure, I did meet an old man at a reunion many years later who thought he remembered seeing a woman pulling her dead child on a sled through the wintry dunes. But all he could tell me was that the sled had suddenly gone over the edge of a foxhole and the woman had sat on the edge as if paralyzed while the last groups were pushing on to the harbor, to the last landing boats that had tied up in a hail of artillery fire. So I had no explanation, no news of the end. They simply disappeared behind a shroud of uncertainty . . .

But what did I want to say? Oh, yes, our convoy steamed along the channel, the icebreaker clearing away the ice layer that was already forming over the water, and the two ship's rumps, which could not be steered, ramming against the sides of the channel. Marian and I stood at the stern and could not take our eyes off the ship behind us, lying low in the water and plowing through the ice mush while the cable held taut.

Gradually the coast flattened out, the jetty seemed to shrink, and the columns of smoke above the town looked smaller. Seagulls provided an escort for us. "You'll see," Marian whispered, "they'll be coming along on the next transport; we'll wait for them in Pillau." He kept talking, trying to reassure me. He told me that with the help of his special authorization he had been allowed to take the Tartar Stone on board; it was on the deck of the ship behind us. Though, of course, he had not been permitted to take all the baggage; like everyone, we had had to leave some behind, but he was sure it was the items we could most easily do without.

When the yellow and white flames eased up along the dark line of coast, we had the impression at first they were spurting up out of the interior of the earth, but immediately afterward we heard heavy missiles shooting over our convoy, and as they struck, we threw ourselves to the deck. A hail of ice lumps came showering down on us. A long-drawn-out warning shout resounded over the deck. Gripped by panic, people rushed for the stairs to the lower decks. In front of us fountains of water and ice shot up, the fine splinters of ice forming a glittering wall that was driven by the wind. Trapped in our channel without engines of our own, we had to follow the course set for us by the icebreaker. A direct hit ripped away its mast and antenna; a second shattered the overhanging wing of the bridge and twisted its steel supports. The front of our ship was also hit; a bursting grenade hurled the luggage onto the ice of the lagoon, ripped up the deck, and killed Krimkowski's men.

Russian tanks and field pieces were firing on our convoy. They had reached the lagoon, had driven onto the beach, and were taking us on as if for practice drill. And then a shell slammed through the rump of the ship behind us; I saw the jagged hole at the waterline, I saw the people hurtling onto the deck, onto the already overloaded deck of the minesweeper, where there was no protection to speak of.

Suddenly the firing ceased, and we began to assume that we had moved beyond the range of their guns. Over on the other ship a man had gone down on his knees and was praying; no one came too close to him. And at first I thought my eyes were playing tricks on me when the bent figure began to tip and very slowly skidded, but skidded so irresistibly that he had to brace himself with his hands. But as we watched, we noticed the deck actually begin to slope. The ship was listing, and everything started to slide, all the baggage piled up on the deck, and the people perched on top of their possessions.

In the silence we heard a great cry of terror, an end-of-the-world cry, and the ship's rump began to sink. Arms reaching into the air, bodies tumbling, boxes, beds, trunks, and suitcases skidding over the deck and hurtling into the ice mush of the channel. Still no one jumped, although the list was steadily increasing. The rust-red rump still clung to the towline and made headway, while water gurgled into its innards.

Again there were flashes of fire from the coast; apparently they had noticed that one of the ships had been hit, and again their salvos smashed through the ice and surrounded us with a wall of fountains. One grenade hit the icebreaker's superstructure without exploding. Deeper and deeper sank the ship behind us, and we began to lose speed. I could no longer see any of our people there.

Two navy men, who apparently belonged to the icebreaker's crew and had been assigned to our minesweeper for the crossing, came running to the stern and tried to throw off the hawser that bound us to the sinking ship. They pulled and pried with a crowbar, but there was too much tension on the line and they could not loosen it. On the ship behind us people waved and shouted, pointing to the ice and the water, crying for help, as they desperately clung to anything that would still hold them. The navy men found a tool chest and dug out two axes. They took turns chopping at the cable, always at the same spot, until the first twisted layers popped, and finally the whole hawser could not withstand the tremendous pressure on it and snapped. Whipping furiously, it dropped into the channel and sank. Freed of the drag of the other ship, our ship shuddered and picked up speed, while the other ship swayed ponderously and plunged aft up into the water . . .

Yes, Martin, I watched, I did not turn away as the rust-red side dove deeper and deeper, as a hundred arms flew up in the air, as ice water sprayed over the deck and carried off the last possessions. As the boat went down, I saw a few people jump onto the treacherous ice along the channel. I saw them slip, break through, and go under, and those who lacked the courage or the desperation to leap were dragged down by the churning water; still, a number of people managed to stay on top of the ice, and from the distance we could still see them waving to us from the boards and ladders on which they were lying.

You see, what went under and perished there was not just half of our Lucknow group, it was part of Lucknow itself, of its past and its unique character. At that moment we knew instinctively that even if we should be allowed to return someday, Lucknow would never again be what it had been for us. Everything would be different, had to be different, for no one would be able to overlook the tragedy engraved forever on our memories.

In any case, Marian and I remained sitting in the stern, looking back until the tiny dark spots along the channel dissolved in mist, and even after that our pain and our emptiness tied us to the spot, although soon there was nothing to be seen but a gray haze through which our meandering wake cut.

Yes, that's how it is, son; divers would be able to reconstruct our path, for at the bottom of the lagoon still lie the countless mute witnesses to our desperate flight to the west—the milestones of our self-induced misfortune, the merciless harvest of the violence we ourselves had sown; ah, how often I imagined descending into the murky, silent depths, down to the underwater trail of death, to find corroboration for the senselessness of those sacrifices. And how often, Martin, have I wished that the sea would dry out or recede far enough so that tragic armada might come to light and tell the story of its undoing for those who on Sundays shower us with extenuations and unjustified optimism.

But we must move on, north over the frozen lagoon, through the canal of Pillau and then into another crowded harbor basin, filled with every imaginable sort of vessel: coastal schooners, seagoing tugs, huge passenger and cargo ships, and among them submarines, frigates, supply ships, and even flat torpedo boats from the last war. Under the cold light of the moon we glided past this seemingly endless fleet. The icebreaker maneuvered us to the pier without itself tying up. We had a long wait before the gangways were shoved into place.

A flashlight flicked on, and in its light I recognized shields with the emblems of the military police. They came clumping on board in their hobnailed boots, and sent all the men to the stern, though we tried to tell them that there were many dead to be attended to. And as if the bitter cold and the thin eddies of snow which the wind whipped over us from the pier did not affect them at all, they began studying our papers with utmost care. Without a word, merely with a curt wave of the hand, they selected some of us, including Marian, and when I asked them to read the special papers once more, their only reply was to demand to see my papers again. They did not return these until their squad leader had granted us permission to enter the military harbor of Pillau. Marian had only enough time to tell me where our luggage was stored before they bustled him and the others who had been selected down the gangplank.

Everyone gathered up his remaining belongings and hauled them onto land. No one seemed in any rush. We put down our things by the railway tracks, bundled ourselves up as best we could, and tried to orient ourselves among the dimly lit steamships. Near them waited the inhabitants of entire towns. The lines stretched far off into the darkness. We looked around, bewildered and disturbed, and suddenly someone cried, "Where's Hermann? Where's my brother?" He went tearing from group to group, pulling the scarves from people's faces, jerking back blankets. And although his frenzied search did not yield any results, it seemed to spur others to similar searches. They awoke from their apathy, and began milling around, calling out names, sobbing, asking everyone in sight: "Where's Johann?" "Have you seen Karl?" "Does anyone know where Ida is?" "But she was . . ." "He can't possibly have . . ." "Where can she be?"

I could no longer bear all the hands touching me, the disappointments, the pleading looks; when Krimkowski set out to inquire about our prospects for getting onto a ship, I accompanied him to the office of the harbor master. I still remember the wooden barracks to which we were directed and see the old man in his tattered uniform. The narrow ribbon with his medal hung crookedly, his tunic was unbuttoned. He looked at us sorrowfully out of reddened eyes. Behind him hung a map of the harbor for which he was responsible, but over which he had long since lost control. "They come and go, often without letting me know," he said. "Ships come sneaking in, load up whatever happens to be there, and sneak out again." He could not assign us to any ship, not this evening, for first he had to wait for the arrival of the hospital trains, five hospital trains supposed to be coming in from Königsberg, that hard-pressed city they had declared a fortress so as to prolong the final agony.

We were told to wait until the following night. Just as we got ready to leave, a soldier came in, saluted, and reported that all the preparations had been made for the demolition. We recognized him at once by his voice: Simon Gayko. "No, that can't be true!" "But it is, it is!" You can imagine how circumspectly we greeted one another and how little was said for sheer amazement. He nodded to us that we should meet him outside. There was a clear, cold sky. The wind whipped cruelly around us. The shadows of light warships slipped out of the harbor to where a convoy was forming. Now that we were alone with each other and so many things should have been said, the three of us just stood there and looked at one another. Finally Simon asked, "I suppose Luck-now's done for?" "It will be reborn," said Krimkowski. "Where?" Simon asked. "In the west?"

He had to return to his battery, but he promised to come out to the pier the next evening, to the end of the railway tracks. We went back to our people, past heaps of military equipment, past long lines crowding together, hoping to be taken on board. We passed a heap of old carts—handcarts and baby carriages—and stopped to look at them, checking the wheels and handles; we considered borrowing a cart, but a guard who had been assigned to watch the heap shoved us away.

I hurried back to the tracks and the place where the remnant of our group were huddled. I shooed away two people who had taken refuge under my possessions, rummaged through the individual bundles, and with a sudden sense of urgency began to lift lids here, and untie twine there. So the straw crown was still with us, and the Sokolken box, protected by a rag rug, and the folder with documents, and the stuffed black stork. As I groped around and caressed the objects, I felt no calmer, but a thin current of warmth coursed through me. No, I did not count up all the things that remained to me; it was enough to feel some of them, to be reunited with a sampling of them.

And then, shortly before the first hospital train pulled in, an automobile drove up. The chauffeur jumped out to open the door, and out stepped a high-ranking officer, whose insignia were covered by a broad fur collar. The officer went around the car and opened the back door. He crooked his arm like a perfect gentleman and helped a slim lady slide out of the car. He bowed and touched his lips to her hand, and at an impatient gesture from him, the chauffeur lifted several boxes out of the car and set them on the ground near us. Then the officer bowed again as he took his leave.

It's a movie; they're showing a movie for us, I thought. And then the "lady in blue" came up to me, snapped her fingers, and asked me on which of the ships a cabin had been reserved for her. I did not reply; I turned away, leaving her standing there.

All through the night, medics and sailors were carrying the wounded from the trains to a white passenger ship that sailed under the Red Cross flag. After the ship had pulled out, a whaling vessel tied up in its place. It took on the inhabitants of several lost villages, as well as the allowed quantity of baggage, and since it was not yet filled to capacity, a warrant officer came running over to us, quickly counted us off, and indicated who would be taken on board: "Everyone from here on, get on board; the folks over there will just have to be patient." I was not among those chosen, and I was not sorry, since each person was permitted only as much luggage as he could carry on himself. Hardly anyone took the time to say goodbye; they were totally engrossed in deciding which of their bundles they should take along. They seemed to guess that these decisions were crucial, for after this there would be no turning back . . .

Certainly, Martin, but perhaps you yourself realize that it is too easy to phrase the alternative in such terms: people or property. Of course, the last corner on a ship should always be reserved for people, and faced with the choice of saving the luggage, no matter how valuable, or fitting in the people, nowadays I would not hesitate for a moment; not the least of my reasons would be that I have come to recognize how easily one can make do without objects. But at the time I simply could not think of the contents of our museum as my personal property. I felt I did not have the right to let these things be lost or scattered, for these objects that bore witness to our origins and our long path out of the darkness of bygone times belonged to all of us, not just to one person. I saw myself as the guardian of a communal heritage, and I could not simply leave this behind like a basket of linens or a grandfather clock.

The rest of our contingent were apparently situated so handily within sight of the pier that several times smaller groups were taken on board to fill up spare space on large ships. My turn came the next evening. As the turrets of the battle cruiser fired deep into the Samland, as new hospital trains kept pulling in and having to wait for empty transport ships to arrive, as an air raid caused the small armed units to hurry out to the roadstead, Simon Gayko helped me haul my entire baggage to a quiet corner of the harbor basin, where a stocky seagoing tugboat already lay at full steam. On Simon's instructions, all remaining eight of us Lucknowers lugged our things to the tugboat's berth. Simon clambered onto the boat alone and conferred with the pilot. From the way they talked, it was clear they were good friends. It also became clear that our crossing did not depend solely on the good will of the pilot. When he rejoined us, Simon Gayko prepared us for a meeting or a reunion with a man whom he referred to as the Statthalter: "Soon the Statthalter of Lucknow will be here"—more he did not need to say. We knew whom he meant.

Reschat did not appear until the air raid ended. Two limousines pulled up carrying him and his entourage, and without giving us so much as a glance, the man with the golden oakleaves jumped onto the boat and supervised the loading of his suitcases and leather bags. So he had not cared to entrust his safety to the superlative tank ditch dug on his orders. By routes reserved to him and his ilk he had made his way to Königsberg and to Pillau, where, since he could not be expected to wait around, a seaworthy vessel had been put at his disposal.

So he stood there in his long, brown coat, his visored cap stiff on his head, and counted the pieces of his luggage heaved into the tug. None seemed to be missing, for he nodded contentedly, offered the pilot a cigarette, and had him light his in return. He consistently ignored us; presumably we were as uninteresting to him as the long lines waiting patiently on the pier. But the pilot and Simon Gayko pointed us out to him as the last stragglers from Lucknow who, they took care to mention, had in their possession significant items from the Lucknow museum of Masurian history and almost priceless examples of the Masurian rug-weaving art, artifacts they had managed to bring this far and that should not be lost. Then the former Statthalter of Lucknow summoned us to the bridge, wanted to know our names and professions and what had prevented us from being at the front; he called it "the heroically struggling front." Then he gave four of us permission to bring our baggage on board. Besides me, those who were allowed on the boat were Krimkowski, the "lady in blue," and Joseph von Intelmann with his archives.

Yes, Martin, one can't always choose one's traveling companions, and sometimes one has to accept help where one can get it—but enough of that. Those who had been chosen worked together to stow their baggage on the quarter deck; it seemed not to matter that the individual pieces of luggage got mixed up with each other. When the odd-looking heap was finished, we stretched a tarpaulin over it. It seemed not to matter because we felt that from now on we shared a common fate and would find ourselves on the same shore when all this was over. Do you know what I called out to Simon Gayko as we were leaving and he wanted to know where he could expect to find us again? Out of the blue, I promised to leave a message for him in Schleswig, at the Schleswig local history museum, and to my lasting wonder he seemed perfectly satisfied with this address. The pilot waved to him, the hawsers slammed down onto the deck, and as we turned, the bumpers crunched against the quai.

We stood in the sheltered spot under the bridge as the boat chugged between the steamships at anchor and headed out toward the mouth of the harbor.

The arms of huge searchlights raked the sky, transecting each other, forming sheaves, and slicing down over the horizon. In the wake of a camouflaged tanker we glided through the harbor and reached the open sea. Exhausted from the long flight and the many uncertainties, freezing in the clothes we had not changed for days, we nevertheless did not take shelter in the warm crew lounge with its bolted-down tables and benches. Instead, we stayed on deck in a corner somewhat out of the wind and looked back at the land, over which a pale, washed-out red glimmer hovered. Our feeling was less that we had escaped destruction than that this sturdy little boat was taking us westward forever, not only to another world, but to another time as well.

The sea was calm; when toward midnight the sky darkened and snow began to fall thickly, we withdrew to the crew lounge and stretched out on the benches there. No, we had no idea. When I questioned Reschat about our destination, he was evasive, making it sound as though he was still awaiting final orders. Once we spotted a barren stretch of land through the dirty portholes, which Intelmann thought he recognized as the island of Born-holm. From this he concluded that we were headed toward Copenhagen or some Danish island. But after a while we were able to make out a stretch of sand to the portside and decided we must be steering for a port in Pomerania.

The former Statthalter of Lucknow never appeared without his two companions, who were purple of face and seemed pledged to total silence. They could stand on the bridge for hours and stare into the mist or watch the scrabbling little waves in our wake. They were not surprised when Reschat, who had taken over the captain's cabin, came out on deck in the uniform of an infantry captain, a used uniform. He pretended not to notice the impact this change had on the rest of us. After this transformation, it was only a matter of time before his henchmen would exchange their brown party uniforms for the battlefield gray of ordinary soldiers.

Just imagine: shortly after their change of costume, the two of them arrested Intelmann and myself, arrested us with all due form and locked us into a closet. Yes, that's what actually happened . . .

You want to know how it came about? Well, it began after we left the fog bank behind us. We were sailing along in barely ruffled seas when we caught sight of a drifting life raft. Ten or twelve men were on it; when they spotted us, they waved and shouted and fired a signal flare. Several of them began to row, and they moved the inflated yellow vessel so efficiently in our direction that we already had ropes in hand to toss to them. At this point we clearly heard the clicking of our ship's teletype machine. I was not the only one who had the impression that the tug was slowing down and turning in the direction of the raft. A sailor was already throwing down a rope ladder and some of the rowers in the raft were drawing in their oars when a commotion arose on the bridge and immediately afterward the teletype clicked again. The tug speeded up, turned away, and was already sailing past the raft, some of whose occupants stood up, staring in disbelief, as if it were a hallucination. We dropped our ropes and rushed up to the bridge; there stood the pilot, with Reschat's cohorts on either side of him, calmly and inconspicuously holding their revolvers to his sides, while Reschat himself leaned against the compass and stared intently into the distance, as if he had spotted a destination, such a desirable and promising destination that he could afford to disregard the men in the raft.

I need not tell you what rebukes Intelmann and I subjected him to. He listened attentively as always, then gave us to understand that sometimes one had to disregard the normal obligations and regulations in favor of a higher mission—and this was one such case. Moreover, he said, he had the distinct impression that the men on the raft were not in serious danger.

Joseph von Intelmann replied that failure to provide rescue on the high seas could be interpreted as murder. He demanded that the boat turn around at once and pick up the men. Otherwise he would report the matter as soon as we landed. At that Reschat ordered us to leave the bridge. He repeated his order three times in a flat, emotionless voice, and when we refused, he left it to his henchmen to remove us bodily. Not only that: we were under arrest for jeopardizing the completion of a mission. That is how we came to spend the last part of our journey locked into a closet in the aft of the ship, where we felt the vibrations of the screw and were almost deafened by its grinding noise . . .

Just wait a bit, Martin, let me tell you about our arrival; yes, do sit down again, this won't take so long . . .

So we lay there in our cold, unlighted cell and listened, since the tug had begun to slow down. The noise of the screw seemed more bearable now. I was picturing a harbor, a peaceful harbor softly illuminated by the wintry sun, with fishing boats bobbing at their moorings and perhaps a few coastal schooners at the pier. I visualized a black limousine driving down to the dock from the town. There was a clanking as the anchor was let down; the screw churned madly, then stopped.

"They've cast anchor," Intelmann whispered, "they're not tying up." We heard steps on the metal stairways, a thumping on deck as of heavy objects. We tried to interpret each sound. But we could not identify the grating sound, the dull blows up above. The orders being issued were unintelligible. Pieces of luggage fell onto a loose floor board. Apparently someone was scrambling down a rope ladder. Close to the ship a diesel motor started up after several attempts.

Yes, and then we heard quick steps in the corridor and stood up, holding on to each other, prepared to see Reschat's henchmen fling open the closet door and wave us outside. But the man who opened the steel door and held out a hand to us not only gave us time to adjust to the light; he also informed us that it was all over and the situation on board had changed. It was the tug's engineer. We followed him onto the deck. The boat lay at anchor in a calm fjord, with forests reaching down to the water along one side and steep cliffs on the other. On this side, where a steep wooden bridge led up out of the ravine, we saw a fisherman calmly drawing in his eel nets. "Over there, look, there they go in our lifeboat," the engineer said. I followed his pointing finger and there, under the overhanging cliffs, a little gray boat was chugging toward a distant tongue of land.

The pilot, who insisted that we add our names to his report about the incident on the high seas, told us where we were: "This here is the Schlei River, to the west is Schleswig, the town, that is, and over there where the land falls off, by the fishing village of Maasholm, the open sea begins. We've made it this far."

You mustn't think that we were impatient to go ashore, even after this journey and after all we had endured. Everyone wanted to remain on board the tugboat, as long as possible, and you could see them prolonging the necessary preparations and decisions for landing. Our baggage was still scrambled. Leaning over the nautical map, I found the spot where we had anchored, noticed the name Egenlund, and, looking up, saw a stuccoed house with a huge thatched roof and the word EGENLUND painted on its façade. It was a roomy, solid house which seemed to express its builder's intention to stay there and weather all storms. And I recall that for a moment the thought flashed through my mind: perhaps this is where you'll find a refuge . . .

Yes, you're right, that was the house that took me in and that one day belonged to me, or rather was willed to me, because I had cared for its elderly owners until their death, an eccentric veterinarian and his ever-smiling wife. And it was under the beeches in front of that very house that I first saw you.

But what was I going to tell you? Right: when the pilot decided to sail up the Schlei as far as Schleswig, I asked him to let me off with my baggage at the bridge. So we tied up, and they handed my belongings down to me. And only now did I feel a compulsion to check through every box and see what was left. Alone there on the rickety wooden bridge, on a somber, windless afternoon, I sat and took stock and pondered my losses. As I sat there, the fisherman rowed by, and I looked after him and could not quite believe that he could so peacefully lower his nets into the water at a time like this. It was the present, not the past, that struck me as unreal and undecipherable.

Suddenly the veterinarian was there, leaning on his cane. He interrogated me unabashedly. Did I come from far away? Yes, from far away, from Lucknow. Was that a town? Yes, a town in the east, not far from the Polish border. Did I intend to stay in these parts for a while? No, only as long as necessary, only until the end of the war. Was this heap my personal property? Not all of it; much of it consisted of items from the Lucknow local history museum; things which one was reluctant to part with, which one needed in order to live properly.

He asked more and more questions, and then unexpectedly he inquired what I would say to a cup of tea; the baggage would be safe on the bridge. He went on ahead up the path. Yes, Martin, I followed him and did not suspect that I had arrived, not at home, but at the spot for a new beginning.

# 14

Soon they will release me from here; I have another ten days to two weeks, and then I must vacate this bed and this room and look around for another place to stay. I still don't know what I should give as my address—Carola's narrow, crooked little organist's house or the Home for Elderly Men, where Simon Gayko is trying to obliterate his memories—and if neither of these, perhaps just the ashes and charred rubble of Egenlund. I have not yet decided whom I should impose on. As at the end of the war, all my people have been scattered hither and yon, but this time I know where I can find them, which does not mean, to be sure, that we will all come together again in a common enterprise.

Oh, Martin, how easy new beginnings are when need and suffering are commonplace and everyone is in the same boat, and how quickly one finds a direction when one has been deprived for so long. Certainly I did not remain alone for long after my arrival at the house on the cliff.

First there appeared . . . no, let me tell it another way. Let me start with the fish kill that hot summer, when the water in the Schlei turned into thin cauliflower soup, and the water level dropped so low that one could see the algae-covered stack of the submarine that had sunk on the last day of the war. Fish and eels floated to the surface, thrashing feebly, and from everywhere, even from the Holmbek estate, came people with basins and pails to scoop up the exhausted fish. What a scene! People waded out into the water up to their chests, stumbling on the slimy bottom, and the tubs on the shore filled rapidly in spite of the gulls' competition.

As I was struggling toward the shore with my pail of cod and plaice, a head bobbed up in front of me, and out of the shallow water rose a grinning, dripping Simon Gayko, pressing a huge flounder to his chest. He held out the fish to me and said, "What do you think, Zygmunt, how would this fellow taste with May butter?" We waded to land, where he had left his clothes neatly folded: a uniform dyed and converted to civilian style. Only here was I able to produce a suitable greeting; only here did I grasp that he had really come, Simon Gayko, who had picked up the message I had left for him months earlier at the Schleswig museum.

The bowlegged Bosnian was the first one who found his way to me, and I took him along to the big house, where he joined us for a meal consisting of several kinds of fish. We had scarcely done eating when he pulled out his fourteen razor-sharp carving chisels and some pieces of beechwood, which he transformed into marvelous birds, most of them spreading their great tails like peacocks. These he painted and later carried about the countryside in a knapsack, exchanging them for bacon, eggs, and wholegrain bread, with which he paid the ailing veterinarian for his lodgings.

The following spring the white motor launch that occasionally tied up at our bridge to deposit passengers or goods brought us an emaciated man who carried no luggage but had more things hanging from his belt than he could have accommodated in a suitcase —pouches, cans, tin boxes, and the like, which bobbed and jangled with every step he took. I saw him coming over the bridge, not striding along confidently, but meandering hesitantly, as though he expected to be disappointed. As he labored up the path, I could sense his exhaustion, his weakness. It was Marian Jeromin, who had found us with the help of the Missing Persons Bureau. My former pupil was not inclined to talk about the period during which he had disappeared from view. We made up a bed for him under the cobwebby attic window. He just lay there for five days and five nights, dozing and occasionally reading in Sonja Turk's book—aimlessly and with many a sigh, because he simply could not concentrate. And one morning he got up and left the house without telling us what he had in mind. He left right after breakfast and did not return until early evening. He repeated this routine several times, and one evening, when he got home particularly late, he came and woke me to let me know that he had succeeded in locating an old peasant loom and had arranged to buy it in return for the first rug we would weave on it . . .

Yes, Martin, that is how we found each other again and began to establish ourselves in that proud, self-respecting house on the fjord, and not only to establish ourselves: with the consent of the childless elderly couple, we took over the house while they were still alive, turning the largest room into the weaving studio, laying a pipe from the well to the house, enlarging one room to provide a workshop for Simon Gayko. Any sense of impermanence quickly faded; the more we worked on the house and built a life for ourselves, the less we wondered when our time would be up. Even before the first two weaving pupils arrived, we had made up our minds to stay.

One matter that left me no peace was the question of what had happened to Edith and the boy. I found myself missing them more and more as my existence in Egenlund became more satisfying. As I worked at the loom, or walked along the steep banks by the fjord, or slept, I repeatedly saw before me a ghostly image: a woman who dragged a sled through wintry dunes, a sled with a child lying on it, his limp sleeves dragging through the snow. Beneath a lowering sky they were hastening toward a group of dark pine trees.

I had no need to hunt for photographs of them, for I always carried pictures with me. One winter day, sick with uncertainty, I betook myself to the Schleswig office of the Missing Persons Bureau, not really in the hope of good news, merely craving some firm information.

The agency was located in poorly heated rooms under the eaves of a former barracks. The stairwell walls were plastered with notices and posters, and the attic space jam-packed with dossiers, arranged alphabetically on rough wooden shelves in folders, file boxes, even paper bags. Beneath a skylight set into the sloping roof stood an old-fashioned desk with ball feet, and behind the desk sat an accommodating young woman with very light-blue eyes. She wore laced-up boots and a quilted skirt, and in order to free her fingers, she had cut off her knitted gloves at the knuckles. She could lower her voice to a mere breath and still be perfectly audible. As she filled out my search form, she repeatedly nodded encouragingly at me. She looked long and approvingly at the wrinkled photographs of Edith and Paulie, and then she frowned slightly, as if to say that no one should be allowed to go unaccounted for, and she shook my hand as I left in such a way that I was filled with a confidence I had never expected to feel after all this time.

From that day on, I always went to see her whenever I found myself in town, not just to ask if any progress had been made, but to listen to the way she cheered up the others who came to see if a brother, a husband, or a son could be located. One of the key questions she asked was: "Where was he when you last had word of him?" and you should have heard how far and wide the war had scattered people. As if all the place names were familiar to her, she filled in the data, pasted on photographs, and quickly composed printable biographies. Anyone who had been to see her left with the feeling that a call would at once go out through all the lands to find the missing person. "Who can provide information on So-and-so?" asked the posters designed then and there at her desk.

Yes, and one time when I went up to see her, I met an old man on the staircase. It was close to the end of office hours, and as always, I let the other person go ahead of me. The old man held himself upright, and he was smoking some substance whose smell reminded me of mildewed mattresses. Although dressed as though he had escaped from an internment camp in the east, he sat there like one accustomed to giving orders. How circumstantially he untied a bundle of documents he had brought with him! How firmly he pushed a filled-out search form across the desk! The woman read what was written on the card, brought out a folder, glanced into it to make sure, and looking straight at the old man, she named a ship and the date and hour and place where it had been torpedoed. There were said to be more than two thousand refugees on board, most of them from the Memel region. The military escort vessels had rescued only one hundred and eighty.

She said all this very softly, without taking her eyes off the man. He did not sigh or give any sign of sorrow such as would have been natural. But his lips began to tremble, and his fluttering fingers could not manage to tie the string around his documents. Finally, he asked us for a sheet of paper and a pen. He seemed to have long before thought through what he had to write, for he barely hesitated. After he had placed the message in an envelope and sealed it and handed it wordlessly to the woman, he pulled a hunting knife out of the lining of his jacket and stabbed himself in the chest.

Later, Martin, I often wondered whether he would have done the same had the news been given to him differently, for much depends on how such terrible information is transmitted. But I have not found an answer. I assume that the old man had planned everything carefully, from the writing of the testament to the thrust of the hunting knife. By the way, he willed all his possessions—his sewing kit, tin cup, spoon and fork, and stocks in a fish-processing plant in the Memel region—to the Missing Persons Bureau. You will not be surprised to hear that after this episode the young woman was no longer employed at the Schleswig office.

After the authorities had attended to the matter, the two of us remained alone in the cold attic room. I coaxed her from her chair and guided her carefully down the stairway; again and again I had to reassure her that it was not her fault. Not that she blamed herself; yet the question remained whether this act of desperation would have occurred if she had been less explicit.

In front of a crooked half-timbered house she stopped and fished a key out of her pocket. She opened the door and waved me in as if we had agreed I would come along. From the upper story a man's voice called out, "Is that you?" and the woman answered, "Yes, who else would it be?" I would have preferred to say goodbye then and there, but she urged me to come upstairs, and we scrambled up a steep little staircase to a tiny parlor where a delicately made man wrapped in blankets was sitting copying music by the light of a votive lamp. The floor creaked with every step. The room was filled with fragile little chairs. Before the man put aside the blankets, he pointed to the paper-thin, almost translucent cups and plates on a little table and complained that he had never had to wait teatime this long.

And while the woman fetched a third cup from a cupboard, we introduced ourselves to each other, and less out of suspicion than out of sincere curiosity he asked me a few quick questions, some of which struck me as downright indiscreet: Where was I living presently? What was my job, my marital status, the condition of my health? "Father," said the young woman, that one word full of reproof. She reminded him of the bottle of rum he had been saving, and he grudgingly brought it out. As he placed the bottle on the table, he actually said, "This we owe to our frugality; you pour, Carola, there mustn't be any spillage."

Yes, Martin, that was how I came to drink to my future wife, and to a father-in-law who was not much older than I. We talked over the afternoon's events once more. We made no specific arrangements for seeing each other again.

But soon after this, on a Sunday, when Marian and I were having our usual Sunday quarrel . . .

What about? Oh, it was always the same question. Whereas I upheld the tradition of the craft, loyalty to the established conventions and techniques, Marian wanted our pupils to give free rein to their imagination; surface texture, color, and imagery should be there for their own sake, an expression of personal feeling and vision. Their creative impulses should take precedence over historical conventions. All I could do was remind him that in the beginning Masurian rugmaking (and not only Masurian) had drawn no distinction between art and craft, and that the weaving apprentices had made things intended to be admired, to be sure, but meant primarily to be used; first you have your materials and their function, only later elevated feelings. As I said, we were wrangling again when suddenly I saw Carola go by. When she reached the door, she stood there, looking uncertainly at the house, probably hoping that someone would notice her presence. She carried something rolled up under her arm which she was bringing to me, "to thank you for your help." At first she did not want to come in, but who can withstand when a Marian Jeromin insists. Over coffee she unrolled the print; it was a reproduction of an eighteenth-century print of Lucknow—how jumbled it all was, how pathetically narrow the houses, clustered together as if for protection. Saddlers' Lane was tinted in azure, Potters' Lane in light brown. The castle of the Teutonic Order sat stolidly on its island, defending the lake, and from the Borek hunters emerged, shouldering roebuck they had shot.

This was my first view of Lucknow since leaving—the print came from an old calendar featuring "Towns and Cities of the East," and because everything was so unformed, because Lucknow was just in the process of taking shape, I found myself involuntarily completing and revising the picture, filling in details from memory, passing in review Little Grajevo, Castle Hill, the marketplace, and recalling the pedestal of the Bosnian commander, where I had lain with Edith, listening to the June bugs bumping against the bronze. We found a frame for the picture and hung it up in the weaving studio.

That same Sunday, thinking about Lucknow led us to open the seldom-visited room where all the rescued objects from the museum were stored. After being shown the weaving studio and Simon's workshop, Carola entered the room alone, while we watched from the doorway. Full of astonishment, she tentatively ran her fingers over the old wooden household implements, the rusty weapons, rag rugs in all the colors of the rainbow, a Sudauese funerary urn, the dust-catching black stork, the Sokolken box. As she looked inquiringly at the objects in crates, you could see that she was burning to unpack them; she seemed amazed that all these fascinating items should be kept hidden. "You have almost enough to set up a museum here," she said. "Yes," I replied. "This shouldn't be allowed to languish this way," she said. "It's not languishing," Marian answered, "it's just resting." "Many people would certainly love to be able to see all this," she said. "'Twasn't the time for it," said Simon. "But now the time has come," she said.

It was her enthusiasm that showed us our next task. Even before she proposed the idea, I found myself dreaming of the collection displayed and organized, endowed with new power to bear witness, and not just in a room or a storeroom but in a building of its own. It would be a small but stylistically appropriate building by the cliff, under the red beeches, a house with an inviting wooden veranda, a Masurian bower house. It should serve a single purpose: to receive everything which characterized the land of our origins, everything which helped illustrate its uniqueness and its history and which explained why it had been lost and under what circumstances we had been forced to leave.

That same evening I found myself sketching out a design. I

could hardly believe what sheer distance and the impossibility of a return could do. Never before had I seen Masuria so concretely before me, never before had I been able to analyze its secret essence, a mixture of obstinacy and humility, with such ease. In any case—what was I going to say? Oh, yes, our wedding present. When the motorboat brought us back from town on our wedding day, Carola spotted from the landing a loaded rack wagon waiting for us by the house. It was spring, and the wagon was decorated with leafy birch branches and garlands. Simon Gayko, who in legendary times had been my wedding bidder, sat astride one of the phlegmatic Holstein oxen. He was dressed in black and his Bosnian inscrutability was so thick that he looked more like a statue than a living human being. As we approached, he called out some rhyme to us which even I did not understand, something for good luck which contained references to rabbit paws and duck feathers, cock's comb and owl's light. And after Marian, at Simon's bidding, had placed a handsomely carved cradle at Carola's feet, Simon gestured to me to climb up on the wagon. "Well, Zygmunt," he said, "so now you're standing on your museum."

He thumped the hand-hewn tree trunks that had been smoothed into beams, drummed on the boards which had been trimmed perfectly to size, showed me the precut windowframes, and the mortised-and-tenoned exterior members, which had already been painted with creosote. "When you give the word to begin, we'll start building; this is my wedding present to you." Up there on top of the load we shook hands, and when we picked up the first beam to throw it off the wagon, it was intended only as a symbolic gesture. But others were already scrambling up to help, tugging at the lumber, seeing who could unload the cargo the fastest. And if you want to know what was the happiest moment in this marriage, it came while we were unloading the materials for our museum.

But let me tell you what else happened. Although Marian and I had told Carola plenty about the country from which we came, she was still not satisfied. Soon after the wedding, while the bow-legged Bosnian dug out the cellar and poured the concrete foundation and erected the wooden veranda, Carola began to make regular trips to Schleswig, where she combed through libraries and secondhand bookstores for literature on Masuria. And you should have seen what she happily dragged home: novels, yearbooks, war memoirs, forestry and fishing periodicals, a book on "Masurian humor," another with "Masurian recipes." She dug up travelers' accounts, stories, and even a play, all of which she devoured, in order, as she jokingly expressed it, "to learn what sort of people" she was mixed up with. She kept a folder of newspaper clippings on the windowsill near her bed and constantly added to it. She carefully studied the radio programs and marked every item that had to do with the "lost homeland."

One afternoon she came bursting into the weaving studio in such excitement that we were at once prepared to hear some extraordinary news. Without a word she handed me the radio program and pointed with her pencil to the heading "Lost Homeland." As I was reading the title for the second time, Carola asked, "Isn't that him? Mustn't that be the Konrad Karrasch you've told me so much about? And look at his topic: 'Thoughts about Lucknow.' Shouldn't we listen to that?"

We whistled to Simon Gayko to come down from the scaffolding, and we all hurried into the living room and turned on the radio. I listened so hard to his voice that I could not concentrate on what he was saying: only after we had had a shot of brandy was I able to take in his words. "Our Conny," Simon whispered. "Any guy who sounds like that must be in good shape." No doubt about it: the voice was Conny's. But the longer I listened, the harder I found it to believe it was really our Conny, for this Conny was pleading a case I could never, in all the time I had known him, have imagined his espousing.

He conjured up a heritage, a historical and cultural heritage. A distant town called Lucknow was cited as an example. Here was a place, a way of life, which, once established, could prevail through the ages, buffeted, to be sure, by the winds of fate, plundered, ravaged, conquered by various neighbors, but indestructible in its innermost core, for the simple reason that the "city was borne in the hearts" of its inhabitants. He pointed out that possessing anything could take many forms, and that the homeland should not be considered lost until no one spoke of it any longer or it had been forgotten. He defined homeland as the locus of wordless ties: ties to custom, language, landscape, and the recognizable accomplishments of earlier generations. He spoke of "pride of homeland." A person deprived of his homeland was more wretched than one afflicted with misery and poverty, he found; and any person sincere about preserving peace, Conny said in conclusion, must grant a "right to one's homeland."

You can imagine how hard it was to recognize my sardonic old Conny in this speaker, but at the end of the program the announcer gave his name. That same day I wrote to him, in care of the station. I gave a detailed account of our tragic flight, of how Marian and Simon and I had found each other, and of what we were up to now. I sent along a photograph to give him an idea of our house. But I received no reply. The letter was not returned, but neither did I hear from Conny . . .

Meanwhile, work on the museum continued. The old veterinarian and his wife died, and the house and grounds became ours, although the will was contested by relatives for four years. But long before we could properly call our new home our own, the museum was completed—the first, and so far as I know, the only museum of Masurian history. The wooden exterior was finished with clear varnish and gleamed in the sun. The wood itself had been cut and worked entirely by Simon; it came from a little forest nearby, and in spite of the knots and cracks, one could see how hard and durable it was. Even if the building appeared modest by contrast with the imposing house nearby, its form always aroused interest. As boats passed, people would come out of the control room to point it out: "Just take a look at that!"

We gave names to all the little rooms, with their shelves and tables; there was the Document Room, the Jewelry Room, the Prehistoric Collection. We displayed the weapons and the toys in "chambers," and the animals and relics of local customs were given "corners." Handsome single pieces that would catch the eye were displayed against the wooden wall, and some smaller objects dangled from wires from the ceiling.

Great was our pleasure and our satisfaction when we finally gave our memories of Lucknow a home. We were delighted to see how much still remained to us. And we made the exciting discovery that our memory could find its way back to the lost town, but that the town itself kept changing as we recalled it to life; for the first time I realized that every past one reconstructs contains a good measure of invention. To be sure it was still Lucknow we reconstructed, but one could not deny that it was both richer and poorer than the actual town had been.

The inauguration of the museum did not go as we would have wished. Had it been up to us, we would have chosen some Sunday morning for making a ceremonial tour of the rooms, then we would have had black pudding on the veranda and later Masurian pastries, and that evening we would have sat down with a bottle of Nikolaschka to go over all the old stories which we never tired of hearing, with slight variations.

But the Schleswig newspaper made sure that the inauguration of the museum did not remain a local affair. A series of articles with photographs helped magnify the occasion, which later a number of people did not hesitate to call a "great day."

So you must picture garlands, blue and white flags, and pine boughs decorating the veranda, a little band made up of former graduates of the Lucknow Firemen's Academy, also the so-called Lucknow Youth, for the most part straw-blond teenage boys and girls in traditional Masurian costumes, as well as the Council of Elders of the Lucknow Homeland Association, which had long since been reconstituted, without our having heard anything about it out there in Egenlund. The Council of Elders was behaving as such groups do when waiting for the arrival of a representative from the state government. The local press seemed well pleased with the combination of brandy and sliced liverwurst. Out on the Schlei bobbed sailboats and rowboats attracted to the spot by the sight of the gathering up on the cliff. I must not forget to mention the hastily knocked-together tables and benches under the red beeches, or the rented field kitchen in which the former chef from the Hotel Queen Luise had been simmering tripe with marjoram for several hours...

Acquaintances? . . . Oh, you wonder whether any old acquaintances turned up. You'll be amazed to hear how many people felt it necessary to journey to Egenlund for the opening of the museum. By the way, many of them had heard of the event through the newly founded newspaper, the *Lucknow Messenger*, which we likewise saw for the first time that day. You probably realize that although we had planned to set up the museum, the program for this particular event had slipped from our hands. We had been shunted aside with the explanation that this event had a significance far beyond the merely private, and in the end we had to stand by helpless while the Council of Elders of the Lucknow Homeland Association drew up and printed the seven-point program, including the entertainment portion. Once again we almost had the impression that the museum no longer belonged to us. But enough of that.

When the modest vehicle of the representative from the state government pulled up under the red beeches, the Council of Elders moved forward hesitantly to greet him. Przytulla led the procession, his hands clasped mildly over his paunch. Simon Gayko and I were allowed to follow. The government representative appeared bareheaded and wearing a dark pinstripe suit. He was helped out by the chauffeur and stood there alone for a moment, looking helpless and embarrassed. Not until he could put one arm over the shoulder of the chauffeur did he advance toward us with a smile, or rather, he was half carried toward us and shook hands attentively with everybody, although I did have the feeling he shook my hand a bit longer than the others.

Not effortlessly but skillfully the chauffeur carried the double amputee—he was missing an arm and a leg—up the steps to the veranda. There he leaned him against the balustrade and straightened his jacket, while the man raised his gaunt face and intently surveyed the audience gathering round. I, too, looked down at the crowd and suddenly recognized Krimkowski, the former fire-fighter general, and Joseph von Intelmann, former chief of the Lucknow detective division. They were laughing together, finding more and more things to laugh about. Over by the well, all by himself, stood a man who resembled Toni Lettkow.

After the words of welcome, the band earned a scattering of applause for Gluck's "Joy Resounds with Festive Sounds," and then the representative of the state government spoke. He brought greetings and best wishes from his colleagues, who were of one mind in viewing this event in Egenlund as an expression of justified longing. The state government, he declared, found itself in full agreement on the point that nothing was truly lost so long as it remained the object of our longing. In that sense the "land of dark forests and crystal lakes" was likewise not permanently lost.

What did we mean by longing? he asked, and he answered his own question: We longed for something unattainable or absent, which was not, however, the same as irrevocably gone. To long, he said softly, was to turn back the hands of time and bring the object of our longing into our present. To cross boundaries in order to take possession or to be taken into possession: that was another sense of longing. But above all, he saw in longing those forms of expectation and yearning which determined every wish-dream. Anything that no longer found a place in our longing was dead and gone, he asserted, and in this sense he wished to speak of Egenlund and of the museum established there as a place where longing had become an active force. "Why are we here?" he asked, and again he answered his own question: "To celebrate something created out of longing." But what testified here to the old homeland he could not regard as a substitute, for substitutes are always suspect; rather, he said, persistent longing had succeeded here in giving form to the dream of the homeland.

With narrowed eyes and stony face he let the applause roll over him. He did not seem surprised at it. We were already shifting our weight to the other leg and looking toward Przytulla, who according to the program was to speak next on "Our Lucknow: Yesterday, Today, and Tomorrow," when the representative from the state government began to speak again, softly. He wanted, he said, to make a few personal remarks of a purely confessional nature. Throughout history, he said, people had been deprived of their native lands. There had been no epoch without its exiles, its refugees, its banished peoples. People had always been forced from home, to wander in foreign lands, and they had survived only if they had ceased to see the past as their only truth. After Biblical typhoons, after the blind outbursts of rage and madness that characterized history, many people once swept away had never found their way back. Everyone had respected their sorrow for what they had lost, but everyone had also hoped they would show themselves ready to forge new ties in their adopted lands.

He went on, "Your beautiful homeland is not unknown to me. I was severely wounded in the charming town of Dippelsee, only a few miles from Lucknow. It was the last winter of the recent war. In Lucknow itself I received the transfusions that saved my life. A lovely town, a lovely, quiet region. Already tens of thousands of Poles have been born in Masuria, people who now regard this land as their own homeland and indeed must do so; for who would want to tear it away from them again? I know your lovely land," he said again; "now it is a neighboring country. We are not indifferent to it, but the true task that lies before us is this: to transform our longing for the old homeland into new neighborliness."

No protest was voiced, but a pained hush fell. People exchanged looks of astonishment and indignation; it was clear that these words were considered thoroughly out of place at a moment like this. The representative from the state government was not disconcerted by the silence. He simply sat down on one of the canvas chairs and wiped the sweat from his brow.

If you recall the arguments between Przytulla and Joseph von Intelmann during our flight, you will guess that the next speaker, Przytulla, served up an entirely different message. Our museum, he said, represented not an expression of longing but a proof of loyalty to the lost soil of the homeland, the temporarily lost soil, as he put it. He found that loyalty had always been rewarded, simply because "no misfortune lasts forever," and because any misfortune created by human beings could be corrected by human beings.

Unfortunately, he went on, he also had to regard the existence of this museum as a silent refutation; for the documents and the entire inventory of the museum refuted those who viewed Masuria not as their booty of war but as reconquered territory. Any people that believed this land had been uncontestedly theirs from time immemorial was invited to come to the mute witnesses in the museum and learn the truth. After a quotation from Kant, after alluding to the moral and creative forces engendered by the sense of homeland, after a description of past and present conditions in Lucknow, Przytulla mentioned the Polish territorial losses to the east and the initial incredulity of the Polish settlers who were told that the new land they had received in the west was to be theirs for keeps. Then he concluded his speech with the public vow to preserve and protect the rich heritage of Lucknow's past and to keep it alive in everyone's memory. "Our museum of Masurian history," he said, "is already part of this vow."

Who knows how long the applause would have lasted had the band not struck up Lortzing's wooden-shoe plattler from "Czar and Carpenter" to conclude the speeches. The next item on the program was a tour of the museum. I was supposed to act as guide . . .

Really? So the newspaper archives have photos of the occasion . . .

And Henrike got hold of them and had them enlarged? . . . She mounted them in an album? . . . Then I presume you have looked through them, and there is a picture among them of a certain encounter, perhaps even of an embrace, at the sight of which I had to close my eyes and hold my breath . . .

You did not notice any such picture? Well, then I will have to tell you what happened right at the beginning of the official tour. We had just looked at the blotched and discolored old documents and were moving on to the jewelry room, which also held the ceremonial costumes, when I suddenly spotted a face, half concealed behind one of the costumes, a face which on this day of all days I had not been prepared for. The words froze on my lips, and I could not even move in the direction of that face, that older but still smooth face of the former Statthalter of Lucknow. So Reschat, the man with the golden oakleaves, was also on hand for the opening of our museum of Masurian history. He conducted himself with uncharacteristic modesty, and his appearance scotched a number of rumors that had sprung up concerning his probable fate: for instance, that he had been caught by the British and upon the Poles' request sent to Warsaw for trial; that he had been in hiding disguised as a woodsman and had committed suicide upon being exposed; that he had escaped to South America and risen to new power and prosperity there.

So there he stood, moved if not overwhelmed by the occasion, making no effort to be noticed; he actually seemed to have come in order to be quietly transported into another time and place. Yes, and then I noticed that Duddek was a few steps behind him, the former local physician with his quaking dewlap and his shapeless lips, whose contours seemed to have been rubbed away with

sandpaper—Dr. Anton Duddek, who had been sent to the Kreuzborn concentration camp in the last months of the war and had
emerged from it with his face partially paralyzed. In a moment, I
thought, the old doctor will brush past the Statthalter, in a moment they will both look up and recognize each other and stand
there frozen, swept by memories and resolutions, and even if the
Statthalter has forgotten the part he played in the doctor's life,
the doctor will certainly not have forgotten.

Well, and then they did bump into each other and turn around.
They recognized each other at once, just as if they had anticipated this moment countless times, and I would have expected
anything but what occurred: their hands reached out, a smile
gradually formed on both their faces, and then, as though their
memories had retained nothing, they embraced, and for longer
than was customary, too.

I speeded up my tour, cut short my explanations, even left out
some points altogether, constantly dreading that the two, who
now seemed inseparable, might push their way to the front and
try to speak to me—you can imagine why. When at the end of
the tour I stood at the door to receive everyone's thanks and
congratulations, I could not shake hands with Reschat. I simply
overlooked his outstretched hand. I heard him saying, "You have
done the homeland proud," but I could not bring out any reply; I
just thought to myself: And you did your bit for the falsification
and the loss of the homeland. Those hermit crabs, each of them
inside his shell of memories: they met and mingled at the museum
as though nothing stood between them. Overwhelmed by a past
they did not even grasp, they simply forgot there were any accounts to be settled . . .

I know your doubts, Martin, but you must take my word for it
that the objects we had collected conveyed something that
affected us all deeply. The day of the inauguration enabled some
of our fellow countrymen to return, in dreams, in secret, to the
lost town. We had the sense that we all shared something, something that belonged to us alone, an indivisible treasure of allusions
and customs.

Did I mention that we had set up a temporary dance floor
under the red beeches?

Yes, Simon had smoothed out the ground and laid boards, had

stretched cords between the trees from which hung homemade paper lanterns shaped like pears, apples, and cucumbers. As dusk fell, the band struck up the dance music. Down below, along the banks of the Schlei, boats tied up wherever they could, and people returning from boat trips or water sports scrambled up to join us and strolled about amused between the field kitchen, the dance floor, and the illuminated museum, although they could not partake of our high spirits. The music did not stir them, even the mazurka which Marian Jeromin requested and then led, giving the signal for slapping the ankles and stomping the feet. How gallantly he caught Carola every time she seemed about to collapse with exhaustion! How challengingly he looked at her as she came toward him! When the two of them danced, even the Council of Elders paused in its cud-chewing deliberations. "New Lucknow," Przytulla suddenly called out to me; "how would it be if we founded New Lucknow here, in Egenlund," and from then on I had to think of that name whenever I looked at the dancers and the eaters and the folks dredging up their memories at the tables and beneath the listening trees. That name, just tossed out that way, seemed to carry a promise.

But what else was it you wanted to hear about? Oh, yes, the other music, the party which the so-called Lucknow Youth wanted to celebrate on its own, late, after many people had already left, after they had thanked us profusely and promised to come back soon. As if upon a secret signal the young men and women in their blue and white costumes got up, one or two at a time, and strolled off, not in any great rush, but with a clear purpose. They slipped into the museum through the back door and had the place to themselves. The electric lights were out, and all that could be seen was the glow of candles behind the checked curtains, which they had drawn. At a certain point I felt I had to look into this conspiratorial gathering. I walked toward the museum in the shadow of the beeches, so that no one noticed me, and I managed to open the door silently and stand there behind the felt curtain that served as a windbreak . . .

Pardon me? Oh, all right, I'll let you guess what was going on.

Yes, exactly; they had appropriated some bottles and a few platters of bread and cold cuts . . .

Right, they were dancing, to phonograph records; yes, it may have been Glenn Miller, I wouldn't know. But you should have seen the way they danced—fiercely, acrobatically, pitilessly, or else with a kind of obscene languor, their open mouths pressed against one another's, their movements like deep-sea plants in a gentle current . . .

You like that kind of dancing? Oh, well, as far as I'm concerned, let everyone do what feels best to him; all I'm saying is that I found it peculiar. I would not have objected, if only they hadn't made free with the museum pieces, slipping the scimitar and the two-handed sword into their belts, putting on the historic costumes. A plump girl was sitting on the floor cracking nuts with an old Masurian rolling pin. A group was sitting as if in a trance around the Sudauese funerary urn, which they were using as an ashtray.

Yes, Martin, and as I stood there, feeling not so much angry as hurt, yes, hurt, I heard someone calling my name: "Zygmunt, where are you? Zygmunt, company for you!" but I could not budge. I just stood there, feeling hurt and downcast, and then I heard shouts from the veranda, and a moment later the front door of the museum flew open, and there, illuminated by the candles which flickered in the evening breeze, stood Conny, Konrad Karrasch, with a package under his arm.

With what calm he took in the entire scene, and what a reprimand he expressed in the way he surveyed the assembled Lucknow Youth. Shamefacedly they pulled themselves together, tried to replace the museum pieces where they had found them, and gathered up their plates and bottles under Conny's steady gaze. Now and then he pointed to something he wanted picked up or removed. When he finally stood aside, they trotted obediently through the door. "I should hope so," Conny remarked. "This is not a haymow."

So there he was, with his package under his arm, and you should have seen us move toward each other across the entire length of the museum, slowly at first, then faster and faster, and before we shook hands we actually pummeled each other lightly on the chest: "Is it really you? Really?" "Yes, Conny." "Well, well, Zygmunt." He handed me the package, saying, "A contribution for the wonderful work you're doing here. It won't be the only one."

I could not take my eyes off him as I loosened the string. What he had brought me was a piece of inlay work, the most beautiful piece of inlay we ever had in our museum. It was a small panel from an old Masurian peasant wardrobe, blue with delicate tendrils. Red and white flowers framed a central medallion, where, surrounded by budding leaves, a man and a woman walked toward each other, arms outstretched. Conny's car had broken down on the way and he had had to reach us by bus, arriving much too late for the opening. Now he asked me to give him a private tour of our museum. Almost at once he found a spot for the piece: "Here, Zygmunt, it would look nice here, wouldn't it?" and he stood back with his head slightly tilted and admired the effect.

As we went through, every item seemed worthy of his attention. He touched some of them dreamily; others, which he thought he recognized, he winked at. He patted them as though he was greeting old friends. He snapped pictures and took notes. Finally, I had to ask him, "What's this about, Conny? You aren't planning to write something on the opening, are you?" He put his hand on my shoulder and genially wagged a finger at me, as if to warn me not to hold him to something that was no longer true. "Yes, Zygmunt, that's why I'm here. You'll have no cause for complaint; our museum will be described as what it is, the most important and comforting establishment of its kind." And before he was through, he had me subscribe to the homeland newspaper which he had founded and of which he was chief editor; place of publication: Lüneburg, independent, non-sectarian . . .

Yes, Martin, the paper still goes on, though it no longer appears weekly but rather every two weeks, probably because everything one can say about Lucknow has already been said a dozen times over. Readers can guess exactly which topics will come up when. The article on the summer regatta will be followed by the one on the autumn hunt, the love song to our tiled stoves promises a think piece on the Masurian rug-weaving art in the next issue, with the obligatory paean to Sonja Turk. But enough of that; the insect trapped in amber cannot be made to fly again.

I must tell you how that very evening Conny persuaded the Council of Elders to establish a Lucknow medal, a stylized shield with a cross in the middle and three leaping fish above it, and suggested that I be the first recipient. The proposal was accepted without dissent and a date fixed for the awarding of the medal. I still remember how Conny insisted on being the first to congratulate me, with a formality that made me uncomfortable. For I often felt uncertain or uneasy when it came to interpreting his actions or deciding whether his words should be taken at face value. Do you see what I mean? I simply did not know what to make of it when he went into the children's room and kissed the sleeping Henrike and pressed a two-mark piece into Bernhard's clenched fist and congratulated me on "these children." And he told Carola in my presence, "When need be, we Masurians always find a way out." What in the world did he mean by that?

But anyway, after I had shown him the house and we had had a few drinks with Marian and Simon, we went into the weaving studio and sat down by the open window in that indecisive darkness which, as you know, is characteristic of summer nights on the Schlei. "Well, Conny." "Hm, Zygmunt."

Ridden by memories as we were, how quickly we traced things back to the last time we had seen each other—that coffee break on snowy Castle Hill when our former classmate came to fetch Conny, to take him to Goldap.

And looking out into the light fog over the Schlei, Conny described his adventures in Goldap, and how the Russian soldiers relieved him of his handcuffs and his watch and, after going through the entire villa, shoved him into the mailroom, where they made him open all the packages sent by soldiers' families. He had to hold the contents up to the light and taste all the liquor to make sure it was safe for them to drink. Finally, they took him outside and had him join a band of prisoners who were marching past, hands clasped behind their necks.

Conny, the civilian, tramped along with the military prisoners through the destroyed town and out into the snowy fields; they marched parallel to the roads and highways, jammed with columns of reinforcements, artillery, and tank divisions. Whirling snow muffled the men's groans. They were forbidden to speak, and it was each man for himself.

But as they passed through a sparse forest, an older soldier spoke softly to Conny. This was his second time in Russian captivity, and he simply wanted Conny to know that it was not advantageous to be dressed as a civilian in this situation. He had no need to say more. From then on Conny tried to stay in the middle of the group, even after sunset. At night they were led to a barn, where they spread out whatever hay they could find and crept into it, then lay chewing the bread crusts the Russian guards had tossed to them before closing and barring the door. Conny could not sleep. Near dawn he was lying there wide awake when he recognized the voice of the older soldier. He got up and followed the moving shadow.

He was led to a crooked ladder, and a poke in the side indicated he was to climb up it. There in the loft lay the body of a soldier who had hanged himself from a beam. All his clothes had already been stripped off except for his underwear. The older soldier, who had followed Conny up the ladder, again nudged him, whereupon Conny undressed and put on the soldier's quilted pants, his jacket, boots, and coat. They clothed the dead man in civilian dress. By the light of a match Conny read the papers, memorizing his new name and serial number and the unit to which he had been assigned. Then they tore up the man's pay book and stuffed the scraps and the dog tag between the loose planks of the loft floor.

The prisoners marched eastward for five days. At first no notice was taken of their names or their units, but before being loaded into a freight car they had to pass through a barracks where military clerks listed the relevant data and their gear was checked expertly and suitably lightened. Conny was registered as Robert Feller, former corporal in a so-called maintenance company; he boarded a train which unhurriedly clicked along through vast wintry spaces; soon they gave up counting the nights they spent on sidings in the middle of nowhere. When the older soldier died, apparently no one remained who knew about Conny's switch of identity; the other soldiers displayed the same indifference toward Conny that they showed to each other.

Conny described the prison camps, camps of the sort everyone knows from somewhere or other, huddled outposts in the midst of endless stretches of desolation, with wooden towers looming over them. He marched in, was assigned a cot identical to the one he had had at the last place, determined the prevailing hierarchy among the prisoners, and gained advantages for himself by vol-

unteering for any job that came up. Under his assumed name he
was willing to try anything. If at roll call a medic's aide was asked
for, Conny stepped forward. If they needed an electrician, a
mason, an assistant to the camp clerk, Conny raised his arm and
was excused from the work of the other prisoners. He escaped
the constant supervision by the guards and could avoid the roll
calls; he did not have to leave the camp before daybreak, returning from hard labor only after nightfall. Several times he was
transferred to even more isolated camps, and each time, he
thought, he left a piece of himself behind. He was growing into
his new name and identity. He remembered with gratitude the
older soldier who had found him his uniform, for in the meantime he had had occasion to see the automatic suspicion to which
civilians on the front were subject, and what followed from that.

When the first lists of prisoners to be shipped home were
drawn up, Conny had no difficulty finding out that his name was
on them. He gave away his secret hoard of razor blades, his
writing paper, and his two homemade knives. But before the
transport was put together, the Russians did a final thorough
check. They summoned each prisoner to the commandant's
office, not so much to obtain new information as to confirm
information already a matter of record. Conny slipped through
the nets of their questions and they had already called the next
prisoner when an observer inquired once more about the number
of Conny's unit and then asked where he had been stationed
during a certain autumn.

At random, Conny said, he named a place in the Ukraine,
whereupon the observer without a word shoved his papers over
to the commandant, who glanced through them, handed them on,
and finally quietly called in a guard. Conny had miscalculated by
about 185 miles, and not only that; he had not known that the
maintenance company had been involved that fall in a punitive
operation against civilians, deep in the hinterland.

After receiving his sentence—twenty-five years at hard labor—
Conny was transported to a camp located at the fork of two
rivers, a forgotten camp, Conny said, surrounded by the silence
of primeval forests and several days' march from the nearest
railroad station. The commandant, a short, stocky, melancholy
man—him, too, one felt one knew from somewhere—seemed to

view his assignment as a sort of exile, and he vented his ill humor on the prisoners. The prisoners came from all over Europe; there were Spaniards, Dutchmen, and Danes among them, most of the men sentenced by military courts to terms of ten, twenty, or twenty-five years. Conny found himself assigned to a group of Hungarians. He set up his cot among theirs, and winter and summer he marched with them to the woods, where they had to fell gigantic trees with nothing but handsaws, wedges, and axes, according to an inflexible quota.

Conny described the Hungarians' spokesman or elder, to whom the others were devoted. When the elder stepped in, quarrels were appeased; he had advice for those who needed it, and for those in despair he always found strengthening words. Beside that, he was skilled with his pencil.

Even after a hard day's work, his hands sticky with resin, he would take his pencil, find some light to see by, and invite one of his countrymen to describe the region he came from, with its landmarks and secret places, the features no one forgets. As the man spoke, he would be sketching rivers and vineyards, plains, ponds, and cottages. He would keep on asking if he had it right, modifying the picture if necessary, coming closer and closer to an accurate image. Many of the pictures shared a certain quality of stillness; something seemed to be waiting, holding its breath.

Each of the Hungarians had such a picture, no bigger than a postcard. Some men carried their pictures around between two pieces of cardboard, others pinned them over their cots. Out of politeness or compassion, Conny, too, was asked to describe the place he wanted fixed on paper, and he decided against the well-known silhouette of Lucknow and asked instead for Castle Hill and the seven giant spruces.

Then came a winter so cold that the birds dropped dead from the trees, and the Hungarians' elder fell ill. Since the hospital was already overcrowded, he was taken straight to the room for the dying. After work the prisoners went all together to see him, but he wanted to speak with each one separately; sometimes he would keep a visitor with him an entire evening, so that almost three weeks passed before each had seen him. No one would say what had been discussed.

And then their elder died, and the Hungarians buried him in

the camp cemetery, where the two rivers joined, and they tended and decorated his grave through all the seasons. It was no surprise, considering their feeling for the dead man, that when they unexpectedly were given their release the Hungarians asked the commandant to allow them to take their leader's remains with them. The commandant refused, and instead of the Hungarians the Rumanians were shipped home, long before their terms were up. The Hungarians salvaged some hardwood and pieces of tin from the camp workshop and made a sort of coffin, which they set up in the middle of their barracks.

Soon they were called again, and again passed over because they refused to forsake the grave of their elder, and nothing would shake their resolve, not a higher work quota, not reduced rations, not the various hardships the melancholy commandant invented for them.

Conny inquired cautiously of individuals among them, and discovered that they had all promised their elder of their own free will that they would not leave without him; they believed that this was what was expected of them by their kinfolk. And they stuck to it. For Conny this proved that Hungarians could tolerate punishment better than other nationalities. The fifth time they were called they threatened to stage a hunger strike if their only wish was not met, and this time the commandant capitulated. Soon after their departure Conny was assigned to a train headed for the west. The Russians impressed it upon him that he owed this extraordinary reduction in his sentence solely to the generosity of the Soviet government . . .

Yes, Martin, I asked him that, too: how he shook off his acquired name and identity, for which he had paid so dear. Had some incident made him decide to give it up? During the weeklong train trip, Conny said, he could not reach a decision. He registered at the transit camp under the name of Feller, and was released under that name to go to Hanover, where he found the undamaged house with a brass plate on its gate: HEINRICH FELLER AND SON, PATENT ATTORNEYS. Instead of entering, he went into an empty little bar across the way, ordered a few beers, gazed over at the house through the dirty gauze curtains, and spent half the afternoon there. Not until he saw a light go on inside did he cross the street and ring the bell. An old man in a smoking jacket opened the door, and even before Conny introduced himself, he heard a woman's voice asking, "Is it him, Heinrich? Quick, tell me who's there."

The old man led him into a crowded study; he seemed to guess why Conny had come. Conny laid his discharge papers on the desk, and let the old man read them before explaining about the switch of papers and clothing and his sufferings under the assumed name.

Can you imagine what the old man finally asked for? For the uniform, or what was left of the uniform; it had been patched and remade numerous times. In return he offered Conny money for a suit. Yes, and Conny told me how shortly thereafter he had new papers drawn up, with the help of Krimkowski, whom he ran into at the Hanover railway station and who was willing to vouch for his identity.

When dawn came, we were still sitting by the open window, not in the least surprised that we had talked through the night. While I started breakfast, Conny went over to the museum once more, holding in his hand the photograph that showed a smiling Edith standing by the bend in the river, trying to fish Paulie's ball out of the water with a pole. "Really, Zygmunt," he said later, "in our museum you feel as if you had firm ground under your feet; something holds you up, makes you stand tall." I thought I had not heard right, but he repeated the confession and nodded at his own words.

He left on the early bus; we walked arm in arm to the bus stop, in silence. Not until we saw the light glittering on the windshield of the bus as it came up the road did we break our silence to promise each other future meetings. And then he was gone, and I strolled back, thinking over the visit with amazement and even incredulity. I felt more and more disturbed and confused; I regretted not having asked Conny more questions, having let him off too easily.

The tables and benches still stood under the beeches, and the whole area was littered with smeared paper plates, empty bottles, crumpled napkins. Seeing the door to the museum open, I wanted to step inside, but I got no farther than the veranda, for down below on the strip of beach I saw two people gamboling, a man and a woman, Marian and Carola. They were chasing each other, running circles around each other, wading out into the water, helping each other tug at large pieces of driftwood lodged in the bank, strange crooked shapes created by ruthless forces. At this early hour they were out looking for driftwood, and leaning over the railing, I saw how they brought their smaller pieces to each other and held them up, giving a meaning to the shapes. I found myself imagining the bold images the "artist" would be offering: "Here you have an extra-long adder with its backbone broken in three places, these here are wishes darting up like flames, and these are crooked surveyors' rods, bent with age, sorrowing for their lost form!"

Oh, that's enough of that. The door to our past stood open and I went inside, intoxicated with the sudden sensation of having fulfilled a mission and finally found a foothold, and I thought of Uncle Adam, seeing his face before me . . .

Recently, you mean? You wonder whether Conny has been heard from since the destruction of the museum?

No, no, don't worry, I fully understand your impatience, and I can certainly answer your question without giving away the decisive point . . .

No, he did not come in person, and he did not write, but an article appeared in his newspaper, the *Lucknow Messenger*, or rather a page-and-a-half open letter to me, under the heading: "To an Untrustworthy Trustee of the Past." I kept the issue here for you, it's in the bottom compartment of the bedside table; you can take it with you after you have heard the whole story. Let me just summarize this much: out of confusion and delusion, he writes, I destroyed an irreplaceable heritage which I had no right to destroy, no matter how deserving my earlier efforts. Overweening presumption, he writes, seduced me into doing away with the collected evidence of eternal truth, thereby rendering many of our fellow countrymen homeless for a second time . . .

But where were we? Right: our museum was now officially opened; Lucknow had been revived on the basis of the scanty evidence that remained to us, touching in its insufficiency, but nevertheless able to represent all the aspects of the life of the past.

None of us had expected the stream of gifts and contributions that began to come in once the papers had printed their accounts of the opening. From far away we received antlers and docu-ments, toys and pieces of weaving, samples of soil, Sunday paint-ings, and preserved fish heads, things our fellow countrymen had taken along and had managed to hang on to when the typhoon of history swept them away and scattered them. Perhaps they parted with these treasures the more willingly because they trusted that in our museum, in proximity to similar pieces of evidence, these objects would testify with greater intensity . . .

All right, Martin, fine: let's call it a day . . . The day after tomorrow? Yes, I'll surely still be here . . .

# 15

You won't be surprised to hear that Conny wrote a total of five reports on our museum, rapturous, lavishly illustrated, attention-getting reports which brought us many visitors, even in our isolated location. Often these people had the reports from the *Lucknow Messenger* with them and used them as guides in the museum. After their visits I sometimes saw them sitting on the wooden benches outside, poring over the articles again, as if they were comparing what they had seen with what they had been promised. Not once did we find the clippings in a wastebasket . . .

Oh, you wonder whether I ever visited Conny at his office? . . .

Yes, Martin, I did, though only once, to be sure. I sat in the visitor's chair and listened while he dictated news bulletins from Lucknow to an apparently completely docile secretary. News bulletins from present-day Lucknow, which its Polish inhabitants have enriched by adding an -o to its name. I should tell you that every time he had visited us in Egenlund, he had urged me to come and see his editorial office, but I had never felt the impulse to go farther than Schleswig, which provided us with all we needed. But then Conny's great day came, and I felt obligated to take the train down to Lüneburg. For it was something entirely new that someone should become an honorary citizen of Lucknow—I mean, an honorary citizen of a lost city which had changed its name, even if only slightly; but our Council of Elders felt it had the power to confer this astonishing distinction on Conny, in recognition of his services to the homeland.

So I went, and found the modest private house on whose top floor the office was located. The little rooms under the eaves had their walls plastered with somewhat out-of-focus photographs showing Lucknow at its most attractive, and the hard-wood floors were heaped high with newspapers and manuscripts. Conny introduced me to his only editor, a heavy-set, introspective type, himself not a Lucknower, but married to one. He also introduced me to the one secretary, who smiled helplessly when he called her the "Lucknow encyclopedia." He had not yet dressed for the gala evening; he still had to dictate the news bulletins, which he translated from reports in the Polish press. He dragged up the chair and said, "Here, sit down and listen: the latest from Lucknow."

And what was the latest? I learned that the upper stories of the buildings in Lucknow had remained without water again in the recent summer, since there was no way of increasing the water pressure. The few taxi drivers in Lucknow had again refused to drive fares into the country, asserting that the bad roads were ruinous to their cars. The former estate was being made into an agricultural school, but classes could not begin yet, since replacement parts for the heating system had not been delivered. The farmers in a small neighboring village had voted to build their own link to the outside world; they had already begun work on a three-mile road. The renovation of the Lucknow railroad station had been completed, in time for winter; the interior walls had been sheathed in marble. The population, by now acquainted with "our" Lucknow winters, was hoping for prompt deliveries of warm clothing.

Were those the most significant pieces of news from our old town? Was there nothing positive to report?

"Here," Conny said with a gloomy expression, "let's add this item: 'On Cathedral Square the grand opening of a new pharmacy was celebrated.' " He turned to me and seemed disturbed at my lack of enthusiasm. He felt he had to justify his choice of news bulletins. It all came from the Polish press, he insisted; nothing was invented or distorted, and he could vouch for the accuracy of the translation. He put his arm around my shoulder and drew me away. I asked no questions, just let him explain what the various little rooms were used for and show me the archives. He pointed out the collection of books on Masuria he had assembled, and called my attention to the portraits of various noteworthy, if not well-known, Masurians. Before we went downstairs I had to promise to come back soon and learn more about the paper.

Downstairs he led me into the tiny furnished apartment which he rented from a woman whose deceased husband had been in charge of a narrow-gauge railway linking the Masurian lakes. His landlady lived across the hall. I had never seen such an imposing wardrobe in all my life. Conny carefully opened its doors and took out a dark suit, a silvery tie, and black dress shoes. As he dressed, I searched the room for a photograph, a print, any object with memories attached to it, but in vain. The room held not one thing that came from Conny and could have helped clarify who he was and where he stood. Everything in the least personal seemed to have been carefully eliminated. Or else, he had consciously avoided, from the very beginning, loading himself down with possessions which testified to experiences or had any emotional meaning. I had to conclude that Conny felt no desire to leave a trace of his own, and that he enjoyed this characterless dwelling, which seemed designed to help a person forget more easily.

But what is it you want to know? Right: the mishap that prevented me from accompanying Conny to receive his award, from being there during his moment of glory.

Suddenly something slipped and began to sway. The monster of a wardrobe appeared about to fall on me. There was a pounding in my ears, and I stood there helpless, too weak to ask for aid. Then a wave of nausea swept over me, and everything went dark before my eyes. My legs were totally numb. Before I fell, I realized it was the dizziness that was making me fall, and I heard Conny's cry of alarm, "For heaven's sake, Zygmunt!" He dragged me to his sofa bed, removed my shoes and jacket, and opened my collar. He went out into the hall to telephone the doctor and waited until the doctor arrived. Not until the doctor had reassured Conny that it was just a passing circulatory problem did he set out, apologizing for having to leave me and promising to be back as soon as he could.

So instead of sitting in the banquet room of the Canoe Inn and listening to a speech by the honorary citizen of the past, I lay in his anonymous furnished room, which was just barely furnished enough to deserve the name. I lay there feeling separated from the rest of the world by a dim, misted-up wall of glass, at least until the injection and the pills began to take effect. Gradually things acquired clearer contours, and I picked out several pairs of eyes focused on me, the friendly eyes of the landlady and the eyes of her dog and her cats. The animals sat there as if carved in stone, following my every movement with utmost concentration.

The woman brought me a cup of linden tea, wiped the sweat from my brow, as if to do so were the most natural thing in the world, and talked in her gently plaintive voice. What I heard was a panegyric to Conny, combined with a lament at the difficulties he had to contend with. Yes, she worshipped him. She understood every sacrifice he made for the newspaper and for that distant town where people had once been so happy. She defended the obsessiveness with which he went about creating monuments to the homeland. She praised his frugal eating habits and his taste in clothing. She marveled at his skill in handling tight finances; he had never yet fallen behind on bills. He always paid the rent on time. She had no worries for the immediate future; she based her confidence on the frequent visits of a polite gentleman who had never appeared without a bouquet of flowers for her and who always left Herr Karrasch in an eased and cheerful mood. I did not even have to ask her the name, for she supplied it herself: "Could be that Herr Reschat is there at the meeting right this minute."

Yes, Martin, she sat there with me until Conny returned, in a rush and full of concern. He casually handed her the scroll he had just received—so that she could look at it, or put it in a safe place, or to compensate her for having missed the ceremony; the woman nodded happily and was already absorbed in reading the document as she left the room with her animals.

From my horizontal position I said, "Congratulations to the honorary citizen of Atlantis." Conny gave this a moment's thought before he answered. "Sometimes, Zygmunt," he said, "I have the feeling that I have the entire ocean above me, and that I must pile myself with weights so as not to float up to the surface."

He was still in his coat, had only dashed back to see how I was feeling; they were waiting for him at the Canoe. Without my asking, he mentioned some of the people there, among them

Reschat; the former Statthalter of Lucknow, now a successful manufacturer, belonged to the committee that had drawn up the charter of citizenship. In my mind's eye I could see them all, sitting at their round table, shoulder to shoulder, in incomprehensible harmony, drawn together and bound to one another only by their common origin. Conny pressed me to come along as soon as I felt up to it. He was sure the gathering would receive me with applause. "Just rest a bit longer and then come over," he said, and was already halfway to the door.

You, at any rate, will understand why I had to call him back and tell him why I could not sit at the same table with Reschat. Conny did not even let me begin explaining. With a sigh of irritation he came back to my bedside, and before I could get a word out, he remarked with quiet decisiveness that he knew perfectly well what I was about to say. In a voice at once impatient and indulgent he begged me to stop dragging around with me all this stale, useless information. He himself was well acquainted with the past of the former Statthalter; in fact, he probably knew more than anyone else about the period in which Reschat had exercised his presumptuous power. Not that he wanted to absolve him of guilt and responsibility, or protect him or even defend him. He just wanted to give him a second chance. That was Conny's present creed: that in times which seemed to give everyone only one chance to prove themselves, we should insist on a second chance. He spoke self-righteously, asking me to examine my own prejudices and discard them. And he pressed me again to come and join them. "Our investment capital, Zygmunt, is hope."

That's right, Martin, I see how well you know me. I did not follow Conny. I lay there quietly for a while longer, feeling not in the slightest torn or indecisive. Then I got up, wrote Conny a note, and went across the hall. I knocked on the landlady's door, and when no one answered, I left the house and went to the station, passing the Canoe on the way without feeling in any way tempted to look into the back room, where those lovers of the unreal were celebrating the first honorary citizen of a city which existed only in their memories . . .

Yes, that may be true; in our memory things lead a purer existence, unimperiled, unharmed . . . But enough of that.

With the autumn storms, life out in Egenlund grew quieter. Only a few visitors turned up at the museum, mostly older people who had to stop and rest several times as they came up the path. I must admit that it was Bernhard, not I, who saw some meaning here; the boy once remarked, noting our visitors' older faces, "Fall is the season of the old frigates, drawn to their home port." Sometimes, when I saw the oldsters sailing over the hill, bent before the wind, more old women than old men, I found myself thinking that the voices of the past might grow softer and softer and finally die away altogether, and that the desire to return to the evidence of one's roots would seem a chimerical undertaking except to those who had once possessed what was now lost. You see, suddenly I had to recognize that our memories and relationships, too, would age and finally pass away, and that everything which had seemed so important to us in the springtime of our venture apparently had value for us alone, not for those we wanted to make our successors. You know, that was when I began to ask myself whether the pain one feels over a loss is inheritable, whether feelings and affections and obligations of this sort can ever be passed on from one generation to the next. It is only a question of time; eventually one's vital experience becomes nothing but a Fata Morgana, a trembling radiance one cannot grasp . . .

Yes, Martin, you are probably right: the value of our experiences cannot be passed on at random. We must be prepared to see others call into question what means so much to us; perhaps everything is condemned to transitoriness, and our attempt to rescue some of what seems to us exemplary and give it permanence is only a futile rebellion against what we secretly recognize to be hopeless. I'm not really sure . . . But enough of that . . .

Oh, yes, so you still remember that; yes, that's what Bernhard called our museum: the relic shack; probably you long ago started to call it that yourself. No? That surprises me, since you and he seem to have so much in common. Still, it was Bernhard who offered to stay up nights to keep watch after someone had broken into the museum. I promised you at the beginning that I would tell you everything, so let me also tell you what happened last night, in a dream I had, a dream surprisingly and painfully clear.

The Tartar Stone had turned up again; it was lying in the shallow water on our beach, licked by the bottle-green waves of the Schlei. There it was, that massive old missile, lost during our wintry flight, and now back with us again. And as if it were the most natural thing in the world, Eugen Lavrenz and Uncle Adam appeared, and they turned up their trousers and waded barefoot into the water and heaved the stone up onto the shore, where they stopped to catch their breath and take some vow, before they braced themselves against the Tartar Stone again. Coughing, they rolled it to the path, the steep, winding path which is tiring even if one is not carrying anything. Summoning up all their strength and skill, they pushed the stone up the hill, inch for inch, an image of extreme torment.

Such determination, such strain! They managed to roll the Tartar Stone as far as the hairpin curve, that is, halfway from the beach to the museum. But there they could not go on; they were exhausted, vanquished. What strength they had left they had to use to prevent the stone from rolling back. Bracing their foreheads against the stone, they called for assistance, called up to me, "Zygmunt, Zygmunt, come and help us!" And when I wanted to jump down to them, I found I was bound, tied by a rope to the red beeches. I strained at the rope, I braced myself and pulled, but in vain; I could not come to their aid, for as soon as I got some slack in the rope, Marian and Carola, who were standing beside me and holding the end of the rope, pulled it tight again, so that I was held close against the tree trunk. From the slope came a warning groan; I saw the two men leap to one side and the Tartar Stone hurtled down the hill and slammed into the waves, throwing up a sheet of mud and water, precisely where I had first spotted it. Twice more they tried to get the stone up the hill, and twice more they failed.

When I woke up, Martin, do you know what was on my mind? The dream had been so distinct that I resolved to go out to Egenlund as soon as possible, for I considered it not out of the question that I might find the Tartar Stone again. Just imagine, for a moment I had forgotten all that had happened. And when it came back to me, I lay there as if paralyzed in the dusk, wondering whether I had only dreamed all the destruction, too, and I heard a voice, unfamiliar yet recognizable as my own, repeating that nothing can be destroyed which has found a safe resting place in memory. My mouth felt parched. I trembled, and fear came over me, and an unbearable sense of pressure as I had to recognize that there was no coming home to Egenlund. I realized that I had become homeless a second time.

But I can see you are eager for other confessions, that you want to hear the rest. All right, I won't keep it from you any longer; you have a right to know.

Just imagine: last summer I received a letter announcing the visit of a Polish television crew. They wrote in that courteous way they have and allowed me plenty of time to answer—again, so considerate of them. I informed Conny of the impending visit, not because I felt I needed support, but because I foresaw that it would be a memorable encounter. Conny, who had his own instincts in such matters, agreed at once to be there, and on his own behest brought along the spokesman for the Council of Elders, Przytulla. There was not much to guess at or to plan in advance, since the letter clearly spelled out the purpose of the visit: our visitors, who had been given Masuria at the end of the war, and viewed it from the first as reconquered territory and rightly theirs, wanted to make a documentary dealing with our approach to the sense of homeland. They wanted to show how we kept alive our spiritual ties with the town we had come from, what hopes we cherished of returning. We would be their last stop on a swing through a goodly number of cities.

So when the motor launch from Schleswig tied up at our wooden bridge, we were there waiting. Since we helped unload the luggage, the greetings and introductions struck the visitors as too rough and ready, and we had to repeat them more formally when all the metal cases and plastic valises were ashore. "Permit me," said the head of the crew—he actually said "Permit me"! And then he introduced the group: himself, Marek Kowallek, Bogdan Czymay, and Karol Neumann. When I gave our names, he nodded with a smile. He seemed familiar with them, this chain-smoking, small-framed, lean young man who cheerfully surveyed the landscape and remarked softly, "Almost like home." When we tried to take some of their gear, he smilingly waved us off; they practiced strict division of labor, and his assistants always attended to the luggage.

We climbed the steep path to the top of the cliff, where Carola was waiting to invite everyone to breakfast. All three Poles kissed her hand. The head of the team admired the location of the house; he established the geological age of the fjord, showed himself a lover of trees and, when we went inside, a connoisseur of tiled stoves.

We had a delicious breakfast of Masurian cold cuts, pickles, and hard-boiled eggs, and toasted the visitors with Nikolaschka and imported buffalo-grass vodka. As we ate, our conversation revolved around food, specifically Polish and Masurian mushroom dishes, which we compared and contrasted; we considered our many ways of preparing mushrooms and finally agreed that nowhere else in the world could anyone claim to know a thing about mushrooms if he had not "experienced" Polish or Masurian mushroom dishes.

We drank to that. But Przytulla only pretended to drink. He was under great strain. He did not care for this kind of small talk; he wanted to come to the point, and by way of steering the conversation in the right direction, he asked how the visitors had liked their four weeks in the West. The head of the crew, who had apparently anticipated this very question, grinned and replied that for the most part his expectations had been confirmed. After this remark, he asked our permission to smoke, for a change. Still grinning, he pointed out the brand-new jeans outfits his colleagues had purchased in Frankfurt.

We did not pursue the matter, and our eyes looked past each other; then Conny abruptly asked whether any of our guests had ever been in Lucknow. Marek Kowallek answered without the slightest surprise, yes, he passed through Lucknow several times each year on his way to his summer place near Mrossen, which for a time had been called Schönhorst. And with a frankness that amazed us, he went on to talk about the reconstruction after the war, about Lucknow's chronic housing shortage, and, winking at me, about a plan of the Lucknow town government to set up a regional museum in the near future. His tone did not change when he responded to Przytulla's remark that this town and this region were only temporarily under Polish administration. "At home we assume that the rectification of borders is permanent," he said quietly. He promised to cook a fish stew for us if we

visited him at his summer place. No insecurity, no guilty conscience. For Marek Kowallek, who was about twenty-five years
younger than we, all the problems in the East were solved. Besides, he suggested, we would have to learn to live with some
unsolved problems; perhaps that was the order of the day.

It was curious; I had prepared myself for this visit, going over
all the questions I wanted to ask, hoping for a real exchange of
views. But now that we were actually sitting down together I had
to content myself with listening. They were young and had been
spared; they did not feel weighed down by experience, for their
world had been a *fait accompli* by the time they became aware of
it. So I decided not to burden them with my questions, questions
that had to do with the meaning of history, with the statute of
limitations on suffering, with the possibility of neighborly rela-
tions.

Conny spoke with great fervor. He called for the recognition
of "historical" or "organically created" rights. Such rights were
everyone's due and should form the basis for any political arrangements. The more warmly he argued, the more interest and
satisfaction Marek Kowallek displayed; it would almost seem as
though he wanted Conny to take this position. So I was not
surprised when at a certain point he proposed that Conny repeat
his statements before the camera. Conny agreed. What followed
proved once more what a strong influence for moderation a
whirring camera can be: Conny offered a measured defense of
historical rights and took the opportunity to remind his presumed
audience of their own trials in the course of history. What had
made their victory possible, he asked rhetorically, if not love of
their own land and their unshakable belief in certain organically
created rights?

The cameraman did not confine himself to Conny's face; as
Conny spoke, the camera examined his posture, wandered up his
body from his feet, rested on his mouth and hands, panned across
to paintings and prints, for instance a tinted Merian print which
showed the borders of Masuria as though they had been drawn
by a wavering, arthritic hand. Since Przytulla refused to say
before the camera what he kept repeating to the head of the TV
crew—"History does not recognize any last word"—they
wanted me to speak about the aims and hopes of the Lucknow

Homeland Association. They gave me about a minute and a half. I asked them to come outside, to the veranda of the museum, where I welcomed them a second time, welcomed them into the presence of the mute witnesses to the past. The camera was running. I opened the door. I stood aside to give them a clear view of the blue and white wedding rug which had mysteriously found its way back to us. "Come," I said, "here we are on home ground, for what is collected in my house involves you, too."

They came in and looked around, not doubtfully or patronizingly, as one might have expected, or with false solemnity, but with frank, thoughtful curiosity, as if injured pride or touchiness were simply out of the question. You can imagine that I had awaited this moment with anxiety, that I had looked forward to it and dreaded it for a long time, for these were not just any ordinary visitors bending over the documents of our past; they were guests to whom we were linked by a thousand years of prejudice. I was glad that they did not act as a group, but went in three different directions, each one spontaneously attracted by something different. I made no attempt to direct their attention, and noticed that they felt no need to point out their discoveries to one another; each one was looking for himself and drawing his own conclusions. At times a sense of unreality overcame me, as if this were all a dream. Did this evidence, sifted down through the filter of time, mean anything to them, did it give them any insight into themselves? I could not tell.

After their tour I said a few words on camera, with the blue and white rug as a background. I talked about that knowledge of one's own region which underlies any understanding of the larger world; about the establishment of our museum, whose contents merely served to show how we had once lived. On a sudden inspiration I proposed that we forge a link with the regional museum in Lucknow to exchange information about our common historical background, not with a view to proving anything, but in the interests of clarification. Marek Kowallek seemed pleased with my statement and asked the cameraman to photograph some of the objects, which he pointed out with a snap of the fingers . . .

What do you mean, Martin? What can you well imagine? . . .

No, not at all. He was by no means choosing only those items that would add up to a negative image of the museum, and there-fore of us—for instance, the yellowed photograph of Hinden-burg and Ludendorff at a briefing during the Masurian winter war, or the propaganda posters Conny had printed and smuggled to us—the ones with "The Enemy Is Listening" and "Wheels Must Roll for Victory." By no means only objects like the Bos-nian attack trumpet or tattered banners from the plebiscite in the twenties. He wanted pictures of the Sokolken box and the Sudauese funerary urn, and the original document describing the donation to the Knights of the Teutonic Order, stipulating their rights and duties.

"Do you really want to show that?" Conny asked. "Can your people handle that?" "Oh," Marek Kowallek replied, "we have a very intimate relationship to history. You might even say many of us are positively addicted to the past. So any historical evi-dence arouses great interest." "Including evidence that might be damaging to your cause?" Conny asked. Kowallek looked at him with surprise, then smiled and said, hesitating slightly, "I don't suppose anyone can have a clear conscience about his own his-tory, or at most a few subsidized residents of the so-called ruling houses. Anyone who has borne the brunt of history must testify, for better or for worse, to the causal connections between events."

They photographed the spinning wheel and a bronze sword and the corked test tubes of Masurian soil people had contributed to replace our original specimens. Then they filmed the building from the outside and asked some questions on the number of visitors, on finances, and on the origins of the exhibits, all of which I was glad to answer.

My uneasiness persisted, for I had assumed that an encounter of this sort could not go off without incident. Even as we were having tea, which Carola had prepared in the Frisian style, I found myself worrying that some misunderstanding might sud-denly lead to an all-out confrontation. But perhaps, Martin, that was what was so extraordinary about this meeting, that nothing out of the ordinary occurred.

So they once more invited us to visit them, kissed Carola's hand, and set out. We accompanied them to the wooden bridge. As we waited for the launch, constraint seemed to descend on us, probably because we were all aware of the things that had gone unsaid, less out of nervousness than out of civility. Our conversation did not flow until the boat tied up and we helped them heave their luggage on board.

As the three of us waved goodbye, we were watching each other sidelong, coldly, in a strangely irritated mood. Even before the launch was out of sight, we stopped waving, as if on command, and trudged back up the path, staring grimly ahead, each preparing a self-defense.

When we reached the museum, Conny undertook to evaluate the visit. At first he complained only of an annoying sense of a missed opportunity, of a bitter taste in his mouth. He could not explain the strange impotence that had kept him from speaking his mind. He looked out over the Schlei and predicted that we and our museum would appear in the documentary as incorrigible dreamers, naïve guardians of the quaint relics of the past, misguided missionaries who thought they could reverse the effects of history by unyielding obstinacy. Yes, that was what we had been guilty of: naïveté. When I countered that nothing we had said on camera would lend itself to distortion, he waved my words aside. He knew from personal experience what film editing could do.

In this state of mind he went up on the veranda. He was too agitated to sit down. He pounded the door frame with his fist and stared into the museum. All at once he swallowed hard, for he had just realized that something in the collection had to go: the propaganda posters he himself had once contributed. They might give rise to misunderstandings. I had better remove them immediately.

I reminded him of where they came from and that they reflected a period in Lucknow's history we ourselves had experienced. But he stood his ground, repeating that the posters might be used against us. Looking for support, he turned to Przytulla, who muttered that Conny was right, the posters should have been removed long ago. I still thought this was only a passing mood of theirs. Did he want to represent Lucknow's history as spotless, I asked Conny, so that everyone would be free of blame? He merely shrugged. It soon became clear to me that this was not the end of it. Their bitterness and disappointment with themselves caused them to find fault with all sorts of items. Things they had previously thought poignant they now saw as tasteless or even incriminating—one could only wonder why it had taken them this long to notice. Conny read the label on the decorated butter crock from the Vistula region and knew why the cameraman had given it such close attention. The same thing happened with the pale-blue corner cupboard, the toothed flax scutcher, the humble peasant chair: they had all found their way to Lucknow from across the border . . .

Pardon me? No, Martin, I had not noticed any difference in the way the Poles treated the various objects. Conny was inventing all this and Przytulla backed him up out of frustration. Now that Conny thought he had discovered the reason for his disgruntlement, he was ready to denounce things he had once praised. He wanted the whole collection reorganized, all those objects that had withstood such trials and tribulations on their way to us.

Now it was Conny who wanted to undertake a purge of the collection, and seemed to think he was the one to decide. He was standing in front of the tubes with soil of the homeland and ranting about stupid sentimentality, when I interrupted him. I reminded him that this museum was a private affair, and that we who had founded it wanted it to serve only one purpose: to preserve the world of Lucknow, as we had known it, from oblivion.

Conny had not been prepared for this objection; he wheeled around, and there was an edge to his voice as he reminded me of the regular subsidies we received from the Lucknow Homeland Association. I suggested something I had long had in mind anyway, that the subsidies be discontinued. Conny replied that that would not change the situation, since too many of the exhibits had been donated by others, and therefore the collection could not be regarded as private property. Besides, the majority of Lucknowers had become accustomed to thinking of the museum as a piece of home that belonged to all of them. Here Przytulla chimed in to say that I had better not take any measures without the approval of the Council of Elders.

As a number of herring boats went by, I wondered once more whether I was hearing my friends aright. Might it be that I was distorting their words? Wasn't all this the product of a passing mood, and soon my old friend Conny would come to his senses and with a tap on the shoulder retract whatever was making me feel so desolate?

But Conny did not stop here. He went on to warn me: where would our visitors come from if his *Lucknow Messenger* stopped steering them in our direction? What if he urged his readers to withdraw their support because the museum no longer served the best interests of Lucknow? Where would we be if the Council of Elders made an announcement to this effect at the next Old Home Day?

I let them go without bidding them farewell. Evening had come, and I walked along the steep cliff toward the sea. I went as far as the hut of the fisherman who had been the first person to wave to us when we reached these parts. The fisherman had died several years earlier, and his hut was still there, or what remained of it when the wind and the cold and the vandals had done their work. I sat down on the doorstep. I heard in the distance our weaving students saying cheery goodbyes to one another. Their voices carried far in the still air.

I sat there until darkness fell, and would have left had I not heard footsteps crunching toward me over the gravel. It was Simon Gayko's tread. He had not been out looking for me, but was not surprised to find me here. He came up to me with a sigh, sat down, and lit his pipe. "Well, Zygmunt." "Well, Simon."

I knew what he wanted; whenever Simon sat down beside me with that Bosnian patience of his, I knew he wanted to go over the old memories, and I had noticed after a while that I joined in all too readily. Without any preliminaries he asked simply, "Remember the royal yacht, Zygmunt, the *Hohenzollern* and the way they smashed it on me?" "Of course," I said. "And remember the ice-sailing race, the regatta with Heini Hauser, and the accident at the bridge? Remember that?" "Of course I do, Simon." "And on the logs that time, when you went under and I gave you up for lost?" "But Sonja Turk was there, and she hauled me out on her drying meadow." "What do you think," he asked, "was everything better back then?" and before I could answer he decided, "Not better, but it sure was homier!"

He sat there in silence for a while, and you could tell he was going over the old pictures, the old names. He ran down the list, as if it were his duty to remember: "Henseleit—what do you think became of him? Eugen Lavrenz—I wonder where he's buried? Heini Hauser—how do you suppose he's making out? Dudei—what would've happened to him?"

Not that he expected any information from me; it was quite sufficient for him to pay tribute to the uncertainty surrounding the fates of these people. Ah, a lost world, a lost time. Little bubbles welled up in the Schlei and burst; waterfowl whirred by, squawking before they landed. "Zygmunt," Simon asked, "if you could go back to Lucknow, say tomorrow, would you go?" and I replied, "I don't know, Simon, I really don't know."

There was a shocked silence. Simon stopped sucking on his pipe, which was drawing poorly, and edged away from me, while peering at me sharply. He could not have been more shocked if I had told him I had an incurable disease. Softly and plaintively he said, "But we've got to go back, Zygmunt, we've got to, because everything's there waiting for us: the trees and the lakes and Castle Hill and the fields, and the old river with the log floats." "No, Simon," I replied, "nothing's waiting for us there anymore. The people who could have waited for us are gone, lost and gone, and that's why the moment you're waiting for will never come."

He pulled himself up by the doorjamb and stood there for a moment as if stunned. Then he left without another word. I realize today what those words of mine must have done to Simon: they simply made the ground cave in beneath him . . .

Maybe, Martin. Maybe that's why he was the only one I took into my confidence when there was but one thing left for me to do: to destroy our museum. Maybe I felt I owed Simon more than I owed any of the others . . .

No, not that same evening. It happened a few days later . . .

Why? No, I don't need to take a break. I've learned to bear up, I can endure the past. But if you want something to drink, there's juice, there's some cold tea—as you see, I no longer have that searing thirst I had at the beginning . . .

Well, it happened in a tent, a huge party tent in which the Lucknowers had gathered for their annual Old Home Day. We from Egenlund were all there, except for Bernhard, who was hitchhiking to Pompeii. We were sitting at long tables, with pitchers of beer within easy reach, listening to the welcoming remarks Przytulla was making as spokesman of the Council of Elders. The elders were seated on a raised platform, Przytulla with the microphone in the middle. We could see him craning his neck to discover who was there so that he could mention people by name and even give their addresses in Lucknow if he knew them. He mentioned me, too, by name, calling me "our esteemed Zygmunt Rogalla, the great rug master from the bend in the river," whereupon the eight hundred guests stood up and clapped until I had climbed up on the bench to acknowledge the cheers.

The greatest applause was for Conny, the first and only honorary citizen of Lucknow since the loss of the city, the man whose *Lucknow Messenger* provided a bridge to the past and biweekly brought them vivid reminders of what they had once been and had called their own.

Although sitting right in front of the speaker, Reschat was one of the last to be greeted. People responded with approval to the straightforward announcement of his presence. I saw him stand up and bow, his key ring in hand.

Sudden gusts of wind brought life to the slack walls of the tent. The canvas billowed and snapped, and the ropes high above us went taut, then relaxed again. The large electric lights swayed back and forth like bells.

After the welcoming words we stood for a moment of silence in honor of our dead, the many who had been shot, drowned, or frozen to death, the many we had left behind, many of them unburied, their souls not laid to rest. For a moment they were there with us, and as we remembered them, we heard the easterly wind buffeting the tent. Then we sang a chorale and the Masurian anthem; the whole tent seemed to float up into the air and drift toward home.

Yes, Martin, that's how it was. And during the intermission almost everybody left their seats and pushed through the narrow aisles to see who else was there, to greet old friends and be greeted. We stayed at our table and let the exclamations flow over us: "Well, well, Zygmunt, to think you're still living! But what else is there to do?"

Suddenly Conny appeared. He embraced all of us, even Henrike; all this was possible in the name of Lucknow, that distant, legendary place that let people forget their differences, made us into a single tribe, a single family, a league of the homesick. Conny motioned to me to come with him to one of the entrances of the tent, whose flaps were waving in the stiff breeze like an elephant's ears. There he let me know that the Council of Elders was about to nominate a new chairman for the Lucknow Homeland Association, an energetic, experienced, dynamic chairman: Reschat. Conny said he was turning to me because he thought he could anticipate my objections. He asked me to let bygones be bygones, for once to overcome my prejudices—"in the best interests of Lucknow, Zygmunt, really, in all our best interests." Conny was wooing me for his candidate.

At this point Conny was swept off by a swarm of people who had to have some words with him, as did half the folks there. I returned to our table, where Simon took one look at me and asked, "Something wrong, Zygmunt?" "No, Simon," I said, "what would be wrong?" The smoke was getting thicker and thicker. At the head table blue slips of paper were being passed around; the agenda was being rearranged. The noise grew deafening. I sat there and followed the program, but I felt as if I were on the other side of the river, separated from what was happening all around me. When everybody sang, I did not sing along, although Henrike nudged me reproachfully. When votes were taken, I forgot to raise my hand. Images from the past besieged me with pitiless charity, but I felt utterly calm, filled with a bitter determination. I was only waiting for the election. Surrounded by my people, I sat there alone and waited for the election.

The election went as Conny had hoped and the Council of Elders had wished. Before the results were announced, there was none of that breathless tension that prevails when the results are in doubt. Clearly, there would be no surprise.

The new chairman rose ponderously. Lifted by the applause, he climbed onto his bench and stood there as if stunned for a moment by the flickering light, his eyes closed. Then he held up his clasped hands in a gesture of gratitude, thanked everyone all around, and let it be known that he accepted, overcome by the confidence they had placed in him. Still standing on the bench, he received the first congratulations. People clustered around him.

They helped him down and cleared a path for him through the crowd. Amid a new wave of applause he seemed to regain consciousness; he looked searchingly at the Lucknowers all around him, apparently sizing them up, and I noticed that he made a point of offering his hand to a few who were not clapping. He seemed to be on the prowl, and to this day I believe it was me he was searching for, me whose hand he particularly wanted to shake, for once he had located me, he headed straight for our table. How easy it was for me to return his gaze, as I suddenly felt a stinging pain on my cheek. He nodded to me, smiling, and left it to Conny to talk with me. He had already passed our table, without having offered me his hand.

Conny, the honorary citizen of the past, put his arm around me, less because he wanted people to see him doing so than to express his satisfaction at the outcome of the election with this confidential gesture. He and the new chairman would be out to visit us right after the celebration was over, he told me. Our museum would be lifted out of its obscurity, not by being expanded or moved, but by being taken under the wing of the Homeland Association. "A new era is beginning," Conny said, and inquired as he turned to leave, "You'll be home?" "Sure," I said, "we'll all be home." He hurried off, and I left the tent.

I went down to the mooring of the motor launch. The wind had died and the languor of August lay over the fjord and its banks with their fading grass. The seaman who hauled crates and metal containers on board winked at me in greeting. A sailboat which had apparently capsized in the wind was being towed in; the light refracted off its shiny hull. Seagulls swooped and dove. I looked out across the water, which glittered like punched tin. Then Simon Gayko came down the boardwalk, strolled over to me, and sat down. He waited with his question until we had pulled out and were headed across the fjord: "Something's wrong, isn't it, Zygmunt?" "Yes," I said, "yes, Simon," and then we sat in silence and watched the other shore retreating in the sun, and not until Egenlund came into view, not until the house appeared, large and self-assured and changeless behind the red beeches, did I tell him what I had decided.

No objection, no protest, not even a justified argument. All I had from Simon was a soft, grim warning: "Don't do wrong,

Zygmunt, don't do wrong." We climbed the steep path to the top of the cliff, and there our ways parted. I went into the museum. I closed the door. I looked at the objects as I had never looked at them before. I made my preparations for the next day . . .

Yes, Martin, I made my preparations calmly, in the certainty that I had to make use of my last freedom, before something was done that I could not tolerate and could assume no responsibility for. I gathered up the colorful scraps of wool, I set out the canisters whose contents would saturate the wool, I decided where the first flames were to leap up. I had to resist countless temptations to smuggle out this or that. But as I made my arrangements, only one wish filled me, and that was to bring the collected witnesses to our past into safety, a final, irrevocable safety, from which they would never again issue forth, but where they could never again be exploited for this cause or that.

My hands trembled, my face burned; all night I had the sensation of having an iron band around my chest. Twice during the night I got up and went into the museum to make sure that I had really made all the preparations, not just dreamed them.

The treasured finds have crumbled away, the traces have been obliterated. The past has received back what was its own to keep and what it had lent us for a while. But already memory has gone to work, searching, gathering evidence in the uncertain stillness of the no-man's-land.